WALLACE the BRAVE

Will Henry

Andrews McMeel
PUBLISHING®

to Grandma Betty

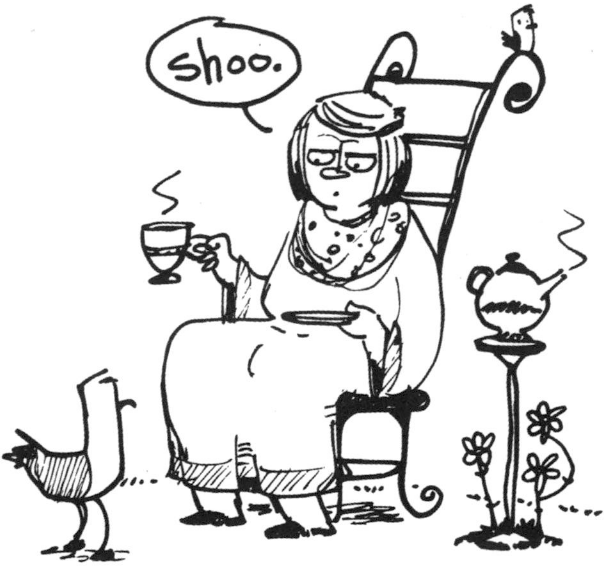
shoo.

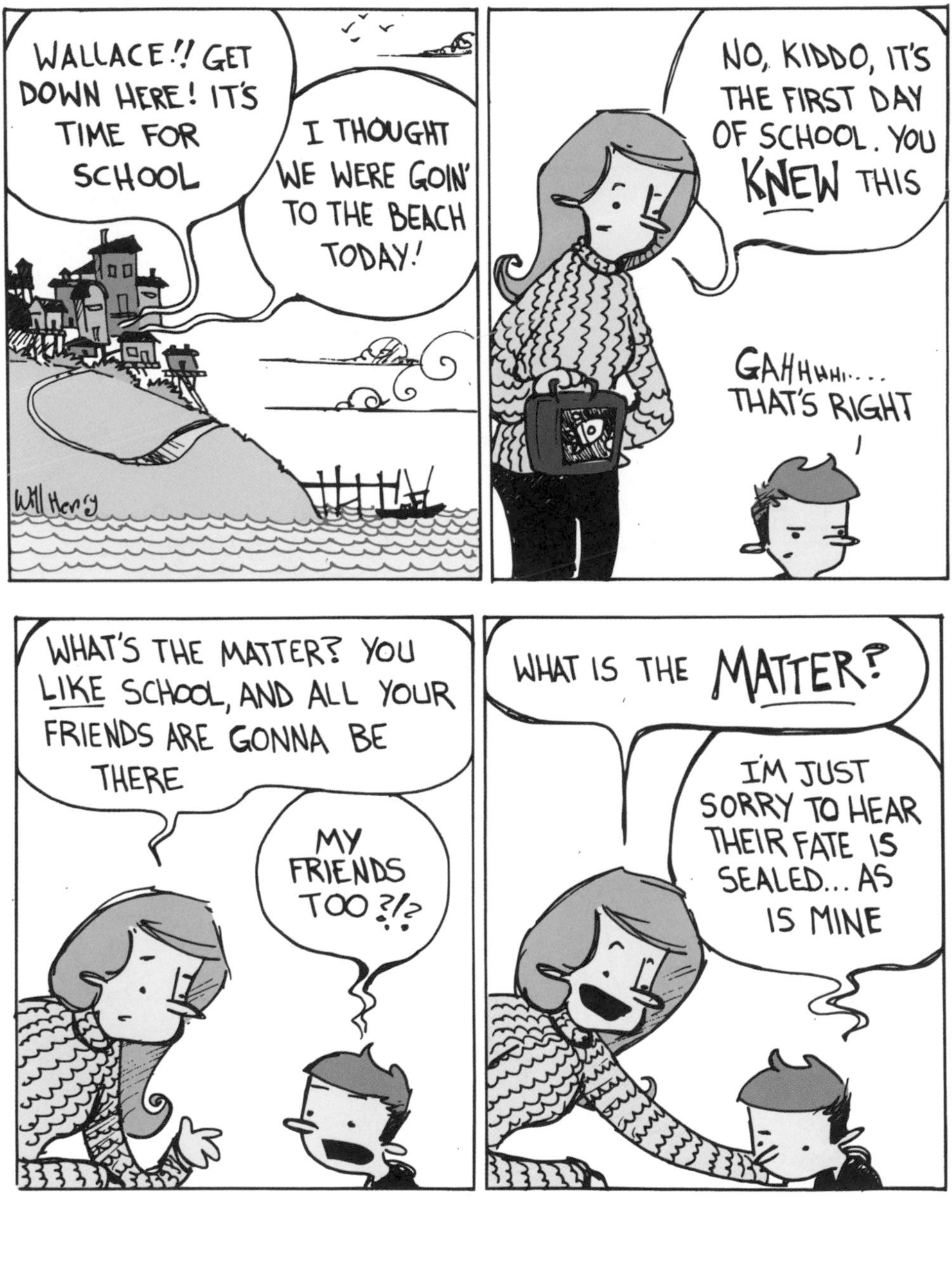
WALLACE!! GET DOWN HERE! IT'S TIME FOR SCHOOL
I THOUGHT WE WERE GOIN' TO THE BEACH TODAY!
Will Henry
NO, KIDDO, IT'S THE FIRST DAY OF SCHOOL. YOU KNEW THIS
GAHHHHH.... THAT'S RIGHT
WHAT'S THE MATTER? YOU LIKE SCHOOL, AND ALL YOUR FRIENDS ARE GONNA BE THERE
MY FRIENDS TOO?!?
WHAT IS THE MATTER?
I'M JUST SORRY TO HEAR THEIR FATE IS SEALED... AS IS MINE

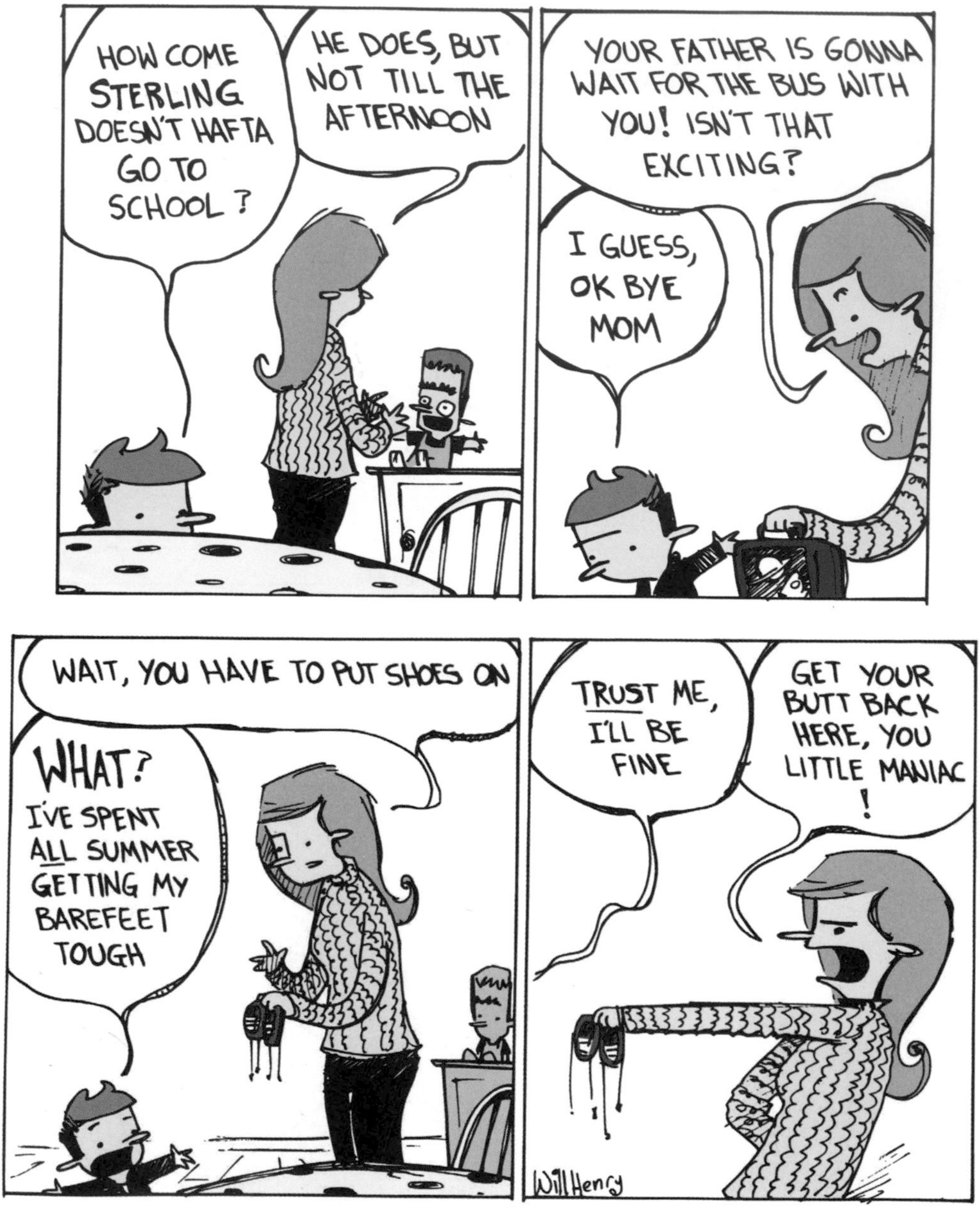
HOW COME STERLING DOESN'T HAFTA GO TO SCHOOL?
HE DOES, BUT NOT TILL THE AFTERNOON
YOUR FATHER IS GONNA WAIT FOR THE BUS WITH YOU! ISN'T THAT EXCITING?
I GUESS, OK BYE MOM
WAIT, YOU HAVE TO PUT SHOES ON
WHAT? I'VE SPENT ALL SUMMER GETTING MY BAREFEET TOUGH
TRUST ME, I'LL BE FINE
GET YOUR BUTT BACK HERE, YOU LITTLE MANIAC!
Will Henry

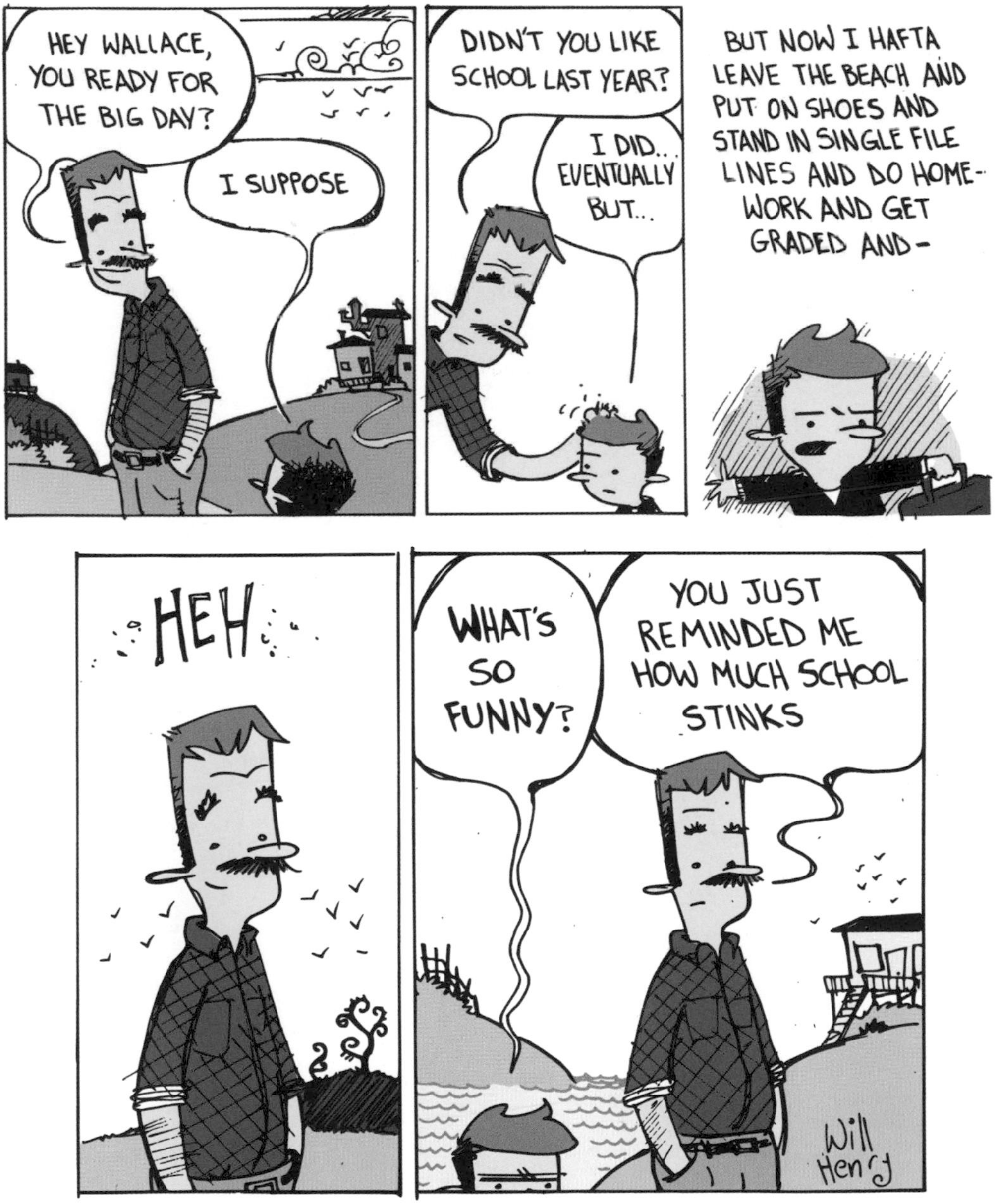
HEY WALLACE, YOU READY FOR THE BIG DAY?
I SUPPOSE
DIDN'T YOU LIKE SCHOOL LAST YEAR?
I DID... EVENTUALLY BUT...
BUT NOW I HAFTA LEAVE THE BEACH AND PUT ON SHOES AND STAND IN SINGLE FILE LINES AND DO HOME-WORK AND GET GRADED AND-
HEH
WHAT'S SO FUNNY?
YOU JUST REMINDED ME HOW MUCH SCHOOL STINKS
Will Henry

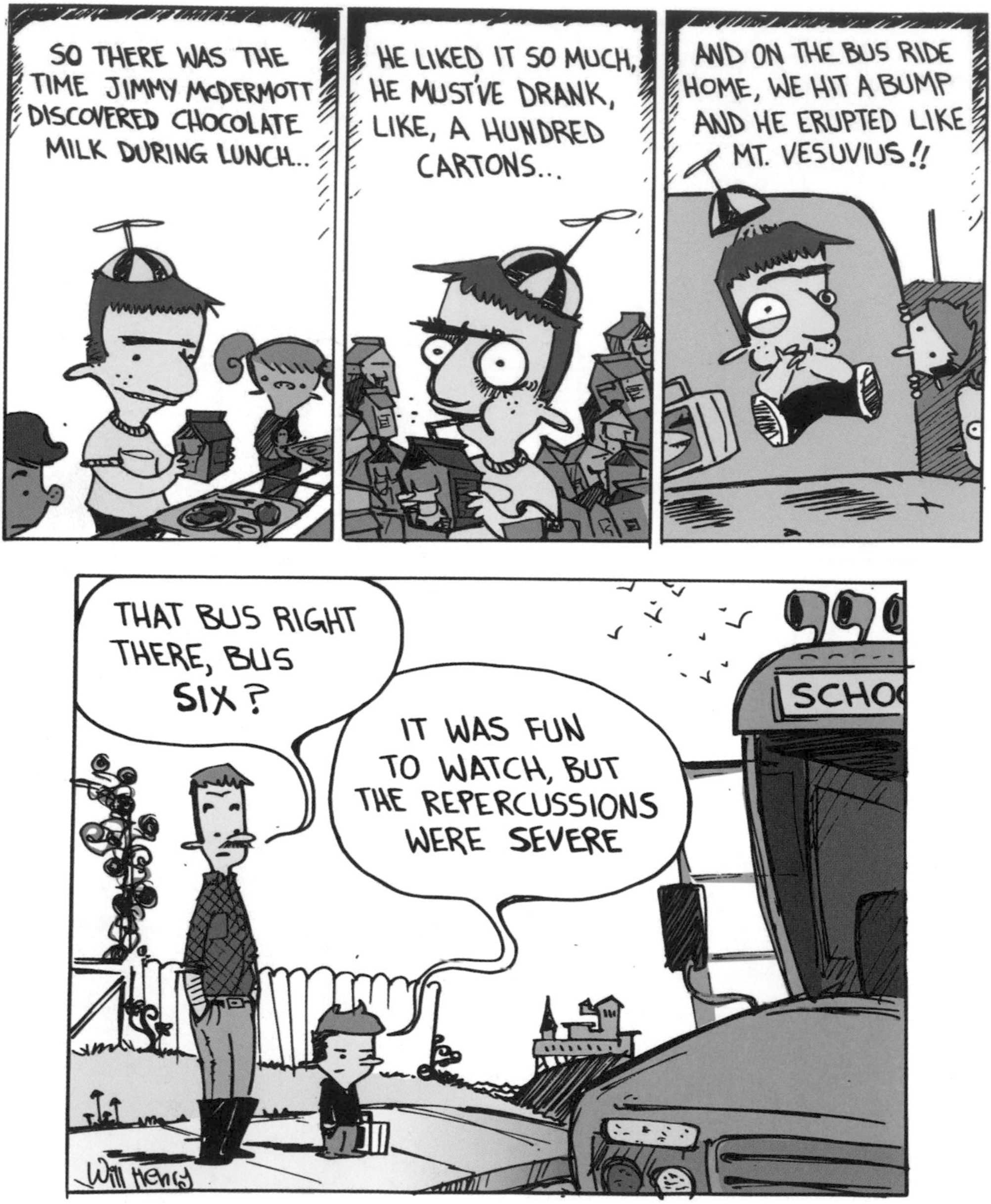
SO THERE WAS THE TIME JIMMY McDERMOTT DISCOVERED CHOCOLATE MILK DURING LUNCH...
HE LIKED IT SO MUCH, HE MUST'VE DRANK, LIKE, A HUNDRED CARTONS...
AND ON THE BUS RIDE HOME, WE HIT A BUMP AND HE ERUPTED LIKE MT. VESUVIUS!!
THAT BUS RIGHT THERE, BUS SIX?
IT WAS FUN TO WATCH, BUT THE REPERCUSSIONS WERE SEVERE
SCHO
Will Henry

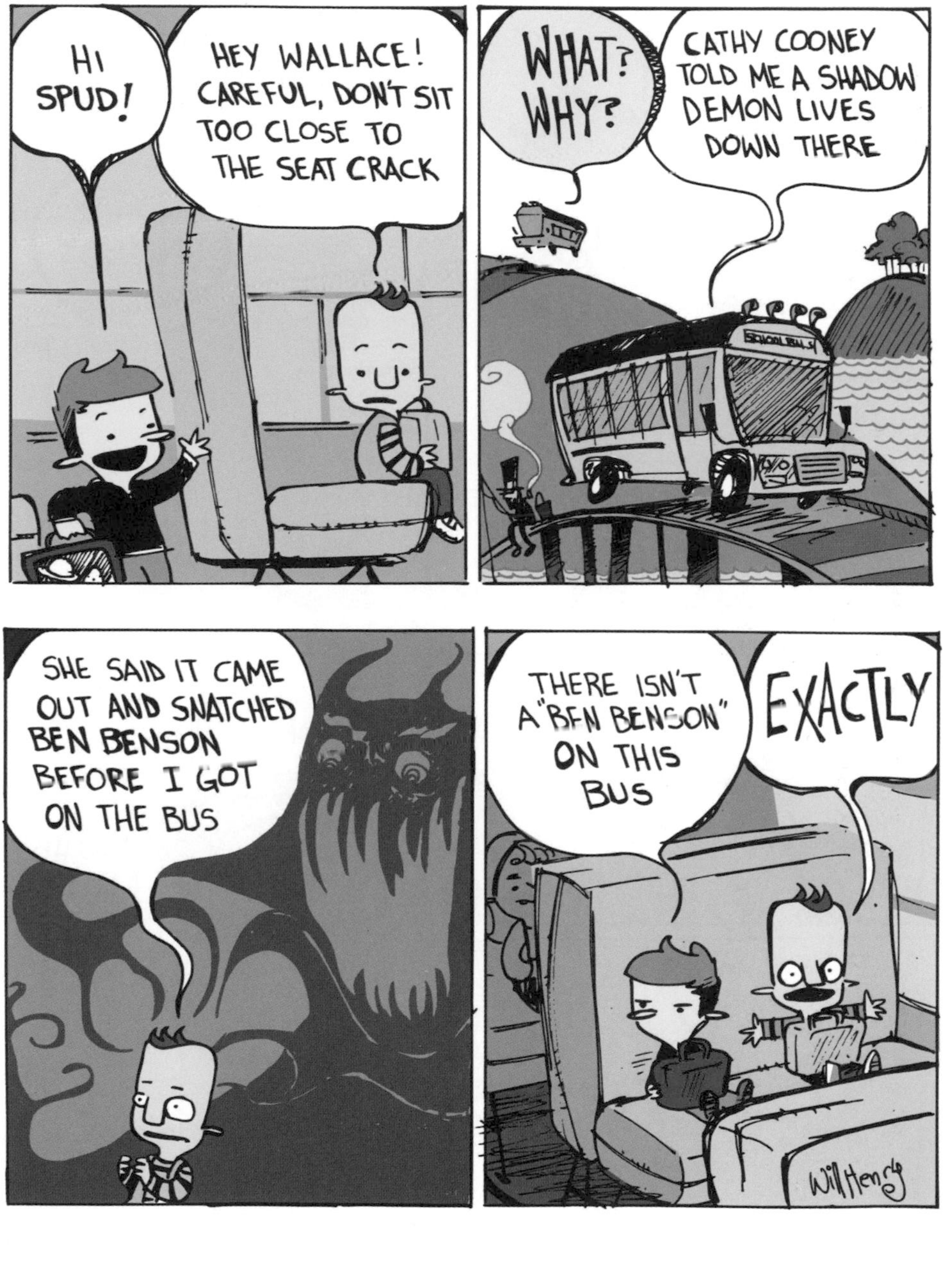
HI SPUD!
HEY WALLACE! CAREFUL, DON'T SIT TOO CLOSE TO THE SEAT CRACK
WHAT? WHY?
CATHY COONEY TOLD ME A SHADOW DEMON LIVES DOWN THERE
SCHOOL BUS
SHE SAID IT CAME OUT AND SNATCHED BEN BENSON BEFORE I GOT ON THE BUS
THERE ISN'T A "BEN BENSON" ON THIS BUS
EXACTLY
Will Henry

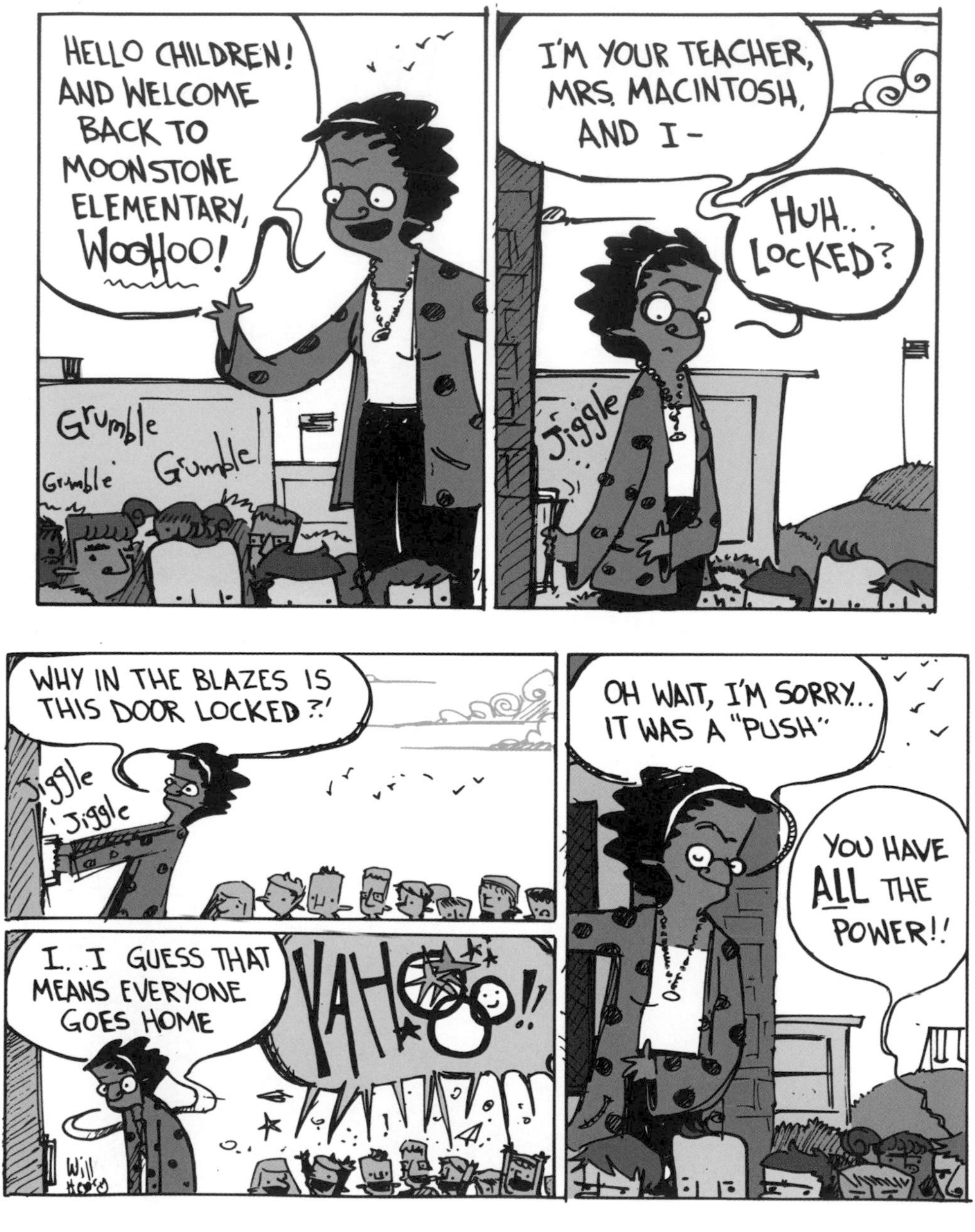
HELLO CHILDREN! AND WELCOME BACK TO MOONSTONE ELEMENTARY, WOOHOO!
Grumble
Grumble
Grumble
I'M YOUR TEACHER, MRS. MACINTOSH, AND I-
HUH... LOCKED?
Jiggle
WHY IN THE BLAZES IS THIS DOOR LOCKED?!
Jiggle
Jiggle
I... I GUESS THAT MEANS EVERYONE GOES HOME
YAHOOO!!
OH WAIT, I'M SORRY... IT WAS A "PUSH"
YOU HAVE ALL THE POWER!!

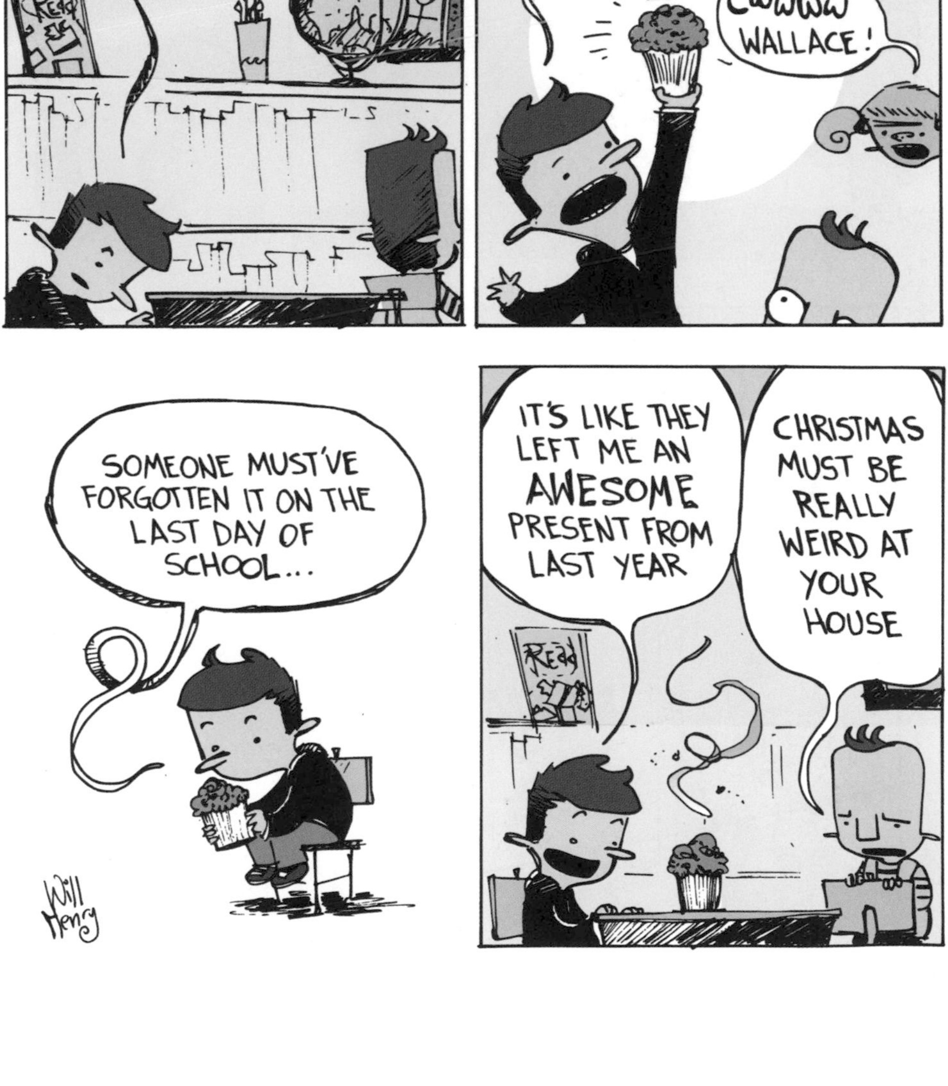
OH WOW! LOOK AT THIS !!!
Mark
Read
IT'S AN OLD MUFFIN! IT'S, LIKE, WICKED HARD
EWWWW WALLACE!
SOMEONE MUST'VE FORGOTTEN IT ON THE LAST DAY OF SCHOOL...
IT'S LIKE THEY LEFT ME AN AWESOME PRESENT FROM LAST YEAR
CHRISTMAS MUST BE REALLY WEIRD AT YOUR HOUSE
Will Henry

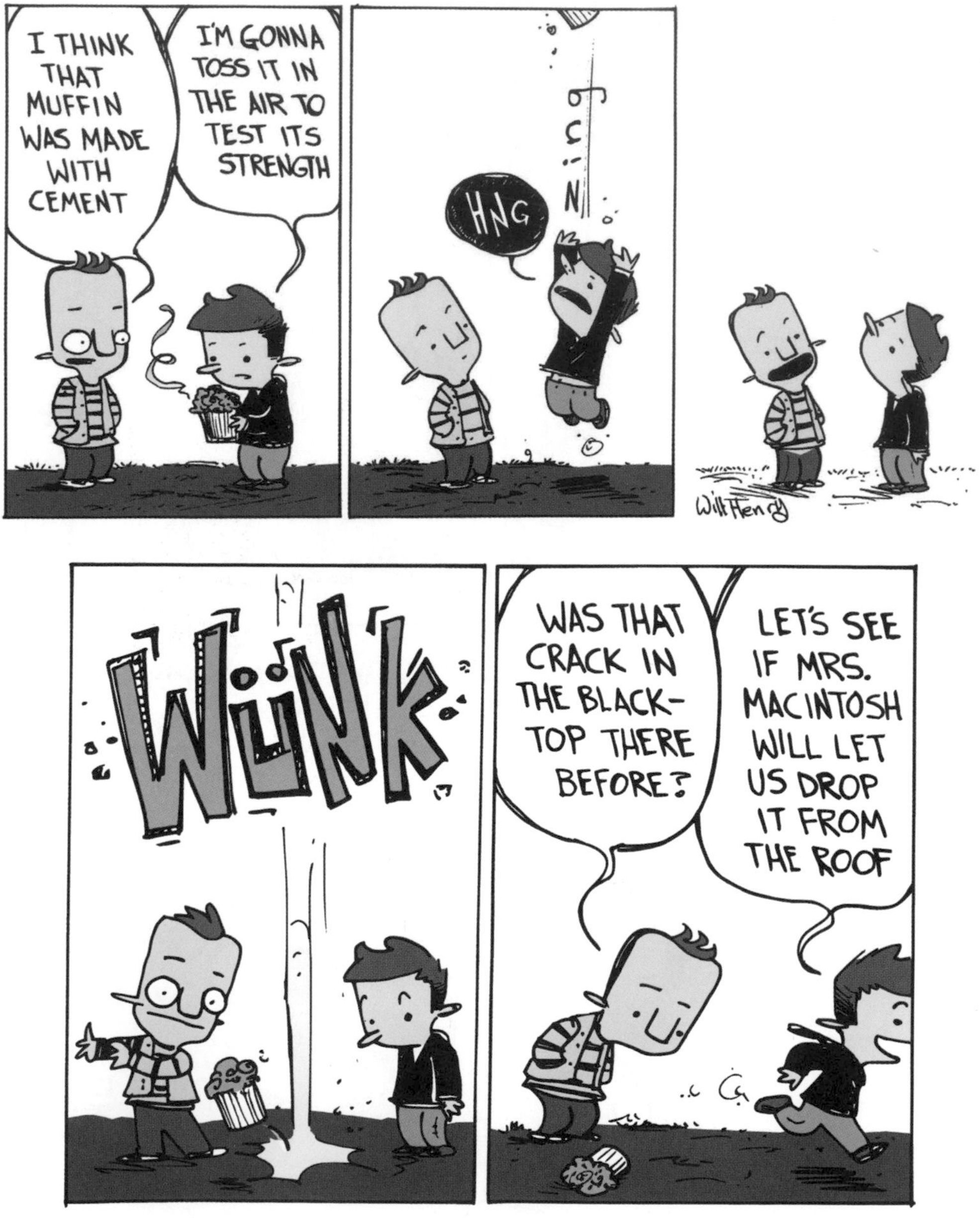
I THINK THAT MUFFIN WAS MADE WITH CEMENT
I'M GONNA TOSS IT IN THE AIR TO TEST ITS STRENGTH
HNG
WUNK
WAS THAT CRACK IN THE BLACK-TOP THERE BEFORE?
LET'S SEE IF MRS. MACINTOSH WILL LET US DROP IT FROM THE ROOF

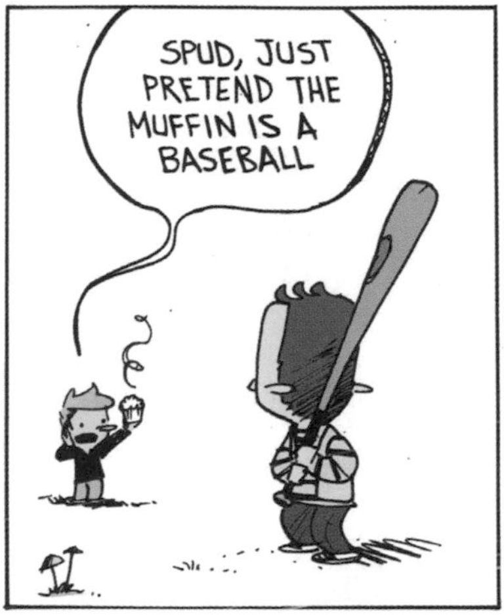
SPUD, JUST PRETEND THE MUFFIN IS A BASEBALL

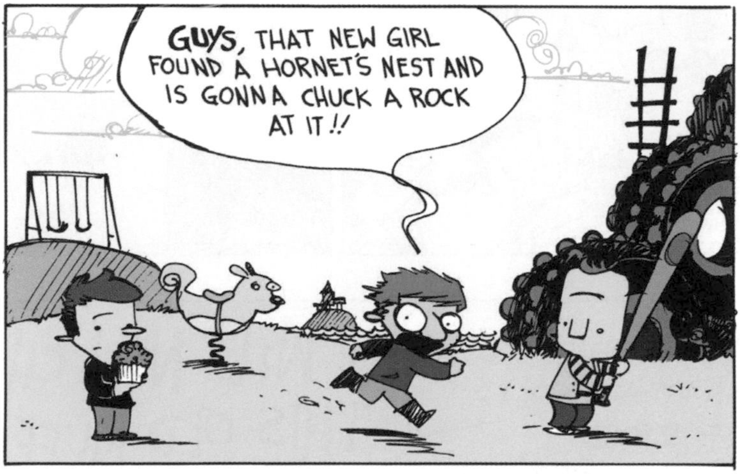
GUYS, THAT NEW GIRL FOUND A HORNET'S NEST AND IS GONNA CHUCK A ROCK AT IT!!

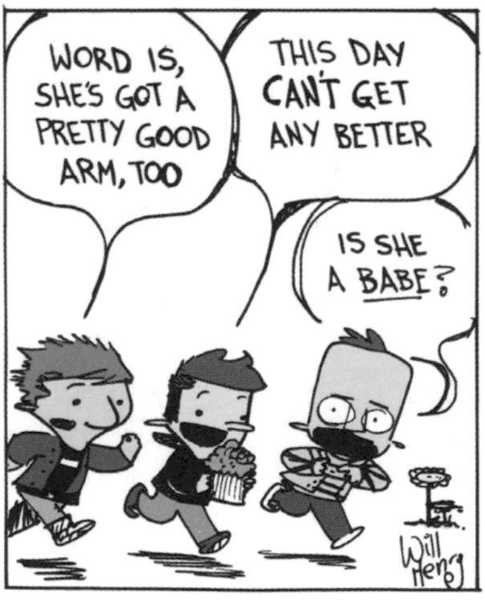
WORD IS, SHE'S GOT A PRETTY GOOD ARM, TOO
THIS DAY CAN'T GET ANY BETTER
IS SHE A BABE?
Will Henry

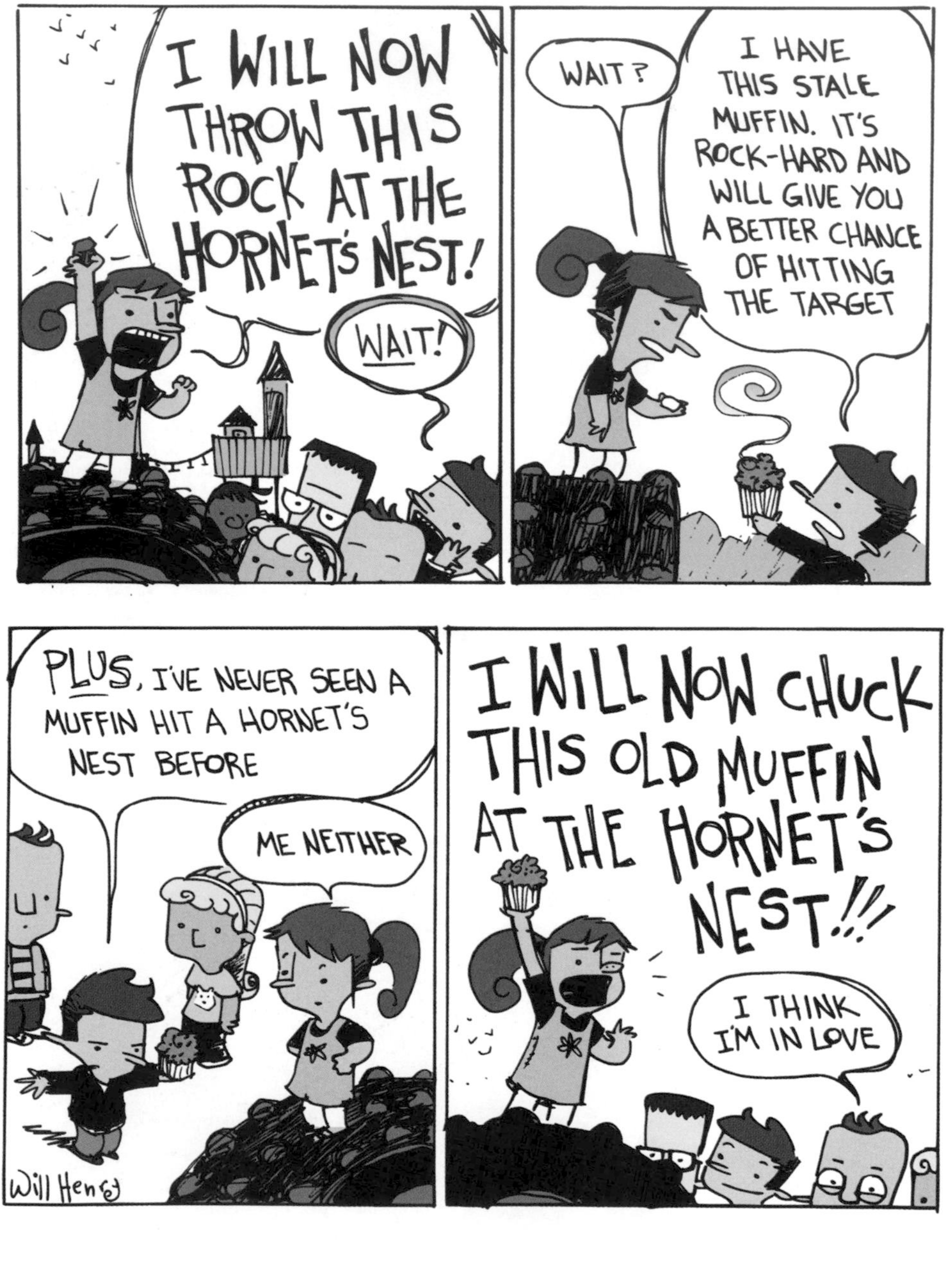
I WILL NOW THROW THIS ROCK AT THE HORNET'S NEST!
WAIT!
WAIT?
I HAVE THIS STALE MUFFIN. IT'S ROCK-HARD AND WILL GIVE YOU A BETTER CHANCE OF HITTING THE TARGET
PLUS, I'VE NEVER SEEN A MUFFIN HIT A HORNET'S NEST BEFORE
ME NEITHER
I WILL NOW CHUCK THIS OLD MUFFIN AT THE HORNET'S NEST!!!
I THINK I'M IN LOVE
Will Henry

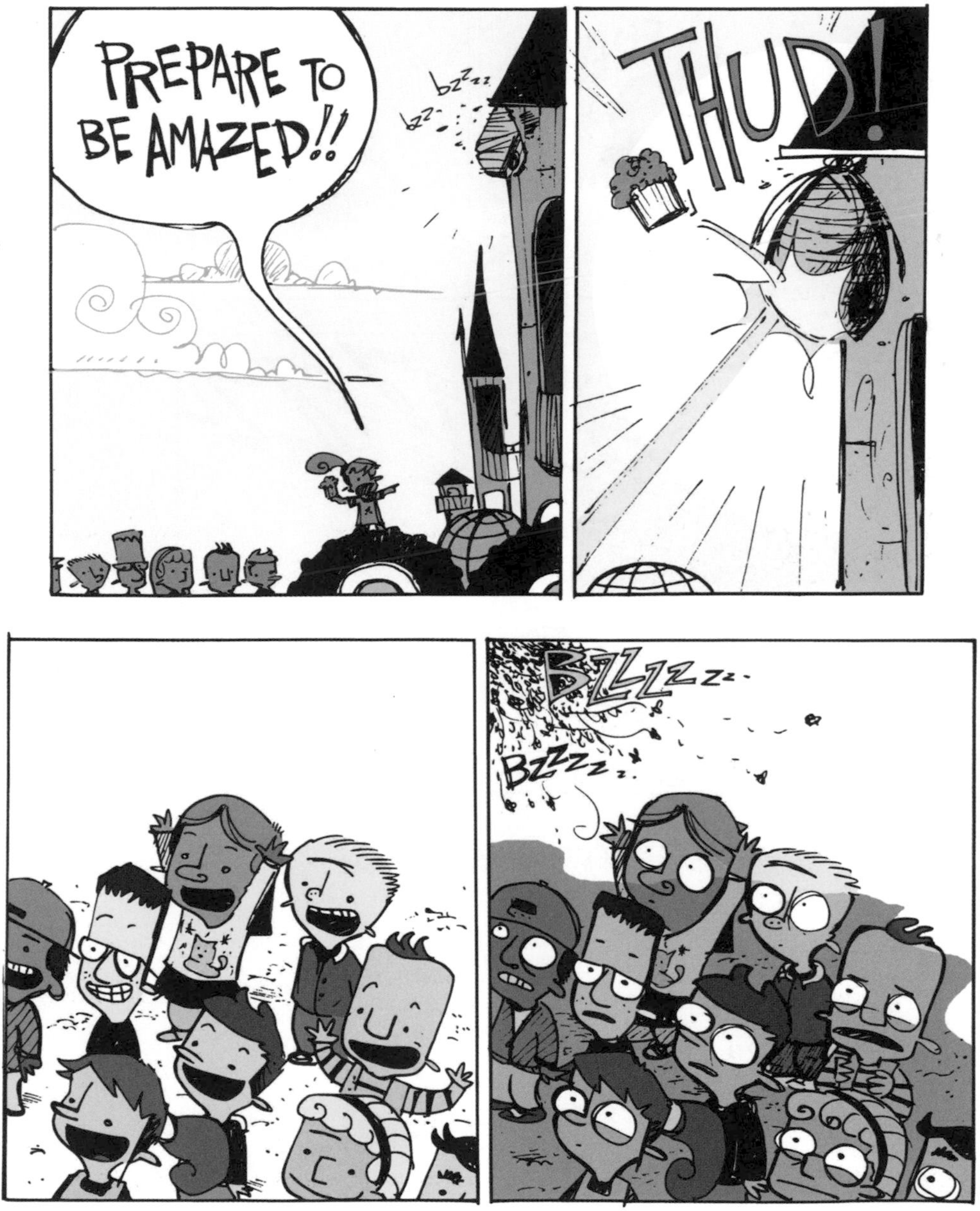
PREPARE TO BE AMAZED!!
bzzzz
bzz
THUD!
BZZZZzz
BZZZZz

BZZZZZ
RUN!
FLIP
BZZZZZ
BZZZZ
THWT
BZZ
BZZZZZZZ
Will Henry
GOT A COUPLE PIMPLES ON YOUR NOSE, EH WALLACE?
MY BABY BOY IS GROWING UP!!

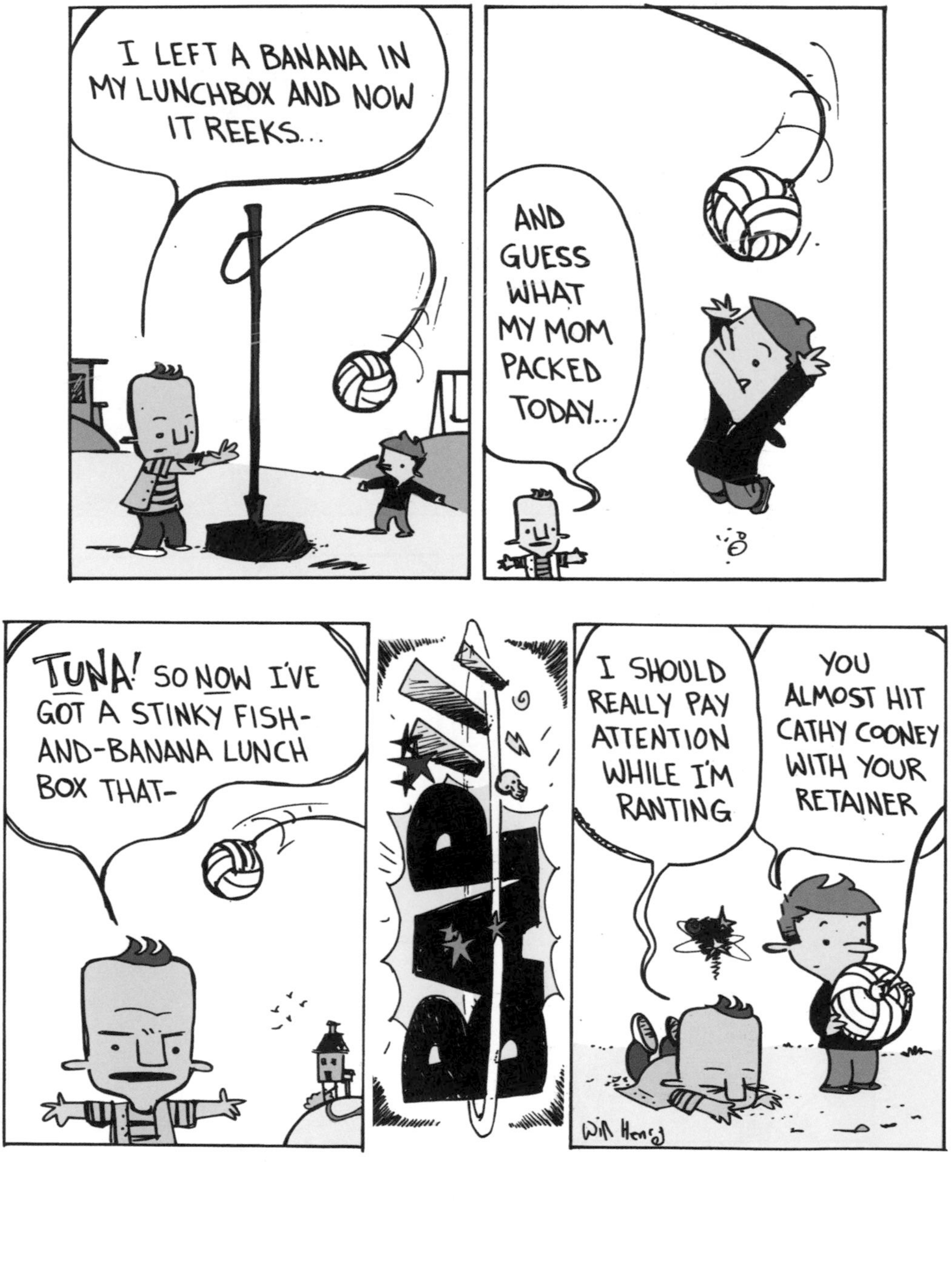

I LEFT A BANANA IN MY LUNCHBOX AND NOW IT REEKS...
AND GUESS WHAT MY MOM PACKED TODAY...
TUNA! SO NOW I'VE GOT A STINKY FISH-AND-BANANA LUNCH BOX THAT-
BAP!
I SHOULD REALLY PAY ATTENTION WHILE I'M RANTING
YOU ALMOST HIT CATHY COONEY WITH YOUR RETAINER
Will Henry

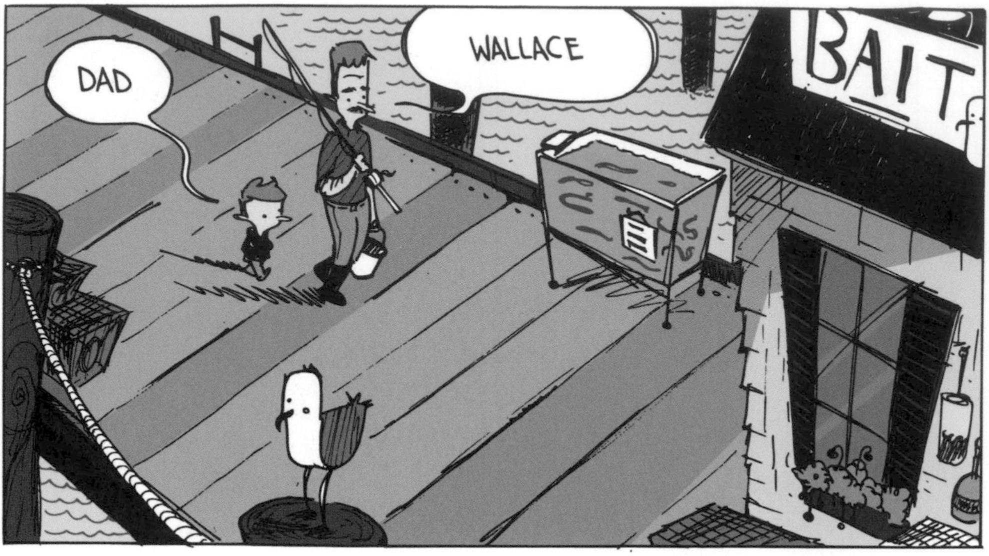
DAD
WALLACE
BAIT

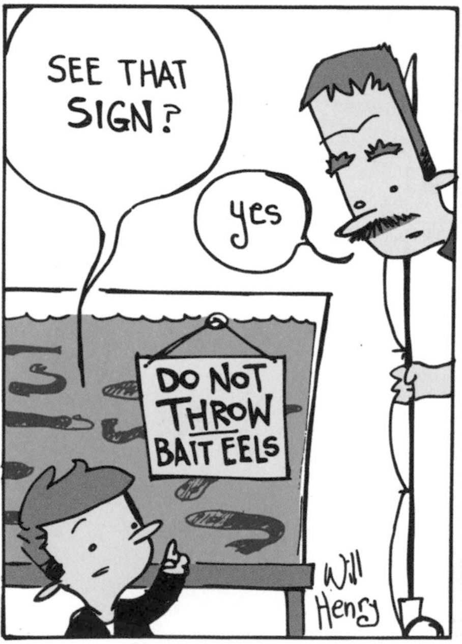
SEE THAT SIGN?
yes
DO NOT THROW BAIT EELS
Will Henry

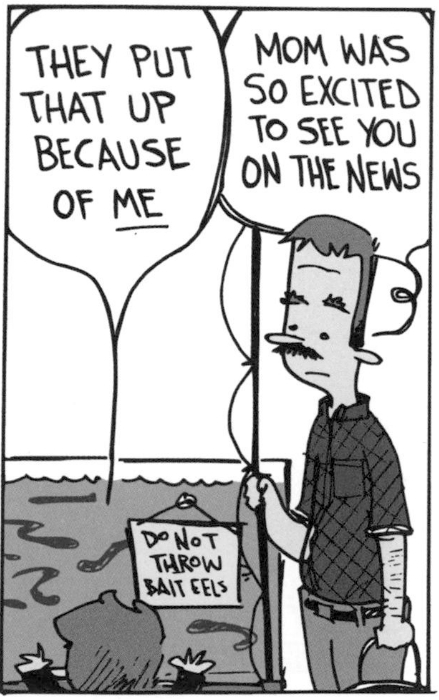
THEY PUT THAT UP BECAUSE OF ME
MOM WAS SO EXCITED TO SEE YOU ON THE NEWS
DO NOT THROW BAIT EELS

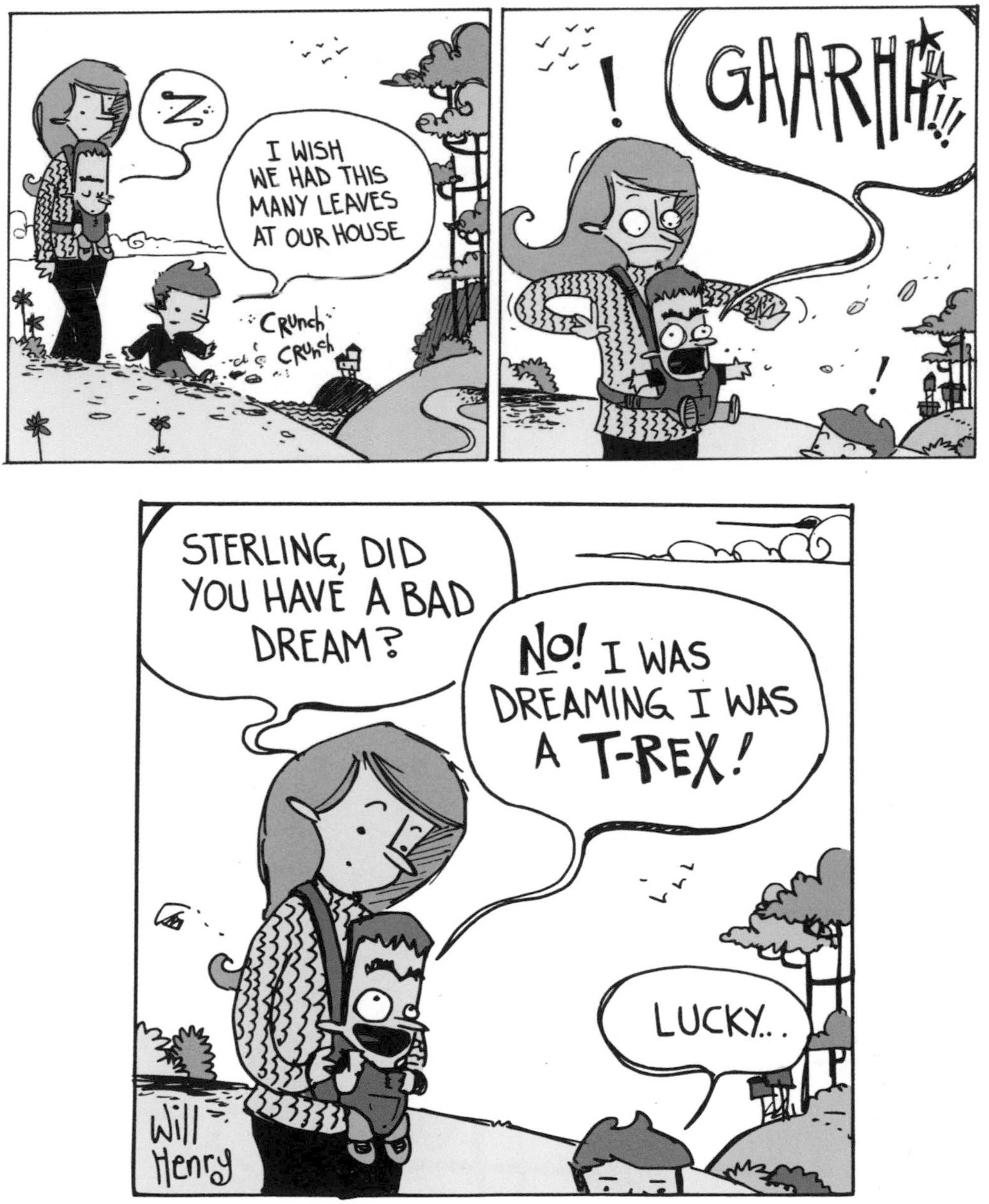
Z
I WISH WE HAD THIS MANY LEAVES AT OUR HOUSE
CRUNCH CRUNCH
!
GAARHH!!!
!
STERLING, DID YOU HAVE A BAD DREAM?
NO! I WAS DREAMING I WAS A T-REX!
LUCKY...
Will Henry

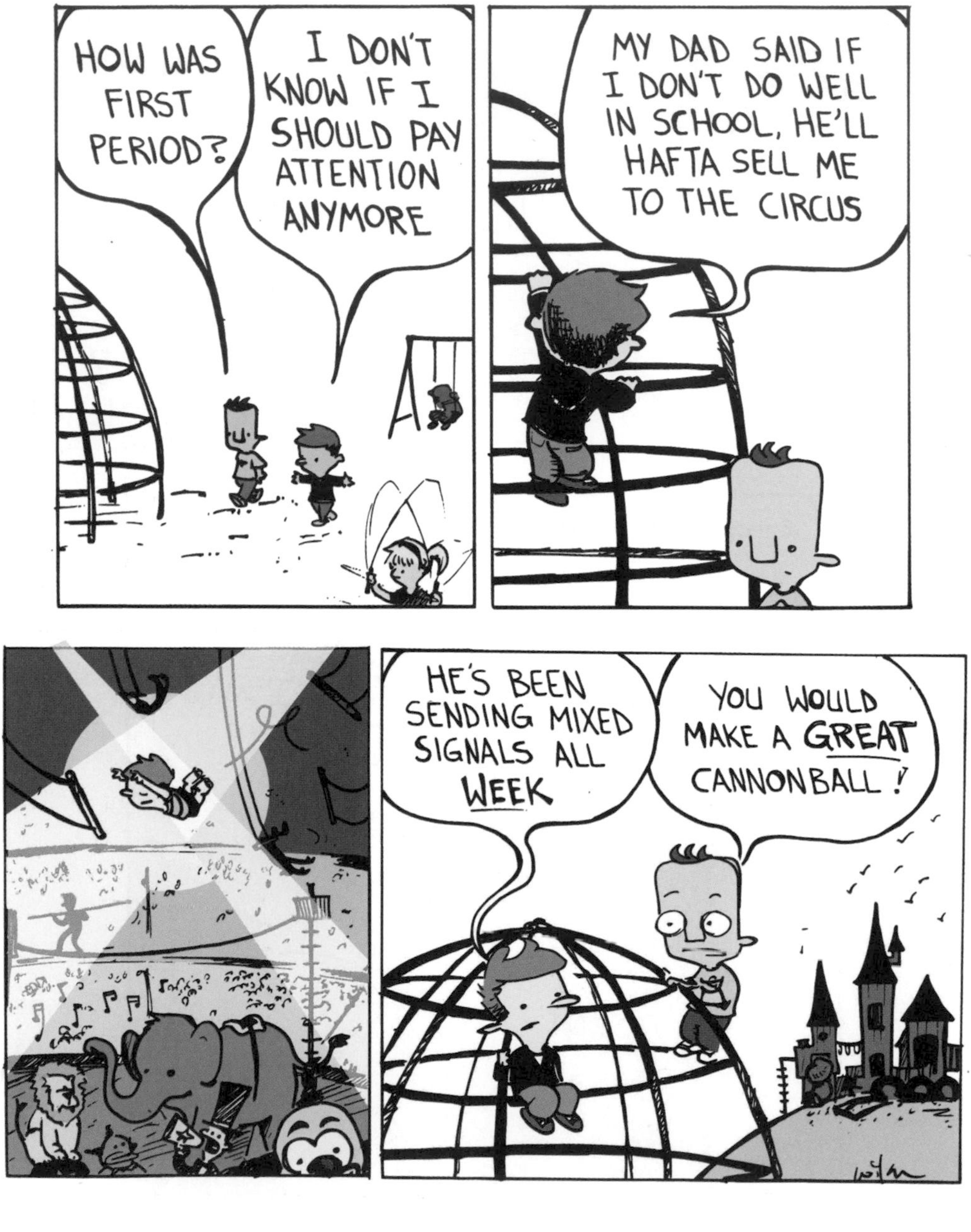
HOW WAS FIRST PERIOD?
I DON'T KNOW IF I SHOULD PAY ATTENTION ANYMORE
MY DAD SAID IF I DON'T DO WELL IN SCHOOL, HE'LL HAFTA SELL ME TO THE CIRCUS
HE'S BEEN SENDING MIXED SIGNALS ALL WEEK
YOU WOULD MAKE A GREAT CANNONBALL!

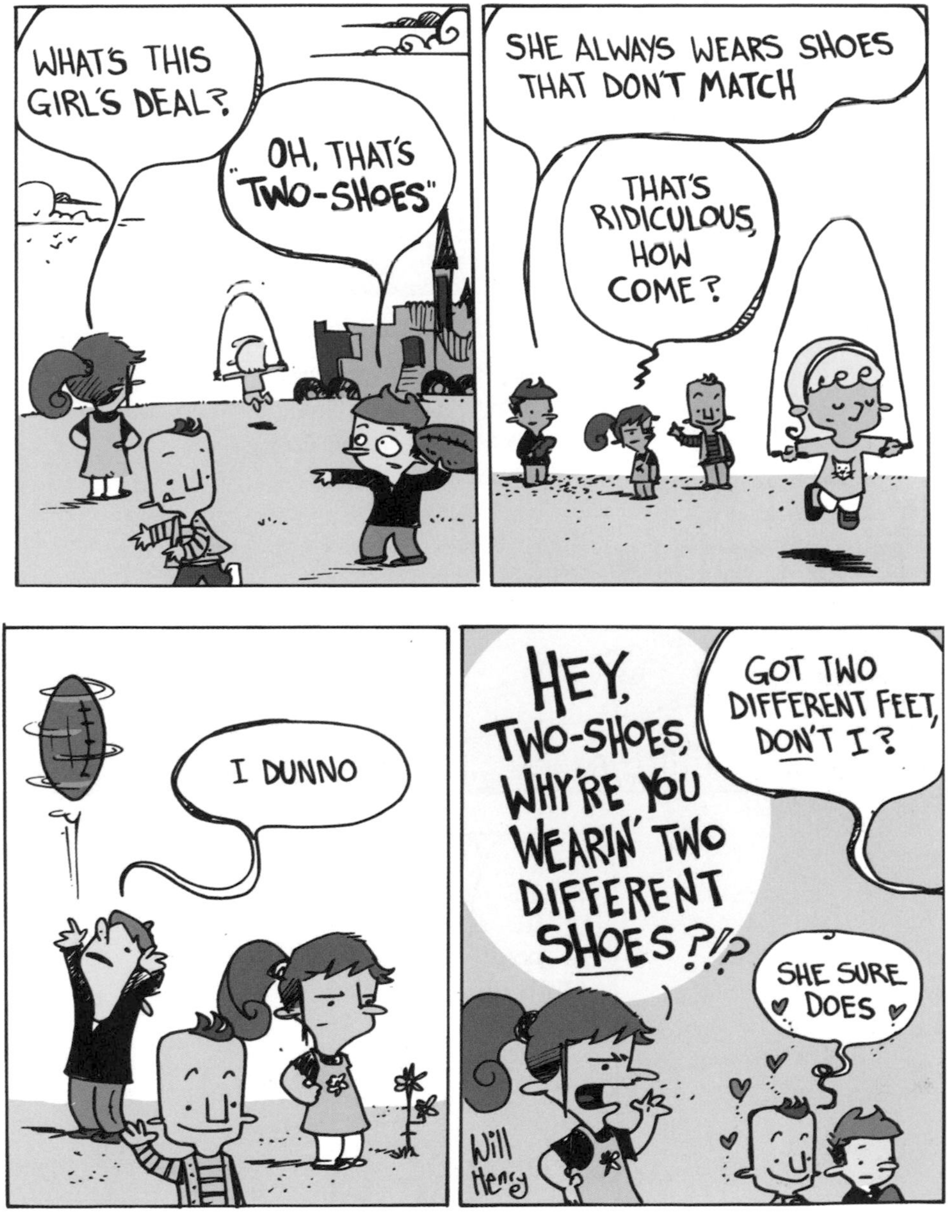
WHAT'S THIS GIRL'S DEAL?
OH, THAT'S "TWO-SHOES"
SHE ALWAYS WEARS SHOES THAT DON'T MATCH
THAT'S RIDICULOUS, HOW COME?
I DUNNO
HEY, TWO-SHOES, WHY'RE YOU WEARIN' TWO DIFFERENT SHOES?!?
GOT TWO DIFFERENT FEET, DON'T I?
SHE SURE DOES
Will Henry

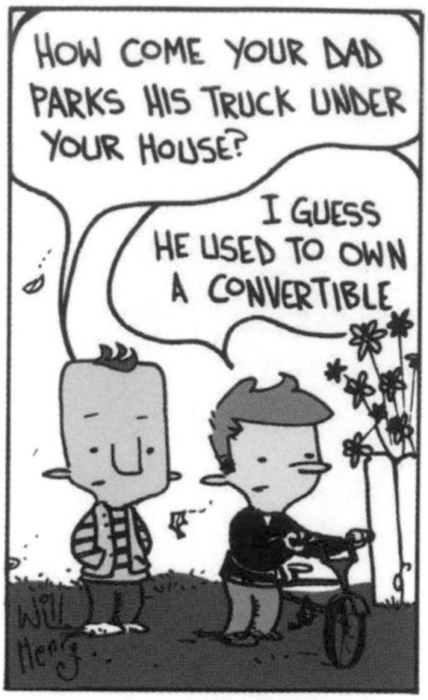
HOW COME YOUR DAD PARKS HIS TRUCK UNDER YOUR HOUSE?
I GUESS HE USED TO OWN A CONVERTIBLE

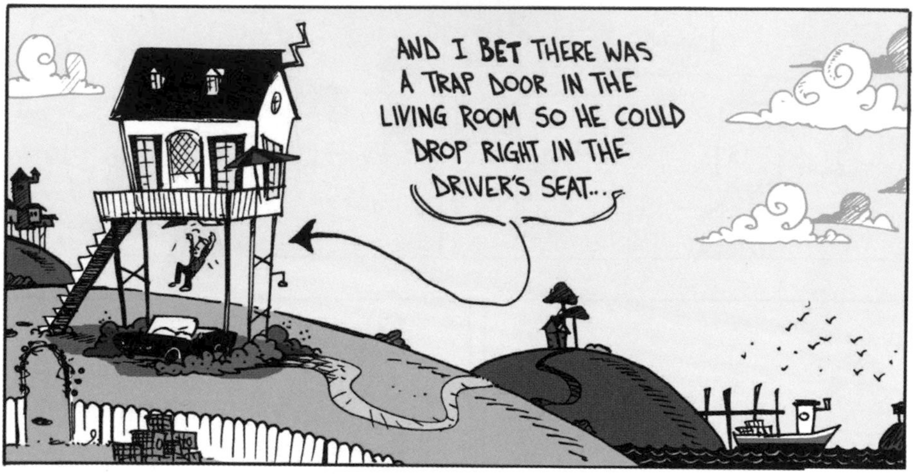
AND I BET THERE WAS A TRAP DOOR IN THE LIVING ROOM SO HE COULD DROP RIGHT IN THE DRIVER'S SEAT...

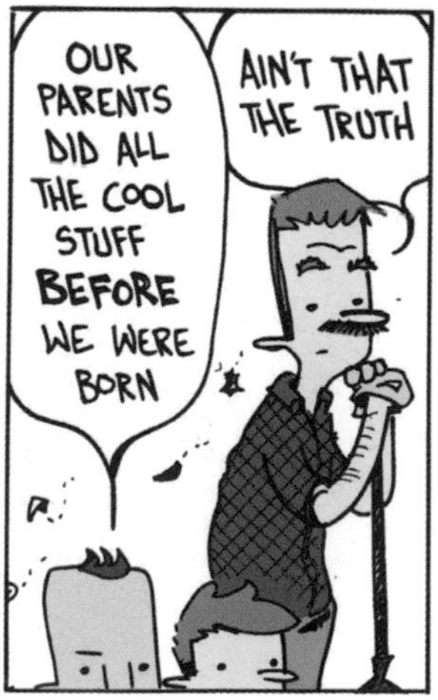
OUR PARENTS DID ALL THE COOL STUFF BEFORE WE WERE BORN
AIN'T THAT THE TRUTH

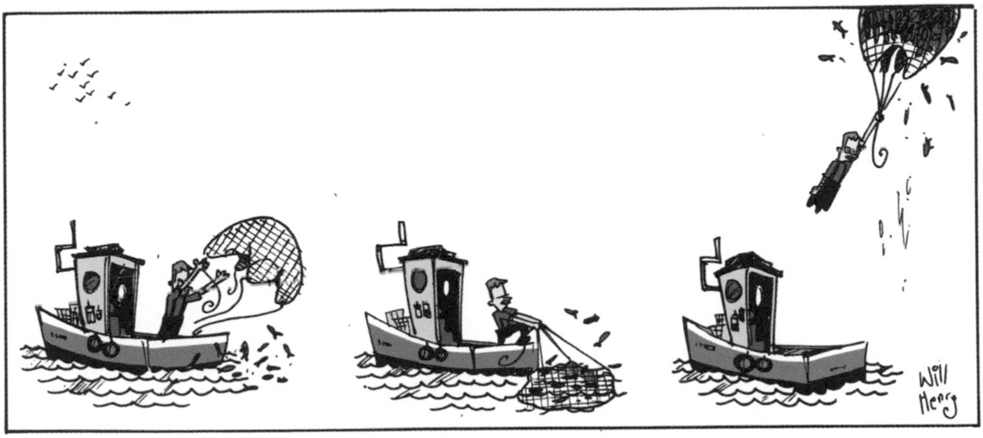
Will Henry

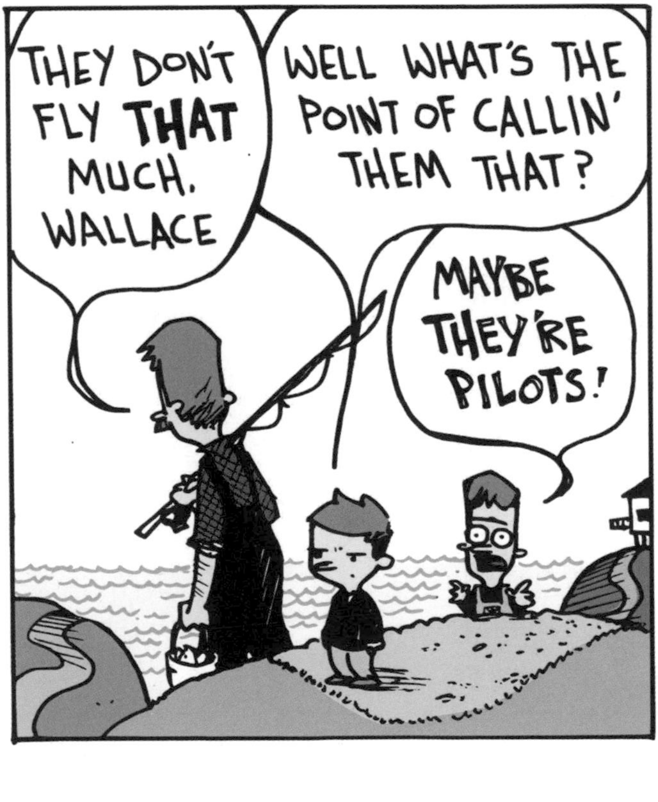
THEY DON'T FLY **THAT** MUCH. WALLACE
WELL WHAT'S THE POINT OF CALLIN' THEM THAT?
MAYBE THEY'RE PILOTS!

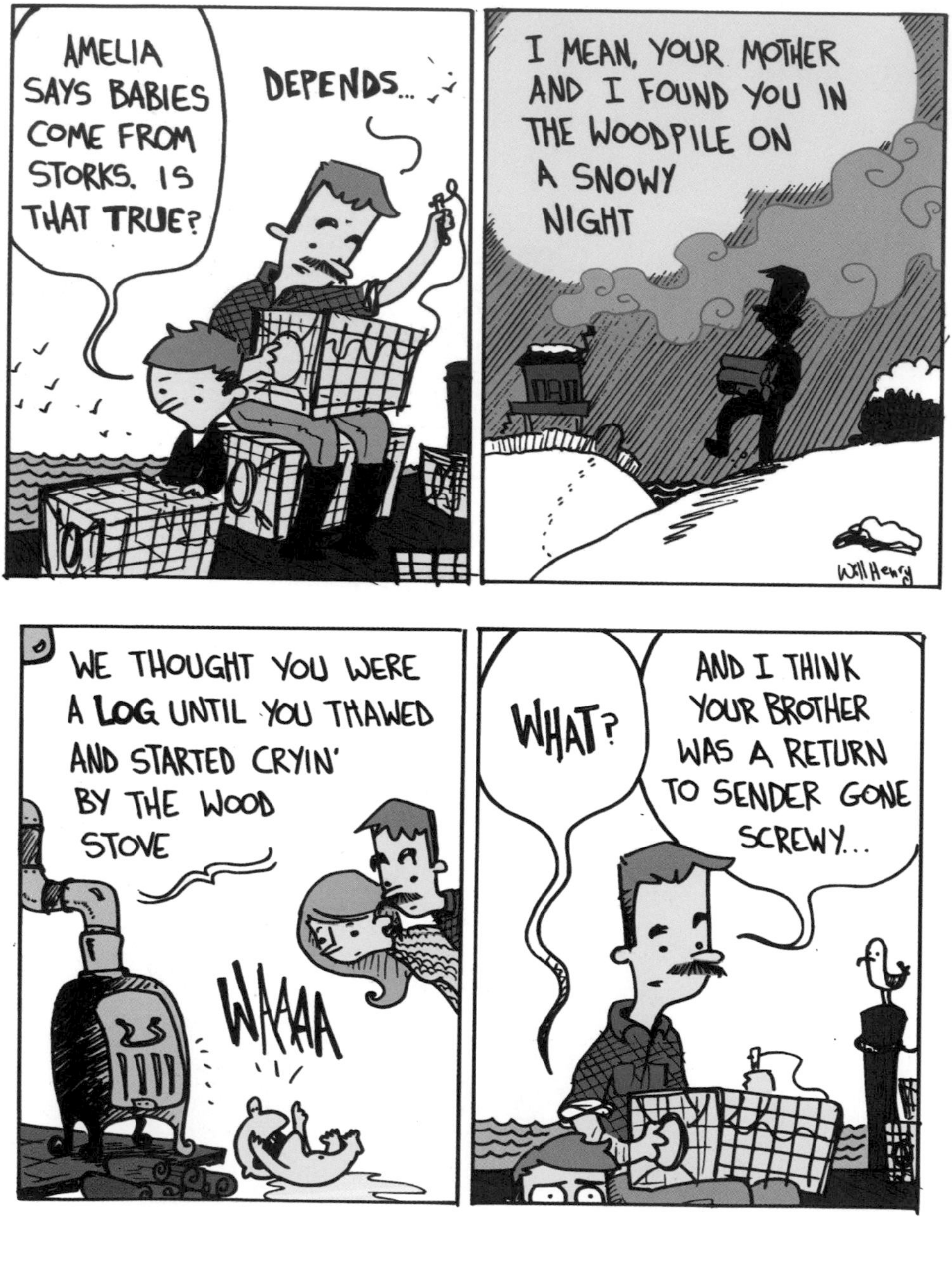
AMELIA SAYS BABIES COME FROM STORKS. IS THAT TRUE?
DEPENDS...
I MEAN, YOUR MOTHER AND I FOUND YOU IN THE WOODPILE ON A SNOWY NIGHT
Will Henry
WE THOUGHT YOU WERE A LOG UNTIL YOU THAWED AND STARTED CRYIN' BY THE WOOD STOVE
WAAAA
WHAT?
AND I THINK YOUR BROTHER WAS A RETURN TO SENDER GONE SCREWY...

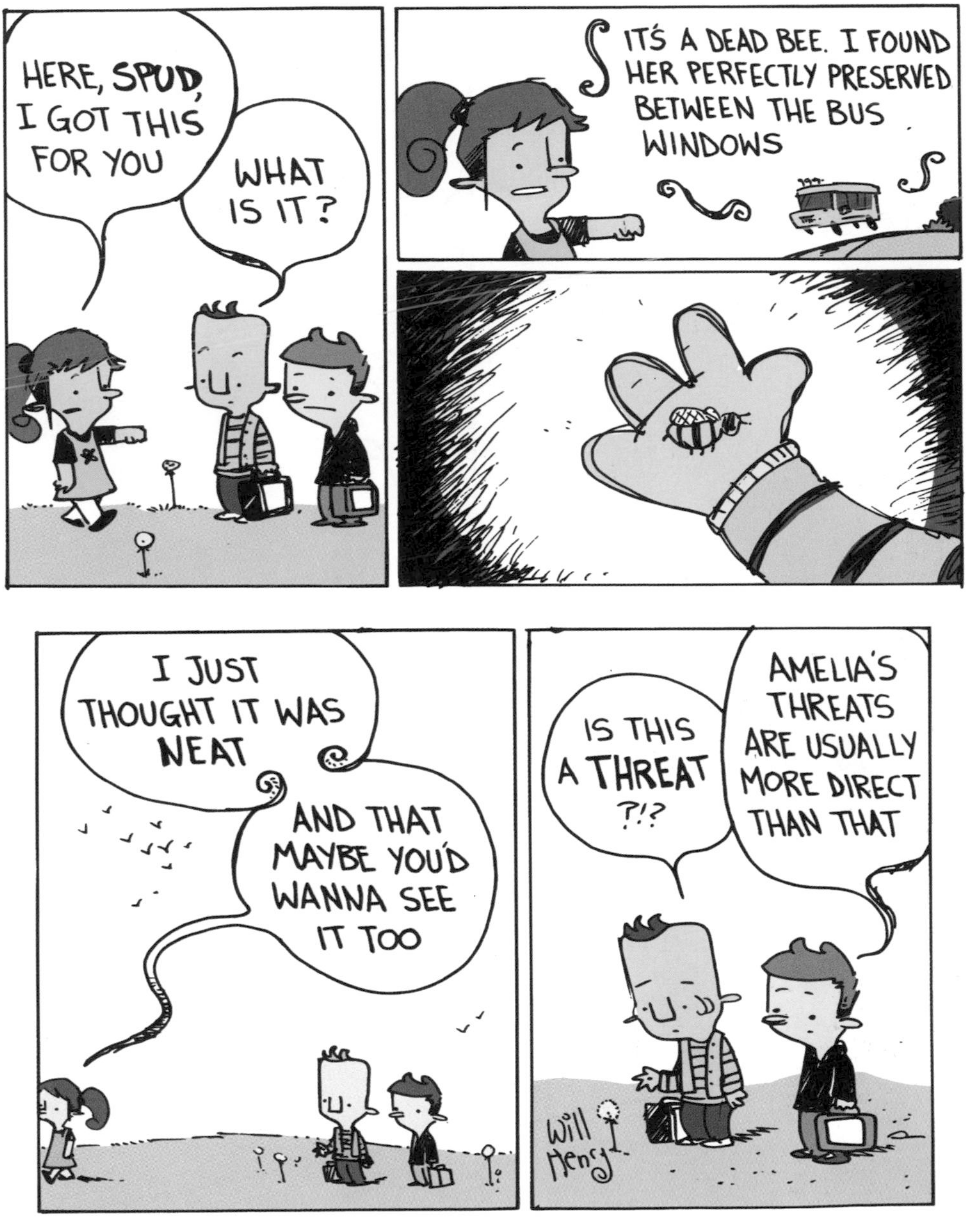
HERE, SPUD, I GOT THIS FOR YOU
WHAT IS IT?
IT'S A DEAD BEE. I FOUND HER PERFECTLY PRESERVED BETWEEN THE BUS WINDOWS
I JUST THOUGHT IT WAS NEAT
AND THAT MAYBE YOU'D WANNA SEE IT TOO
IS THIS A THREAT ?!?
AMELIA'S THREATS ARE USUALLY MORE DIRECT THAN THAT
Will Henry

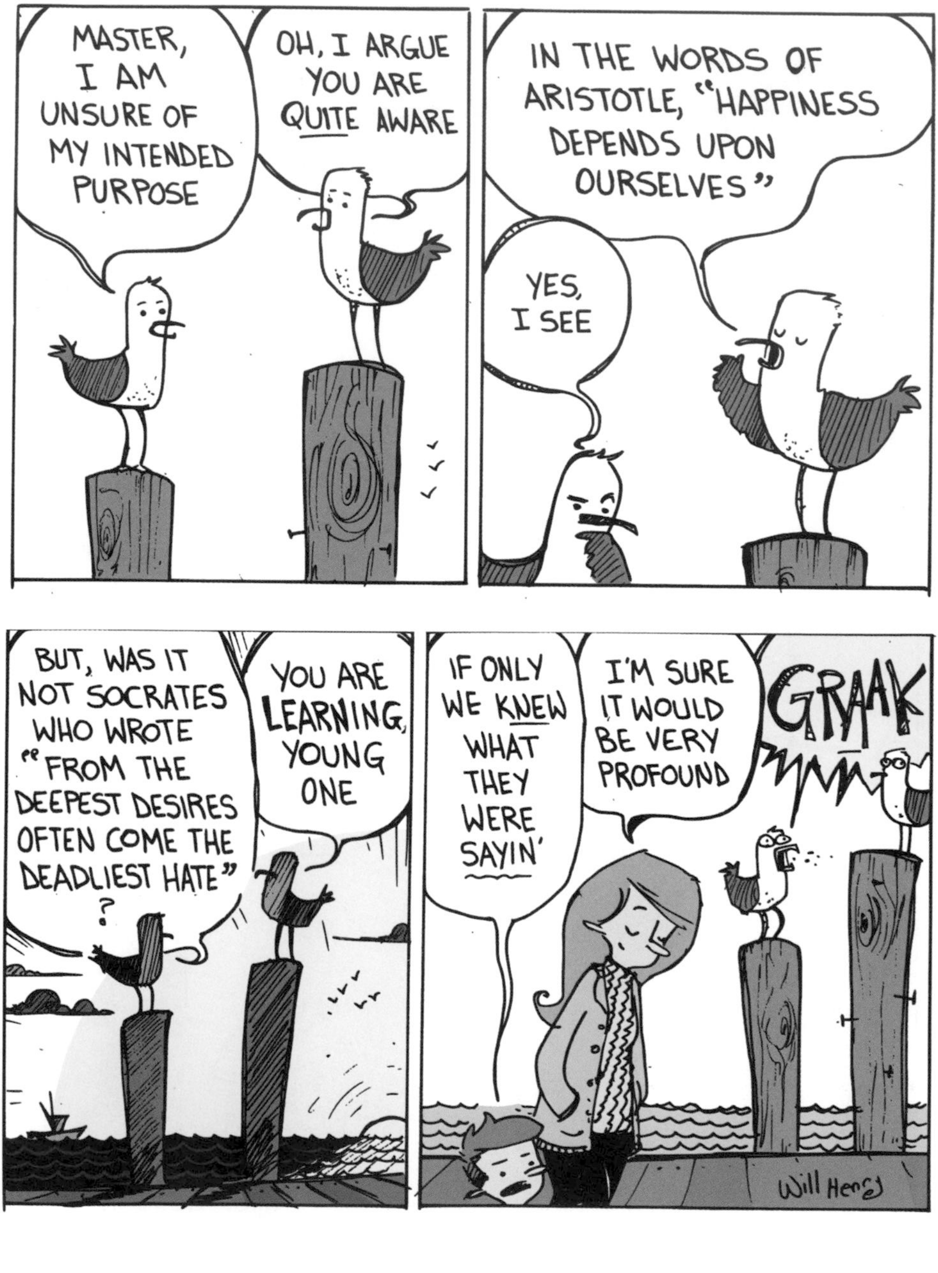
MASTER, I AM UNSURE OF MY INTENDED PURPOSE
OH, I ARGUE YOU ARE QUITE AWARE
IN THE WORDS OF ARISTOTLE, "HAPPINESS DEPENDS UPON OURSELVES"
YES, I SEE
BUT, WAS IT NOT SOCRATES WHO WROTE "FROM THE DEEPEST DESIRES OFTEN COME THE DEADLIEST HATE"?
YOU ARE LEARNING, YOUNG ONE
IF ONLY WE KNEW WHAT THEY WERE SAYIN'
I'M SURE IT WOULD BE VERY PROFOUND
GRAAK
Will Henry

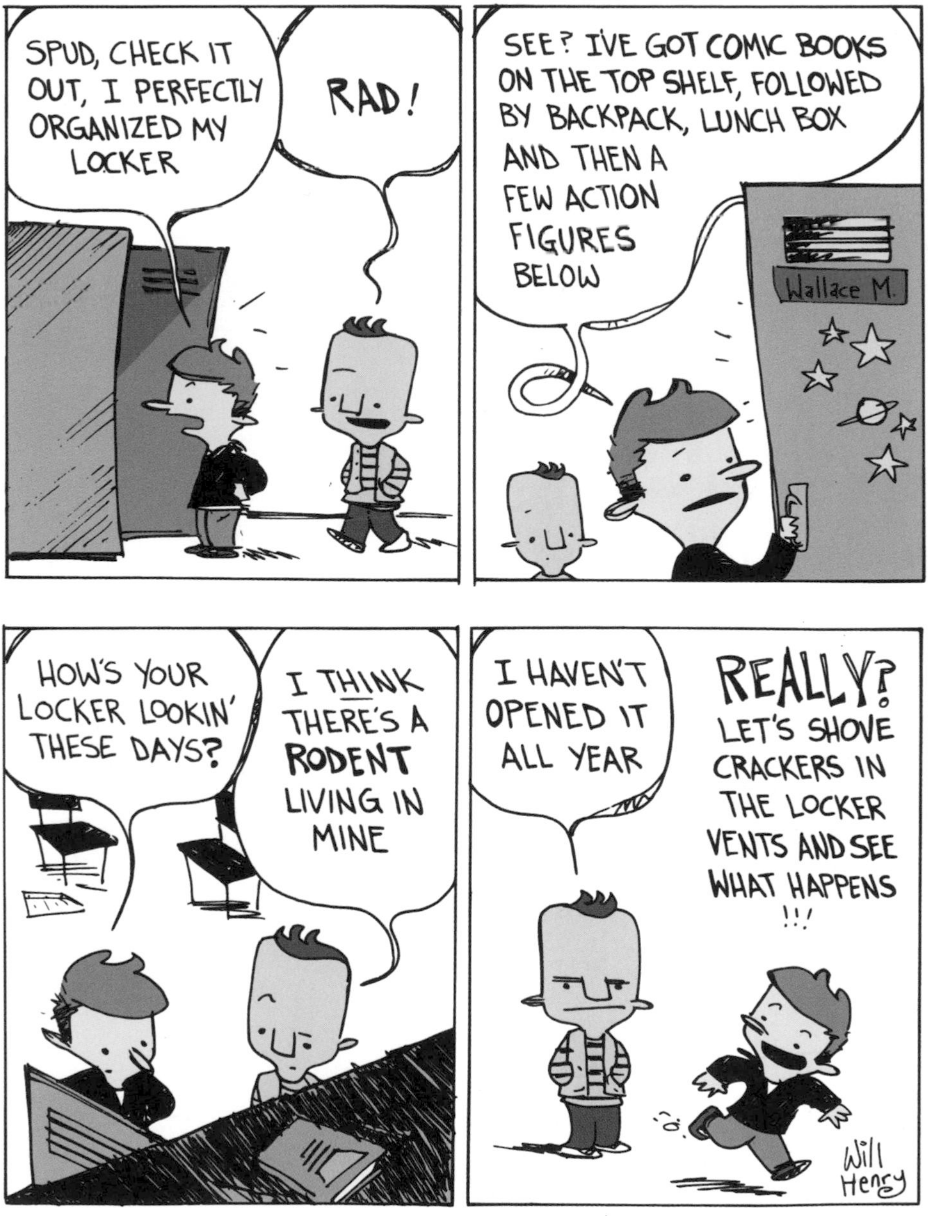
SPUD, CHECK IT OUT, I PERFECTLY ORGANIZED MY LOCKER
RAD!
SEE? I'VE GOT COMIC BOOKS ON THE TOP SHELF, FOLLOWED BY BACKPACK, LUNCH BOX AND THEN A FEW ACTION FIGURES BELOW
Wallace M.
HOW'S YOUR LOCKER LOOKIN' THESE DAYS?
I THINK THERE'S A RODENT LIVING IN MINE
I HAVEN'T OPENED IT ALL YEAR
REALLY? LET'S SHOVE CRACKERS IN THE LOCKER VENTS AND SEE WHAT HAPPENS
!!!
Will Henry

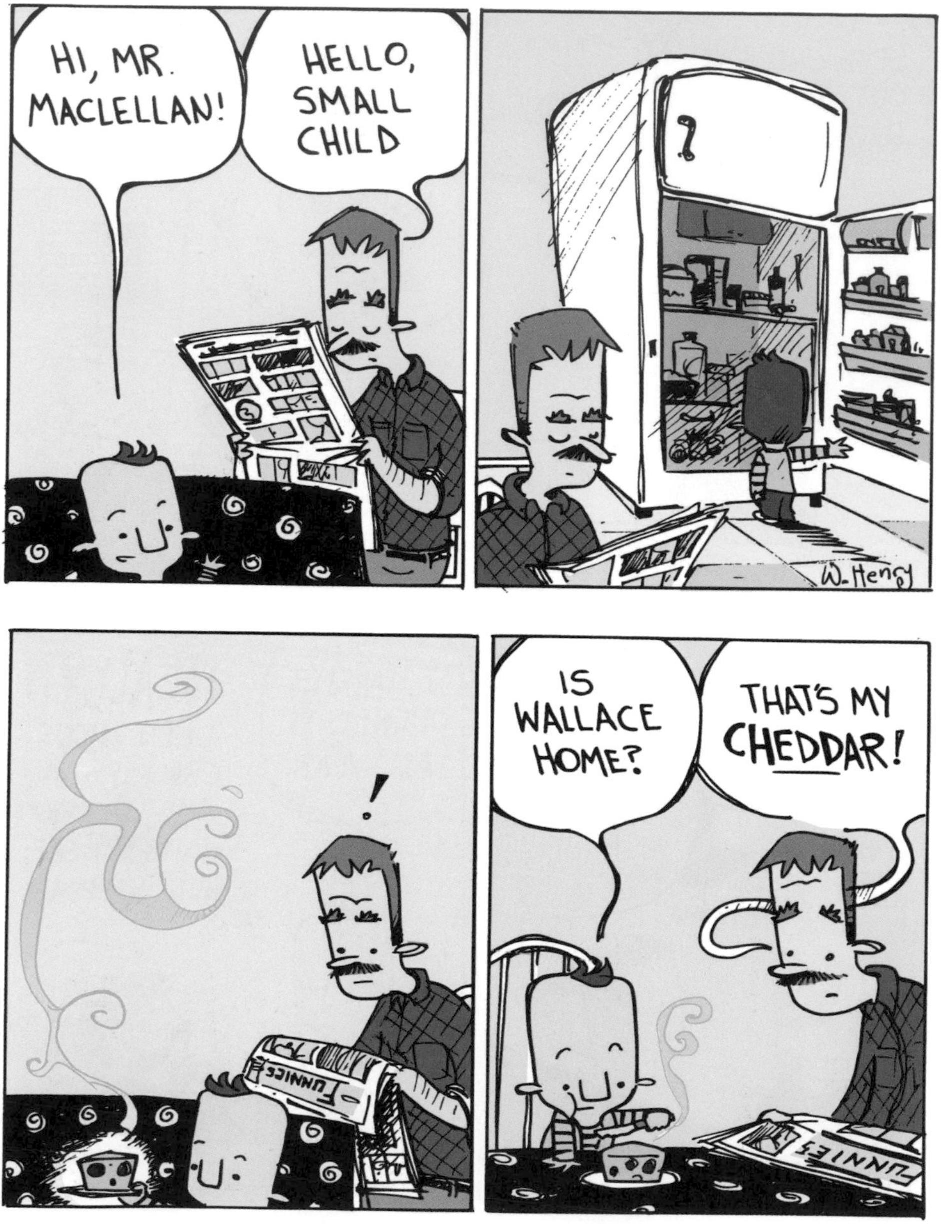
HI, MR. MACLELLAN!
HELLO, SMALL CHILD
W. Henry
!
IS WALLACE HOME?
THAT'S MY CHEDDAR!
FUNNIES

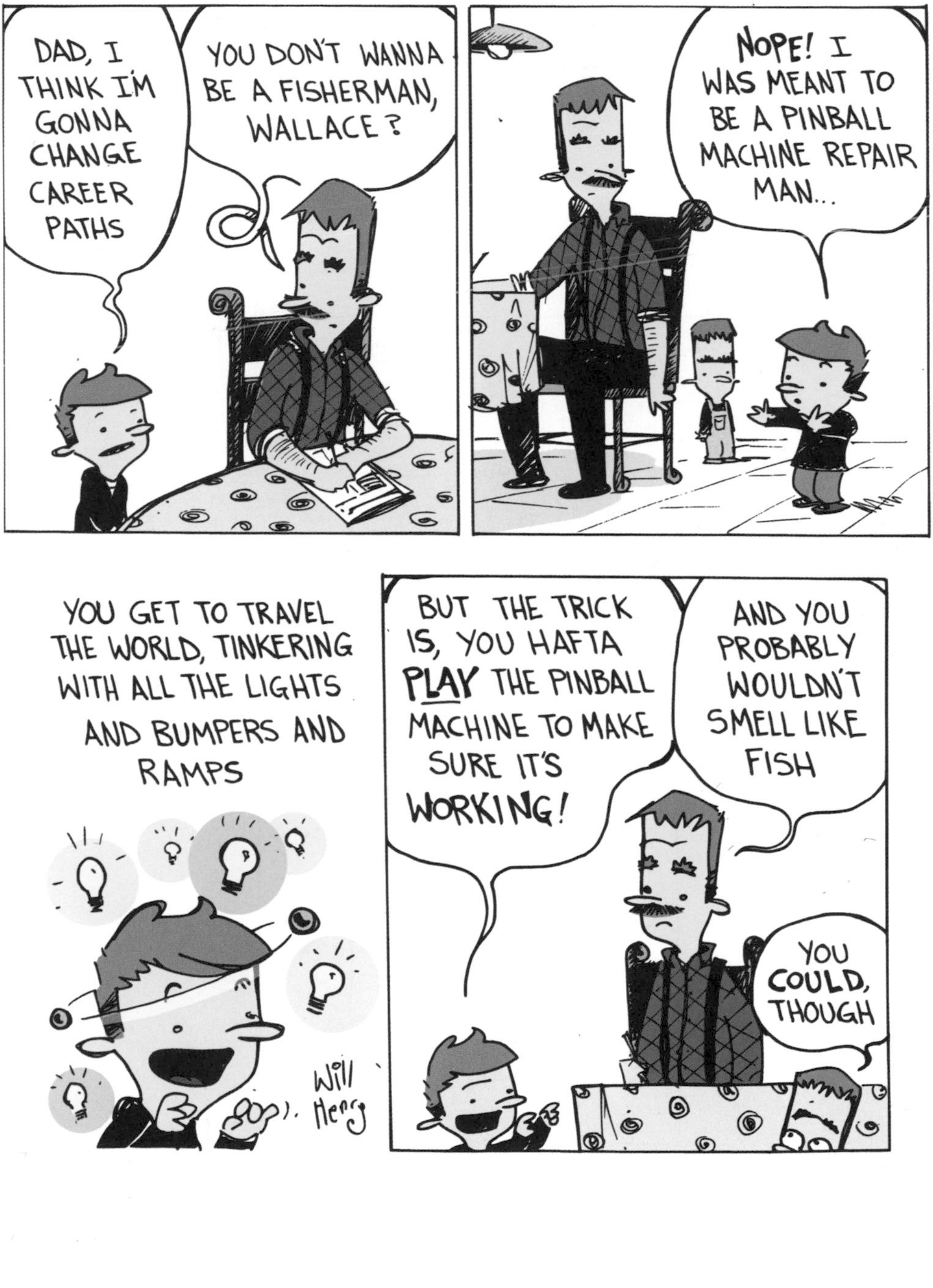
DAD, I THINK I'M GONNA CHANGE CAREER PATHS
YOU DON'T WANNA BE A FISHERMAN, WALLACE?
NOPE! I WAS MEANT TO BE A PINBALL MACHINE REPAIR MAN...
YOU GET TO TRAVEL THE WORLD, TINKERING WITH ALL THE LIGHTS AND BUMPERS AND RAMPS
Will Henry
BUT THE TRICK IS, YOU HAFTA PLAY THE PINBALL MACHINE TO MAKE SURE IT'S WORKING!
AND YOU PROBABLY WOULDN'T SMELL LIKE FISH
YOU COULD, THOUGH

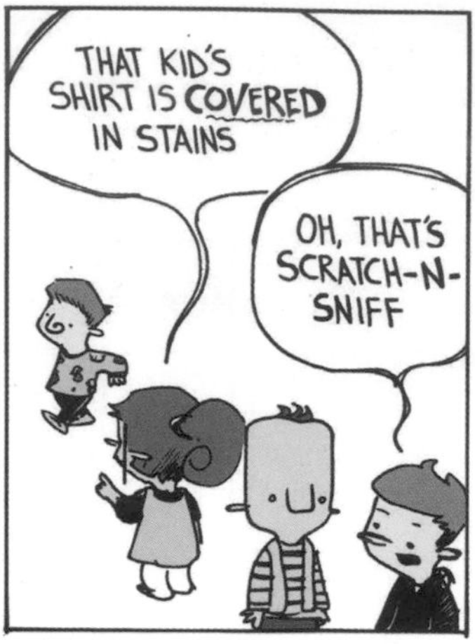
THAT KID'S SHIRT IS COVERED IN STAINS
OH, THAT'S SCRATCH-N-SNIFF

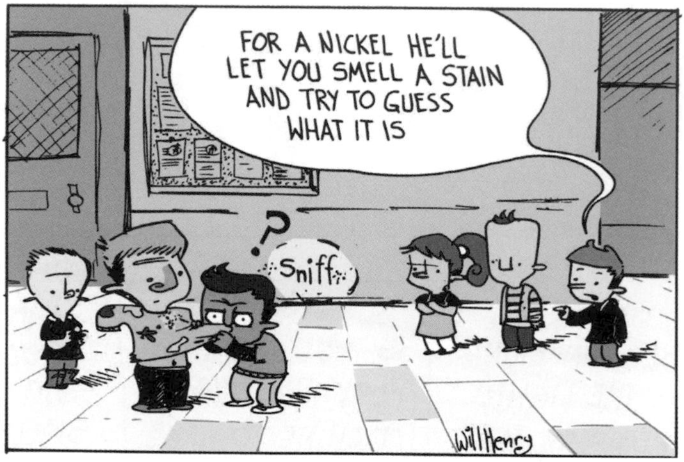
FOR A NICKEL HE'LL LET YOU SMELL A STAIN AND TRY TO GUESS WHAT IT IS
?
Sniff
Will Henry

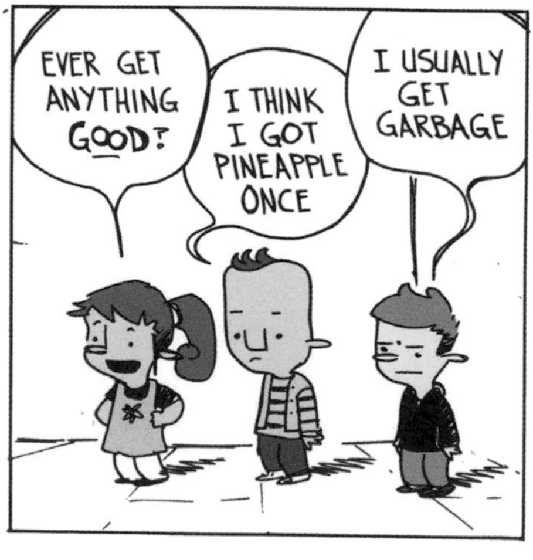
EVER GET ANYTHING GOOD?
I THINK I GOT PINEAPPLE ONCE
I USUALLY GET GARBAGE

SPUD! C'MON UP, WE'RE GONNA JUMP IN THE OCEAN

Will Henry

I'D RATHER NOT

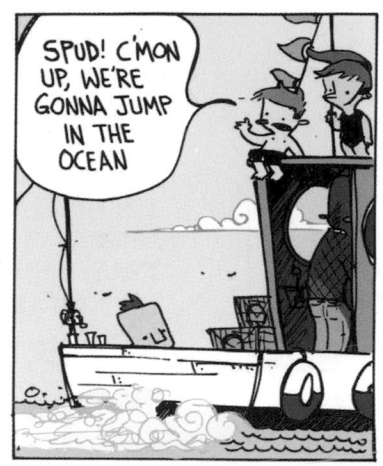

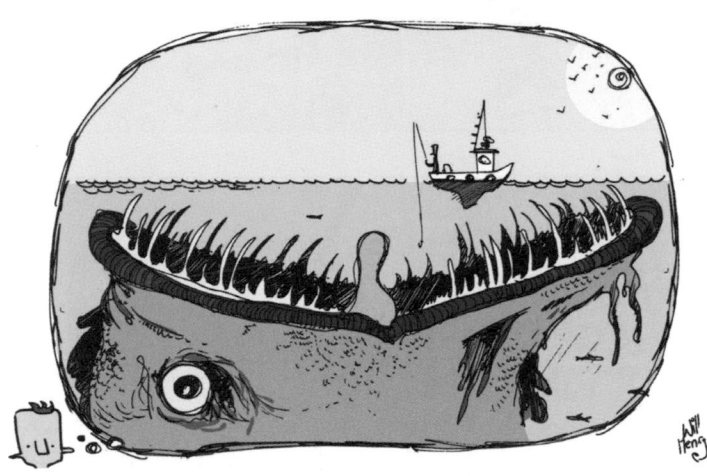

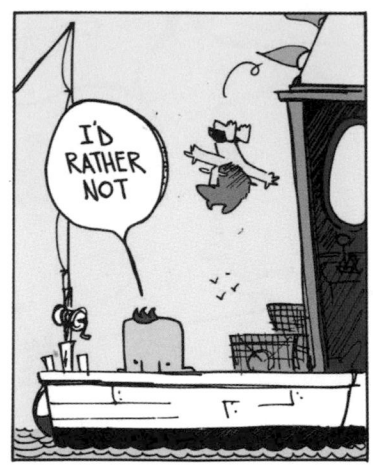

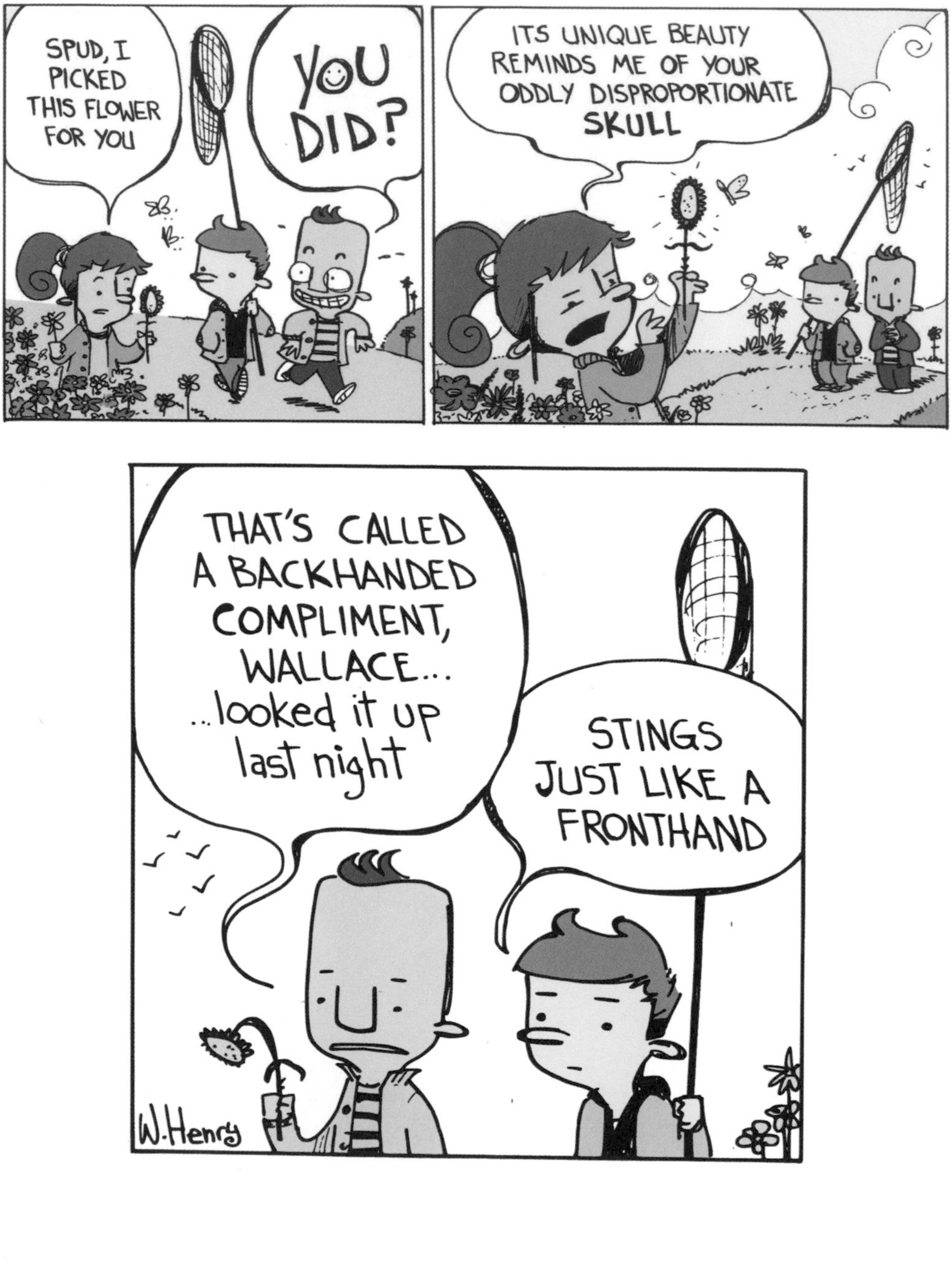
SPUD, I PICKED THIS FLOWER FOR YOU
YOU DID?
ITS UNIQUE BEAUTY REMINDS ME OF YOUR ODDLY DISPROPORTIONATE SKULL
THAT'S CALLED A BACKHANDED COMPLIMENT, WALLACE... ...looked it up last night
STINGS JUST LIKE A FRONTHAND
W.Henry

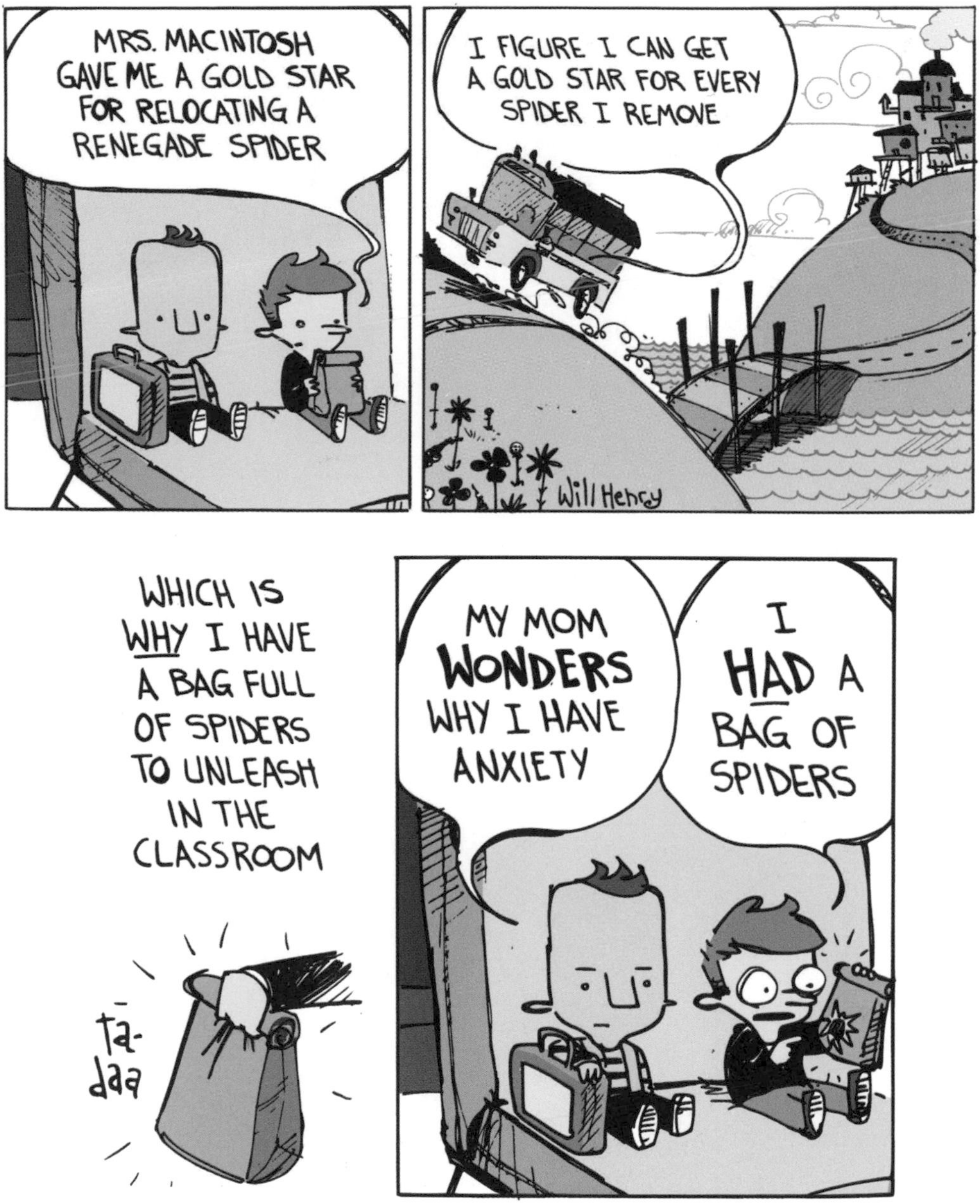
MRS. MACINTOSH GAVE ME A GOLD STAR FOR RELOCATING A RENEGADE SPIDER
I FIGURE I CAN GET A GOLD STAR FOR EVERY SPIDER I REMOVE
Will Henry
WHICH IS WHY I HAVE A BAG FULL OF SPIDERS TO UNLEASH IN THE CLASSROOM
ta-daa
MY MOM WONDERS WHY I HAVE ANXIETY
I HAD A BAG OF SPIDERS

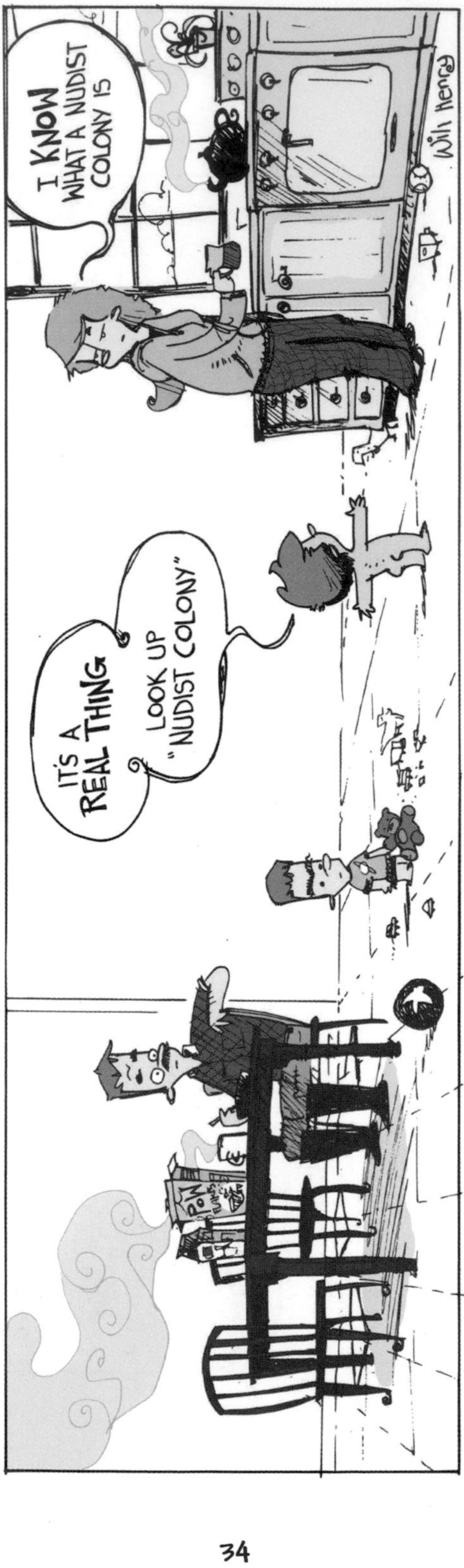
IT'S A REAL THING
LOOK UP "NUDIST COLONY"
I KNOW WHAT A NUDIST COLONY IS
Will Henry

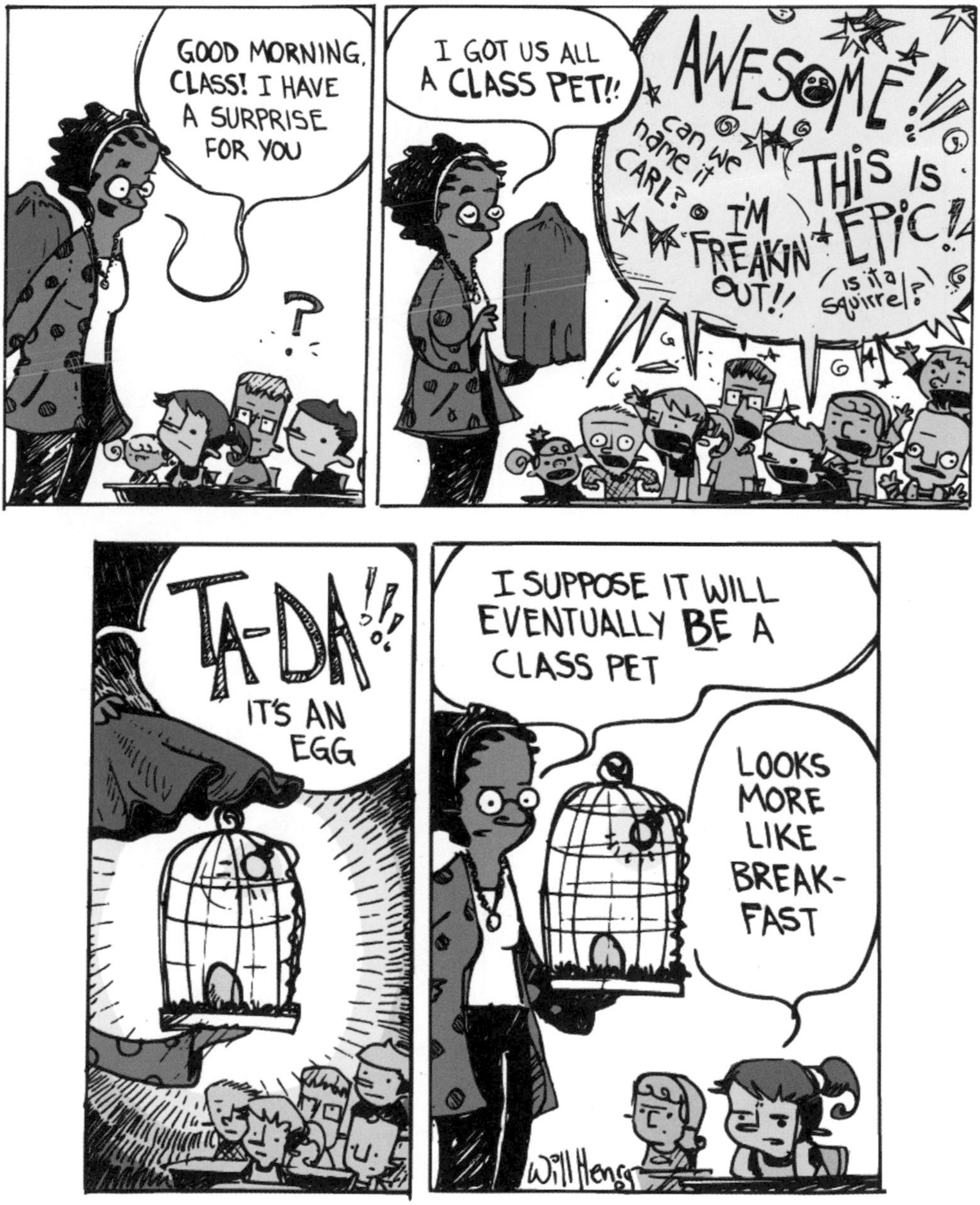
GOOD MORNING, CLASS! I HAVE A SURPRISE FOR YOU
?
I GOT US ALL A CLASS PET!!
AWESOME!!!
can we name it CARL?
THIS IS EPIC!
I'M FREAKIN OUT!!
is it a squirrel?
TA-DA!!!
IT'S AN EGG
I SUPPOSE IT WILL EVENTUALLY BE A CLASS PET
LOOKS MORE LIKE BREAK-FAST
Will Henry

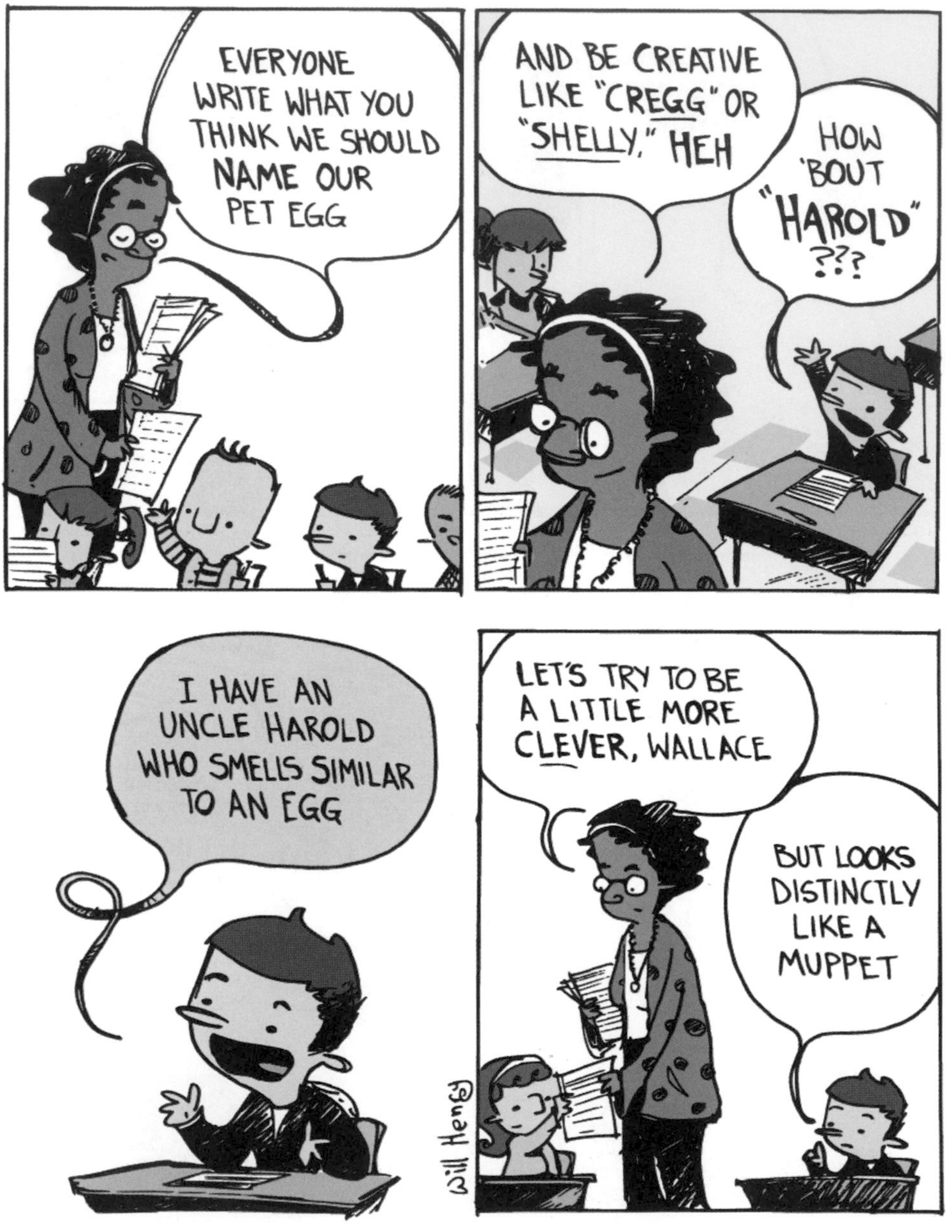
EVERYONE WRITE WHAT YOU THINK WE SHOULD NAME OUR PET EGG
AND BE CREATIVE LIKE "CREGG" OR "SHELLY." HEH
HOW 'BOUT "HAROLD" ???
I HAVE AN UNCLE HAROLD WHO SMELLS SIMILAR TO AN EGG
LET'S TRY TO BE A LITTLE MORE CLEVER, WALLACE
BUT LOOKS DISTINCTLY LIKE A MUPPET
Will Henry

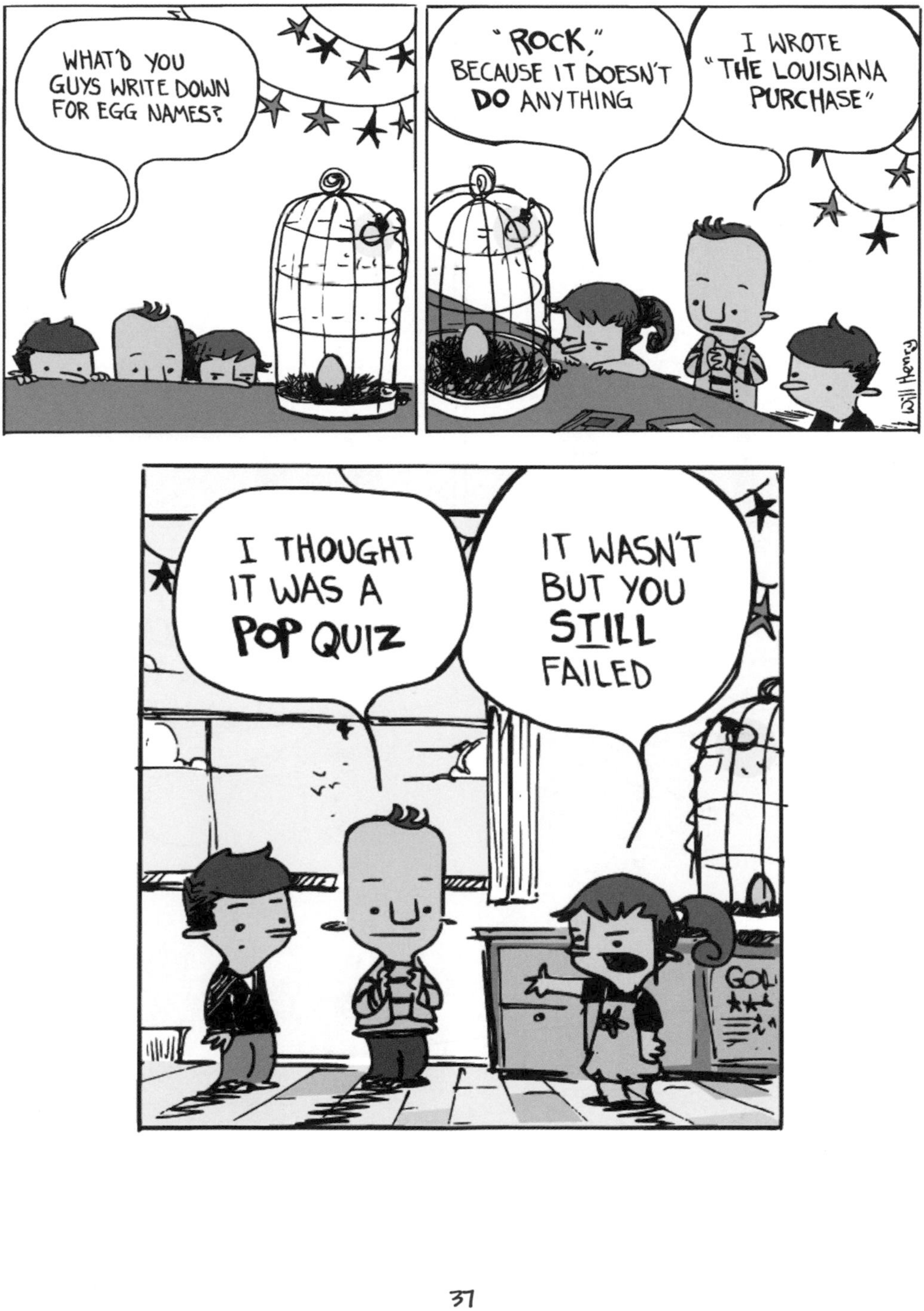
WHAT'D YOU GUYS WRITE DOWN FOR EGG NAMES?
"ROCK," BECAUSE IT DOESN'T DO ANYTHING
I WROTE "THE LOUISIANA PURCHASE"
Will Henry
I THOUGHT IT WAS A POP QUIZ
IT WASN'T BUT YOU STILL FAILED

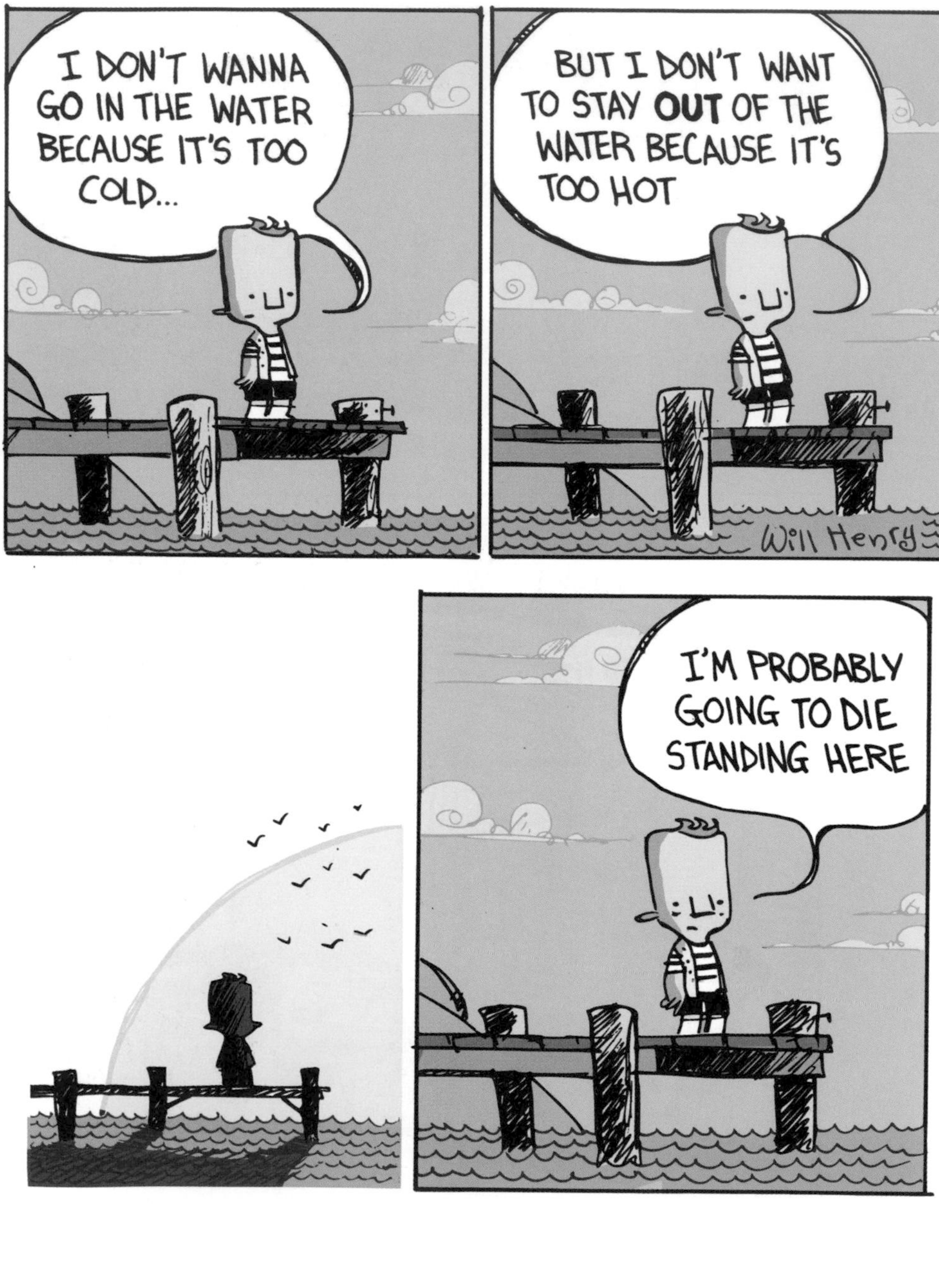
I DON'T WANNA GO IN THE WATER BECAUSE IT'S TOO COLD...
BUT I DON'T WANT TO STAY OUT OF THE WATER BECAUSE IT'S TOO HOT
Will Henry
I'M PROBABLY GOING TO DIE STANDING HERE

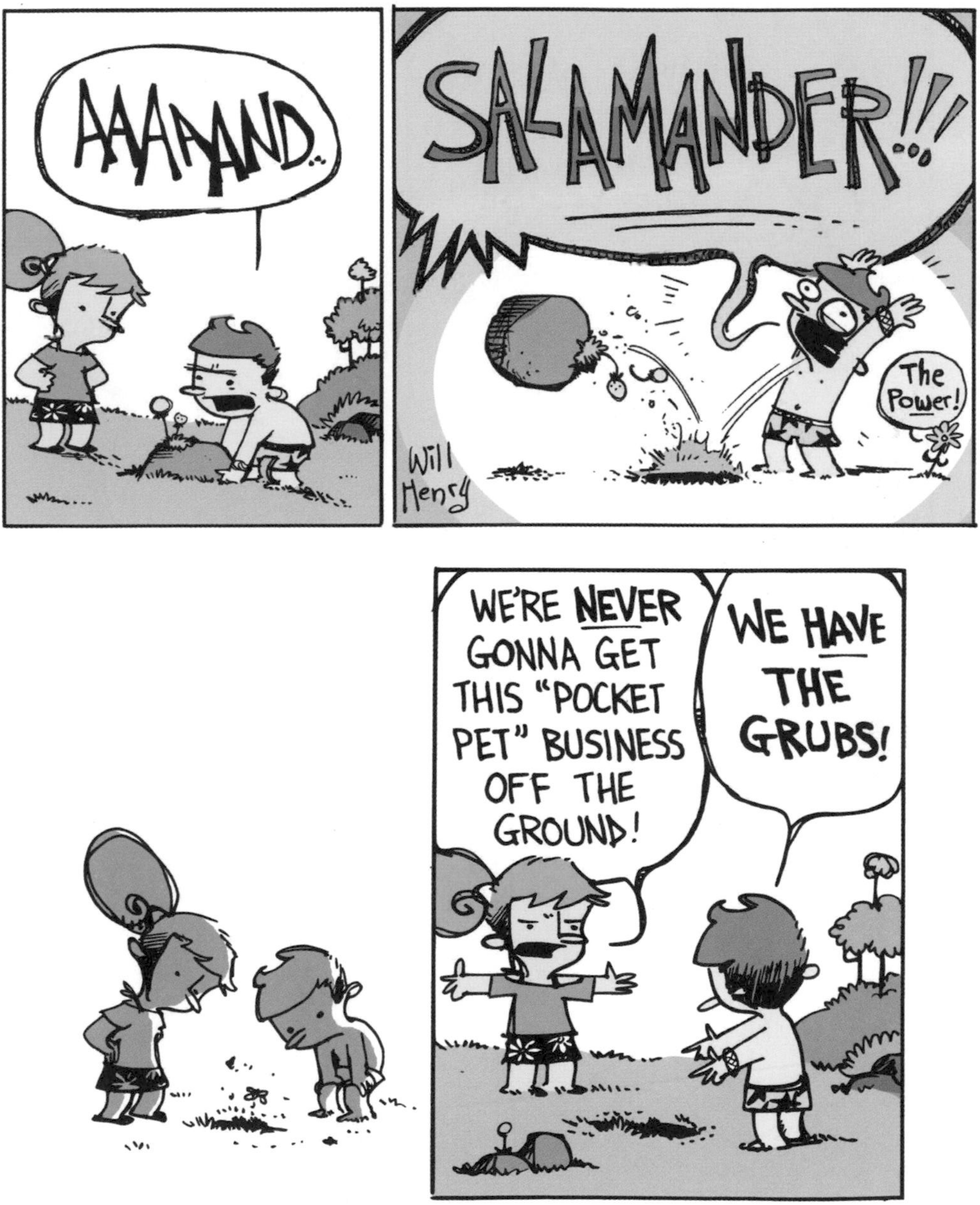
AAAAAND...
SALAMANDER!!!
The Power!
Will Henry
WE'RE NEVER GONNA GET THIS "POCKET PET" BUSINESS OFF THE GROUND!
WE HAVE THE GRUBS!

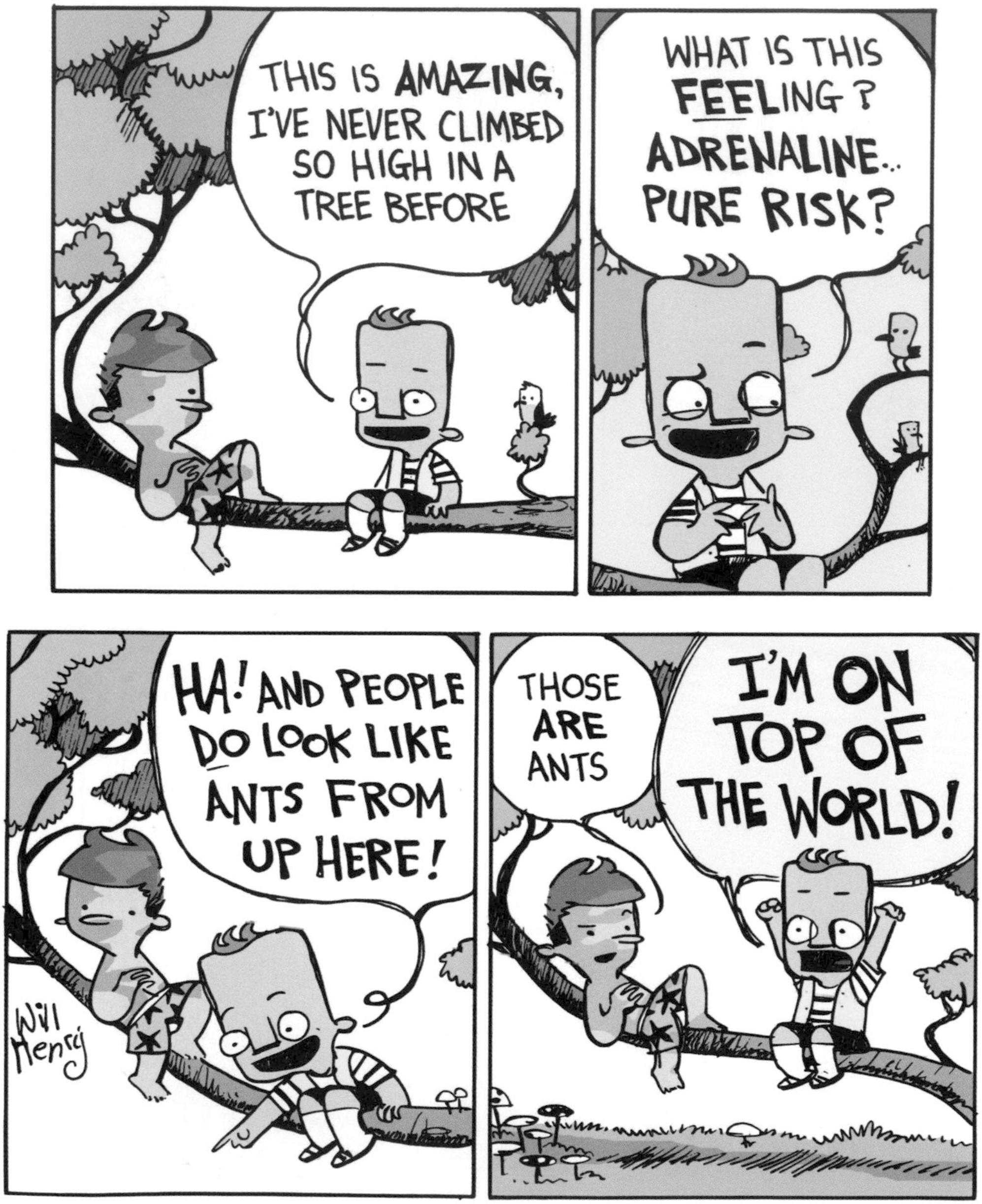
THIS IS AMAZING, I'VE NEVER CLIMBED SO HIGH IN A TREE BEFORE
WHAT IS THIS FEELING? ADRENALINE... PURE RISK?
HA! AND PEOPLE DO LOOK LIKE ANTS FROM UP HERE!
Will Henry
THOSE ARE ANTS
I'M ON TOP OF THE WORLD!

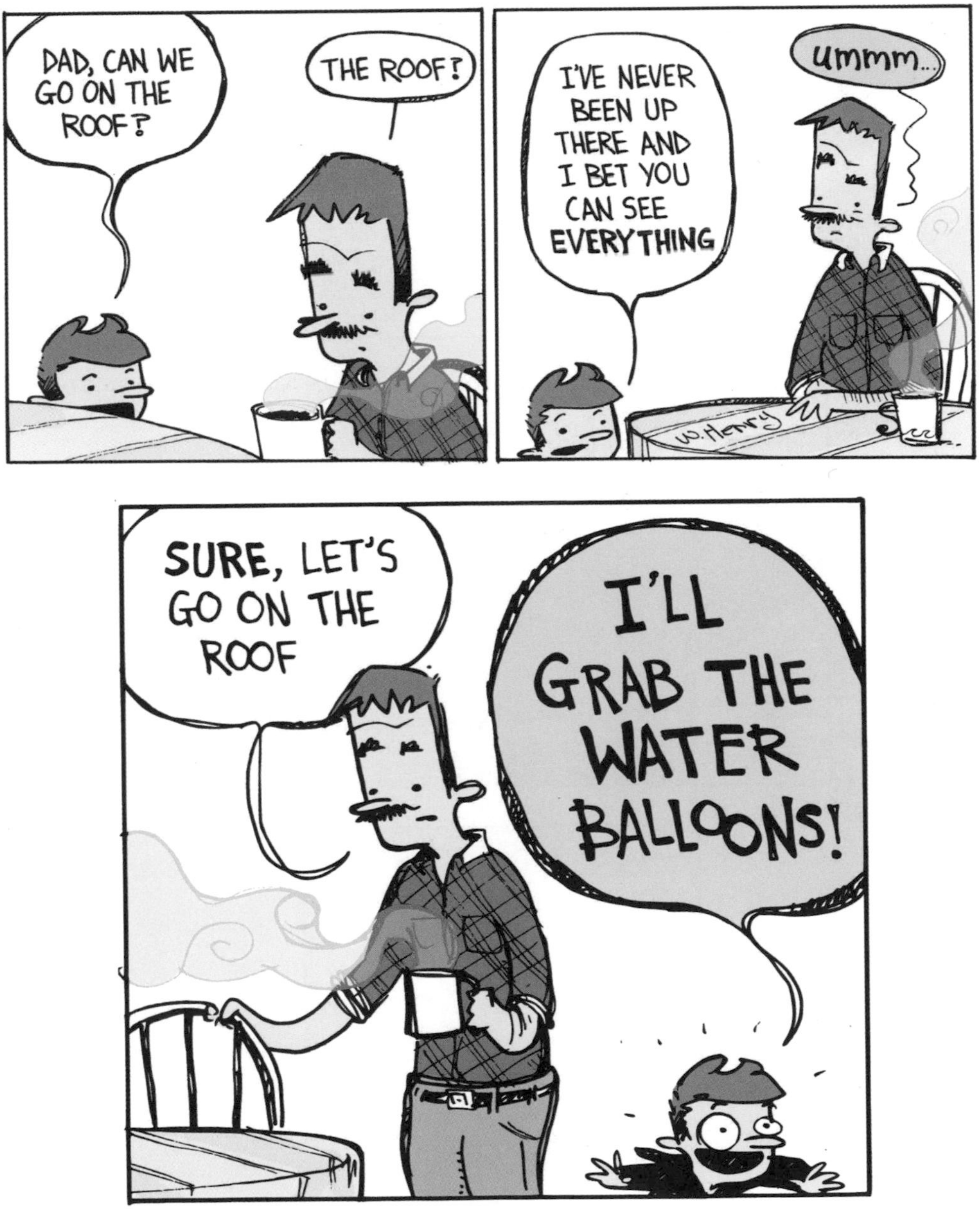
DAD, CAN WE GO ON THE ROOF?
THE ROOF?
I'VE NEVER BEEN UP THERE AND I BET YOU CAN SEE **EVERYTHING**
ummm...
W. Henry
SURE, LET'S GO ON THE ROOF
I'LL GRAB THE WATER BALLOONS!

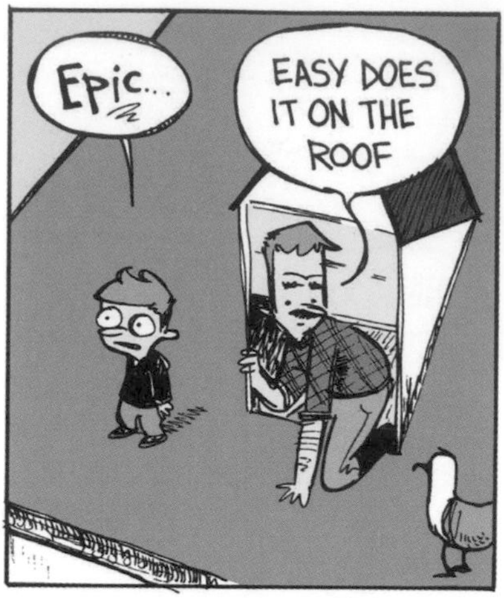
Epic...
EASY DOES IT ON THE ROOF

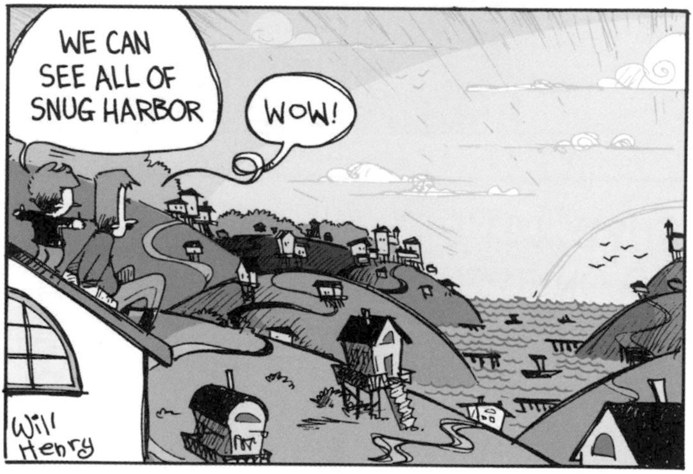
WE CAN SEE ALL OF SNUG HARBOR
WOW!
Will Henry

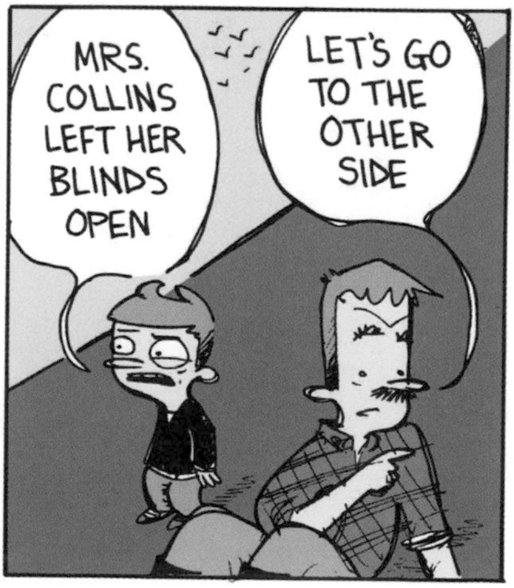
MRS. COLLINS LEFT HER BLINDS OPEN
LET'S GO TO THE OTHER SIDE

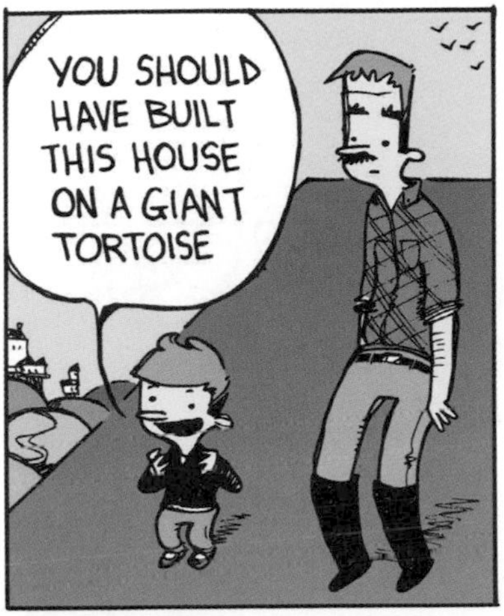
YOU SHOULD HAVE BUILT THIS HOUSE ON A GIANT TORTOISE

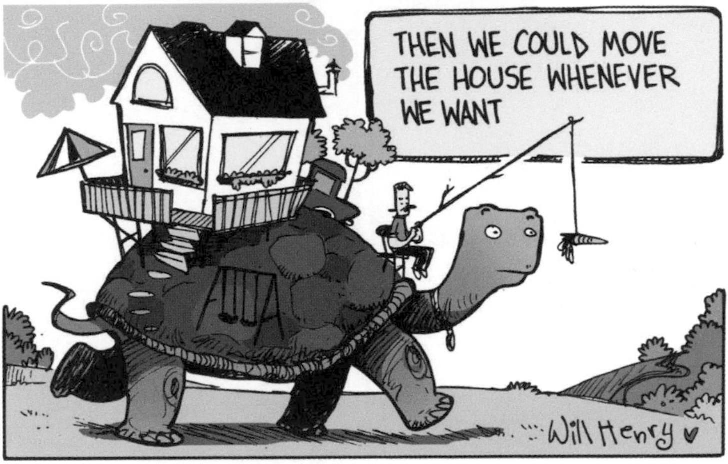
THEN WE COULD MOVE THE HOUSE WHENEVER WE WANT
Will Henry

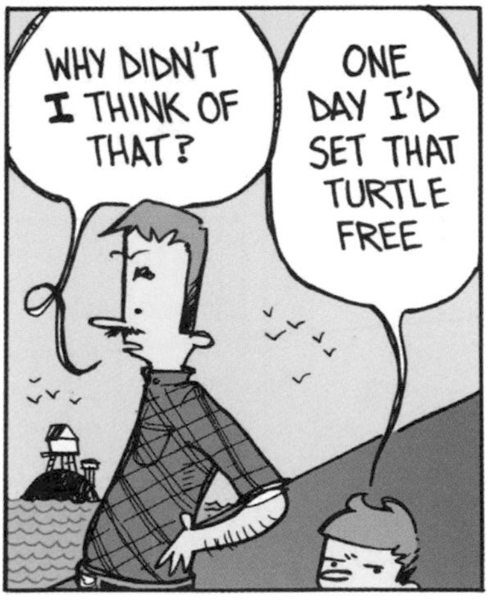
WHY DIDN'T I THINK OF THAT?
ONE DAY I'D SET THAT TURTLE FREE

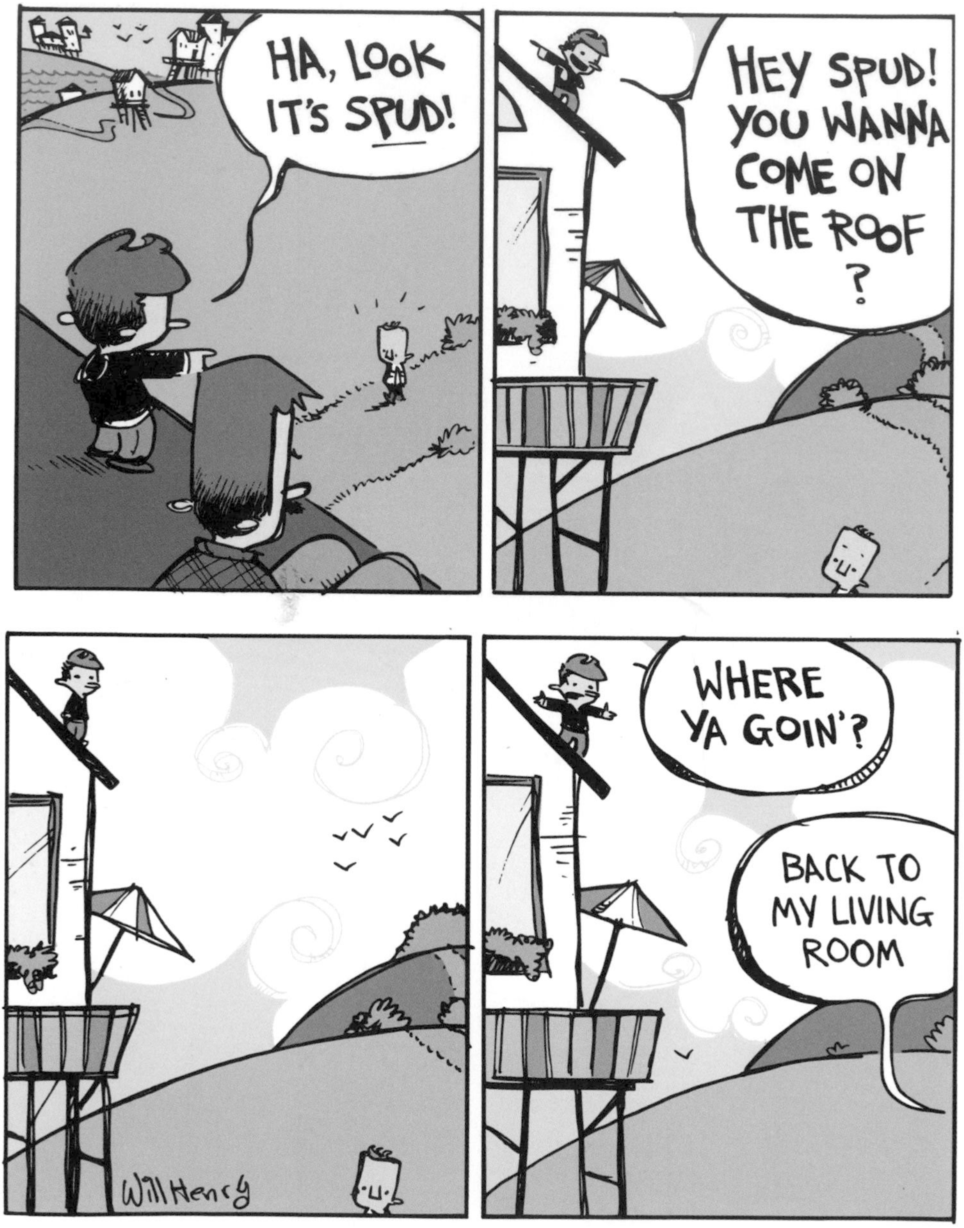
HA, LOOK IT'S SPUD!
HEY SPUD! YOU WANNA COME ON THE ROOF ?
WHERE YA GOIN'?
BACK TO MY LIVING ROOM
Will Henry

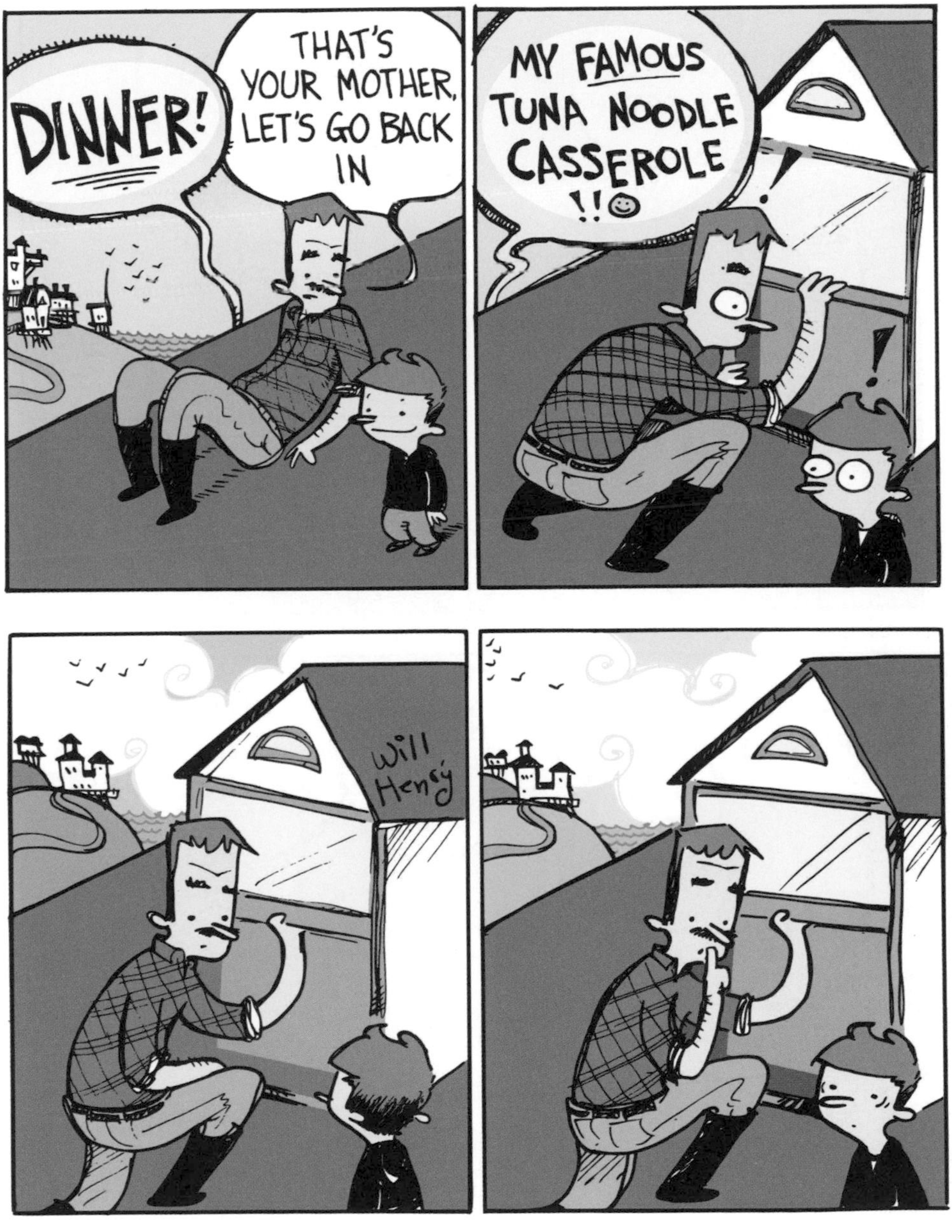
DINNER!
THAT'S YOUR MOTHER, LET'S GO BACK IN
MY FAMOUS TUNA NOODLE CASSEROLE !!
!
!
Will Henry

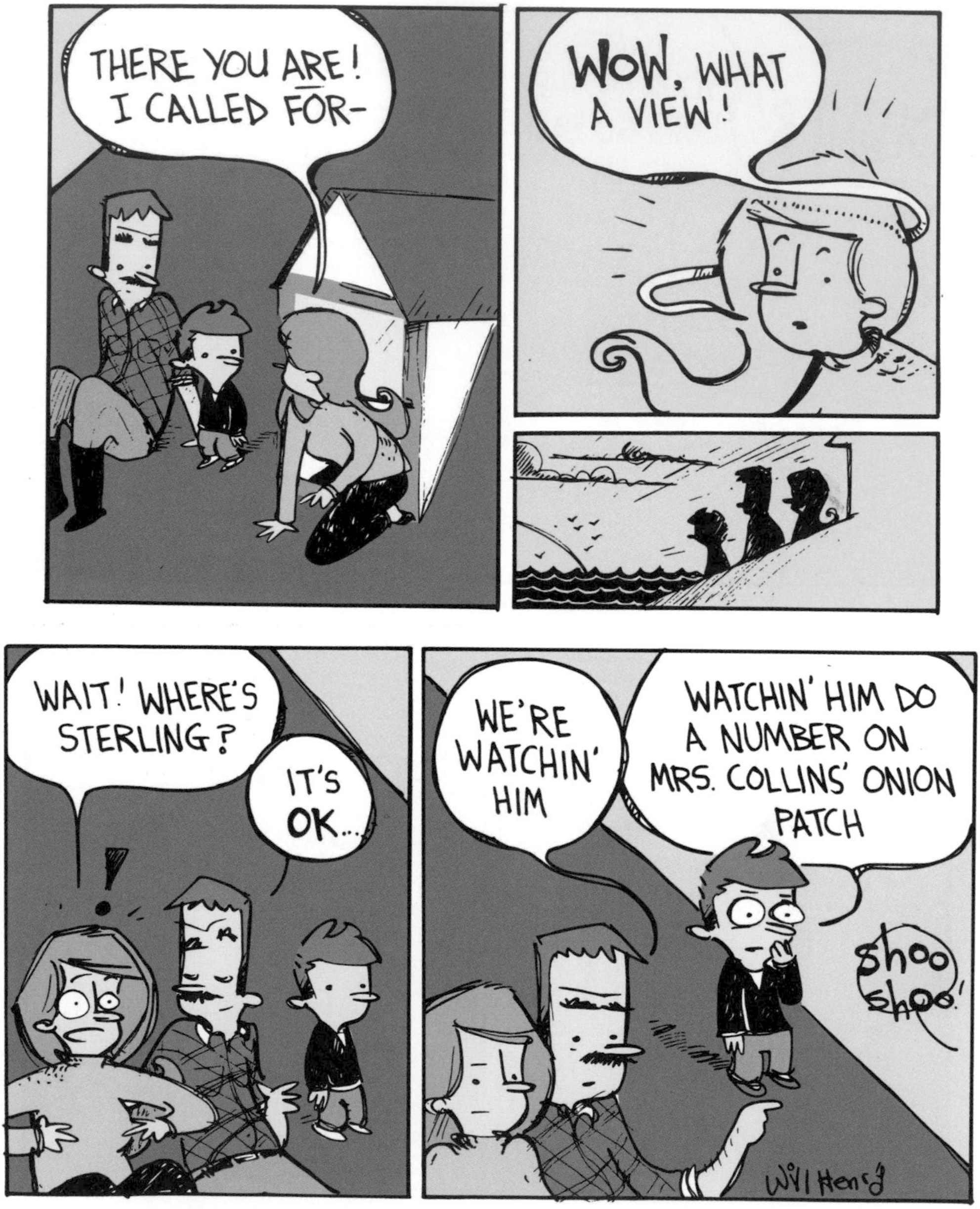
THERE YOU ARE! I CALLED FOR-
WOW, WHAT A VIEW!
WAIT! WHERE'S STERLING?
!
IT'S OK...
WE'RE WATCHIN' HIM
WATCHIN' HIM DO A NUMBER ON MRS. COLLINS' ONION PATCH
shoo shoo!
Will Henry

LOOK AT THAT, SPUD
THE OPEN OCEAN! WHERE THE TIDES CAN TAKE YOU EXPLORING THE WORLD OVER
truth
SOMEDAY I'M GONNA SEE EVERY CORNER OF IT!
I'M MORE THE "GOOGLE IMAGES" TYPE
Will Henry

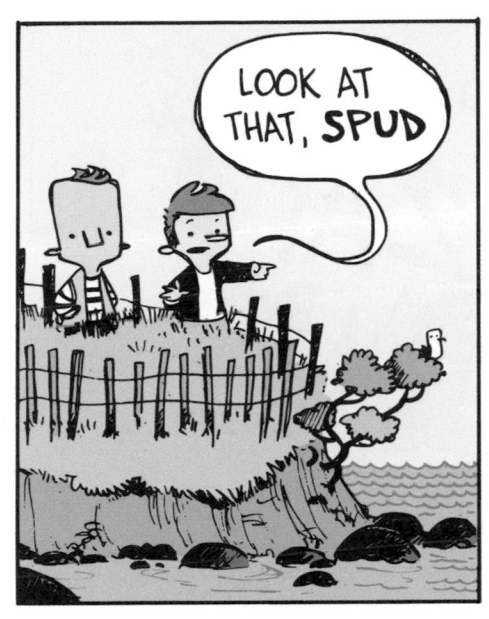

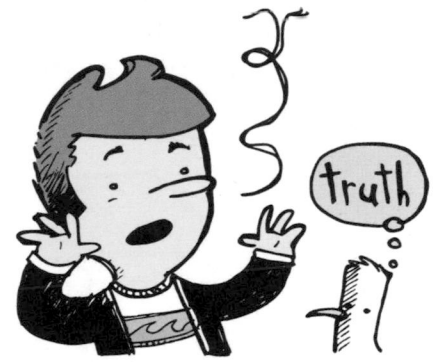

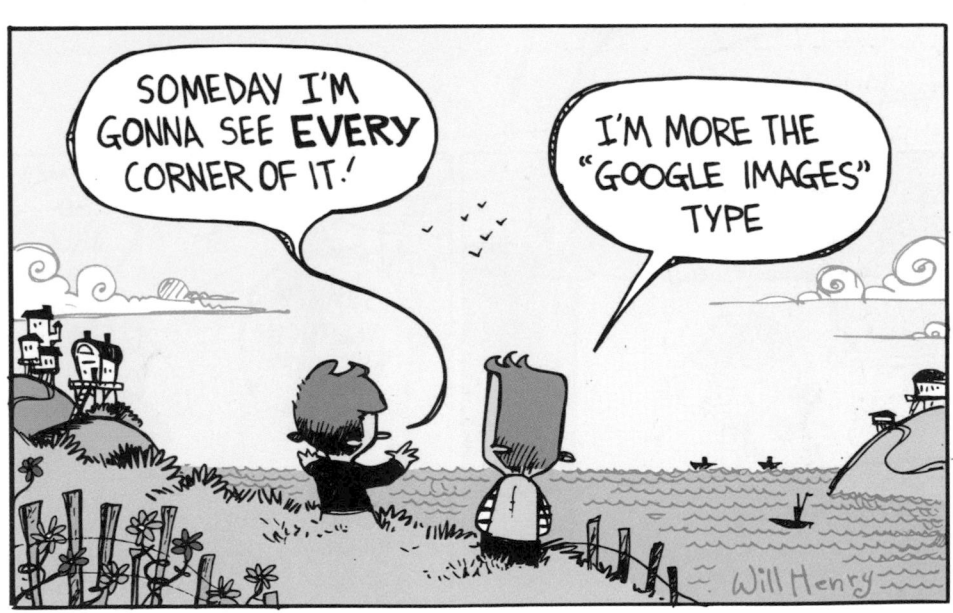

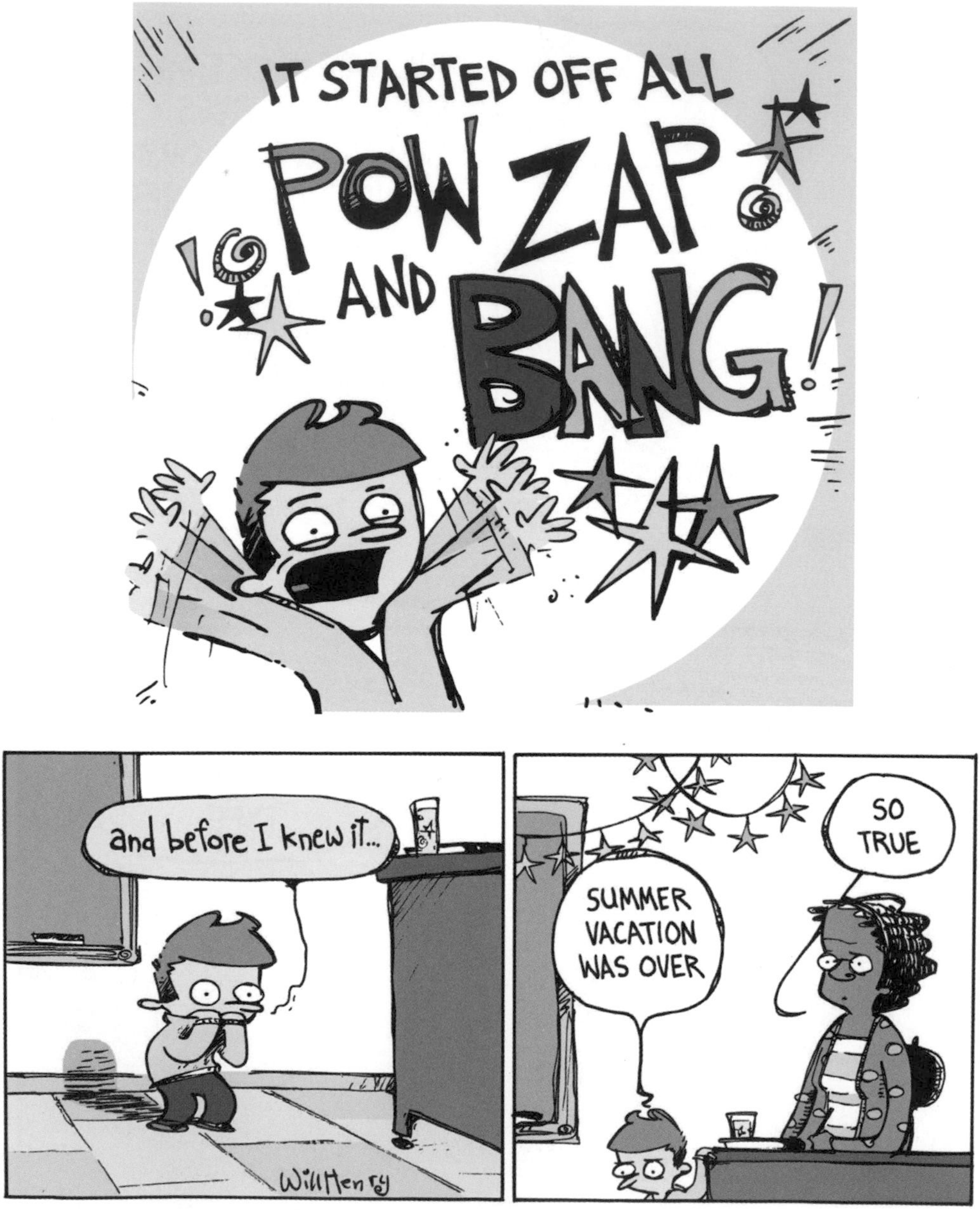
IT STARTED OFF ALL
POW ZAP AND BANG!
and before I knew it...
WillHenry
SUMMER VACATION WAS OVER
SO TRUE

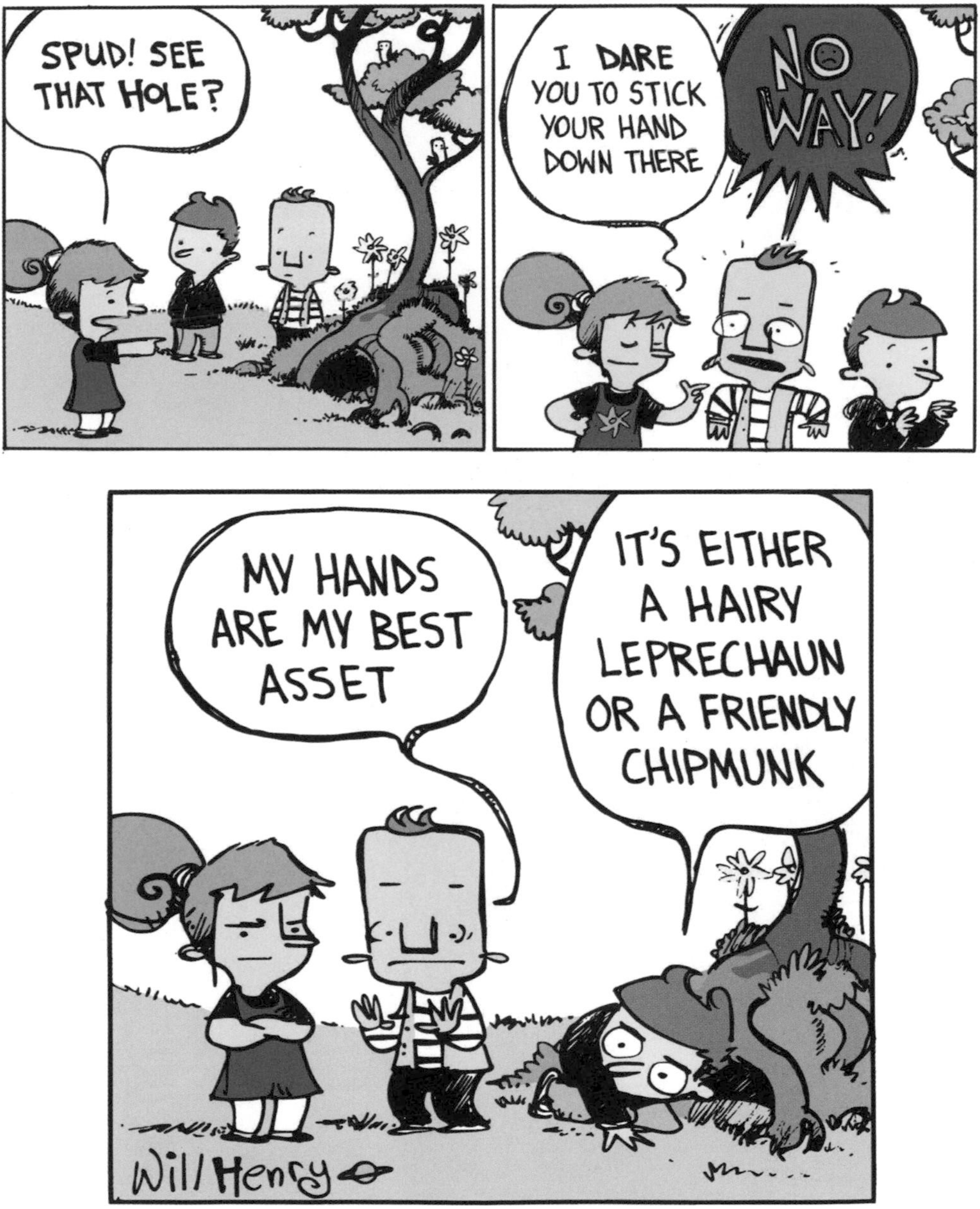
SPUD! SEE THAT HOLE?
I DARE YOU TO STICK YOUR HAND DOWN THERE
NO WAY!
MY HANDS ARE MY BEST ASSET
IT'S EITHER A HAIRY LEPRECHAUN OR A FRIENDLY CHIPMUNK
Will Henry

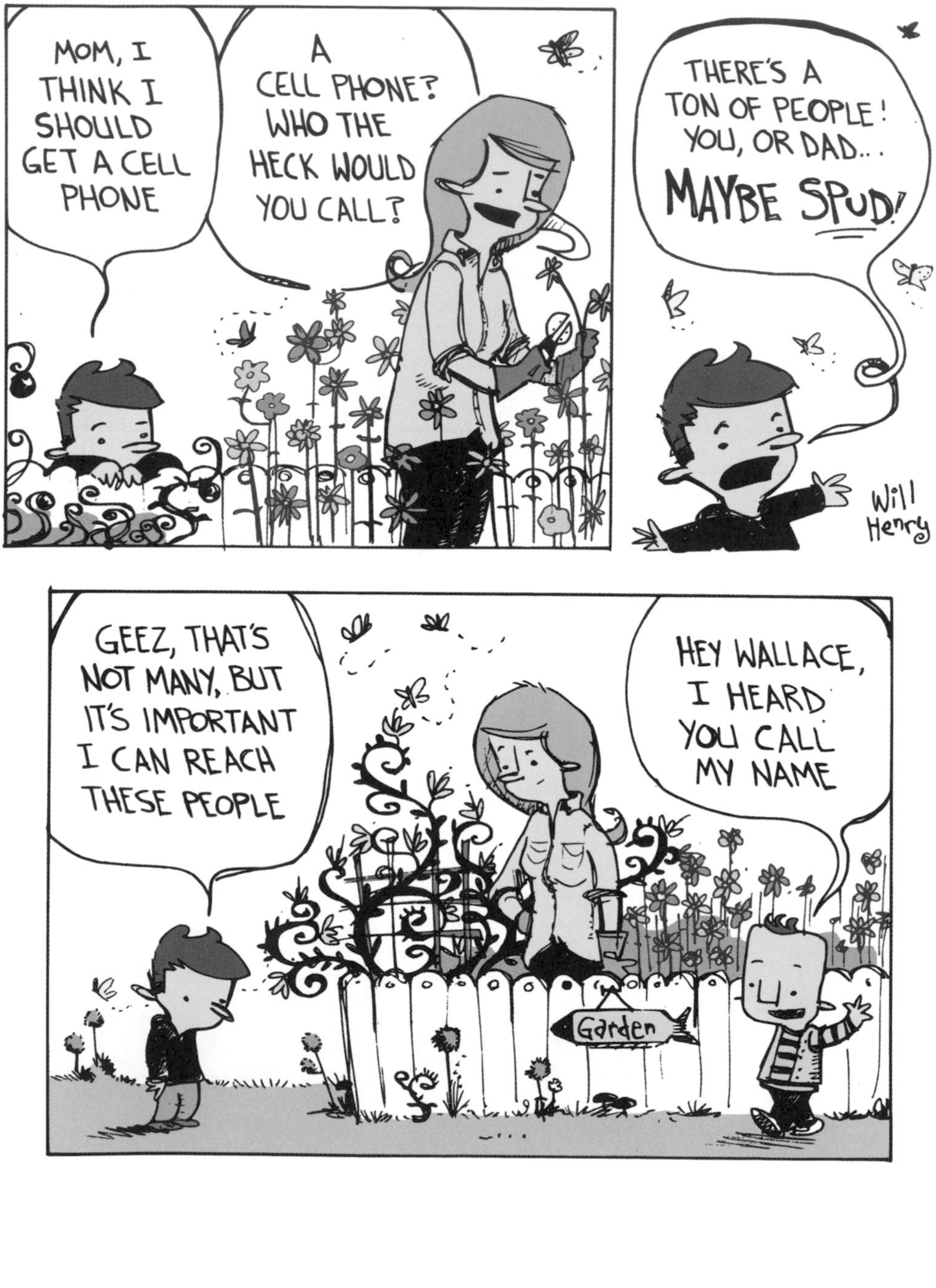
MOM, I THINK I SHOULD GET A CELL PHONE
A CELL PHONE? WHO THE HECK WOULD YOU CALL?
THERE'S A TON OF PEOPLE! YOU, OR DAD... MAYBE SPUD!
Will Henry
GEEZ, THAT'S NOT MANY, BUT IT'S IMPORTANT I CAN REACH THESE PEOPLE
HEY WALLACE, I HEARD YOU CALL MY NAME
Garden

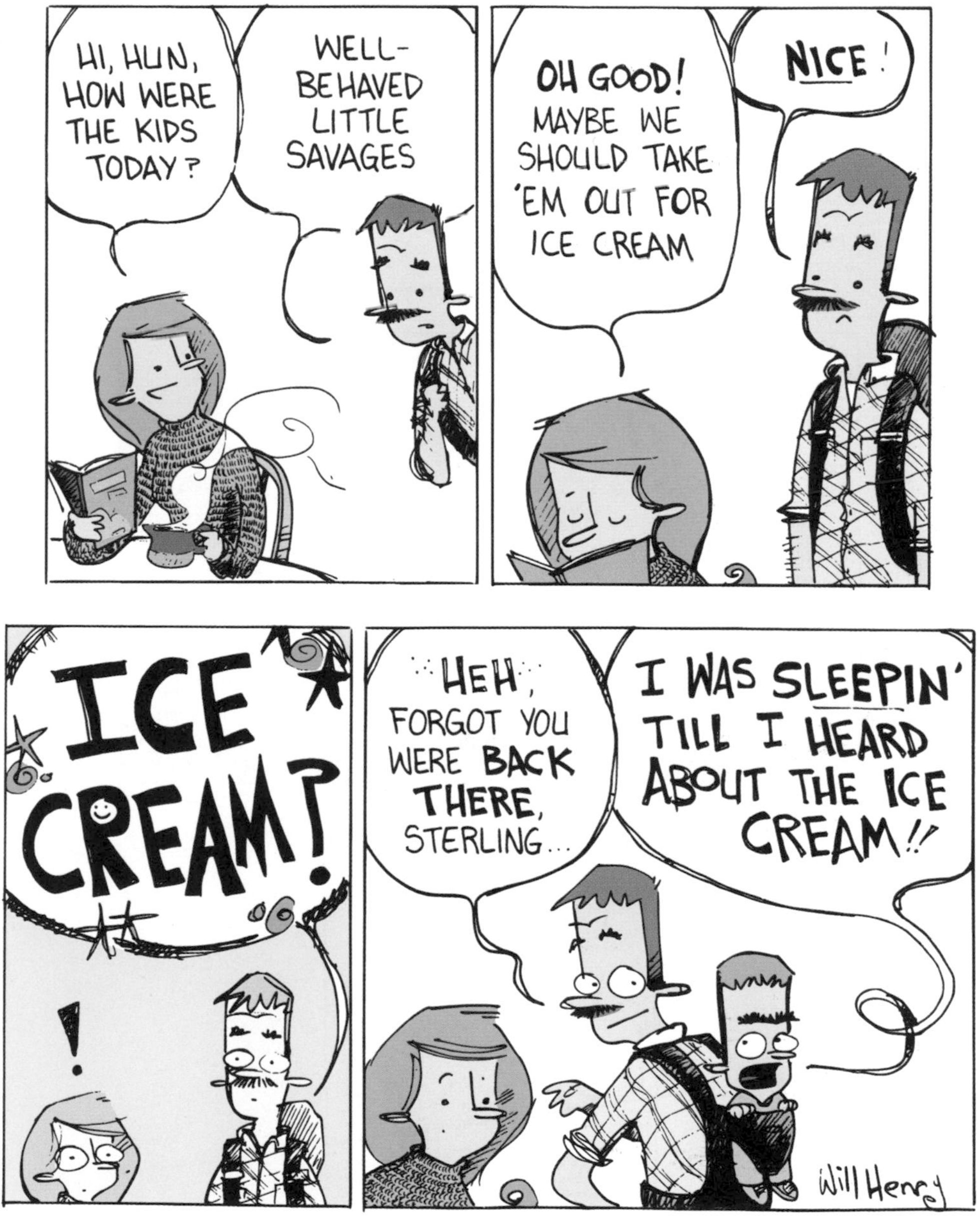
HI, HUN, HOW WERE THE KIDS TODAY?
WELL-BEHAVED LITTLE SAVAGES
OH GOOD! MAYBE WE SHOULD TAKE 'EM OUT FOR ICE CREAM
NICE!
ICE CREAM?
!
HEH, FORGOT YOU WERE BACK THERE, STERLING...
I WAS SLEEPIN' TILL I HEARD ABOUT THE ICE CREAM!!
Will Henry

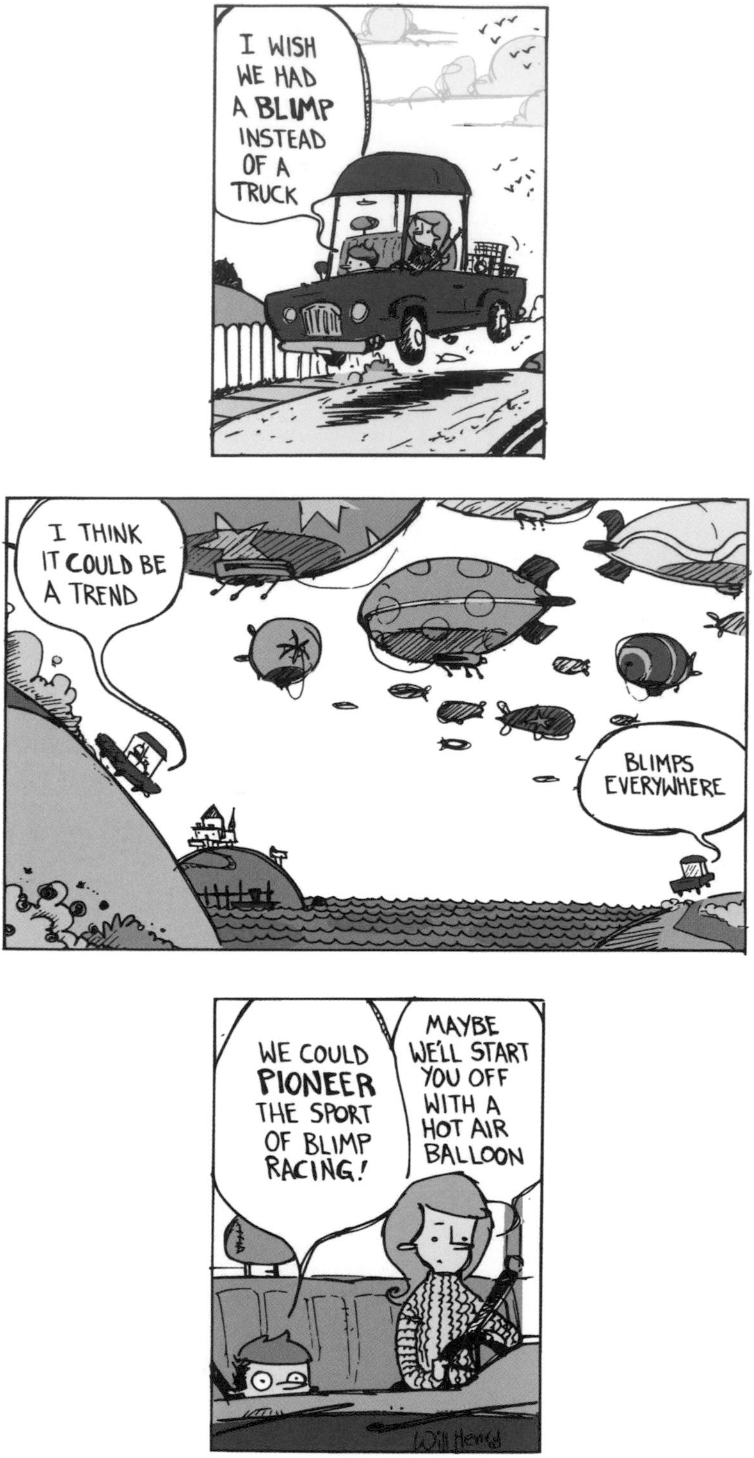
I WISH WE HAD A BLIMP INSTEAD OF A TRUCK
I THINK IT COULD BE A TREND
BLIMPS EVERYWHERE
WE COULD PIONEER THE SPORT OF BLIMP RACING!
MAYBE WE'LL START YOU OFF WITH A HOT AIR BALLOON
Will Henry

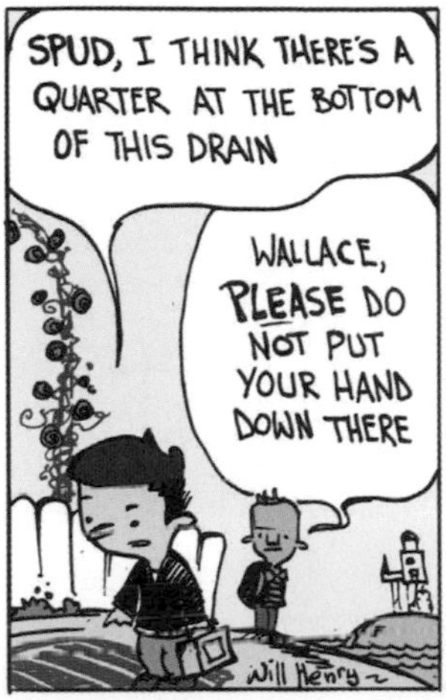
SPUD, I THINK THERE'S A QUARTER AT THE BOTTOM OF THIS DRAIN
WALLACE, PLEASE DO NOT PUT YOUR HAND DOWN THERE
Will Henry

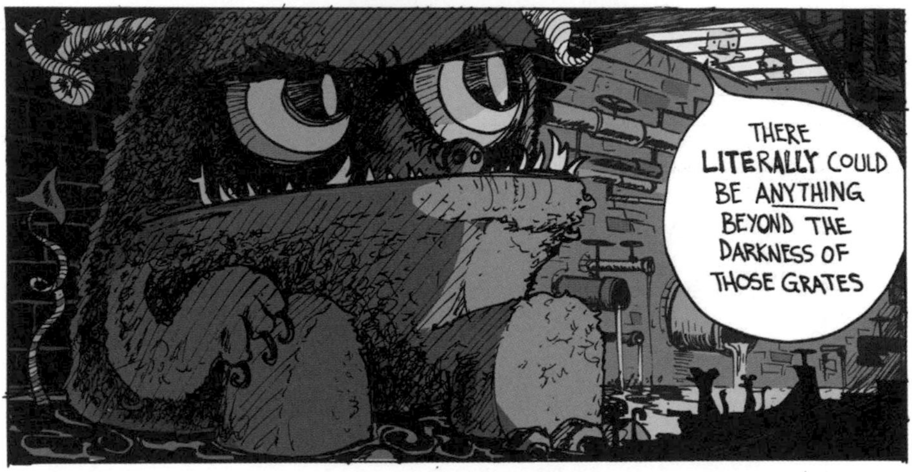
THERE LITERALLY COULD BE ANYTHING BEYOND THE DARKNESS OF THOSE GRATES

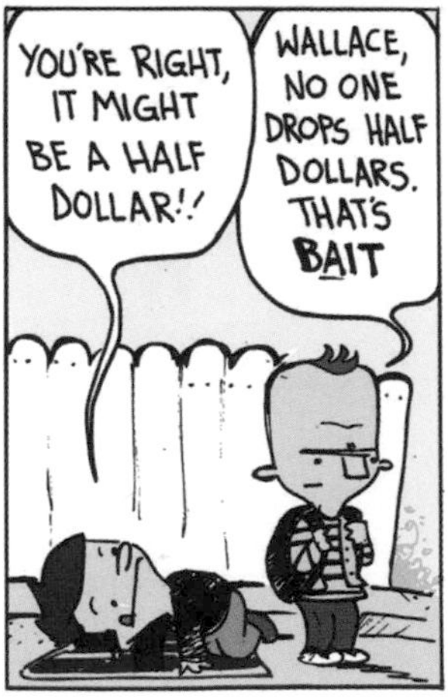
YOU'RE RIGHT, IT MIGHT BE A HALF DOLLAR!!
WALLACE, NO ONE DROPS HALF DOLLARS. THAT'S BAIT

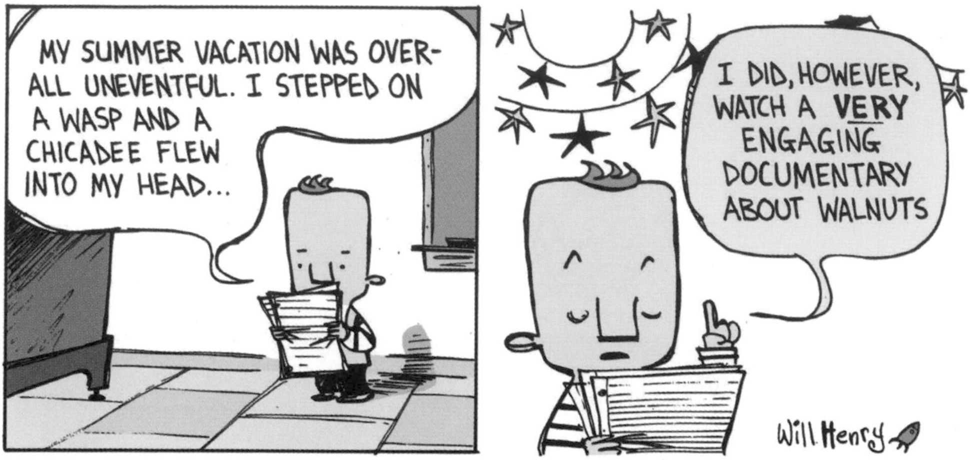
MY SUMMER VACATION WAS OVER-ALL UNEVENTFUL. I STEPPED ON A WASP AND A CHICADEE FLEW INTO MY HEAD...
I DID, HOWEVER, WATCH A VERY ENGAGING DOCUMENTARY ABOUT WALNUTS
Will Henry

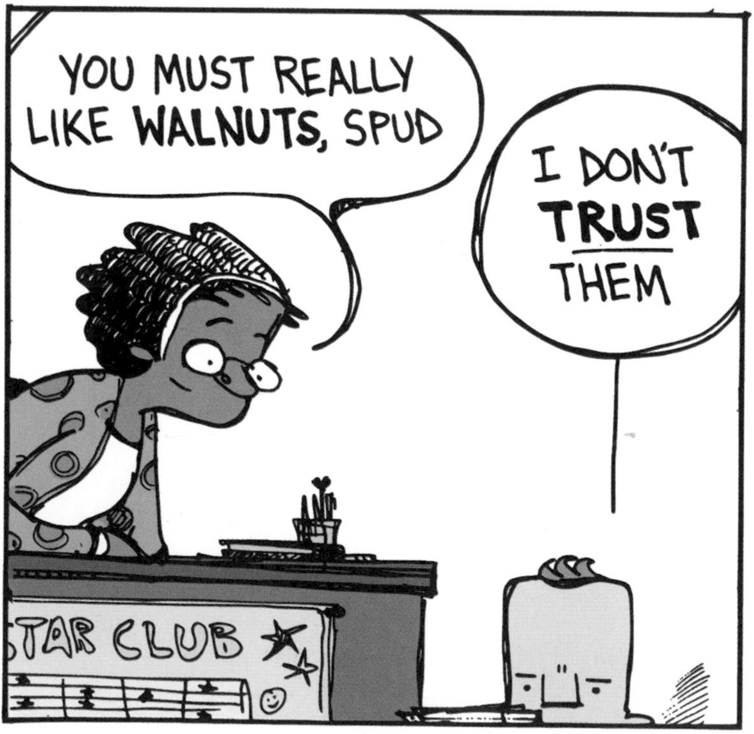
YOU MUST REALLY LIKE WALNUTS, SPUD
I DON'T TRUST THEM
STAR CLUB

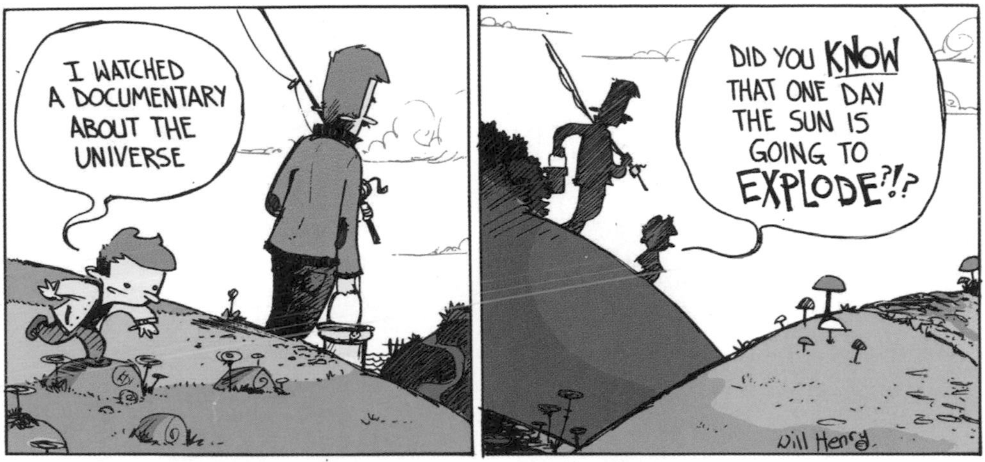
I WATCHED A DOCUMENTARY ABOUT THE UNIVERSE
DID YOU KNOW THAT ONE DAY THE SUN IS GOING TO EXPLODE?!?
Will Henry

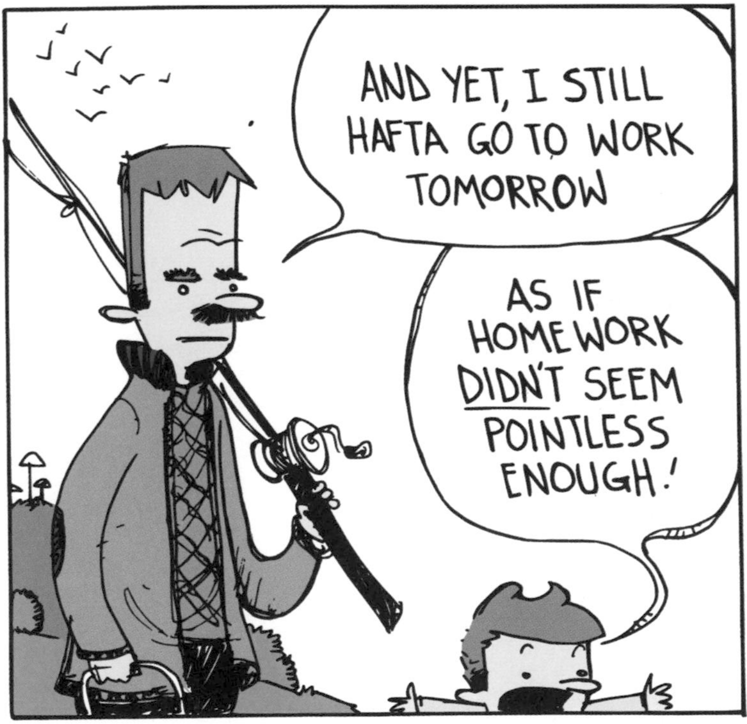
AND YET, I STILL HAFTA GO TO WORK TOMORROW
AS IF HOMEWORK DIDN'T SEEM POINTLESS ENOUGH!

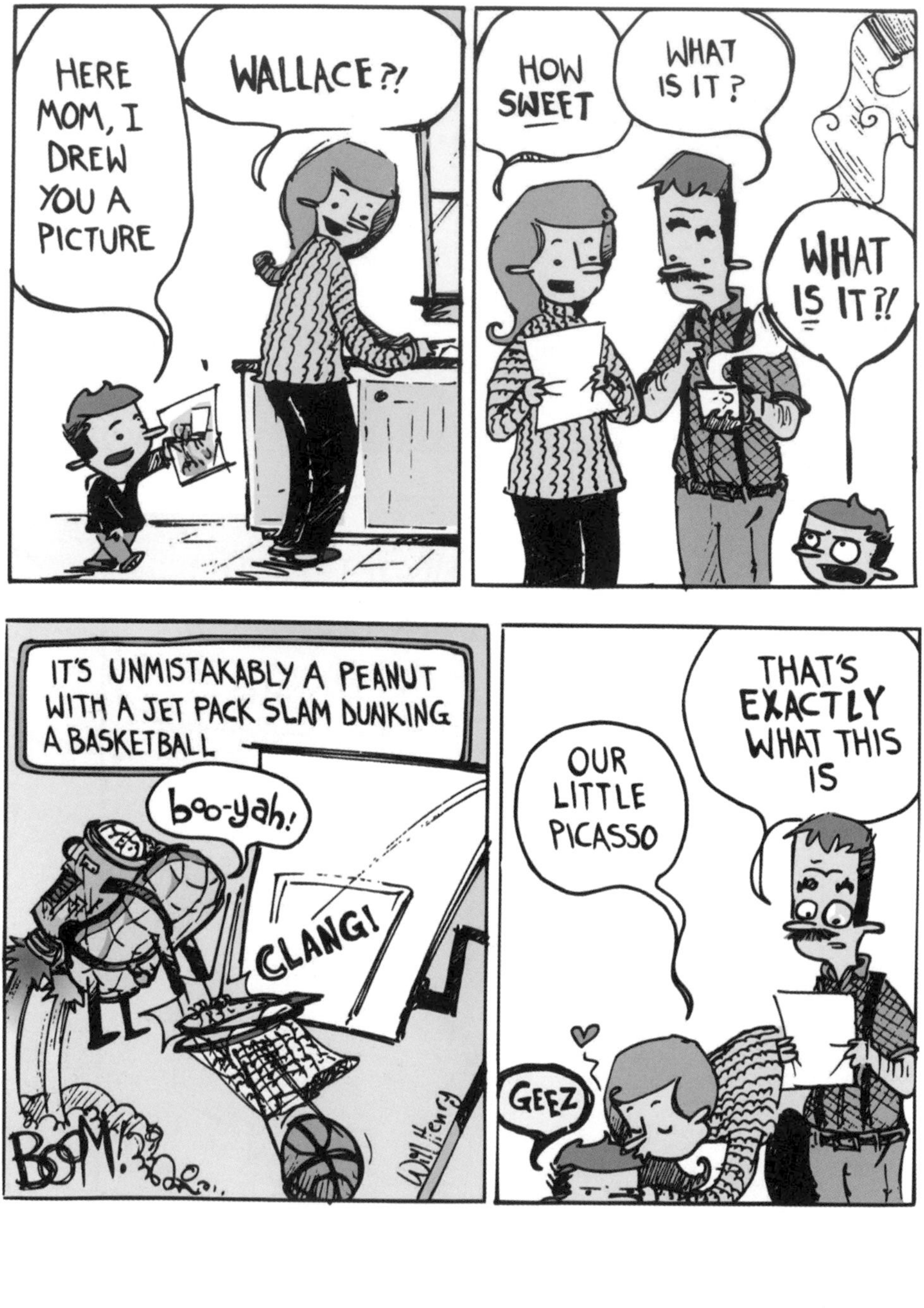
HERE MOM, I DREW YOU A PICTURE
WALLACE?!
HOW SWEET
WHAT IS IT?
WHAT IS IT?!
IT'S UNMISTAKABLY A PEANUT WITH A JET PACK SLAM DUNKING A BASKETBALL
boo-yah!
CLANG!
BOOM!
OUR LITTLE PICASSO
THAT'S EXACTLY WHAT THIS IS
GEEZ

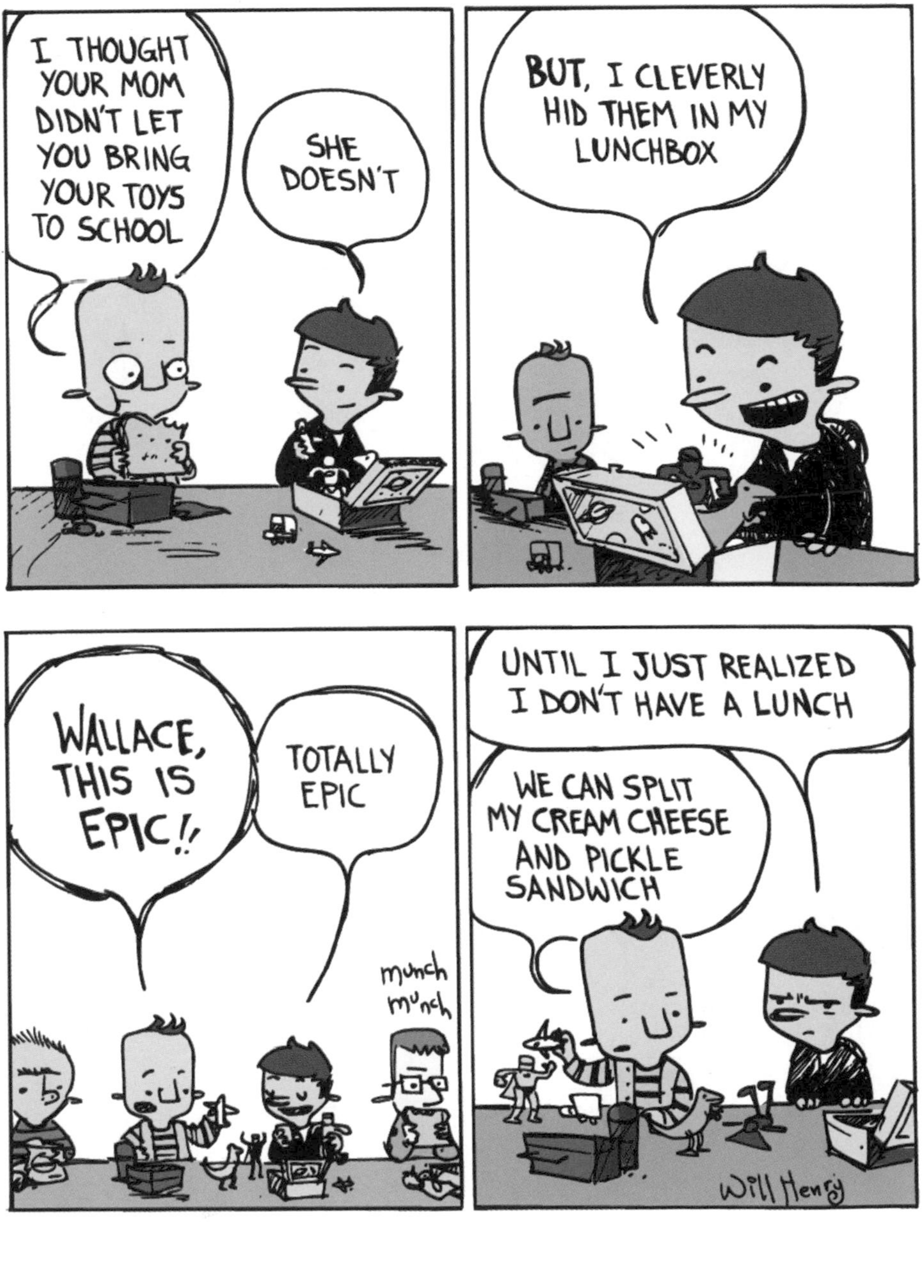
I THOUGHT YOUR MOM DIDN'T LET YOU BRING YOUR TOYS TO SCHOOL
SHE DOESN'T
BUT, I CLEVERLY HID THEM IN MY LUNCHBOX
WALLACE, THIS IS EPIC!!
TOTALLY EPIC
munch munch
UNTIL I JUST REALIZED I DON'T HAVE A LUNCH
WE CAN SPLIT MY CREAM CHEESE AND PICKLE SANDWICH
Will Henry

YOU SEE THIMBLE ISLAND?
YEP...
ONE TIME, FARMER BROWN'S CHICKENS GOT OUT THERE
CLUCK CLUCK CLUCK CLUCK CLUCK CLUC
NO ONE KNOWS HOW
THEY FLEW OUT THERE
THERE'S A HOLE IN THAT THEORY
THEY COULD FLY IF THEY WEREN'T AFRAID OF HEIGHTS
W. Henry

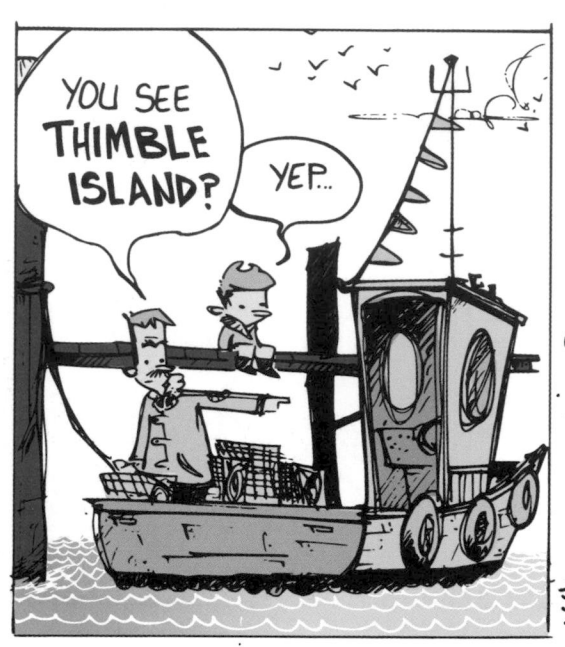

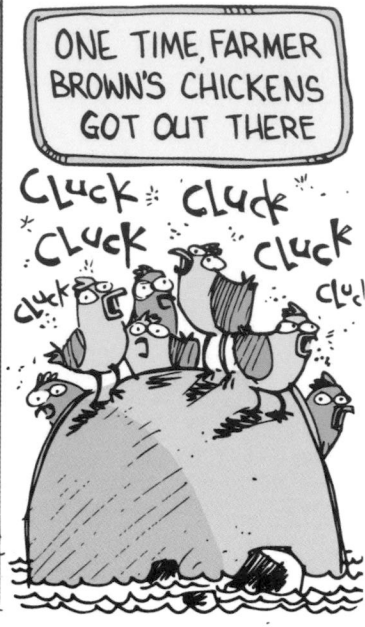

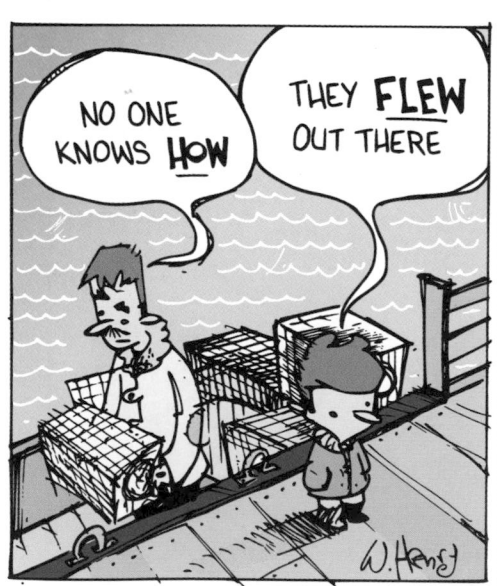

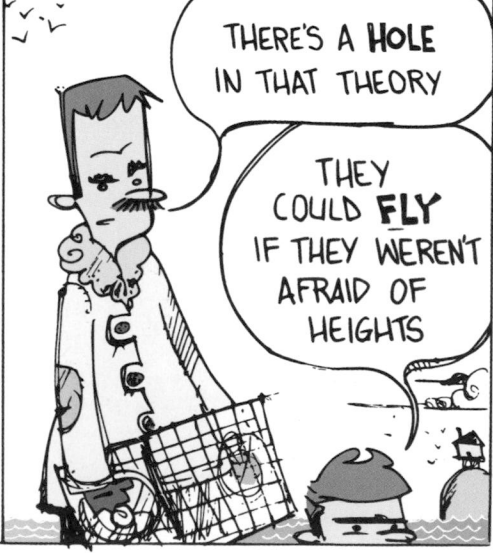

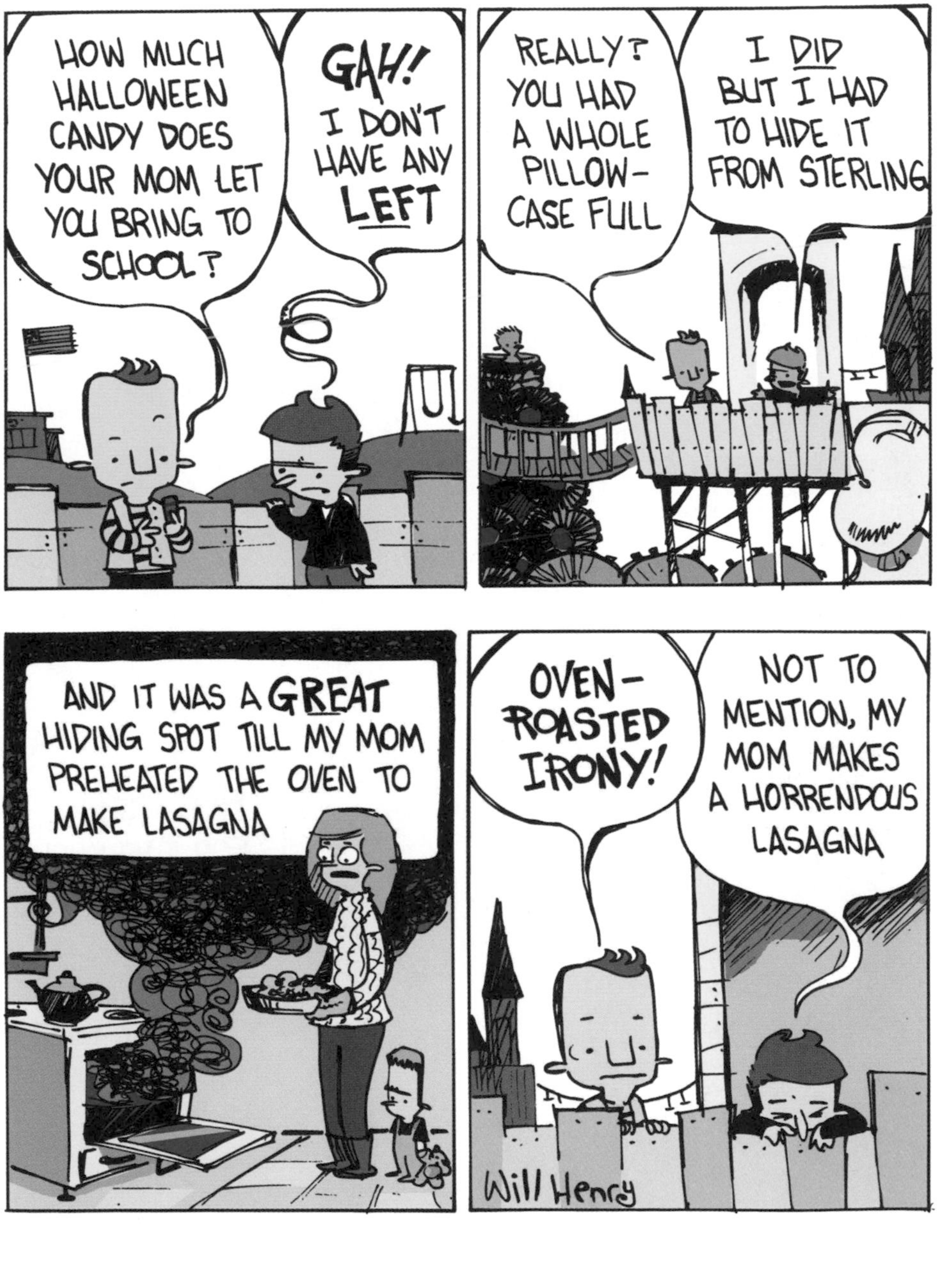
HOW MUCH HALLOWEEN CANDY DOES YOUR MOM LET YOU BRING TO SCHOOL?
GAH!! I DON'T HAVE ANY LEFT
REALLY? YOU HAD A WHOLE PILLOW-CASE FULL
I DID BUT I HAD TO HIDE IT FROM STERLING
AND IT WAS A GREAT HIDING SPOT TILL MY MOM PREHEATED THE OVEN TO MAKE LASAGNA
OVEN-ROASTED IRONY!
NOT TO MENTION, MY MOM MAKES A HORRENDOUS LASAGNA
Will Henry

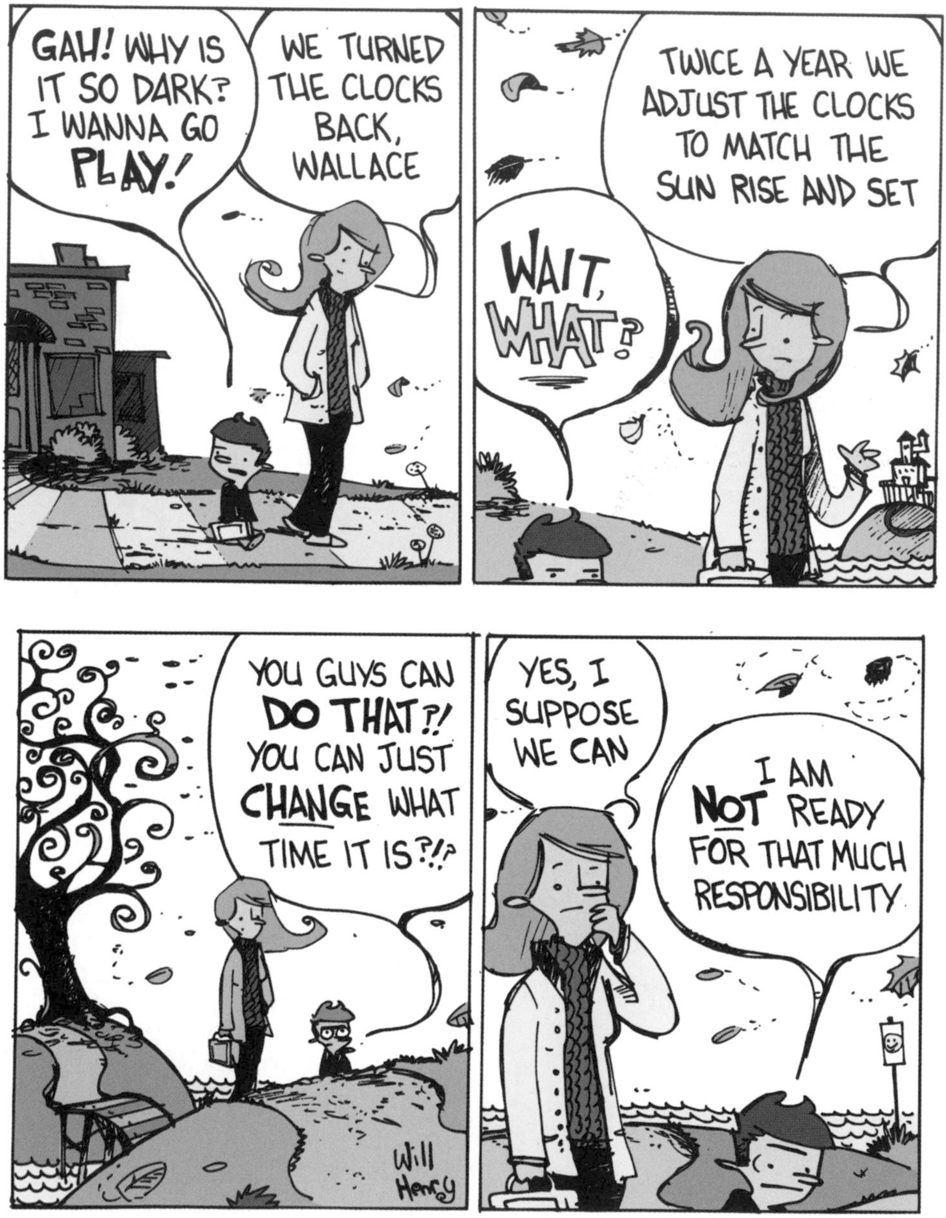
GAH! WHY IS IT SO DARK?! I WANNA GO PLAY!
WE TURNED THE CLOCKS BACK, WALLACE
TWICE A YEAR WE ADJUST THE CLOCKS TO MATCH THE SUN RISE AND SET
WAIT, WHAT?
YOU GUYS CAN DO THAT?! YOU CAN JUST CHANGE WHAT TIME IT IS?!?
Will Henry
YES, I SUPPOSE WE CAN
I AM NOT READY FOR THAT MUCH RESPONSIBILITY

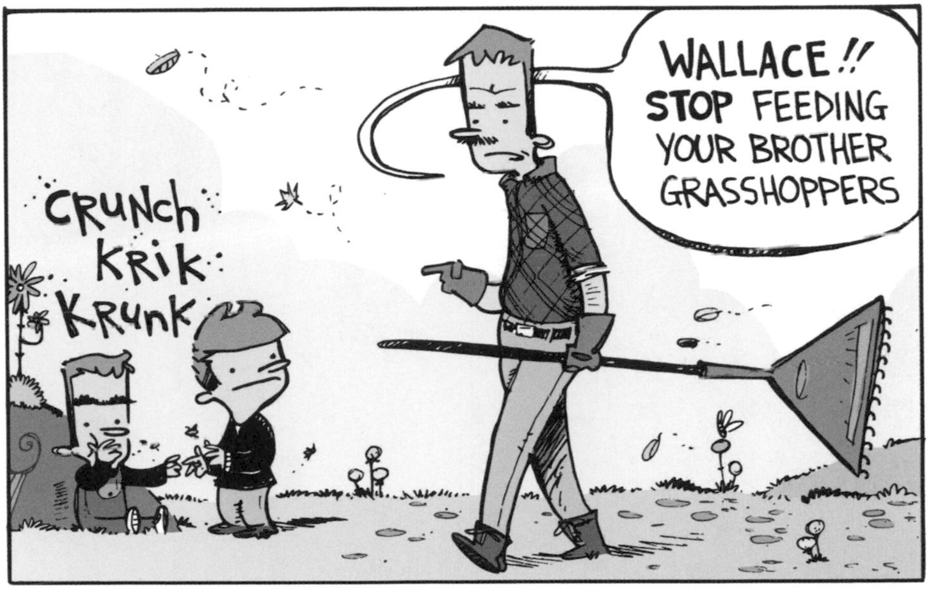
CRUNCH
KRIK
KRUNK
WALLACE!! STOP FEEDING YOUR BROTHER GRASSHOPPERS

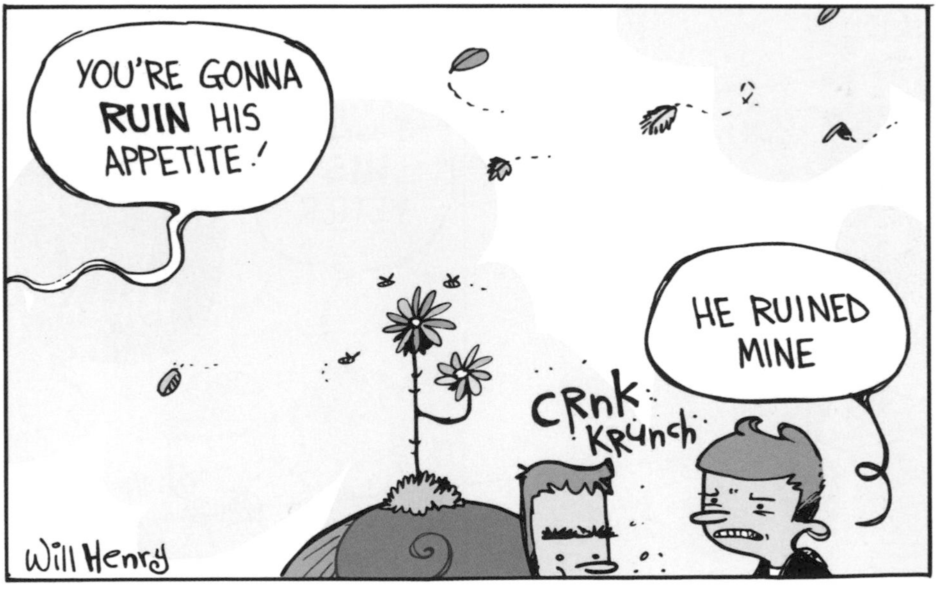
YOU'RE GONNA RUIN HIS APPETITE!
HE RUINED MINE
CRNK
KRUNCH
Will Henry

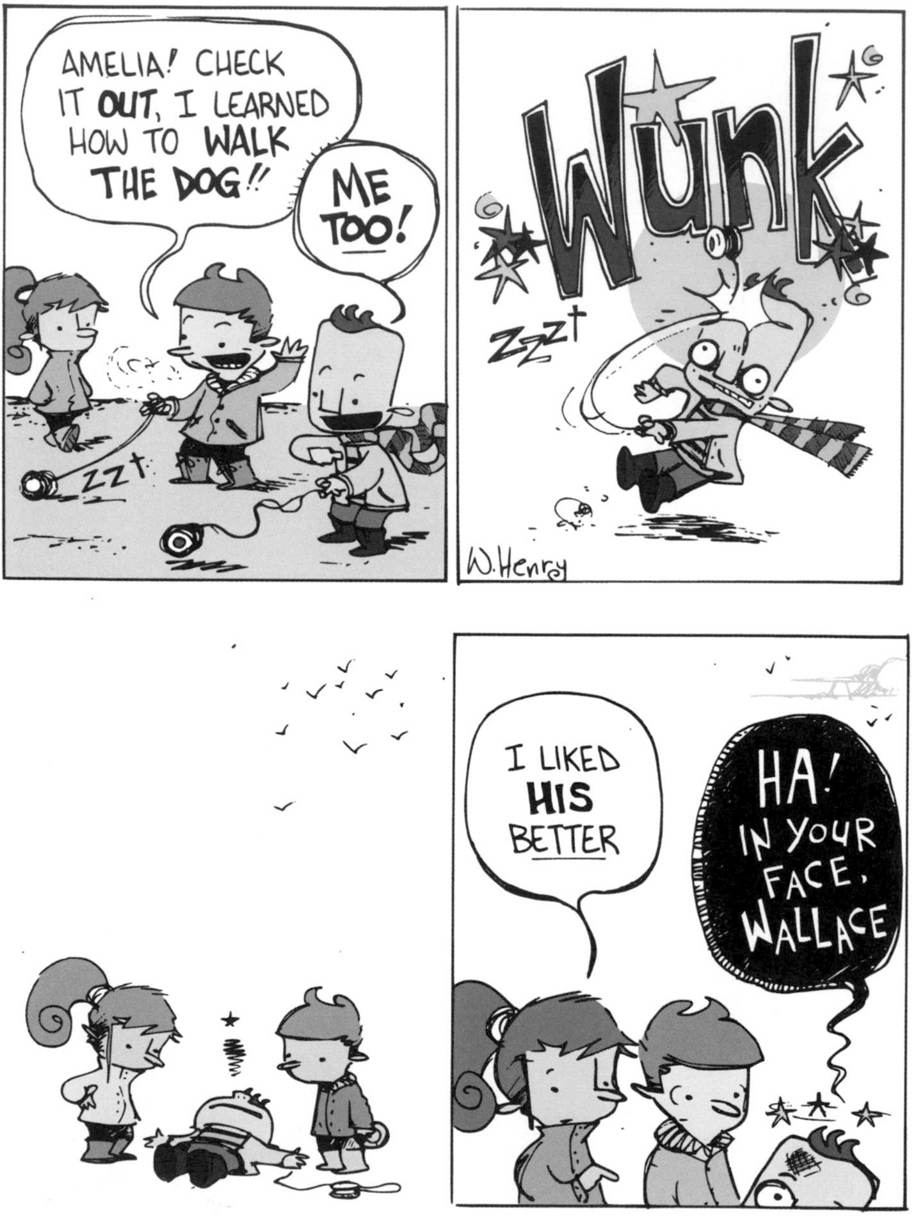
AMELIA! CHECK IT OUT, I LEARNED HOW TO WALK THE DOG!!
ME TOO!
ZZZT
WUNK
ZZZT
W.Henry
I LIKED HIS BETTER
HA! IN YOUR FACE, WALLACE

PSSST SPUD! YOU WANT A SNACK?
ALMOST ALWAYS!
I LACED MY SHOES WITH STRING LICORICE
WALLACE, I WATCHED YOU PUDDLE JUMP ALL RECESS...
OOF, YOU CAN TASTE IT, TOO...
munch munch
Will Henry

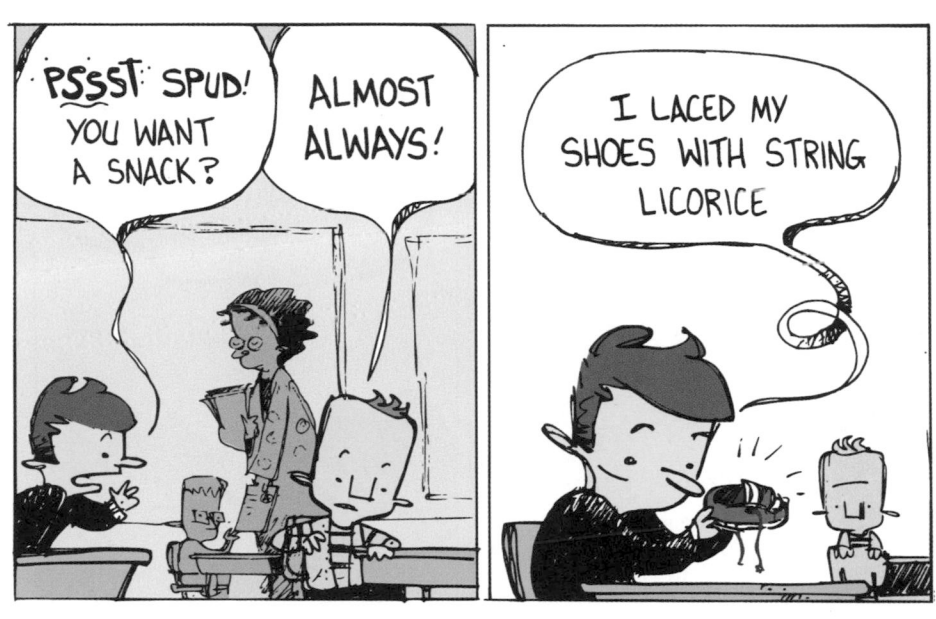

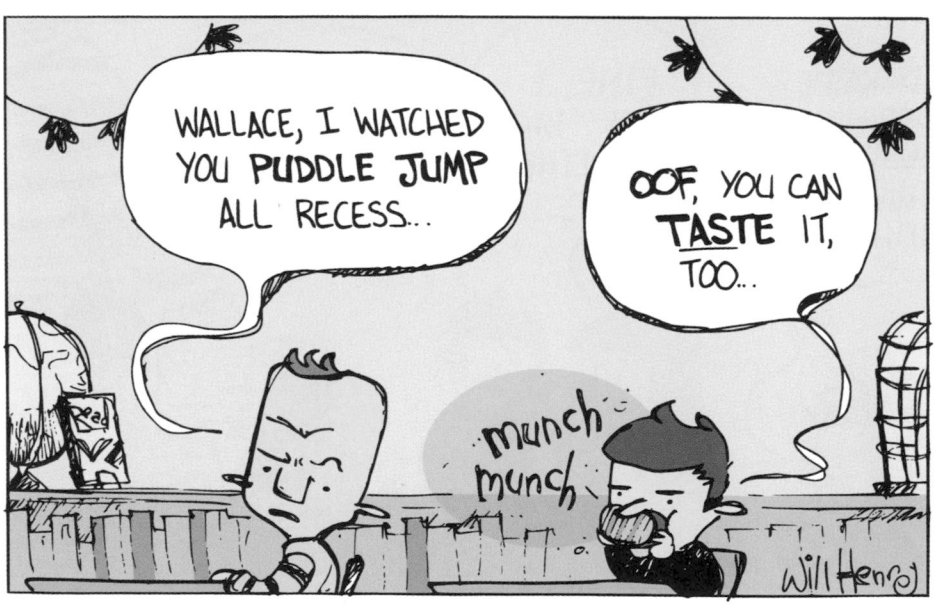

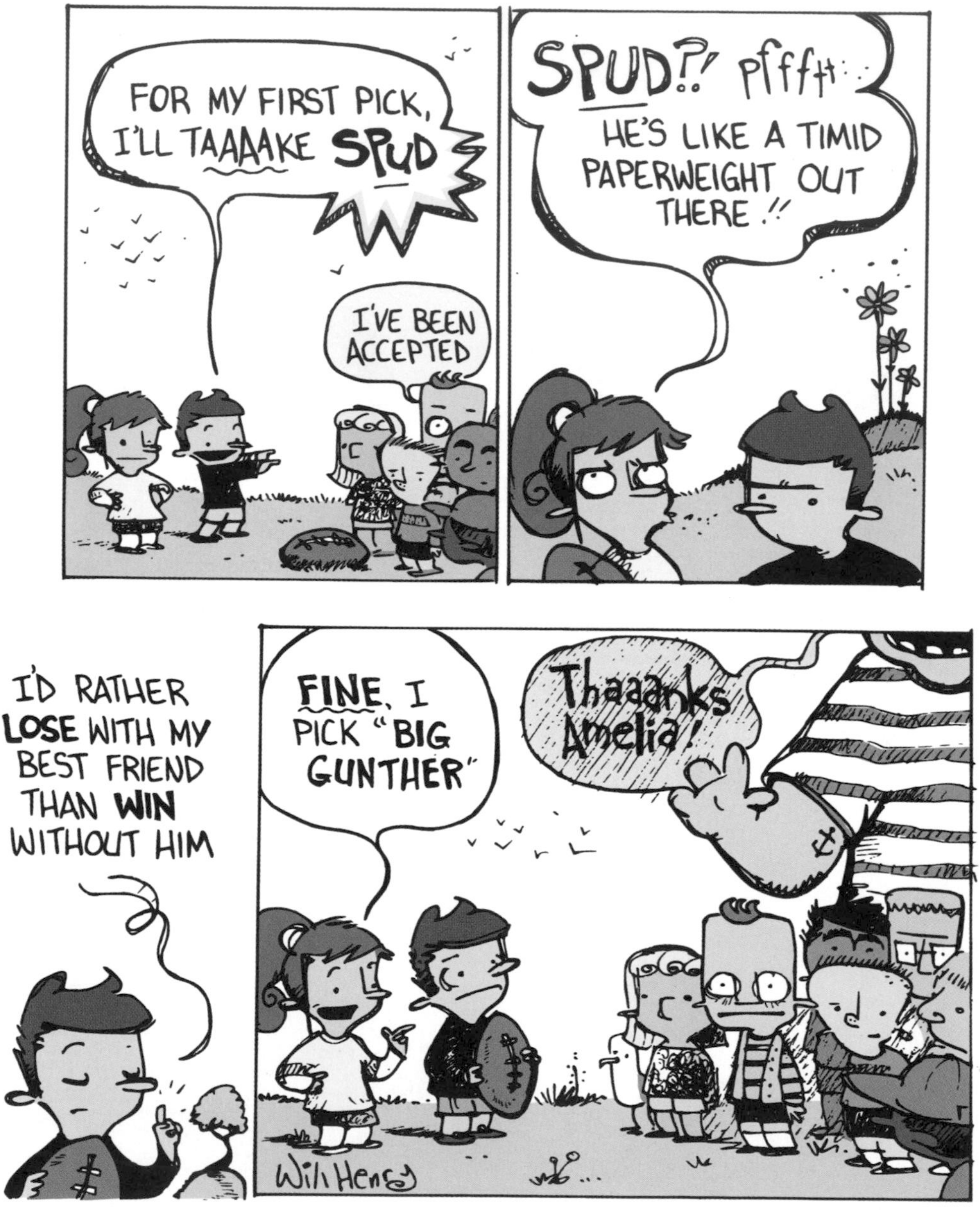
FOR MY FIRST PICK, I'LL TAAAAKE SPUD
I'VE BEEN ACCEPTED
SPUD?! pffft
HE'S LIKE A TIMID PAPERWEIGHT OUT THERE!!
I'D RATHER LOSE WITH MY BEST FRIEND THAN WIN WITHOUT HIM
FINE, I PICK "BIG GUNTHER"
Thaaanks Amelia!
Will Henry

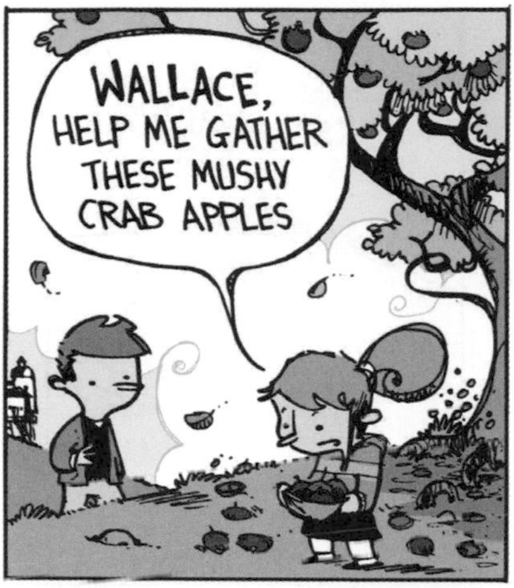
WALLACE, HELP ME GATHER THESE MUSHY CRAB APPLES

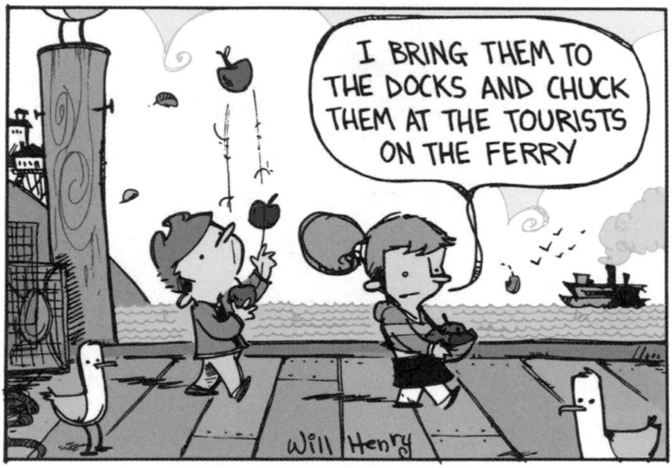
I BRING THEM TO THE DOCKS AND CHUCK THEM AT THE TOURISTS ON THE FERRY
Will Henry

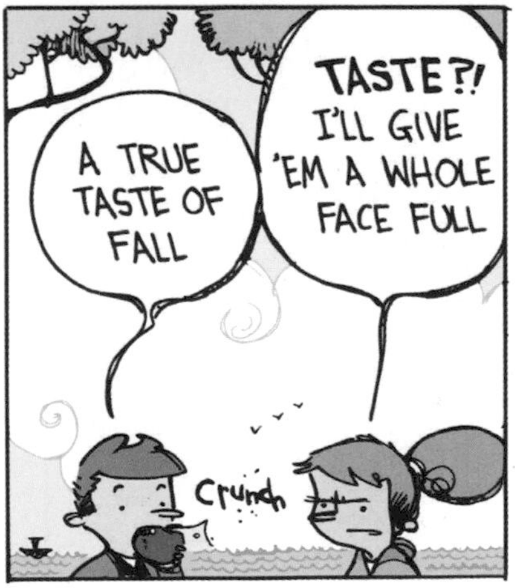
A TRUE TASTE OF FALL
TASTE?! I'LL GIVE 'EM A WHOLE FACE FULL
Crunch

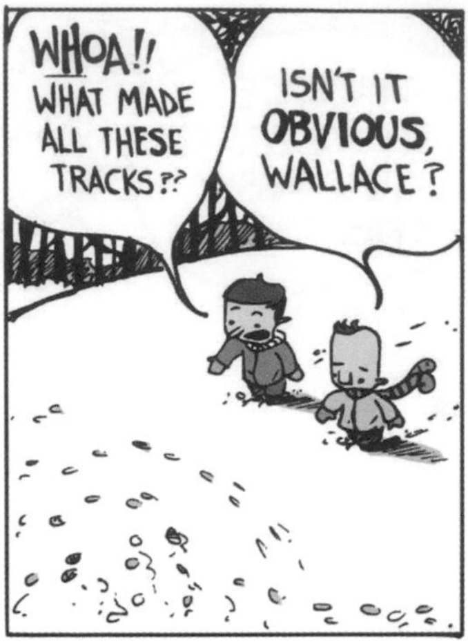
WHOA!! WHAT MADE ALL THESE TRACKS?!?
ISN'T IT OBVIOUS, WALLACE?

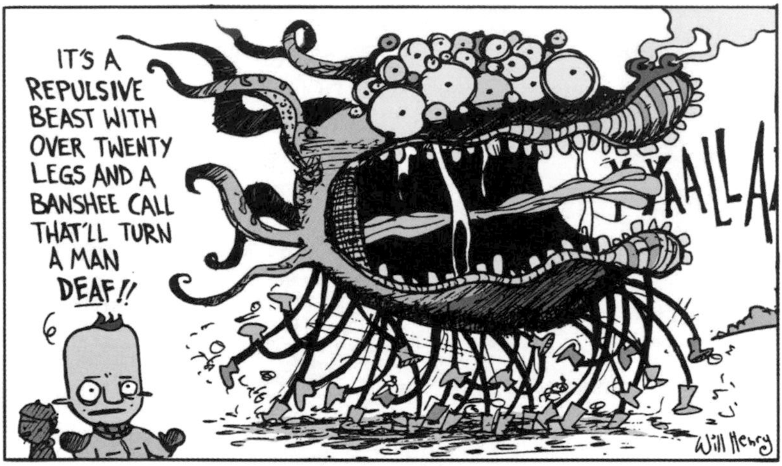
IT'S A REPULSIVE BEAST WITH OVER TWENTY LEGS AND A BANSHEE CALL THAT'LL TURN A MAN DEAF!!
YAALLA
Will Henry

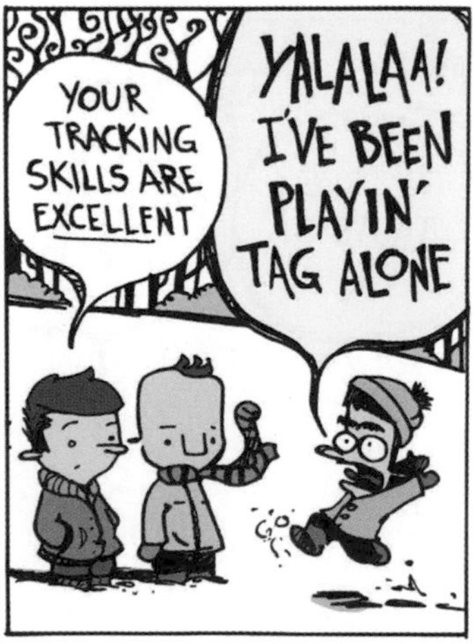
YOUR TRACKING SKILLS ARE EXCELLENT
YALALAA! I'VE BEEN PLAYIN' TAG ALONE

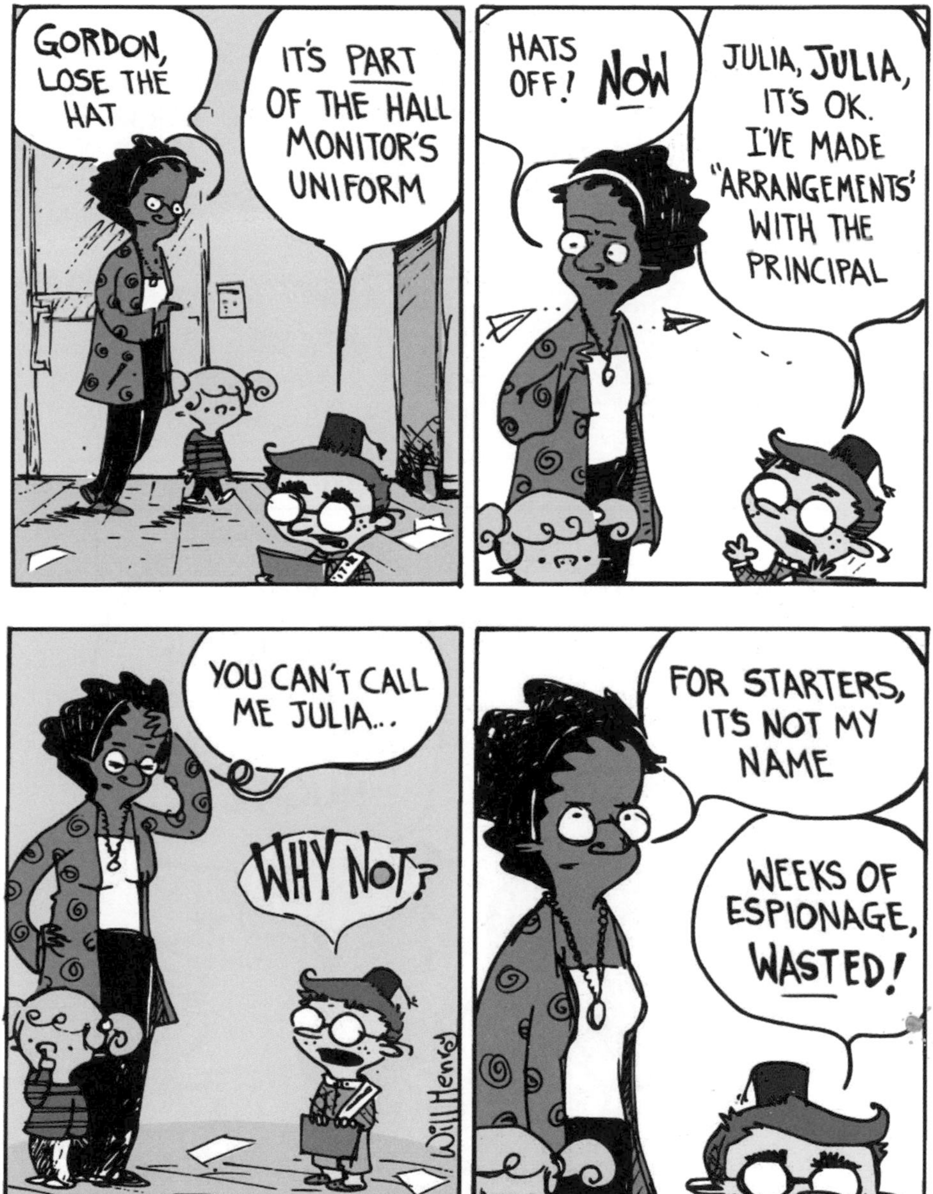
GORDON, LOSE THE HAT
IT'S PART OF THE HALL MONITOR'S UNIFORM
HATS OFF! NOW
JULIA, JULIA, IT'S OK. I'VE MADE "ARRANGEMENTS" WITH THE PRINCIPAL
YOU CAN'T CALL ME JULIA...
WHY NOT?
Will Henry
FOR STARTERS, IT'S NOT MY NAME
WEEKS OF ESPIONAGE, WASTED!

YOUR BUDDY SPUD IS A WEIRD DUDE
ACCURATE
I TAGGED HIM OUT PLAYING KICKBALL, AND THEN HE SAID HE LOVED ME !!
I WOULDN'T WORRY ABOUT IT
ZZZ
Hm, MAYBE I SHOULD'VE SLUGGED HIM
THIS MORNING HE FELL IN LOVE WITH A CHICKEN NUGGET
ZZZ
Will Henry

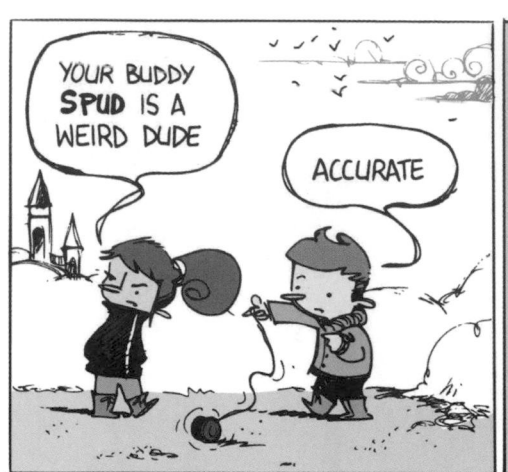

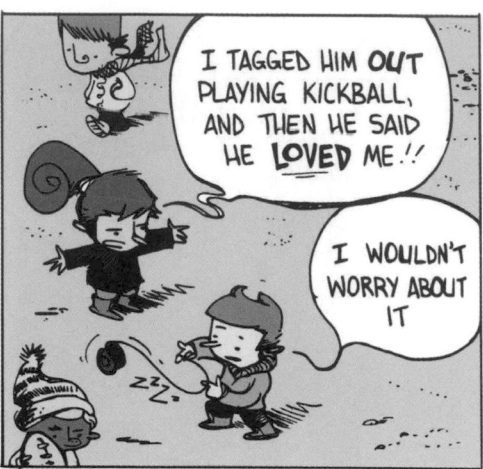

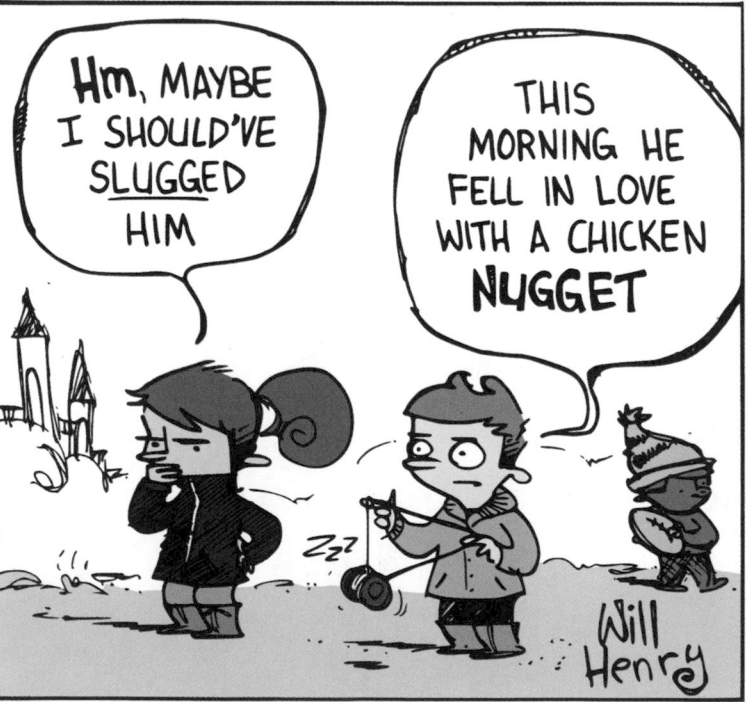

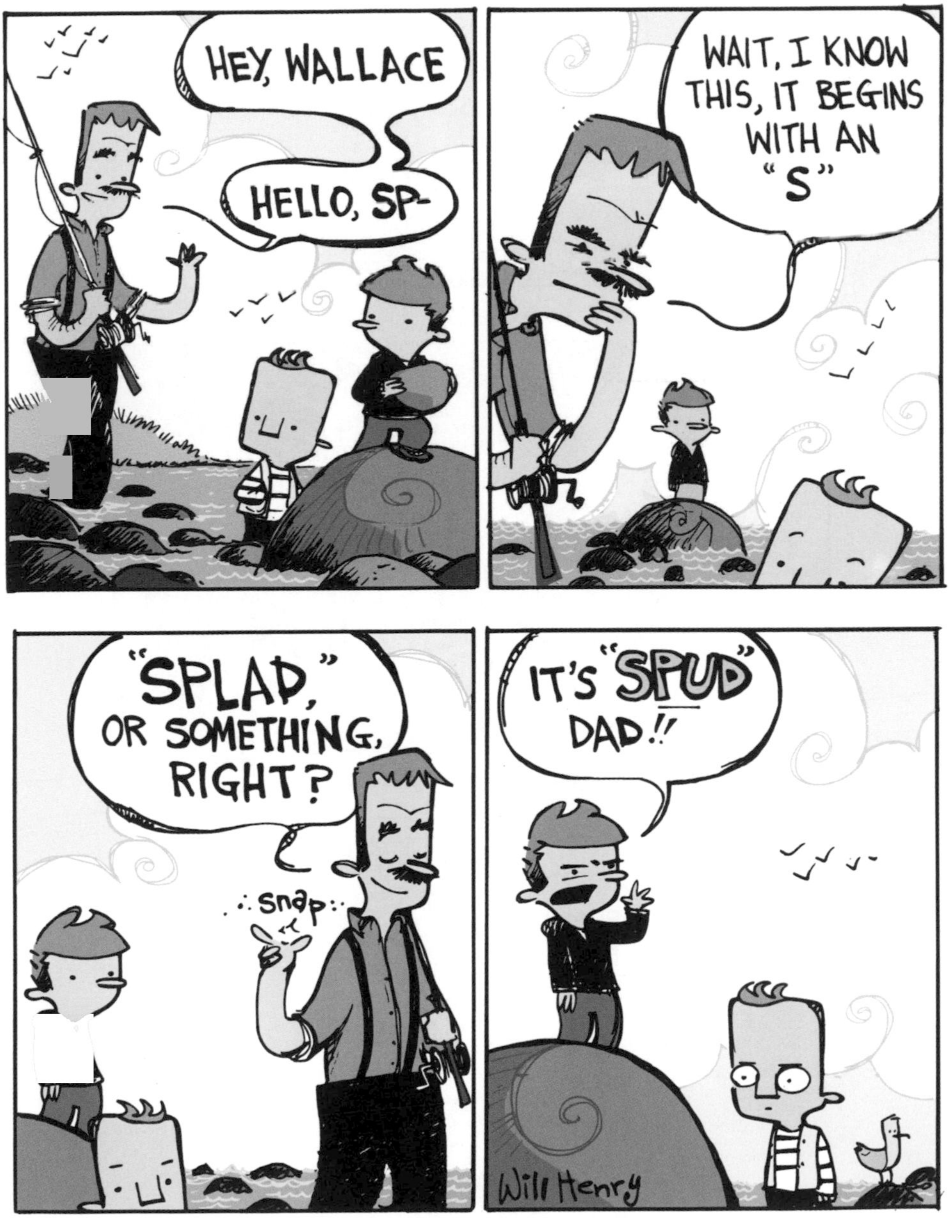
HEY, WALLACE
HELLO, SP-
WAIT, I KNOW THIS, IT BEGINS WITH AN "S"
"SPLAD," OR SOMETHING, RIGHT?
snap
IT'S "SPUD" DAD!!
Will Henry

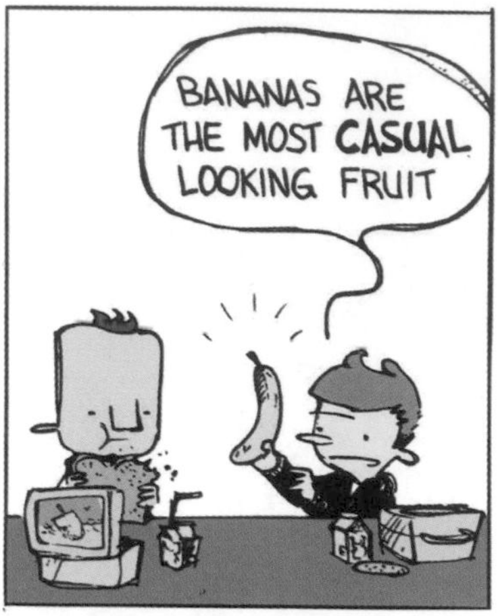
BANANAS ARE THE MOST CASUAL LOOKING FRUIT

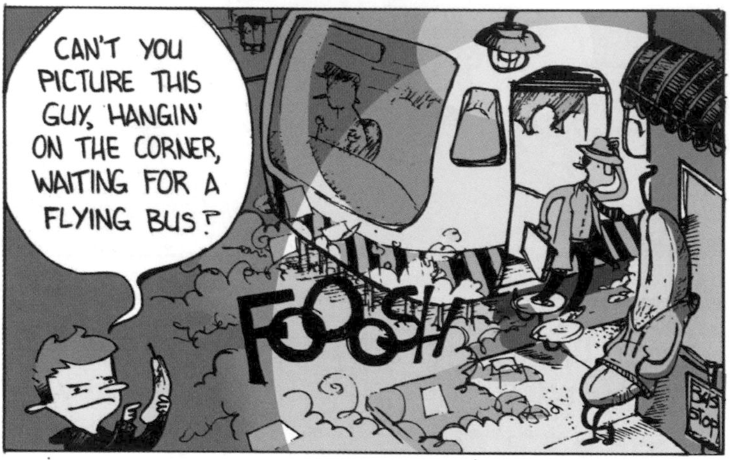
CAN'T YOU PICTURE THIS GUY, HANGIN' ON THE CORNER, WAITING FOR A FLYING BUS?
FOOOSH!
BUS STOP

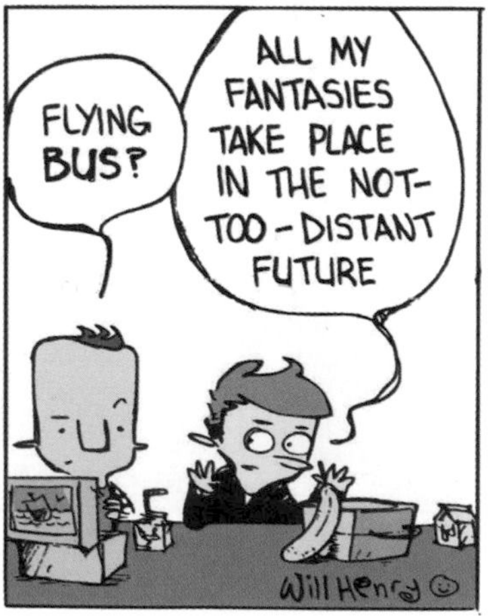
FLYING BUS?
ALL MY FANTASIES TAKE PLACE IN THE NOT-TOO-DISTANT FUTURE
Will Henry

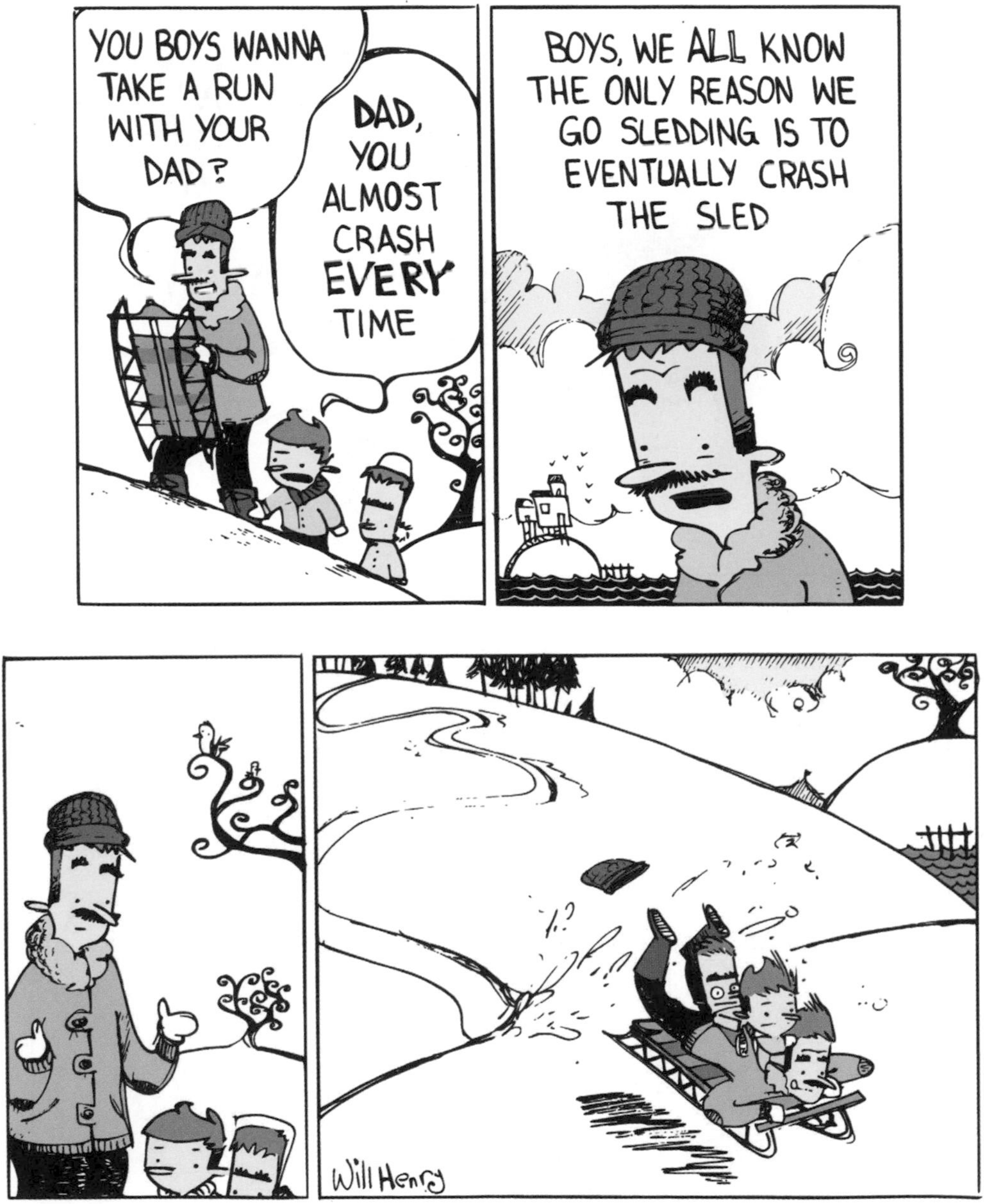
YOU BOYS WANNA TAKE A RUN WITH YOUR DAD?
DAD, YOU ALMOST CRASH EVERY TIME
BOYS, WE ALL KNOW THE ONLY REASON WE GO SLEDDING IS TO EVENTUALLY CRASH THE SLED
Will Henry

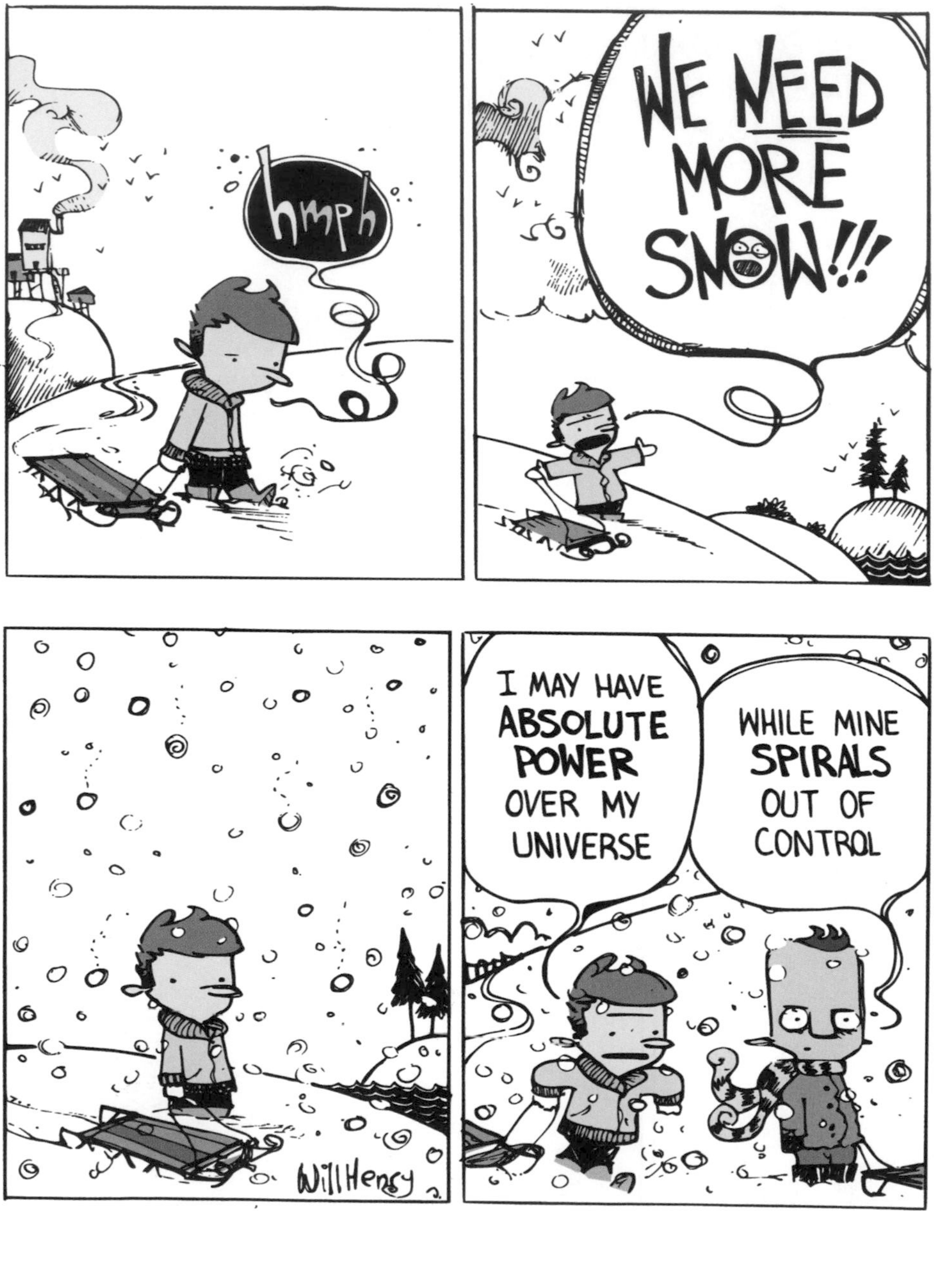
hmph
WE NEED MORE SNOW!!!
I MAY HAVE ABSOLUTE POWER OVER MY UNIVERSE
WHILE MINE SPIRALS OUT OF CONTROL
Will Henry

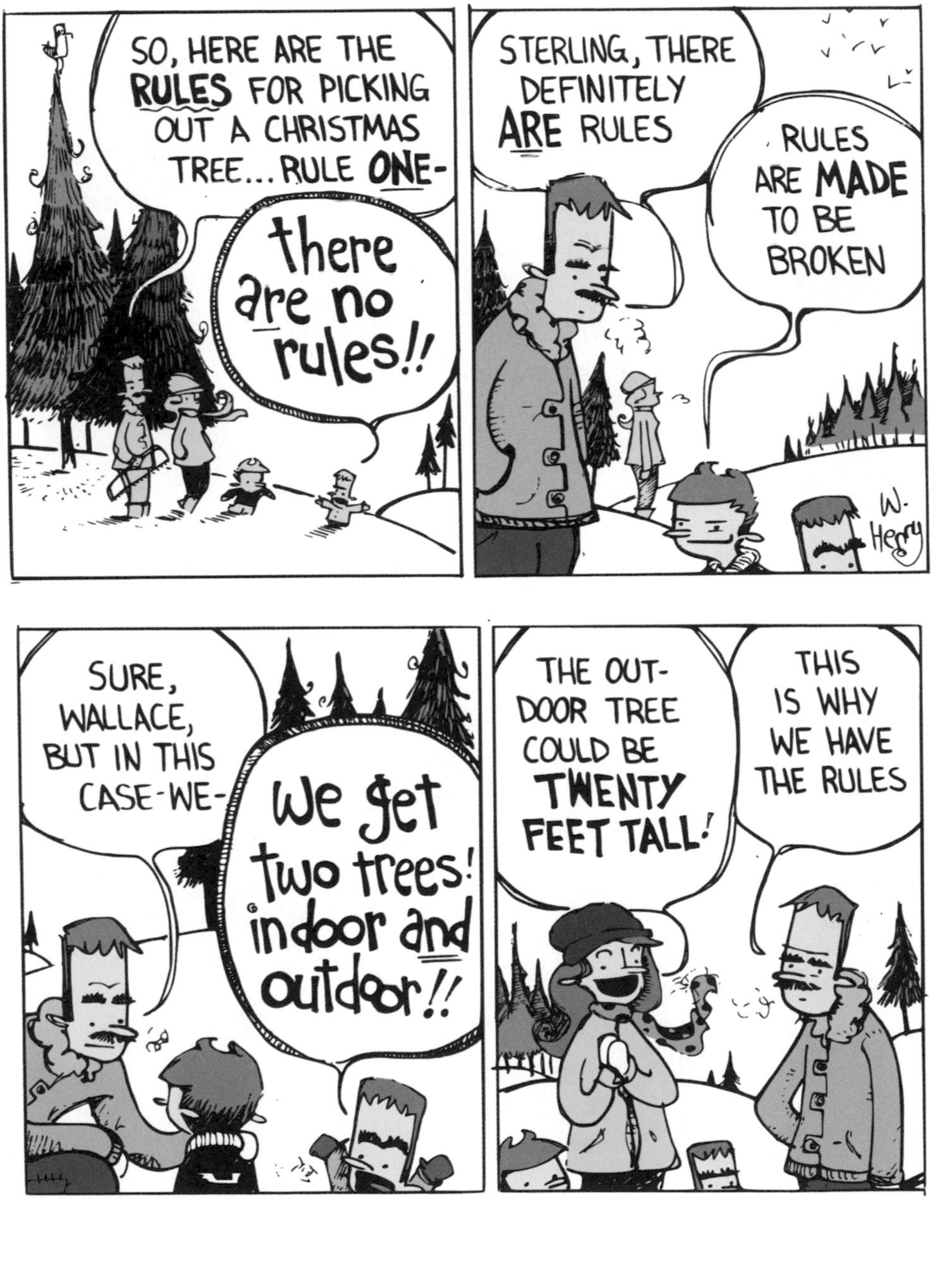
SO, HERE ARE THE RULES FOR PICKING OUT A CHRISTMAS TREE... RULE ONE-
there are no rules!!
STERLING, THERE DEFINITELY ARE RULES
RULES ARE MADE TO BE BROKEN
W. Henry
SURE, WALLACE, BUT IN THIS CASE-WE-
We get two trees! indoor and outdoor!!
THE OUT-DOOR TREE COULD BE TWENTY FEET TALL!
THIS IS WHY WE HAVE THE RULES

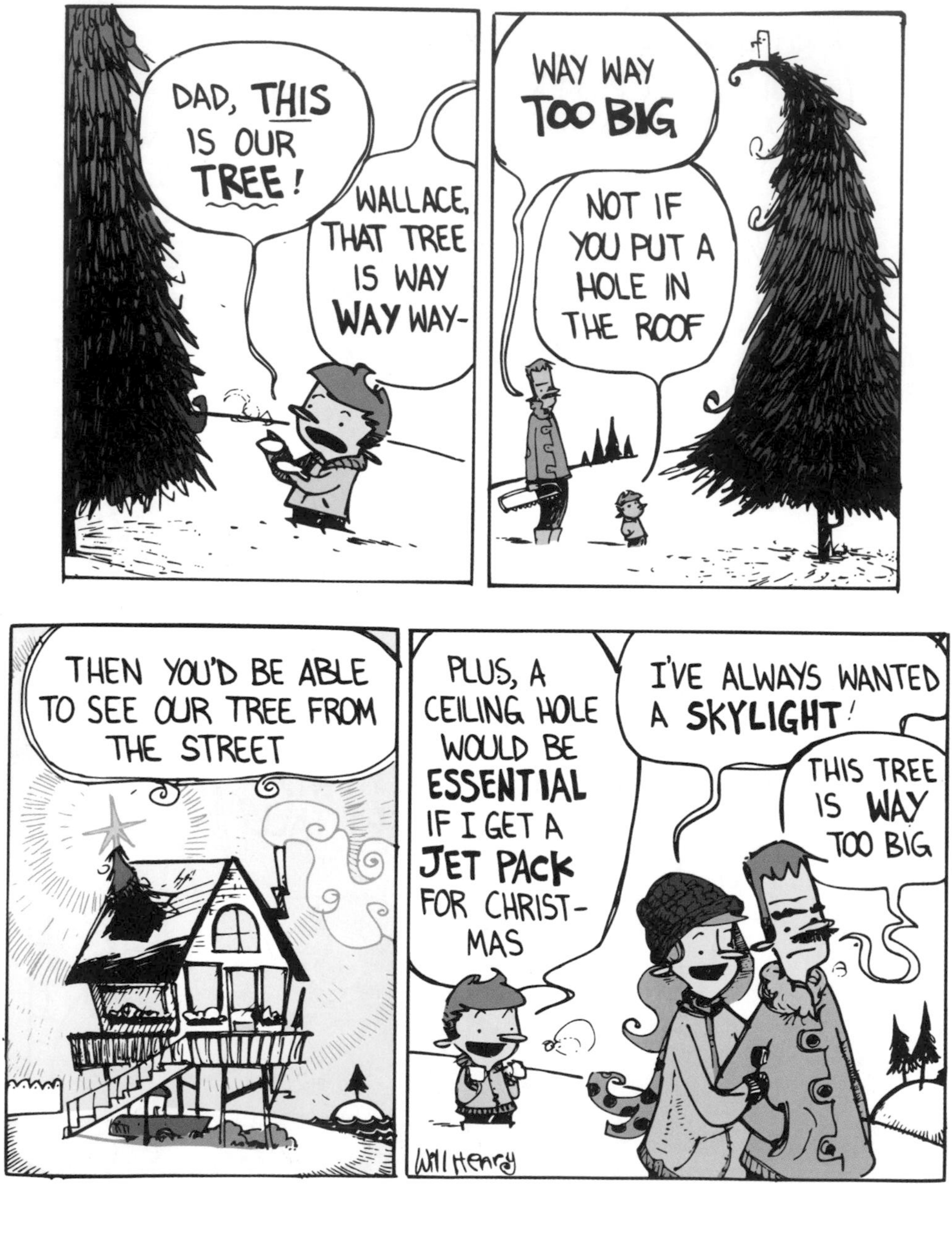
DAD, THIS IS OUR TREE!
WALLACE, THAT TREE IS WAY WAY WAY-
WAY WAY TOO BIG
NOT IF YOU PUT A HOLE IN THE ROOF
THEN YOU'D BE ABLE TO SEE OUR TREE FROM THE STREET
PLUS, A CEILING HOLE WOULD BE ESSENTIAL IF I GET A JET PACK FOR CHRIST-MAS
I'VE ALWAYS WANTED A SKYLIGHT!
THIS TREE IS WAY TOO BIG
Will Henry

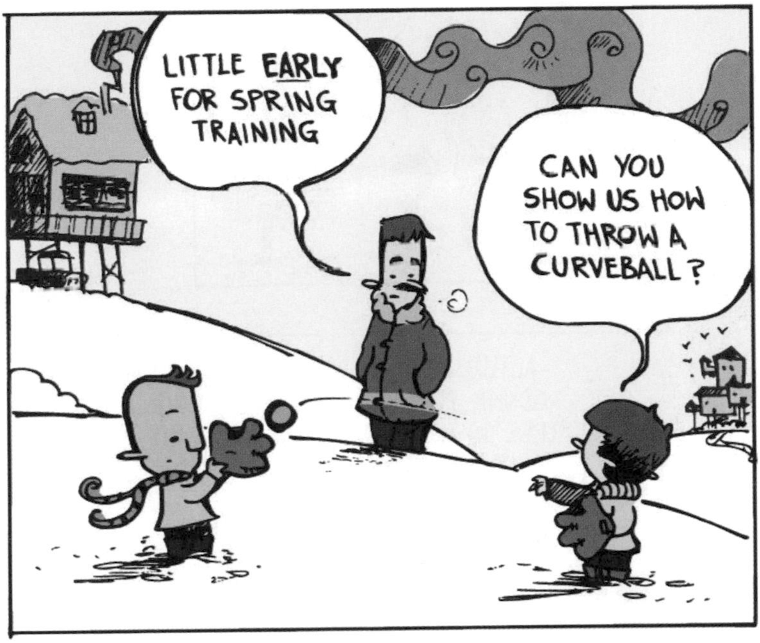
LITTLE EARLY FOR SPRING TRAINING
CAN YOU SHOW US HOW TO THROW A CURVEBALL?

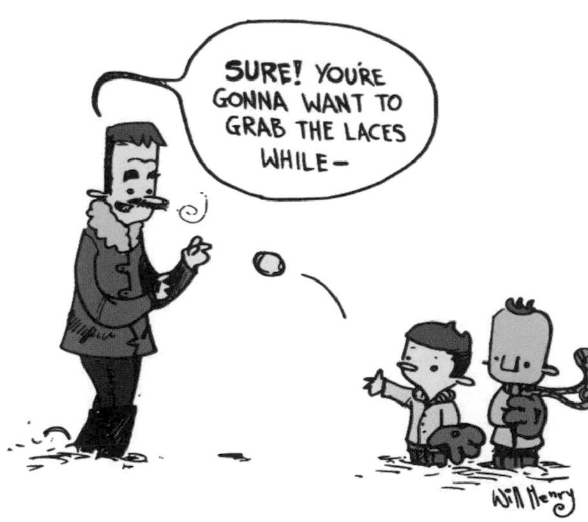
SURE! YOU'RE GONNA WANT TO GRAB THE LACES WHILE-
Will Henry

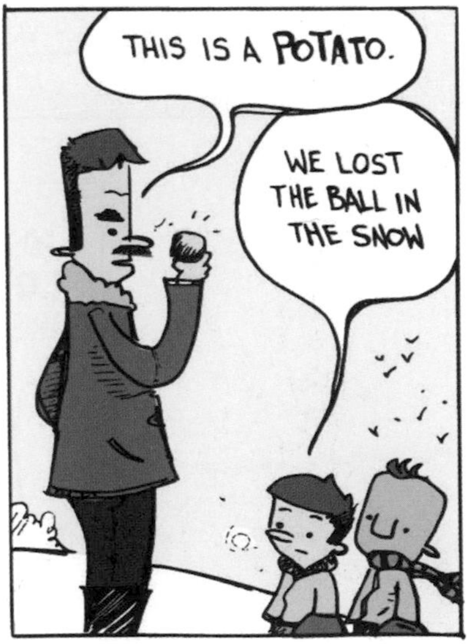
THIS IS A POTATO.
WE LOST THE BALL IN THE SNOW

HOW 'BOUT THIS TREE?
DAD, WE COULD FIT A TREE TWICE THIS SIZE IN THE TRUCK
ACTUALLY, I WAS GONNA PUT THE TREE IN THE FRONT SEAT AND MAKE STERLING SIT IN THE BACK
SO WE CAN BUCKLE UP THE TREE
VROOM VROOM
Will Henry

I POSITIVELY LOVE CHRISTMAS
NOBODY IS RIDING IN THE BACK
please?

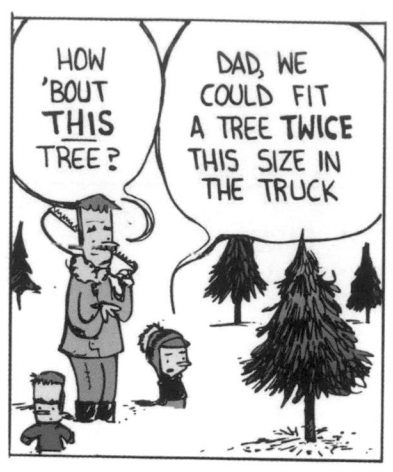

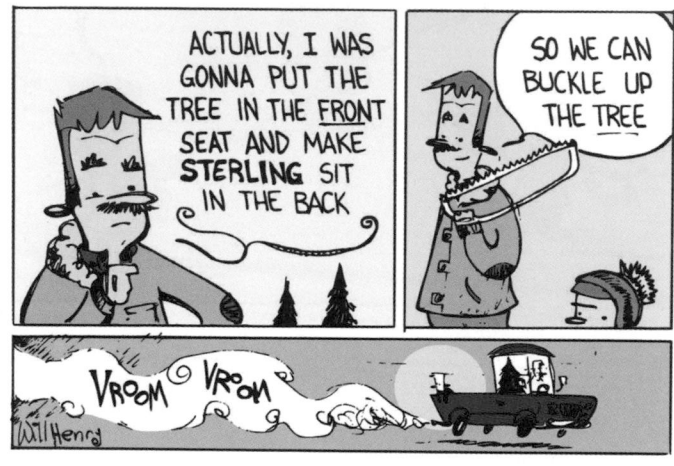

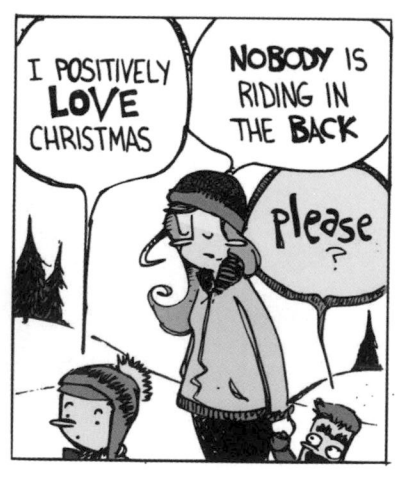

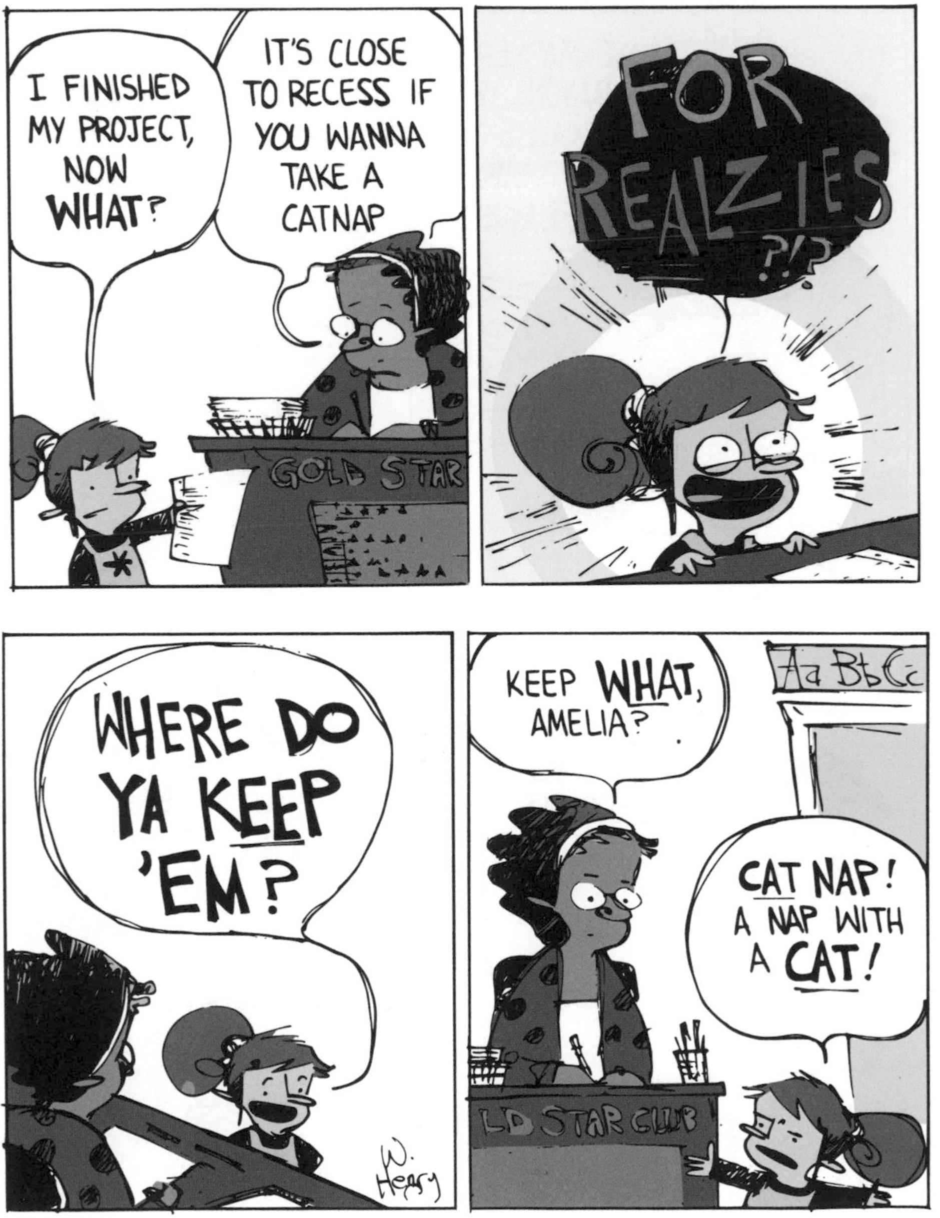
I FINISHED MY PROJECT, NOW WHAT?
IT'S CLOSE TO RECESS IF YOU WANNA TAKE A CATNAP
GOLD STAR
FOR REALZIES ?!?
WHERE DO YA KEEP 'EM?
W. Henry
KEEP WHAT, AMELIA?
Aa Bb Cc
CAT NAP! A NAP WITH A CAT!
LD STAR CLUB

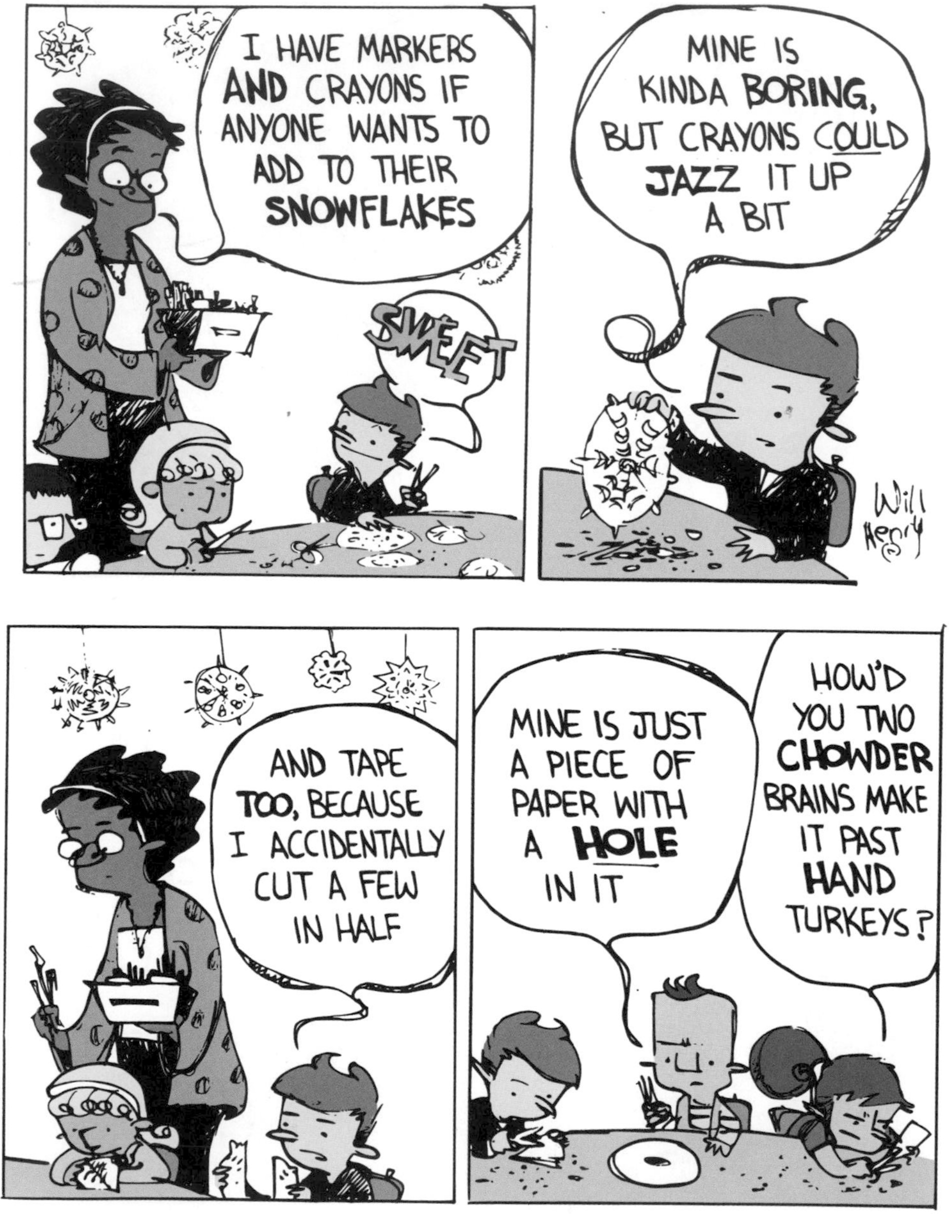
I HAVE MARKERS AND CRAYONS IF ANYONE WANTS TO ADD TO THEIR SNOWFLAKES
SWEET
MINE IS KINDA BORING, BUT CRAYONS COULD JAZZ IT UP A BIT
Will Henry
AND TAPE TOO, BECAUSE I ACCIDENTALLY CUT A FEW IN HALF
MINE IS JUST A PIECE OF PAPER WITH A HOLE IN IT
HOW'D YOU TWO CHOWDER BRAINS MAKE IT PAST HAND TURKEYS?

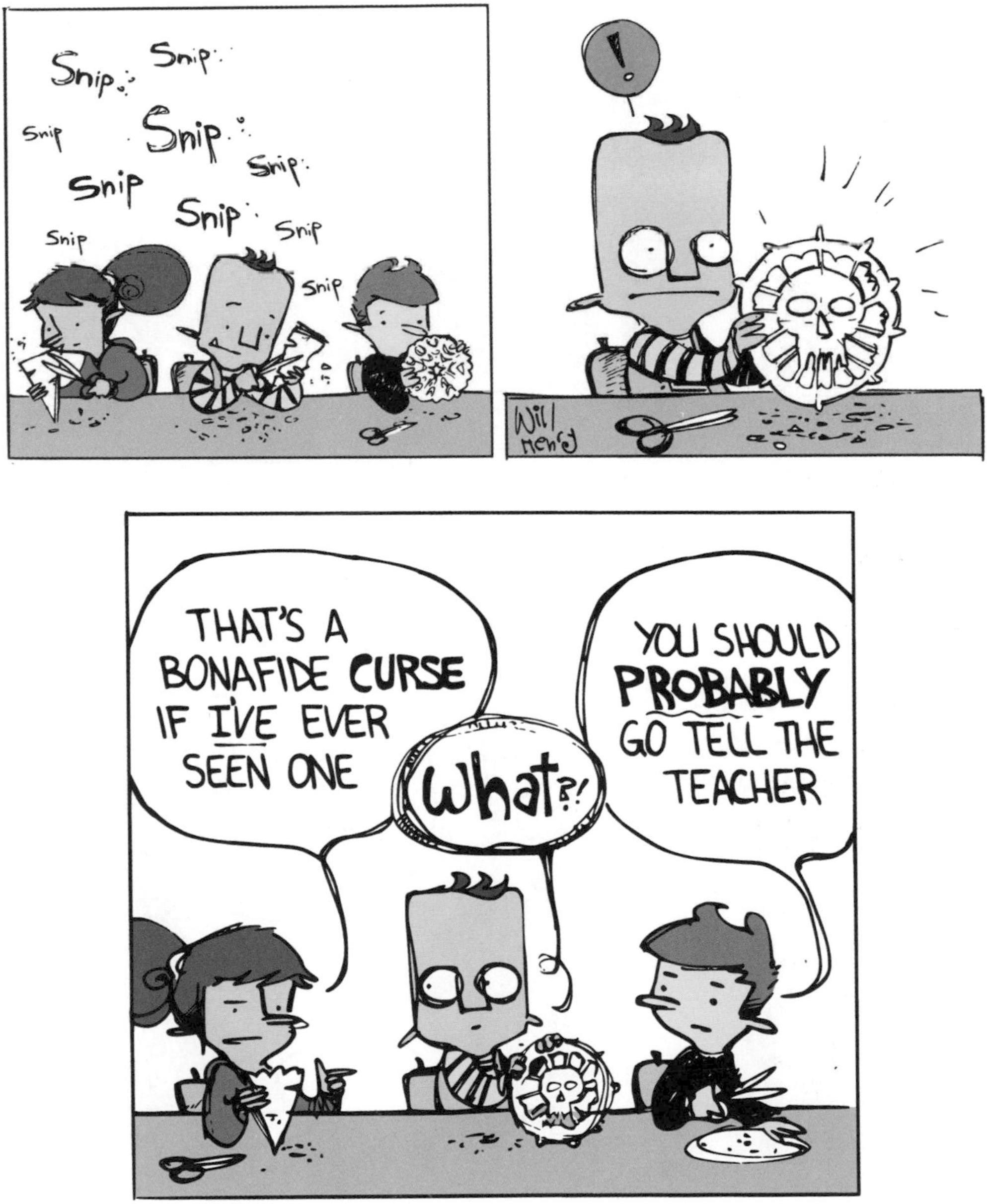
Snip
Snip
Snip
Snip
Snip
Snip
Snip
Snip
Snip
Snip
!
Will Henry
THAT'S A BONAFIDE CURSE IF I'VE EVER SEEN ONE
What?!
YOU SHOULD PROBABLY GO TELL THE TEACHER

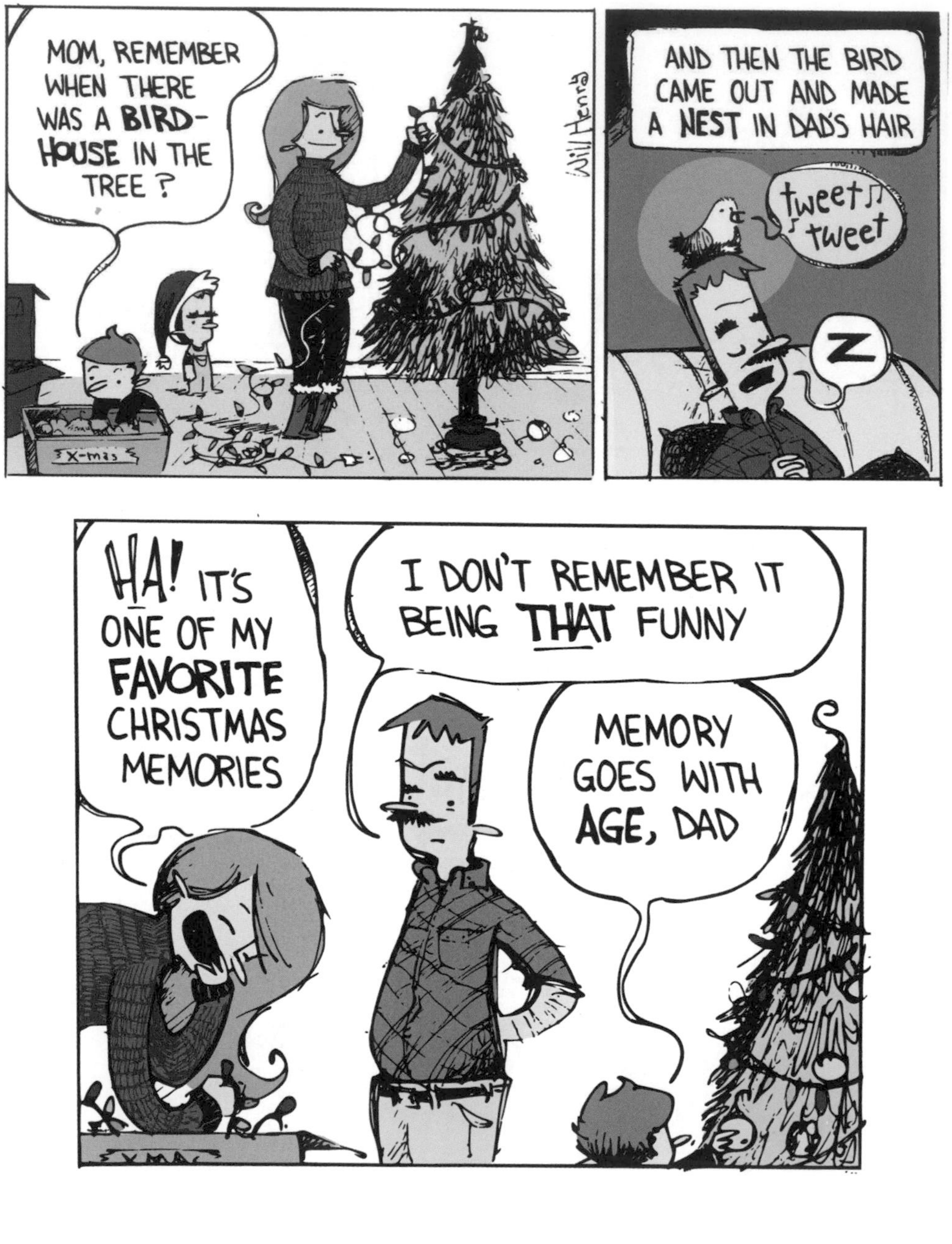
MOM, REMEMBER WHEN THERE WAS A **BIRD-HOUSE** IN THE TREE ?
Will Henry
X-mas
AND THEN THE BIRD CAME OUT AND MADE A **NEST** IN DAD'S HAIR
tweet tweet
Z
HA! IT'S ONE OF MY **FAVORITE** CHRISTMAS MEMORIES
I DON'T REMEMBER IT BEING **THAT** FUNNY
MEMORY GOES WITH **AGE**, DAD
XMAS

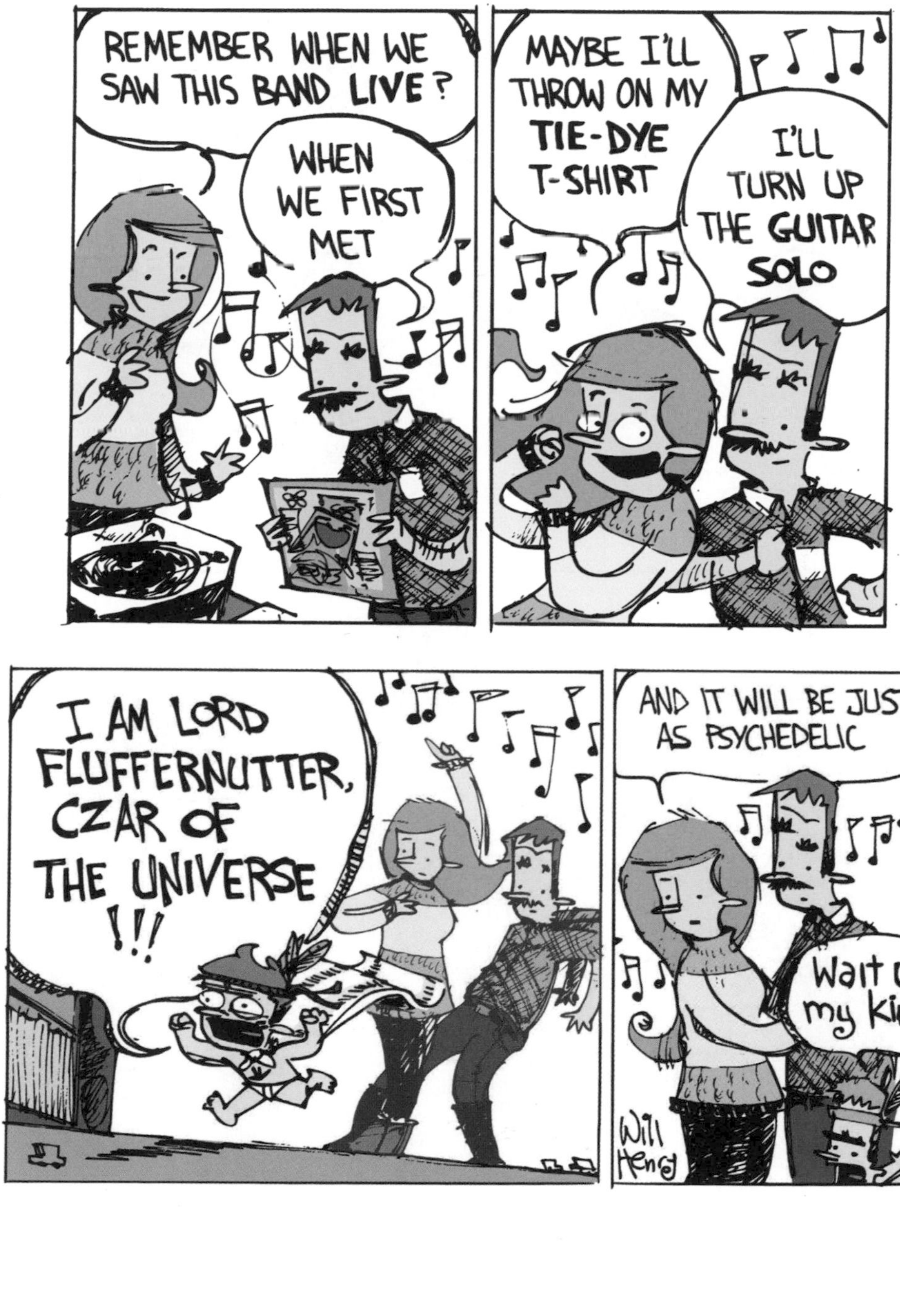
REMEMBER WHEN WE SAW THIS BAND LIVE?
WHEN WE FIRST MET
MAYBE I'LL THROW ON MY TIE-DYE T-SHIRT
I'LL TURN UP THE GUITAR SOLO
I AM LORD FLUFFERNUTTER, CZAR OF THE UNIVERSE !!!
AND IT WILL BE JUST AS PSYCHEDELIC
Wait up my king!
Will Henry

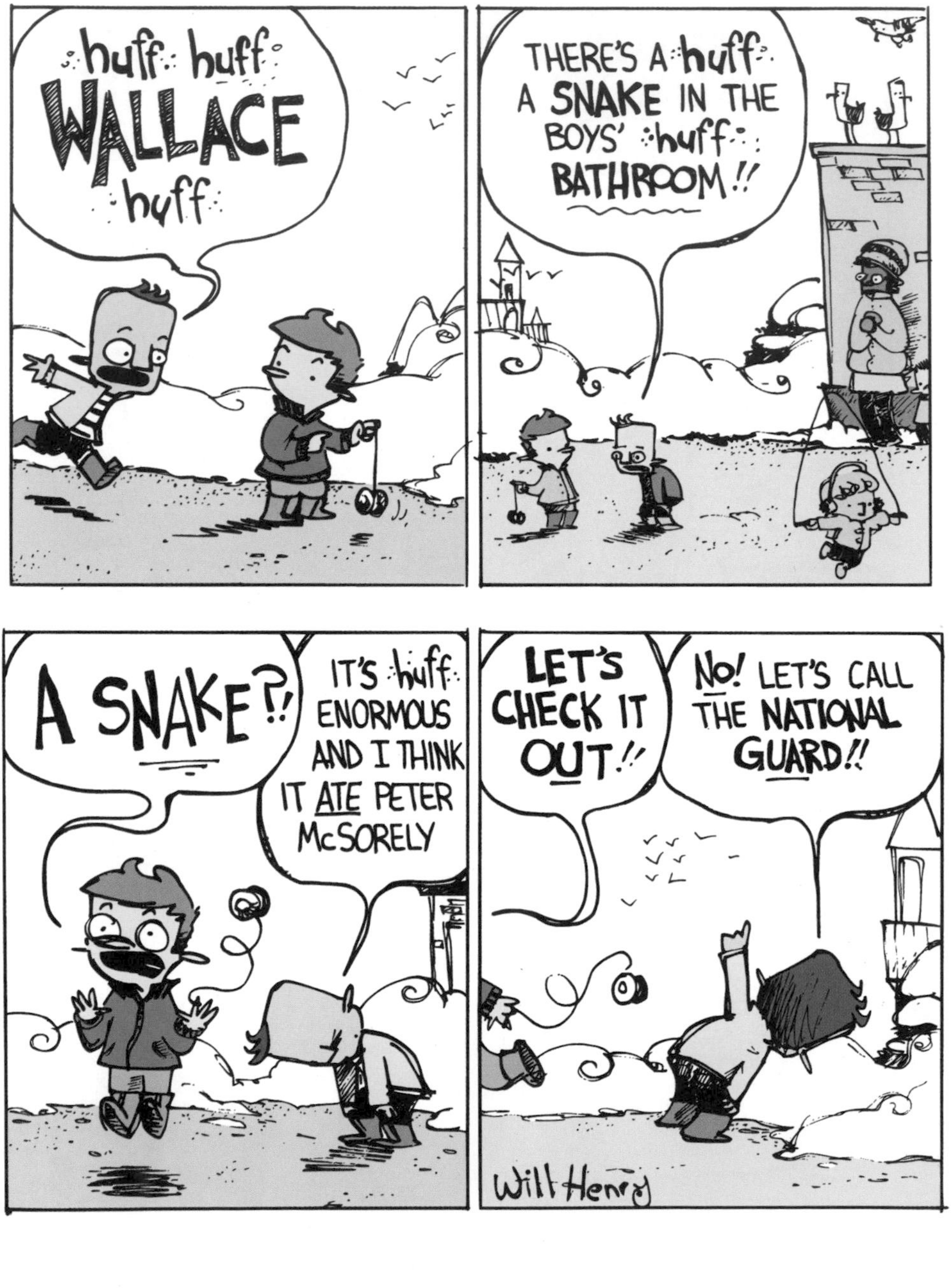
huff huff WALLACE huff
THERE'S A huff A SNAKE IN THE BOYS' huff BATHROOM!!
A SNAKE?!
IT'S huff ENORMOUS AND I THINK IT ATE PETER McSORELY
LET'S CHECK IT OUT!!
NO! LET'S CALL THE NATIONAL GUARD!!
Will Henry

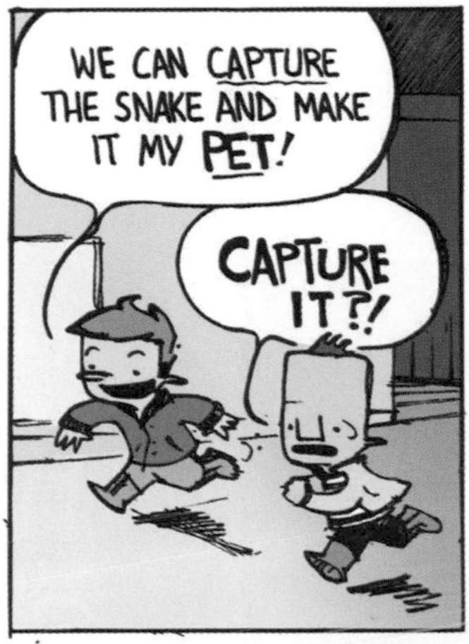
WE CAN CAPTURE THE SNAKE AND MAKE IT MY PET!
CAPTURE IT?!

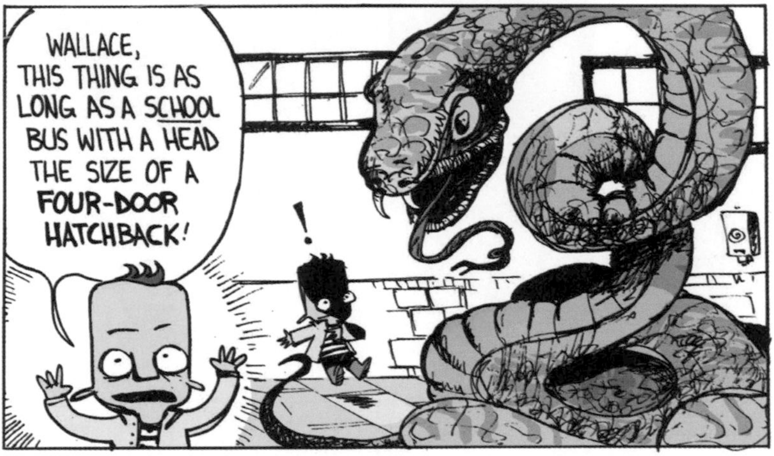
WALLACE, THIS THING IS AS LONG AS A SCHOOL BUS WITH A HEAD THE SIZE OF A FOUR-DOOR HATCHBACK!
!

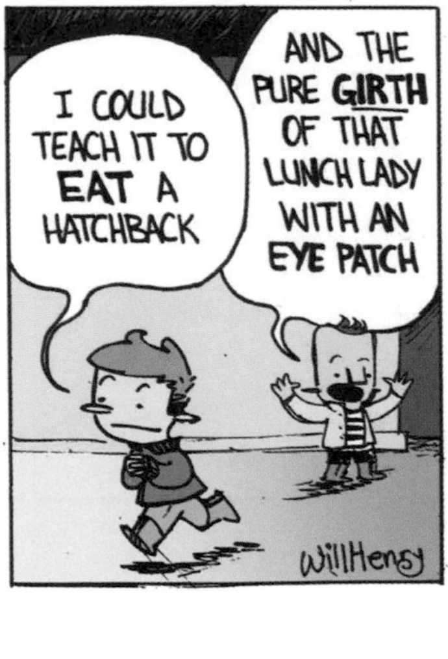
I COULD TEACH IT TO EAT A HATCHBACK
AND THE PURE GIRTH OF THAT LUNCH LADY WITH AN EYE PATCH
WillHenry

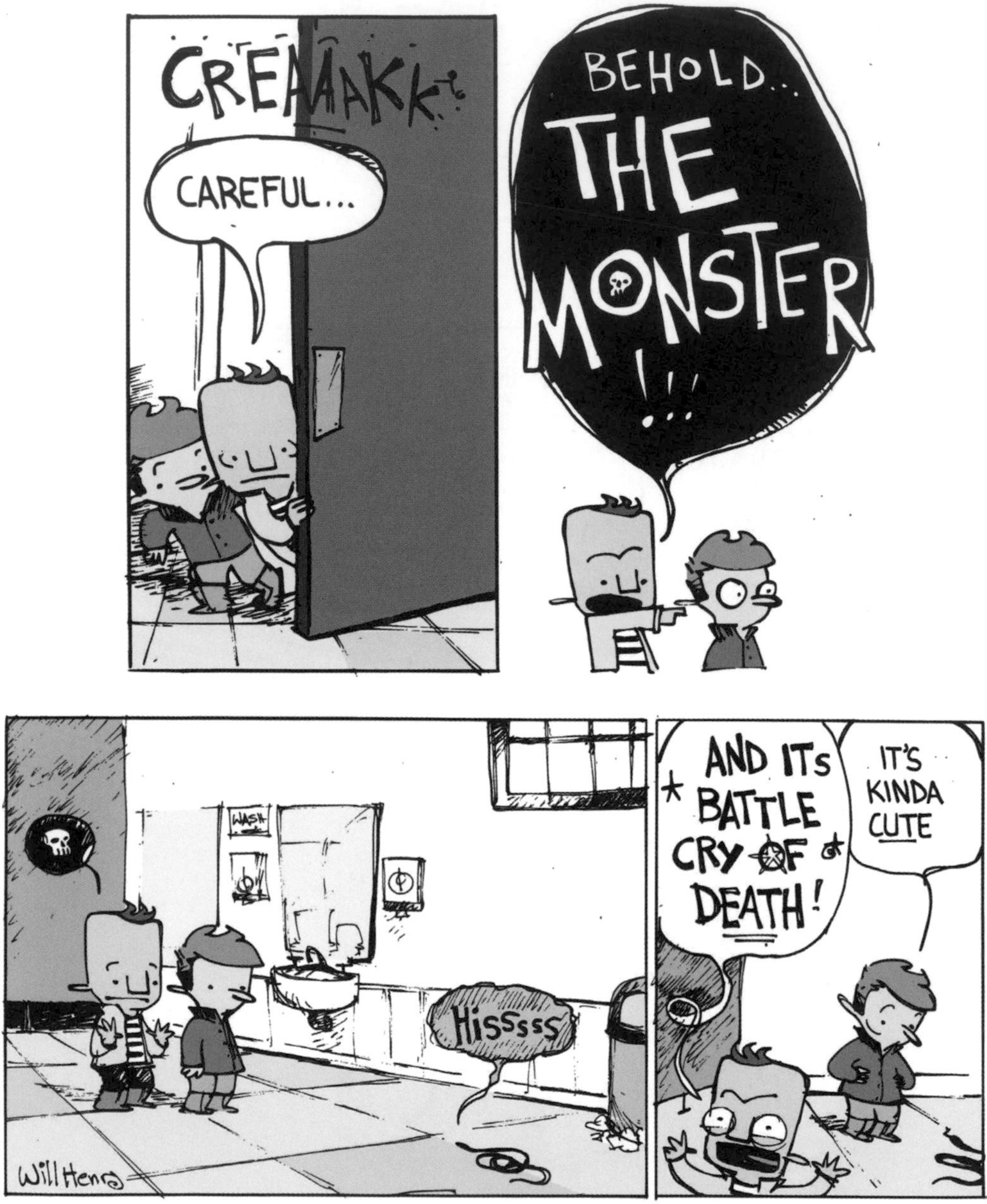
CREAAAKK
CAREFUL...
BEHOLD... THE MONSTER !!!
HISSSSS
AND ITS BATTLE CRY OF DEATH!
IT'S KINDA CUTE
Will Henry

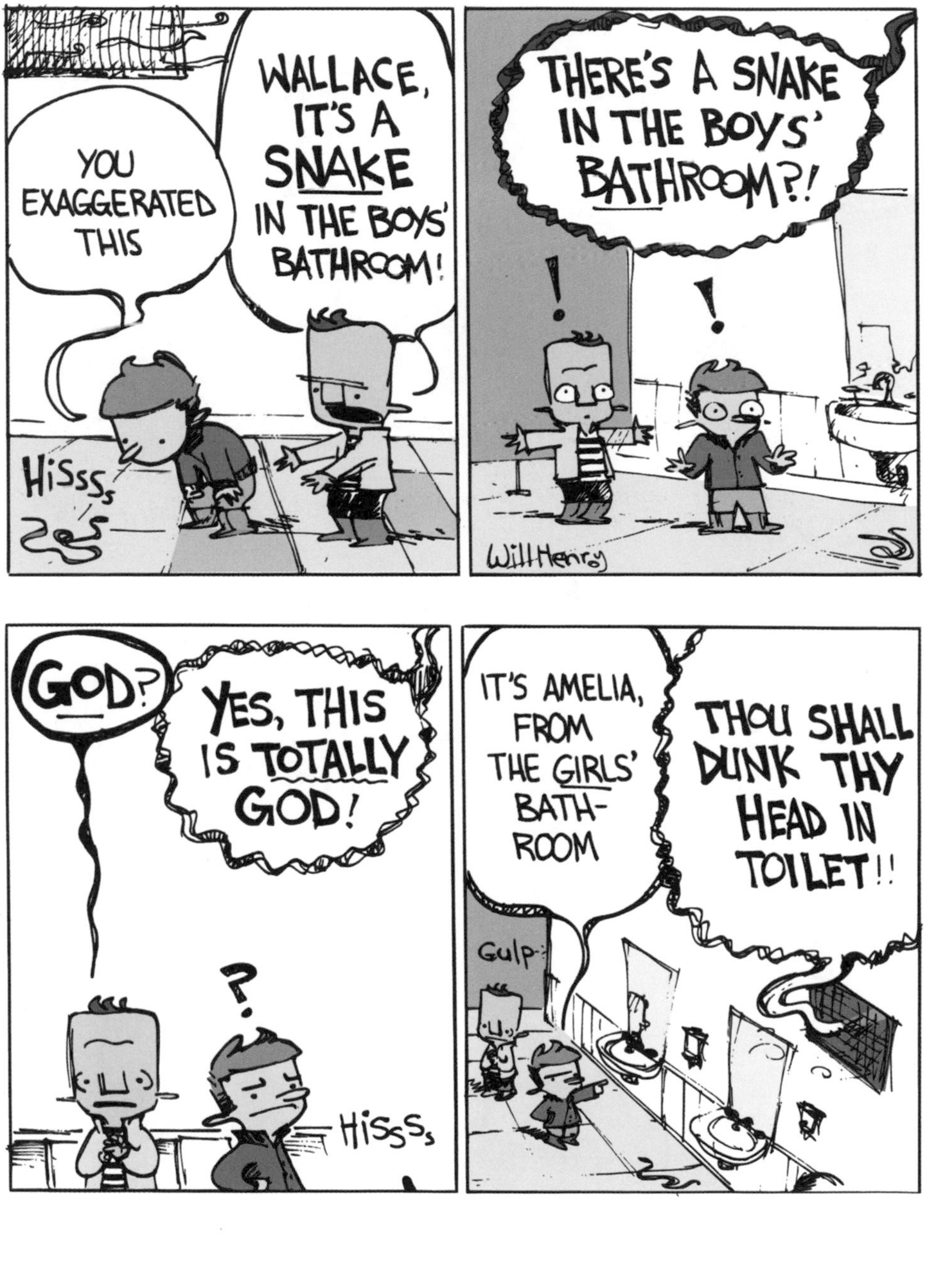
YOU EXAGGERATED THIS
WALLACE, IT'S A SNAKE IN THE BOYS' BATHROOM!
HISSSS
THERE'S A SNAKE IN THE BOYS' BATHROOM?!
!
!
Will Henry
GOD?
YES, THIS IS TOTALLY GOD!
?
HISSSS
IT'S AMELIA, FROM THE GIRLS' BATH-ROOM
THOU SHALL DUNK THY HEAD IN TOILET!!
Gulp

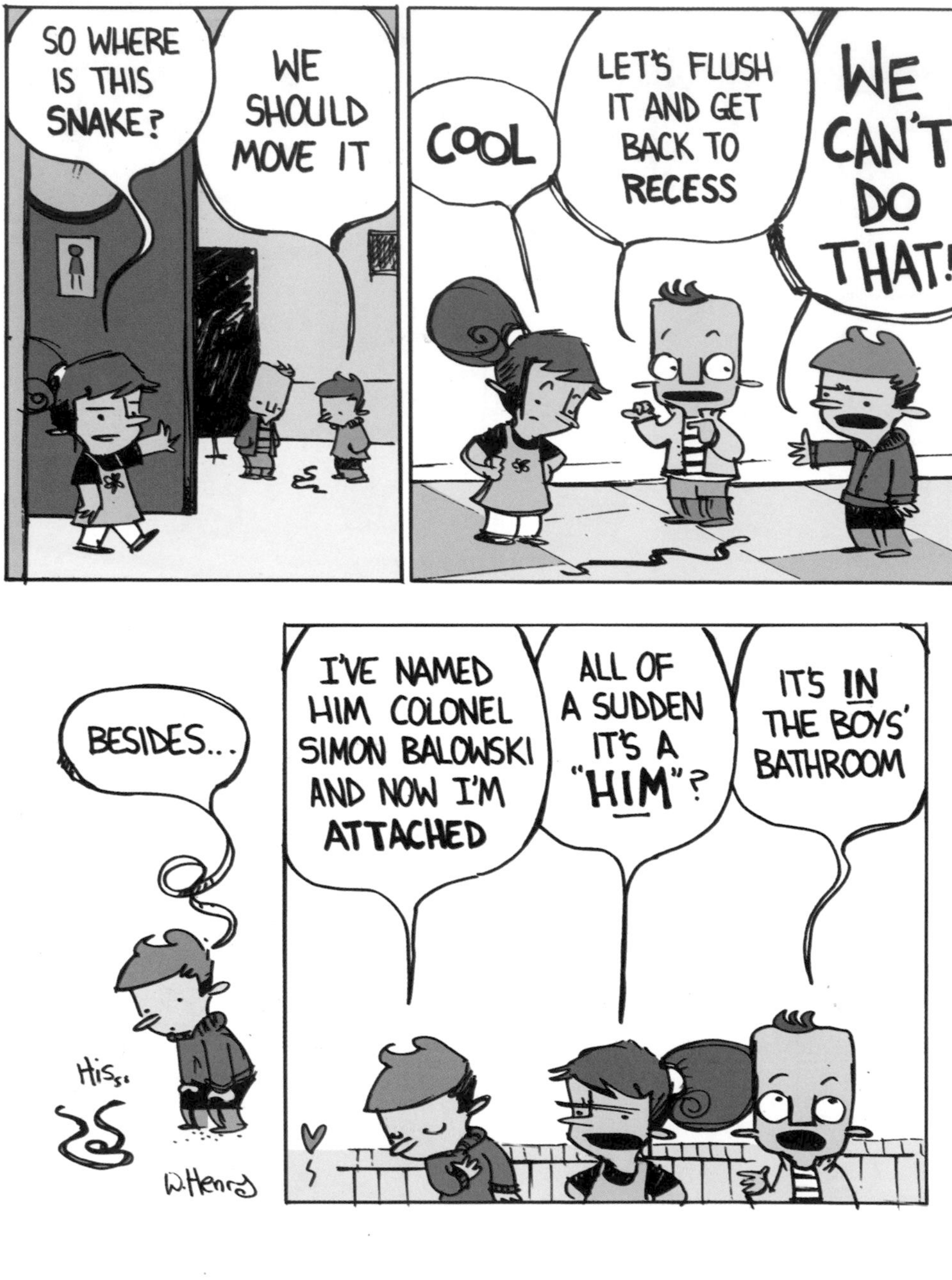
SO WHERE IS THIS SNAKE?
WE SHOULD MOVE IT
COOL
LET'S FLUSH IT AND GET BACK TO RECESS
WE CAN'T DO THAT!
BESIDES...
His...
W. Henry
I'VE NAMED HIM COLONEL SIMON BALOWSKI AND NOW I'M ATTACHED
ALL OF A SUDDEN IT'S A "HIM"?
IT'S IN THE BOYS' BATHROOM

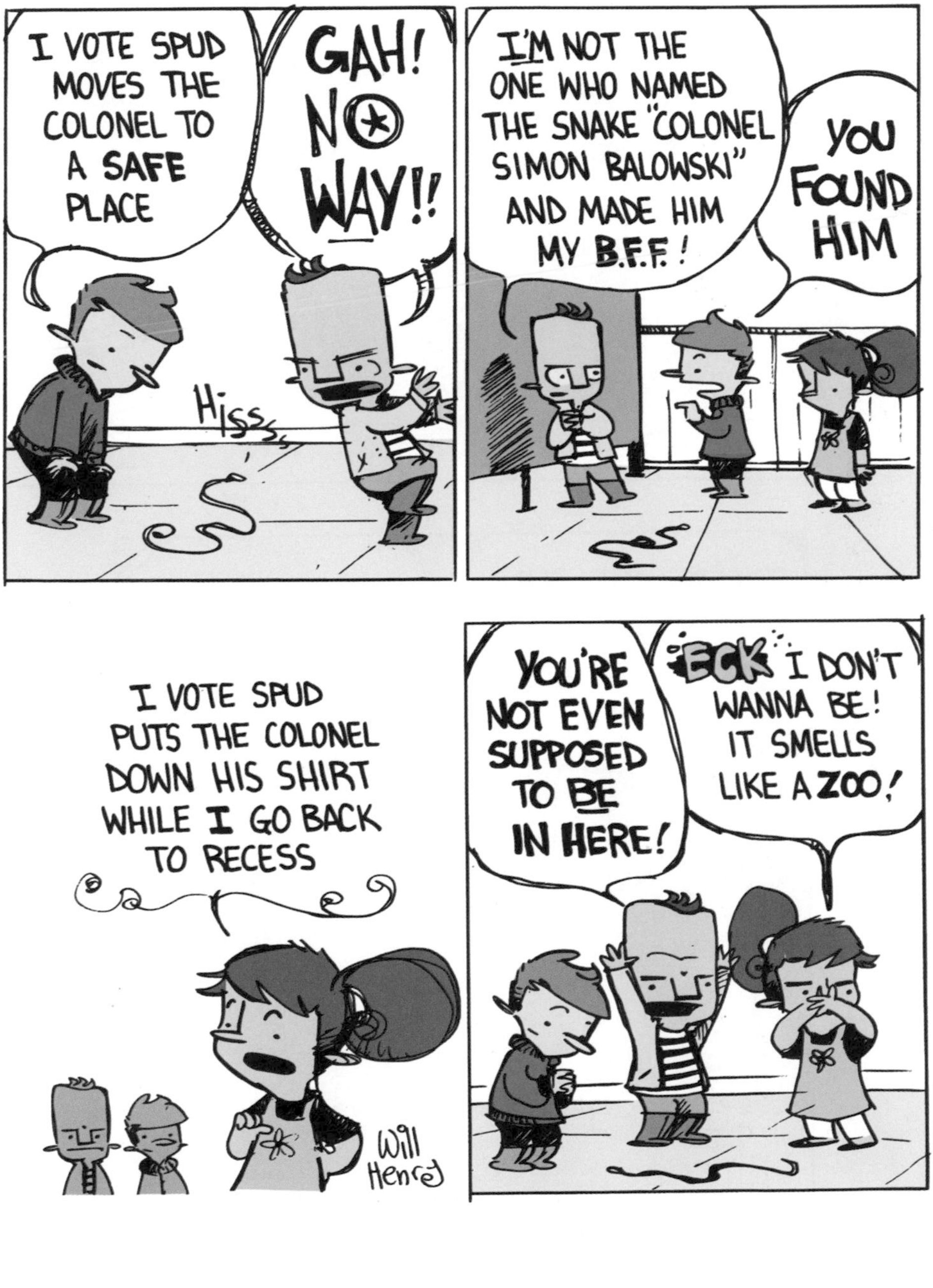
I VOTE SPUD MOVES THE COLONEL TO A SAFE PLACE
GAH! NO WAY!!
HISS
I'M NOT THE ONE WHO NAMED THE SNAKE "COLONEL SIMON BALOWSKI" AND MADE HIM MY B.F.F.!
YOU FOUND HIM
I VOTE SPUD PUTS THE COLONEL DOWN HIS SHIRT WHILE I GO BACK TO RECESS
YOU'RE NOT EVEN SUPPOSED TO BE IN HERE!
ECK I DON'T WANNA BE! IT SMELLS LIKE A ZOO!
Will Henry

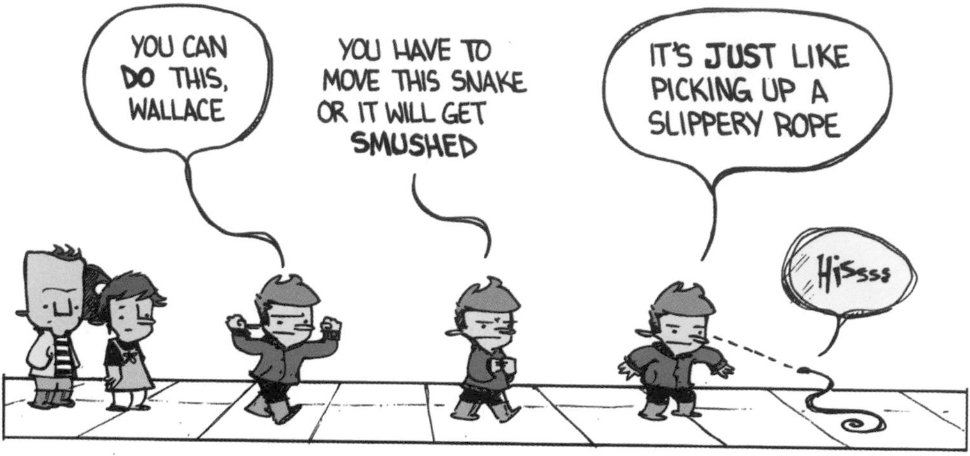
YOU CAN DO THIS, WALLACE
YOU HAVE TO MOVE THIS SNAKE OR IT WILL GET SMUSHED
IT'S JUST LIKE PICKING UP A SLIPPERY ROPE
Hissss

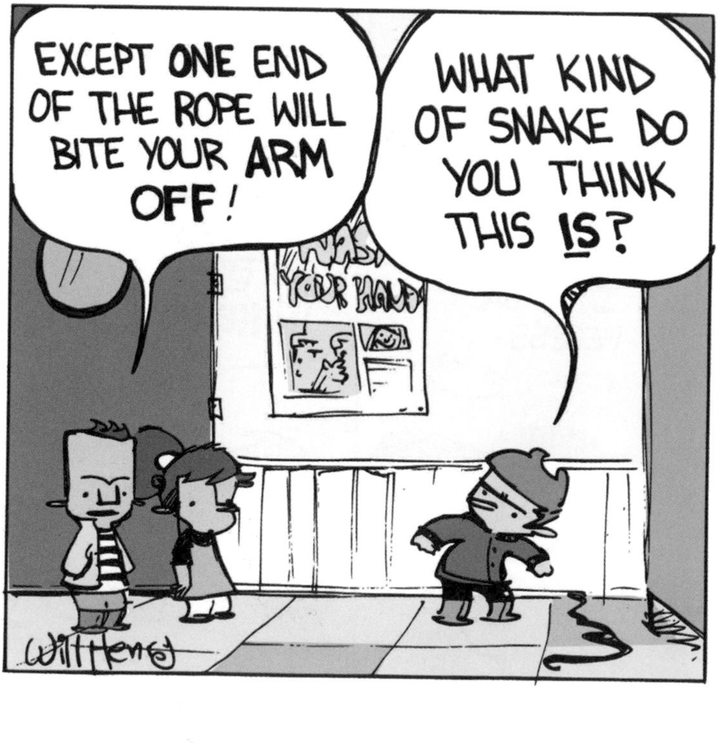
EXCEPT ONE END OF THE ROPE WILL BITE YOUR ARM OFF!
WHAT KIND OF SNAKE DO YOU THINK THIS IS?
Will Henry

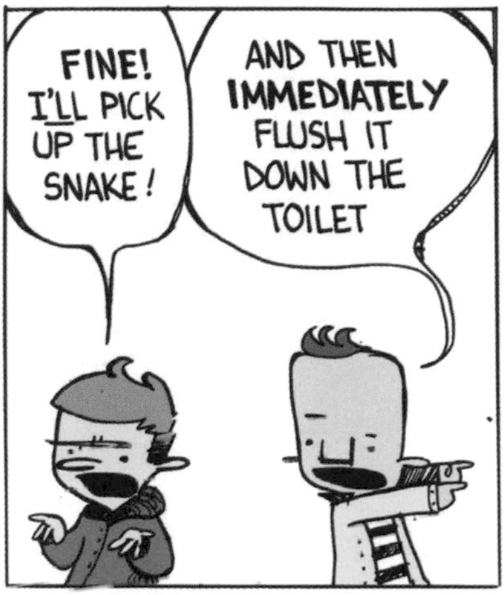
FINE! I'LL PICK UP THE SNAKE!
AND THEN IMMEDIATELY FLUSH IT DOWN THE TOILET

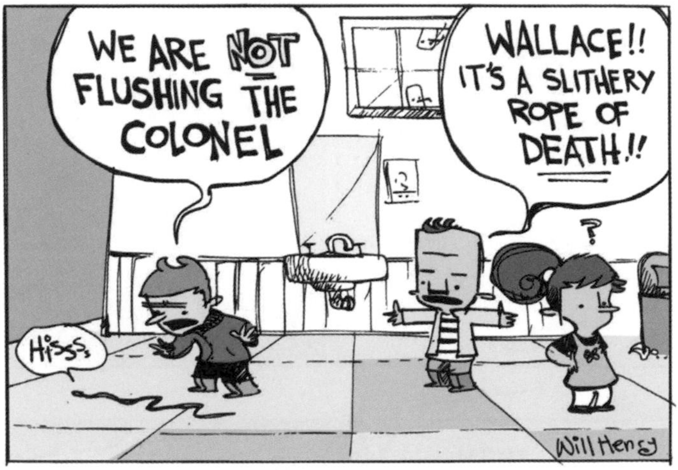
WE ARE NOT FLUSHING THE COLONEL
WALLACE!! IT'S A SLITHERY ROPE OF DEATH!!
?
Hissss
Will Hensy

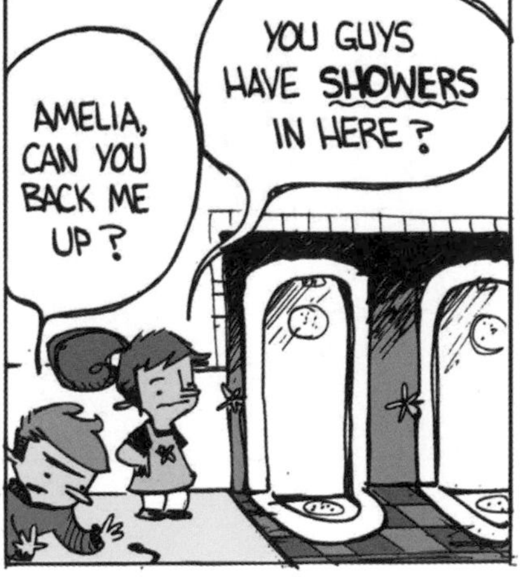
AMELIA, CAN YOU BACK ME UP?
YOU GUYS HAVE SHOWERS IN HERE?

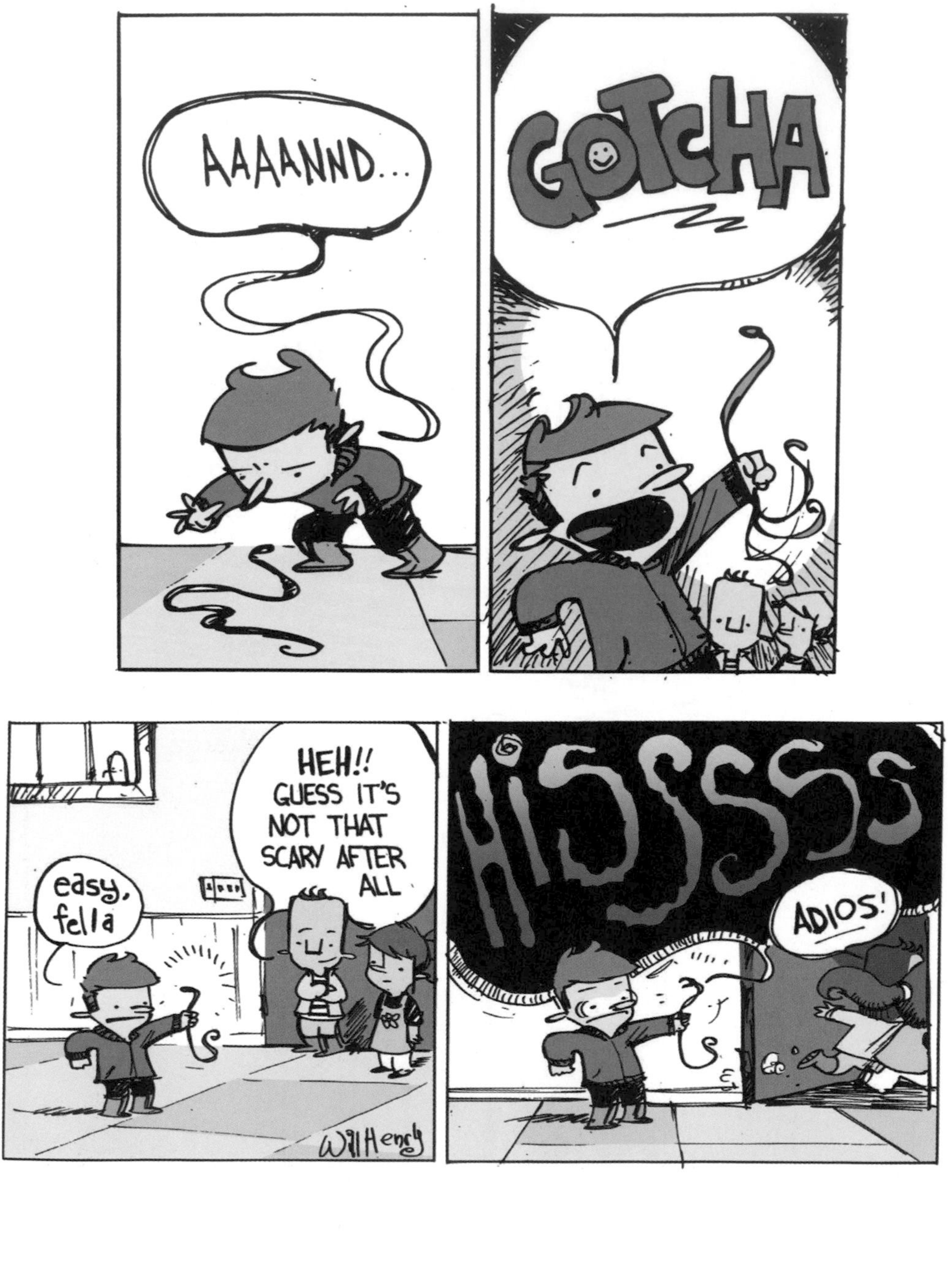
AAAANND...
GOTCHA
easy, fella
HEH!! GUESS IT'S NOT THAT SCARY AFTER ALL
Will Henry
HISSSSS
ADIOS!

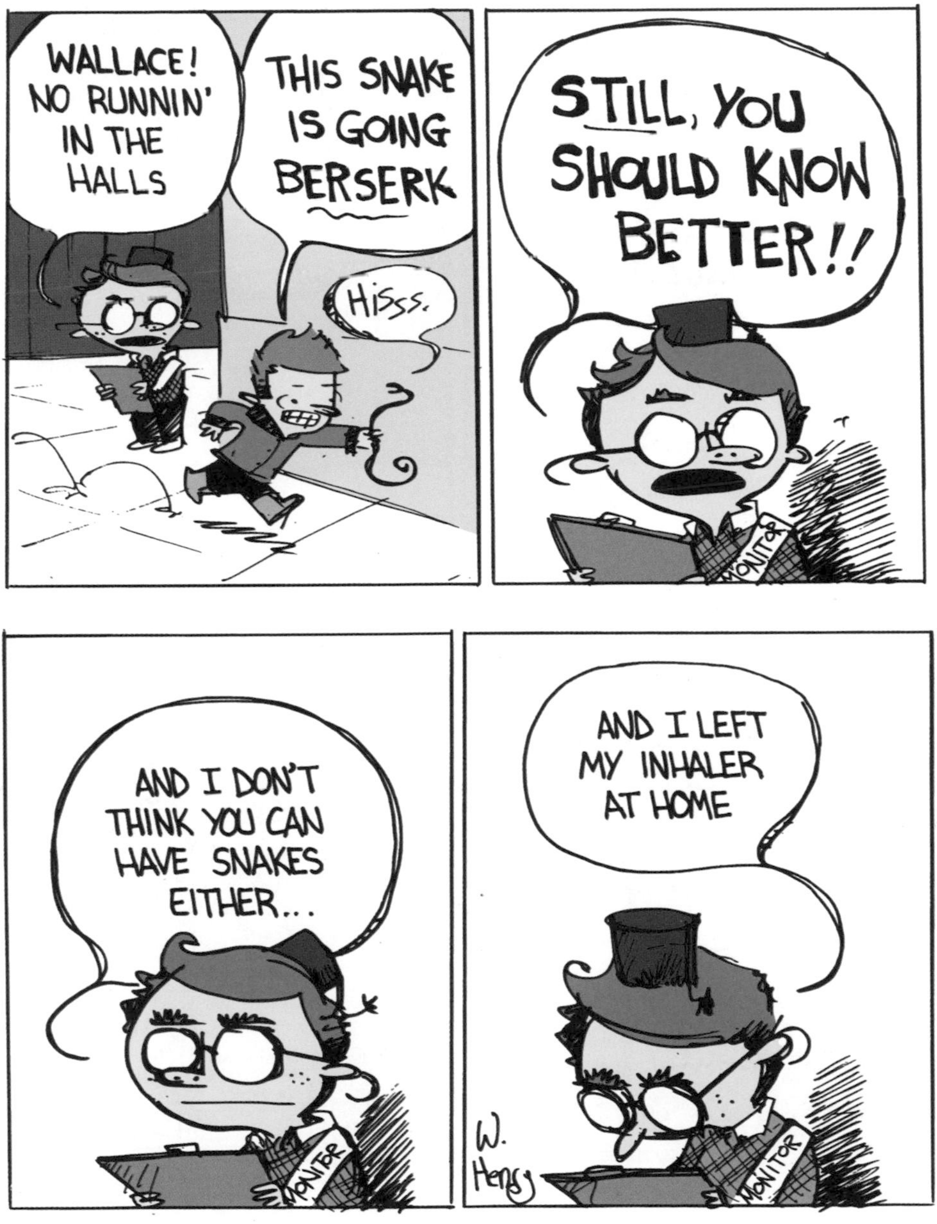
WALLACE! NO RUNNIN' IN THE HALLS
THIS SNAKE IS GOING BERSERK
HISSS.
STILL, YOU SHOULD KNOW BETTER!!
MONITOR
AND I DON'T THINK YOU CAN HAVE SNAKES EITHER...
MONITOR
AND I LEFT MY INHALER AT HOME
W. Henry
MONITOR

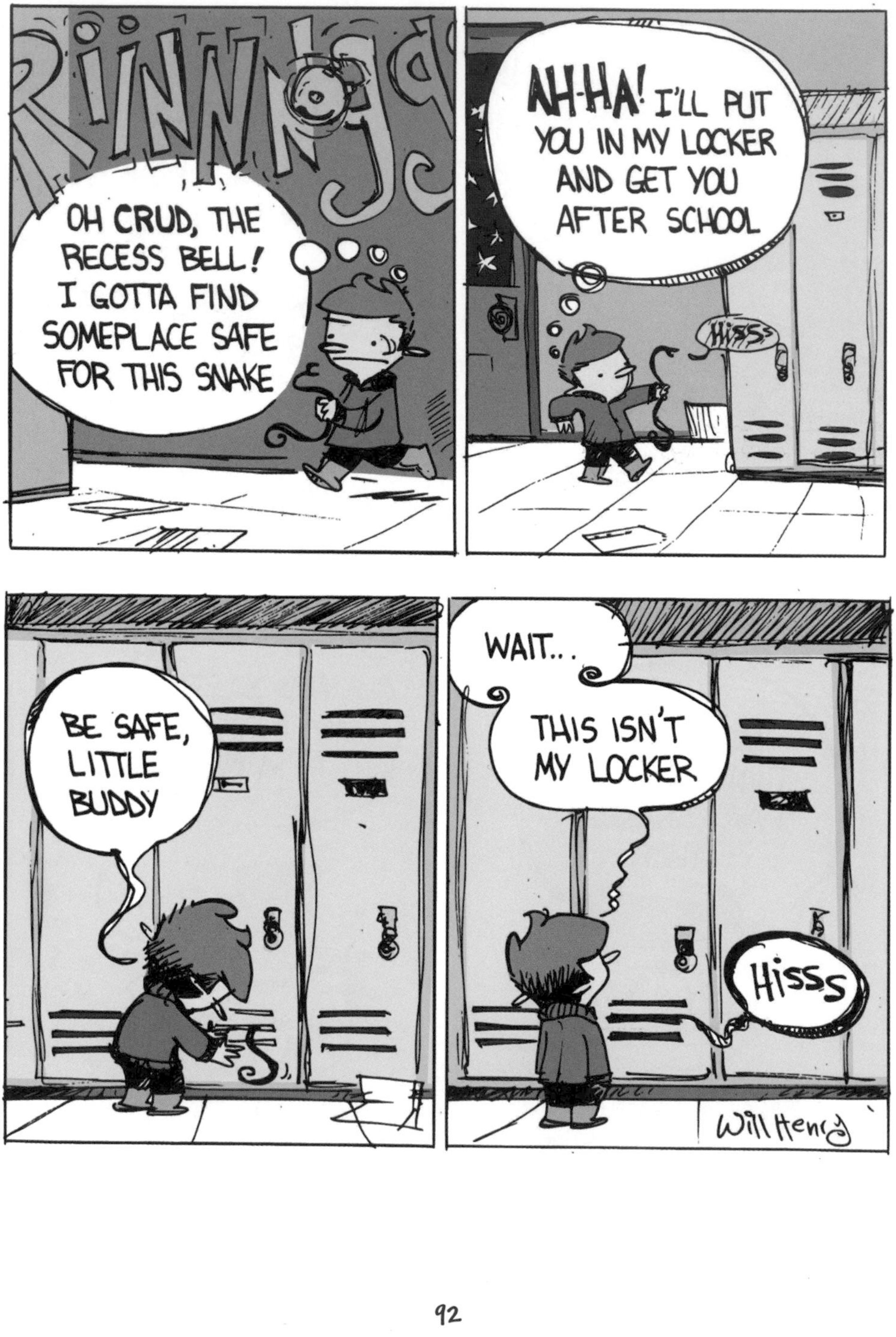
RINNNGG
OH CRUD, THE RECESS BELL! I GOTTA FIND SOMEPLACE SAFE FOR THIS SNAKE
AH-HA! I'LL PUT YOU IN MY LOCKER AND GET YOU AFTER SCHOOL
HISSS
BE SAFE, LITTLE BUDDY
WAIT...
THIS ISN'T MY LOCKER
HISSS
Will Henry

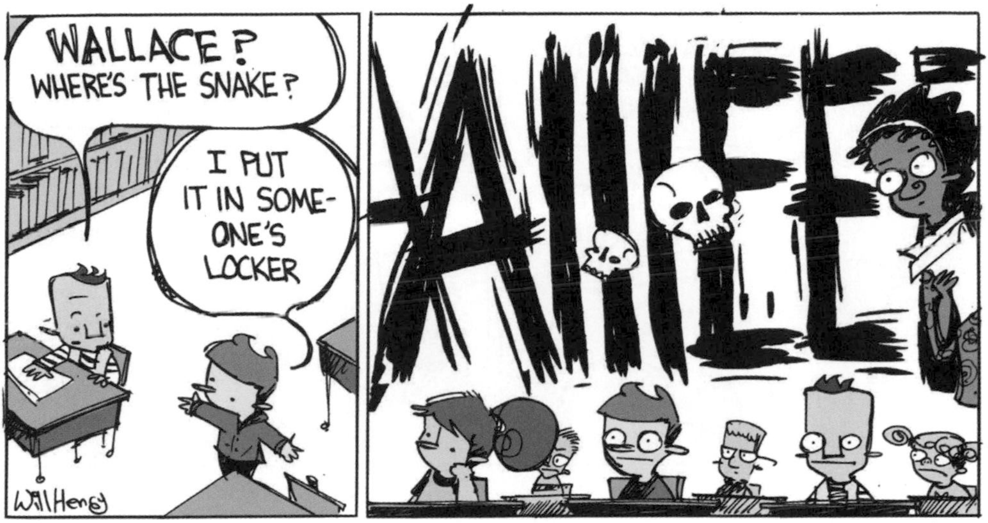
WALLACE? WHERE'S THE SNAKE?
I PUT IT IN SOME-ONE'S LOCKER
WillHenry
YAIIIEE

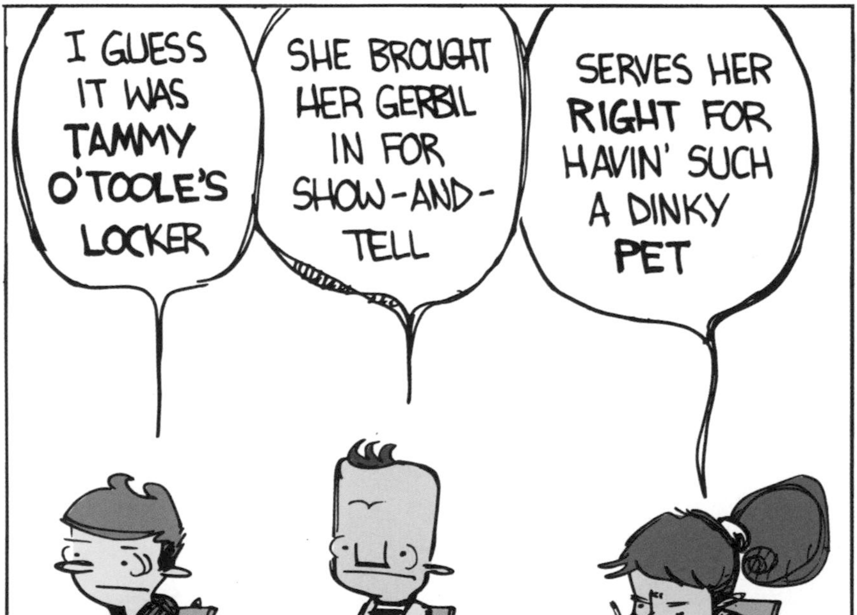
I GUESS IT WAS TAMMY O'TOOLE'S LOCKER
SHE BROUGHT HER GERBIL IN FOR SHOW-AND-TELL
SERVES HER RIGHT FOR HAVIN' SUCH A DINKY PET

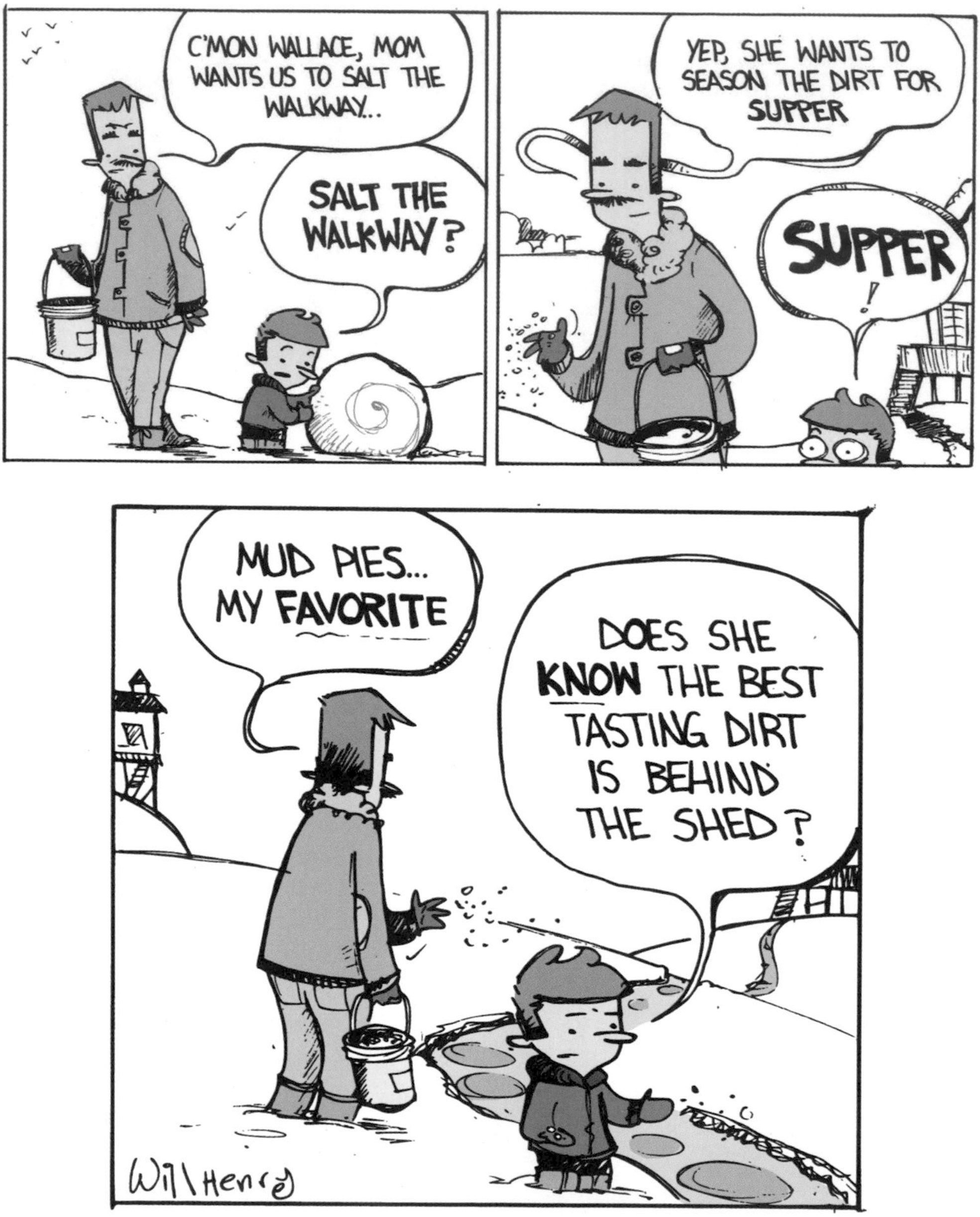
C'MON WALLACE, MOM WANTS US TO SALT THE WALKWAY...
SALT THE WALKWAY?
YEP, SHE WANTS TO SEASON THE DIRT FOR SUPPER
SUPPER!
MUD PIES... MY FAVORITE
DOES SHE KNOW THE BEST TASTING DIRT IS BEHIND THE SHED?
Will Henry

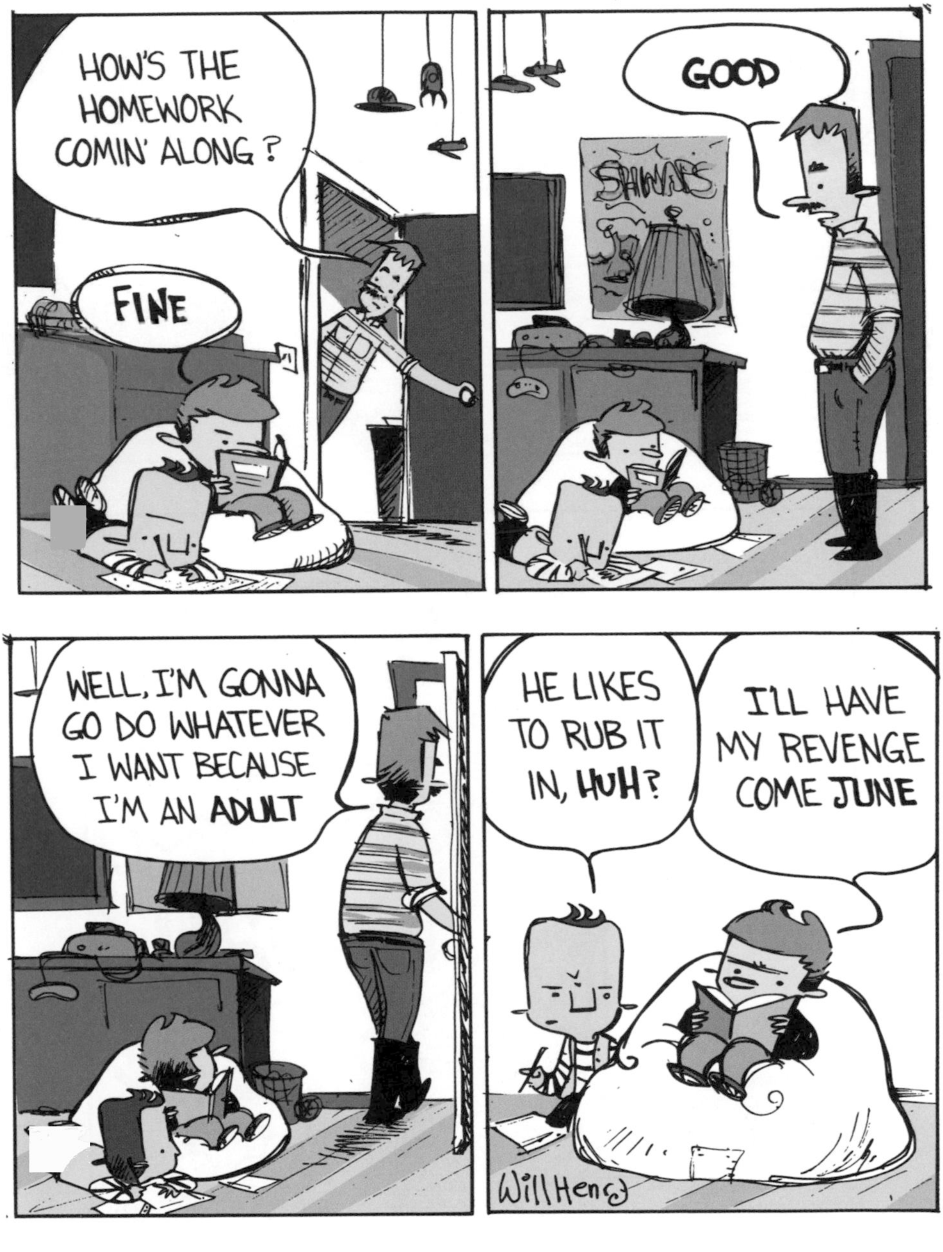
HOW'S THE HOMEWORK COMIN' ALONG?
FINE
GOOD
WELL, I'M GONNA GO DO WHATEVER I WANT BECAUSE I'M AN ADULT
HE LIKES TO RUB IT IN, HUH?
I'LL HAVE MY REVENGE COME JUNE
Will Henry

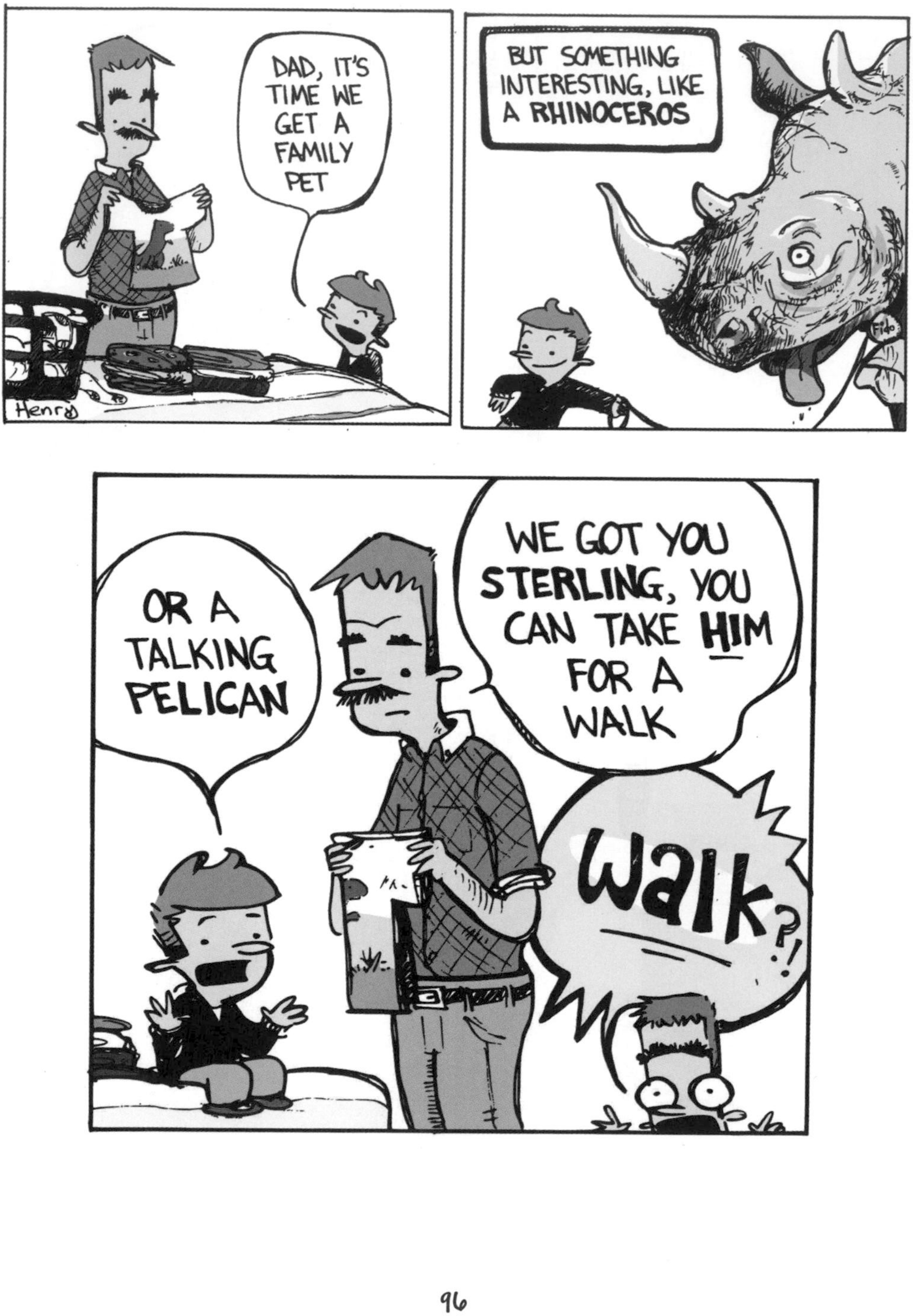
DAD, IT'S TIME WE GET A FAMILY PET
Henry
BUT SOMETHING INTERESTING, LIKE A RHINOCEROS
Fido
OR A TALKING PELICAN
WE GOT YOU STERLING, YOU CAN TAKE HIM FOR A WALK
Walk?!

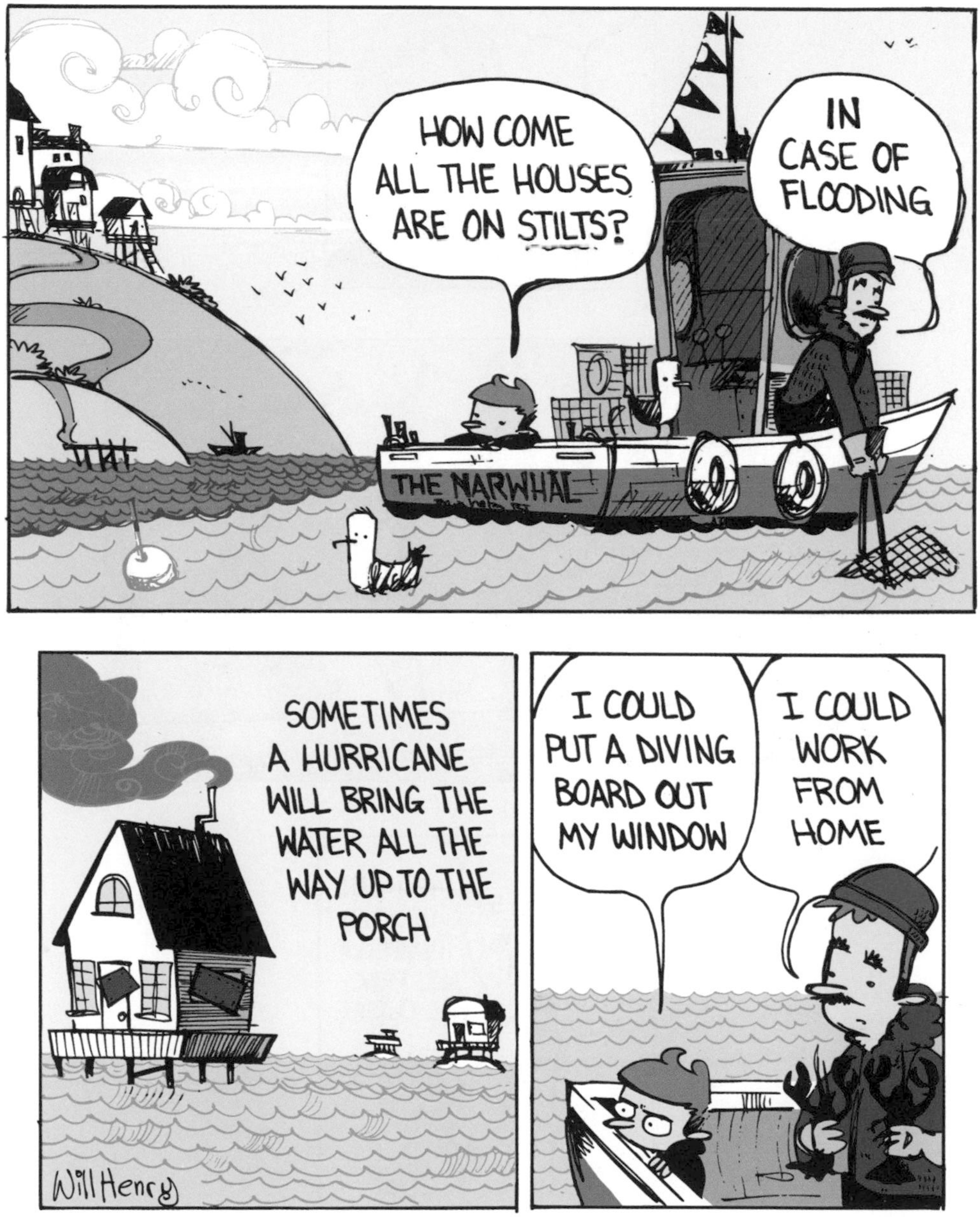
HOW COME ALL THE HOUSES ARE ON STILTS?
IN CASE OF FLOODING
THE NARWHAL
SOMETIMES A HURRICANE WILL BRING THE WATER ALL THE WAY UP TO THE PORCH
Will Henry
I COULD PUT A DIVING BOARD OUT MY WINDOW
I COULD WORK FROM HOME

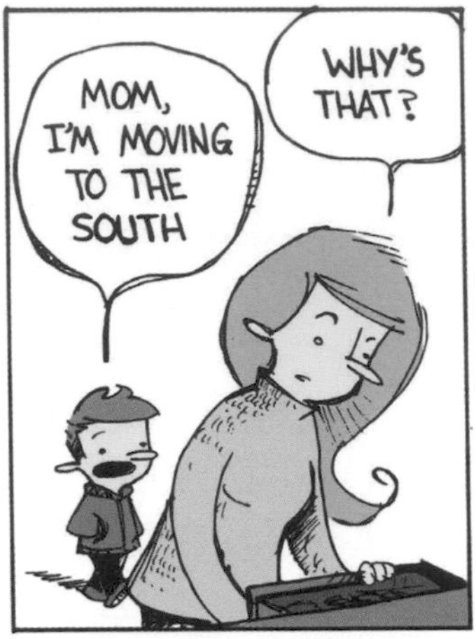
MOM, I'M MOVING TO THE SOUTH
WHY'S THAT?

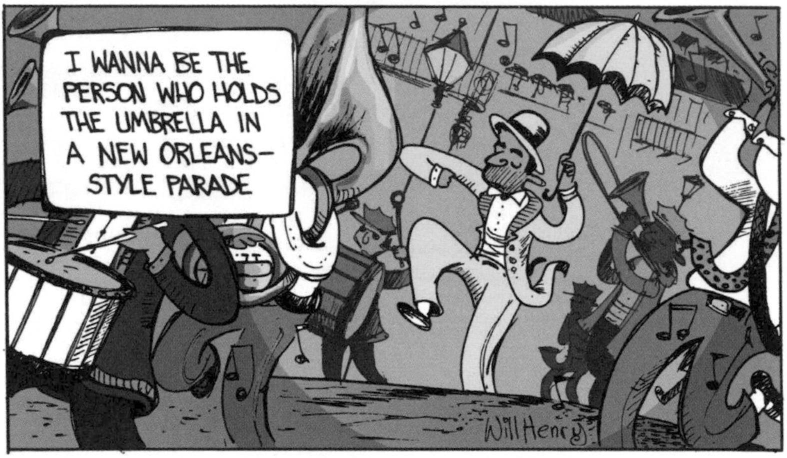
I WANNA BE THE PERSON WHO HOLDS THE UMBRELLA IN A NEW ORLEANS-STYLE PARADE
Will Henry

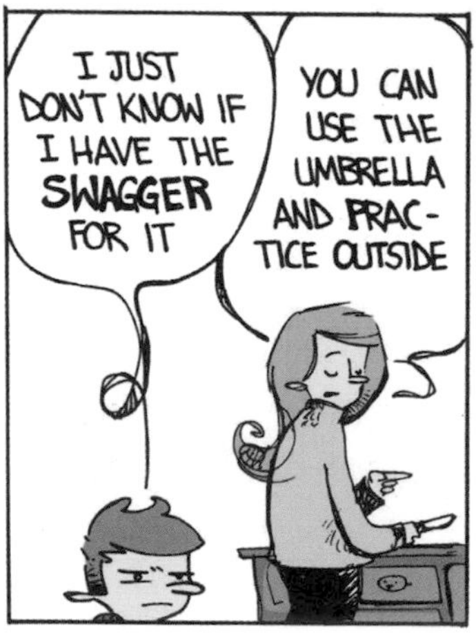
I JUST DON'T KNOW IF I HAVE THE **SWAGGER** FOR IT
YOU CAN USE THE UMBRELLA AND PRAC-TICE OUTSIDE

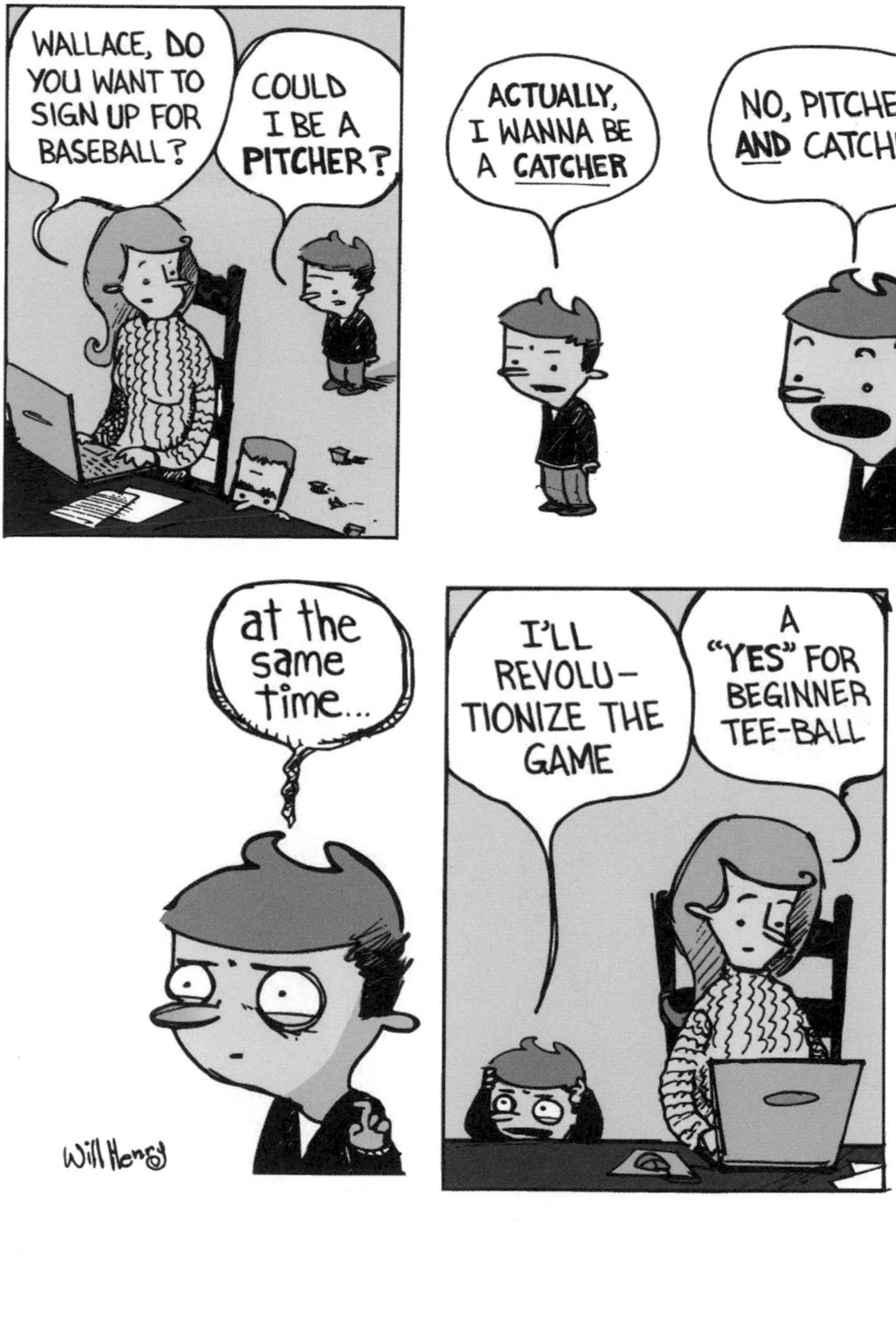
WALLACE, DO YOU WANT TO SIGN UP FOR BASEBALL?
COULD I BE A PITCHER?
ACTUALLY, I WANNA BE A CATCHER
NO, PITCHER AND CATCHER
at the same time...
I'LL REVOLU-TIONIZE THE GAME
A "YES" FOR BEGINNER TEE-BALL
Will Henry

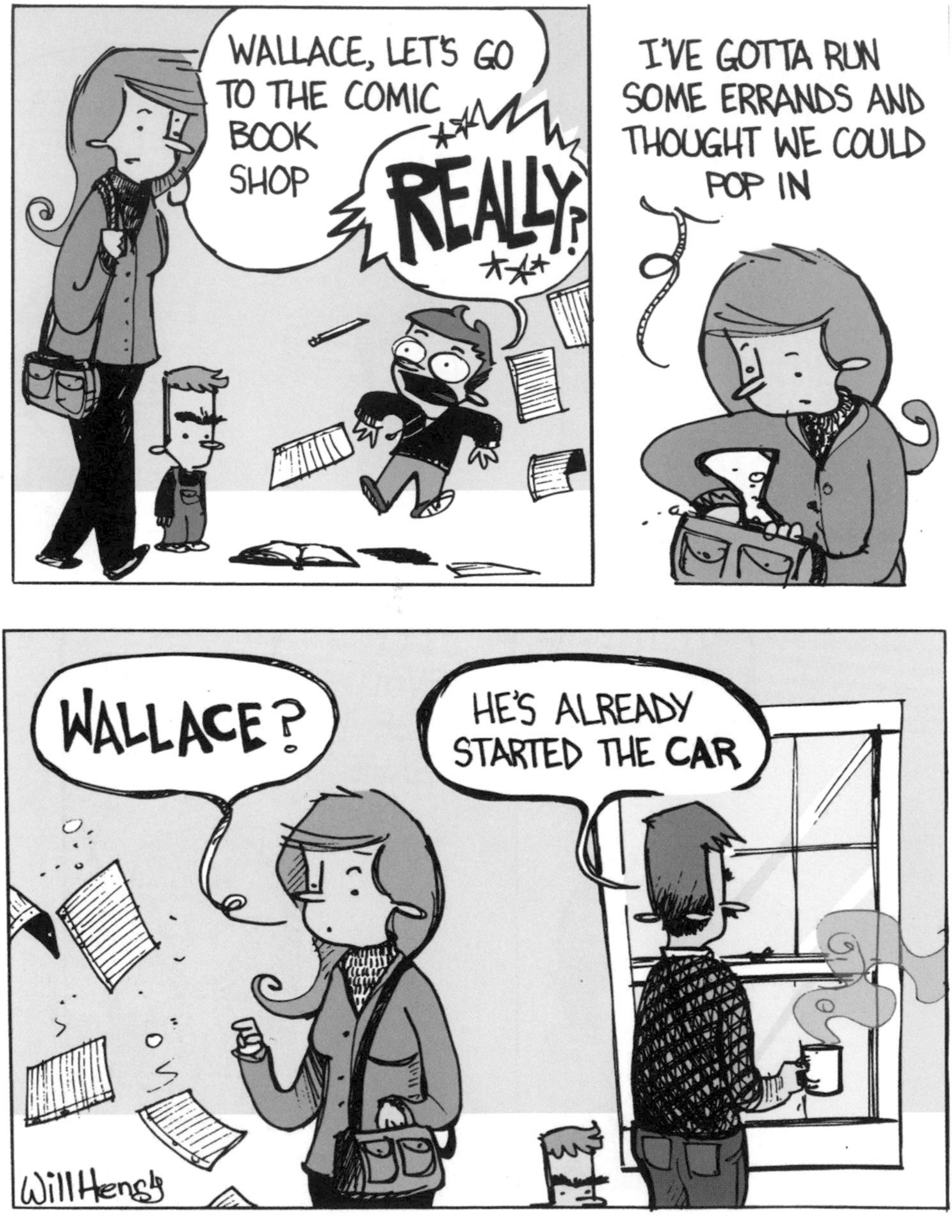
WALLACE, LET'S GO TO THE COMIC BOOK SHOP
REALLY?
I'VE GOTTA RUN SOME ERRANDS AND THOUGHT WE COULD POP IN
WALLACE?
HE'S ALREADY STARTED THE CAR
Will Hensley

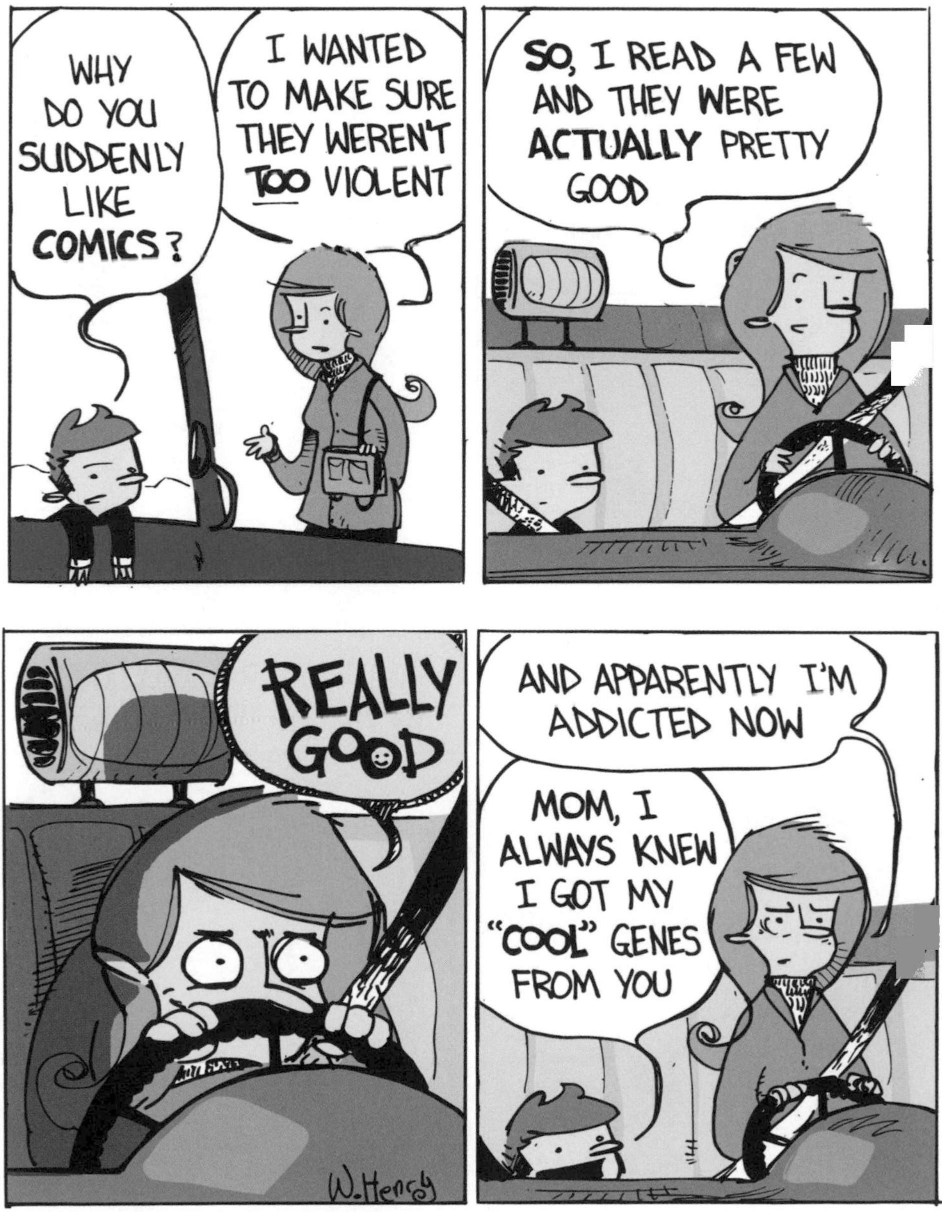
WHY DO YOU SUDDENLY LIKE COMICS?
I WANTED TO MAKE SURE THEY WEREN'T TOO VIOLENT
SO, I READ A FEW AND THEY WERE ACTUALLY PRETTY GOOD
REALLY GOOD
AND APPARENTLY I'M ADDICTED NOW
MOM, I ALWAYS KNEW I GOT MY "COOL" GENES FROM YOU
W.Henry

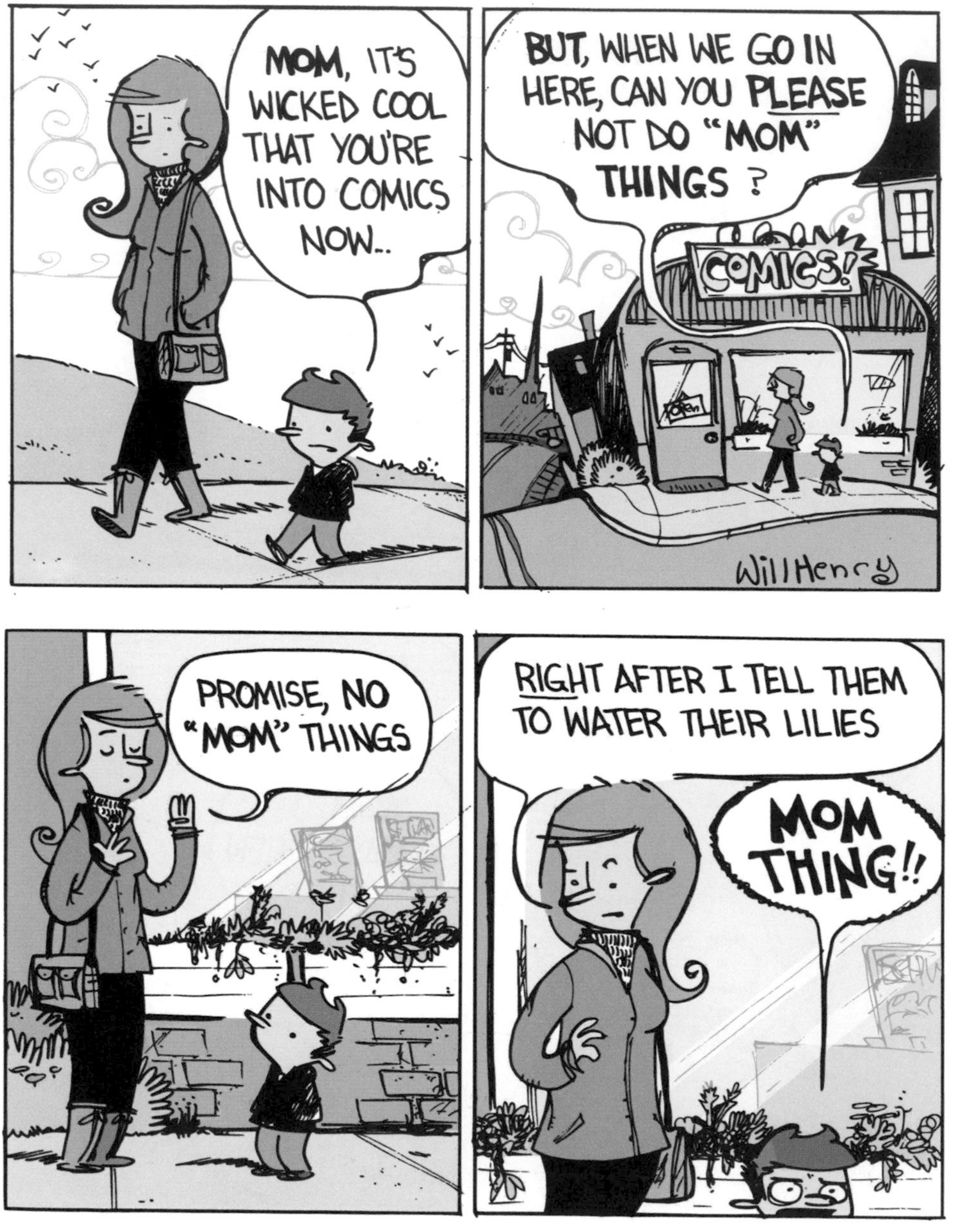
MOM, IT'S WICKED COOL THAT YOU'RE INTO COMICS NOW..
BUT, WHEN WE GO IN HERE, CAN YOU PLEASE NOT DO "MOM" THINGS ?
COMICS!
Will Henry
PROMISE, NO "MOM" THINGS
RIGHT AFTER I TELL THEM TO WATER THEIR LILIES
MOM THING!!

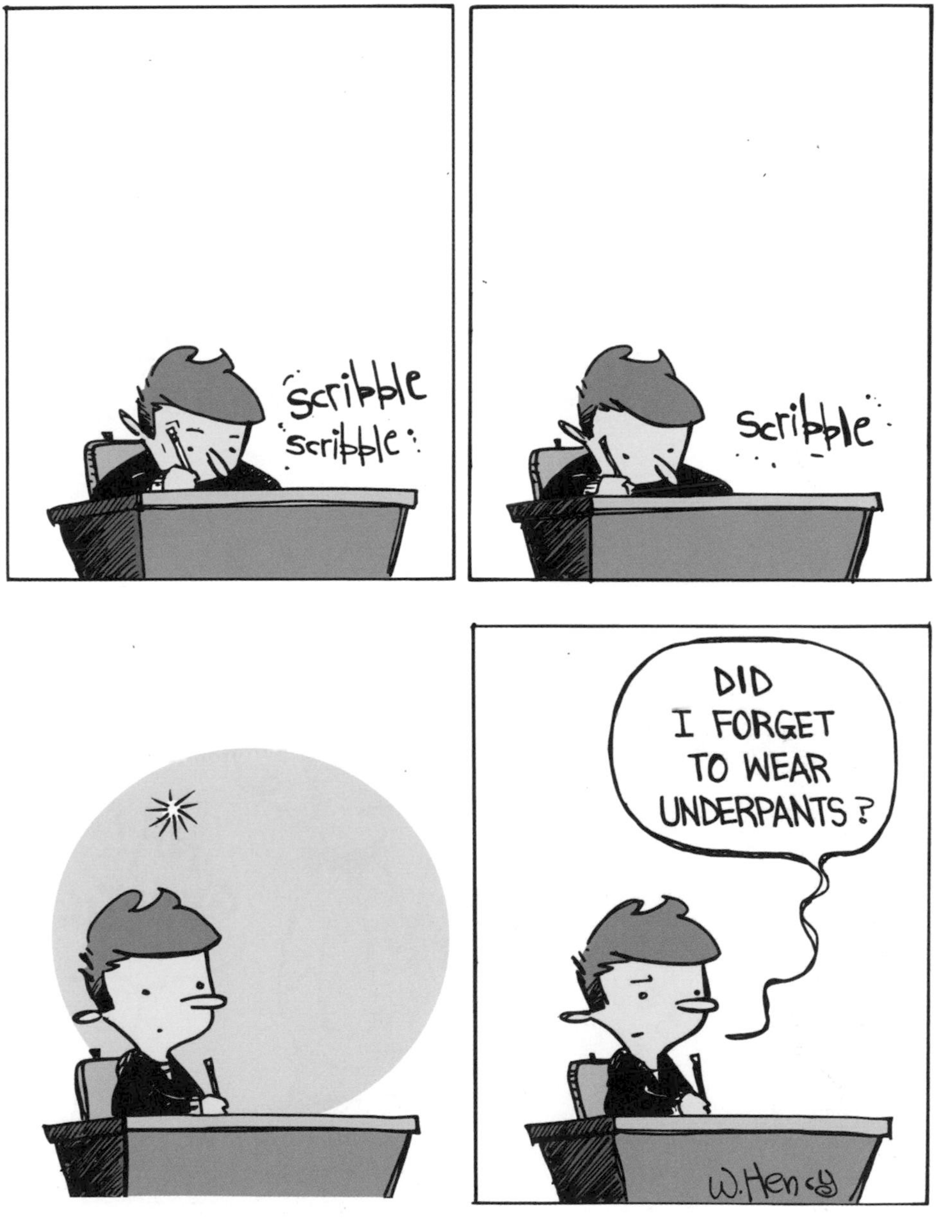
scribble
scribble
scribble
DID I FORGET TO WEAR UNDERPANTS?
W. Henry

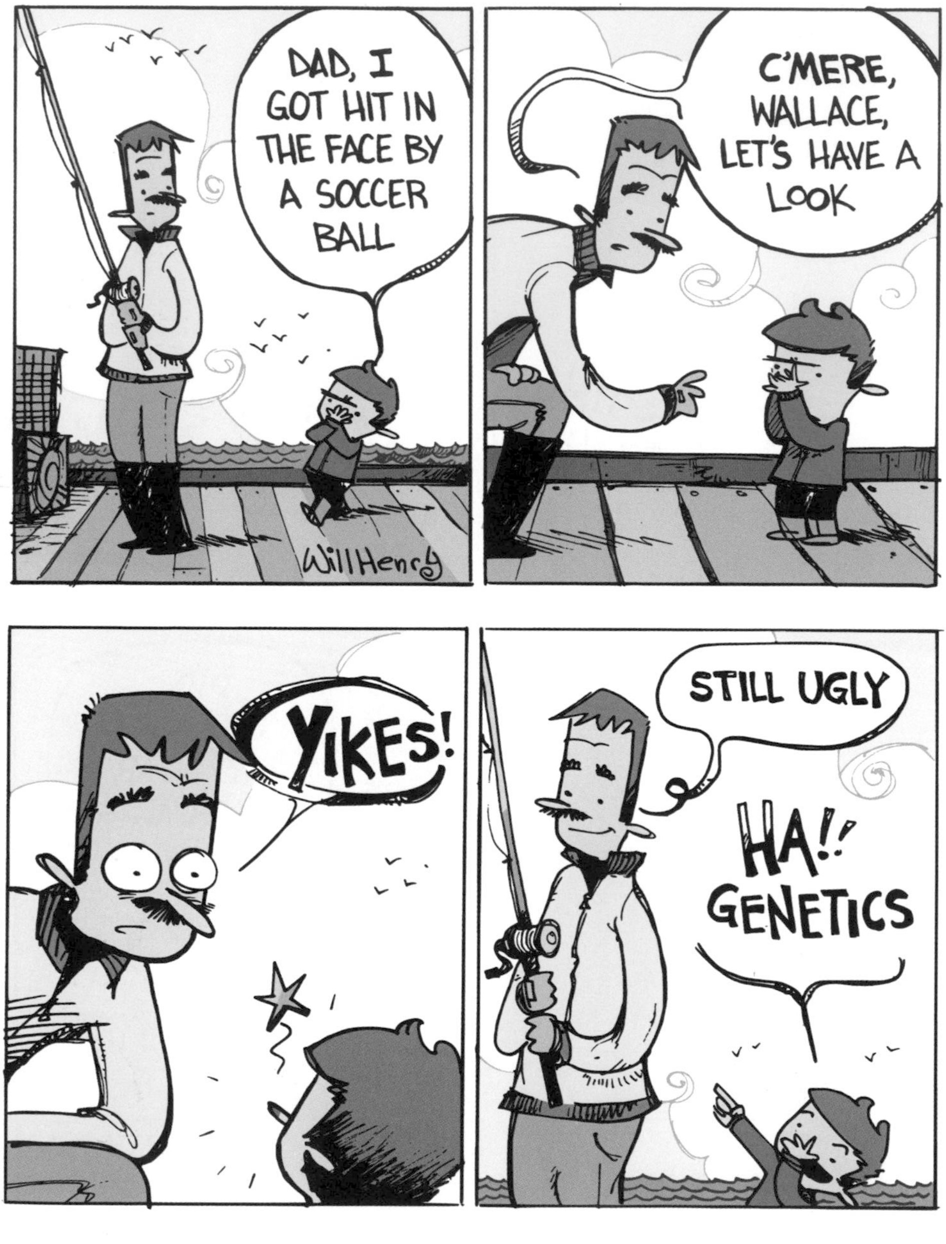
DAD, I GOT HIT IN THE FACE BY A SOCCER BALL
WillHenry
C'MERE, WALLACE, LET'S HAVE A LOOK
YIKES!
STILL UGLY
HA!! GENETICS

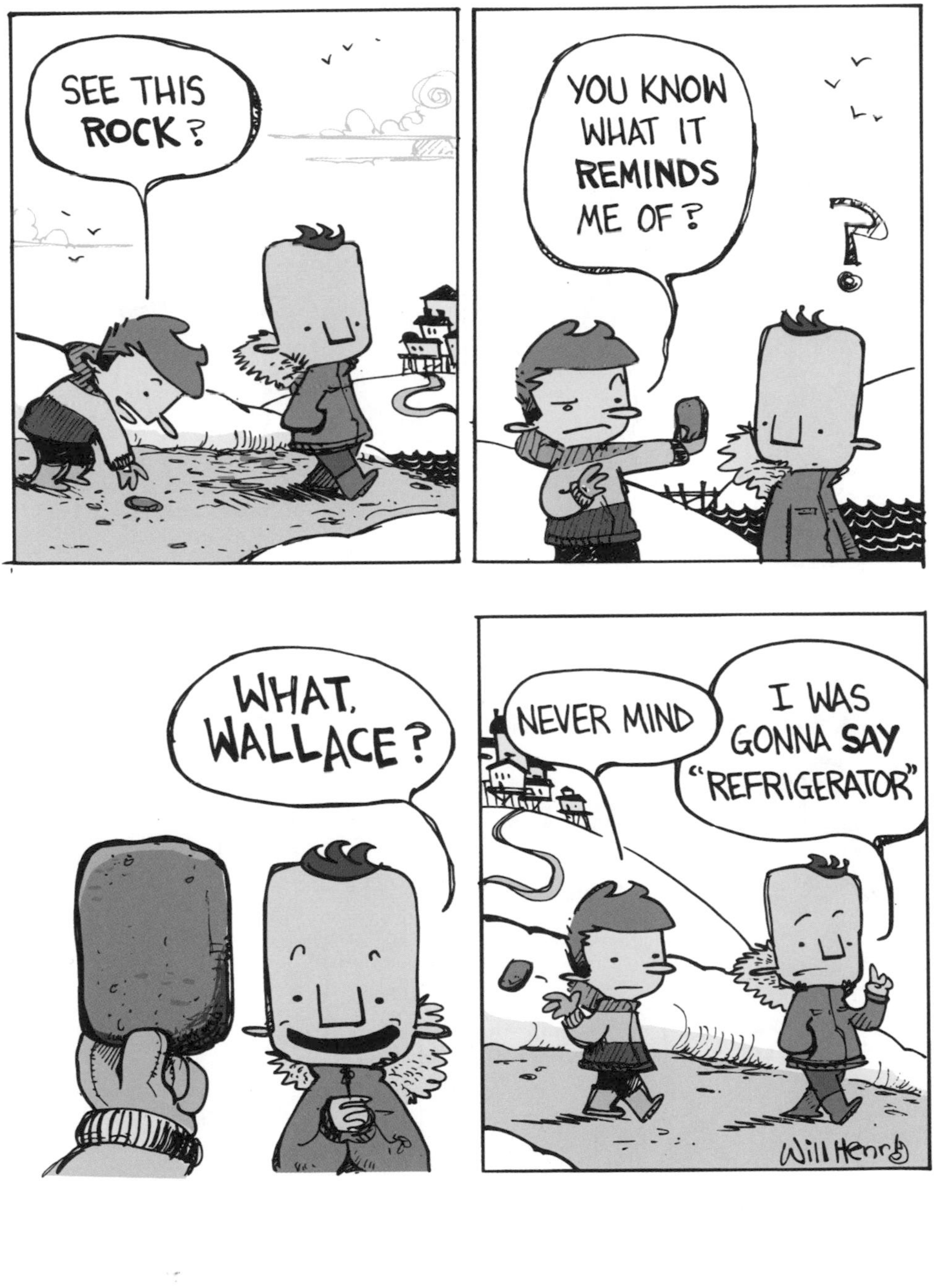
SEE THIS ROCK?
YOU KNOW WHAT IT REMINDS ME OF?
?
WHAT, WALLACE?
I WAS GONNA SAY "REFRIGERATOR"
NEVER MIND
Will Henry

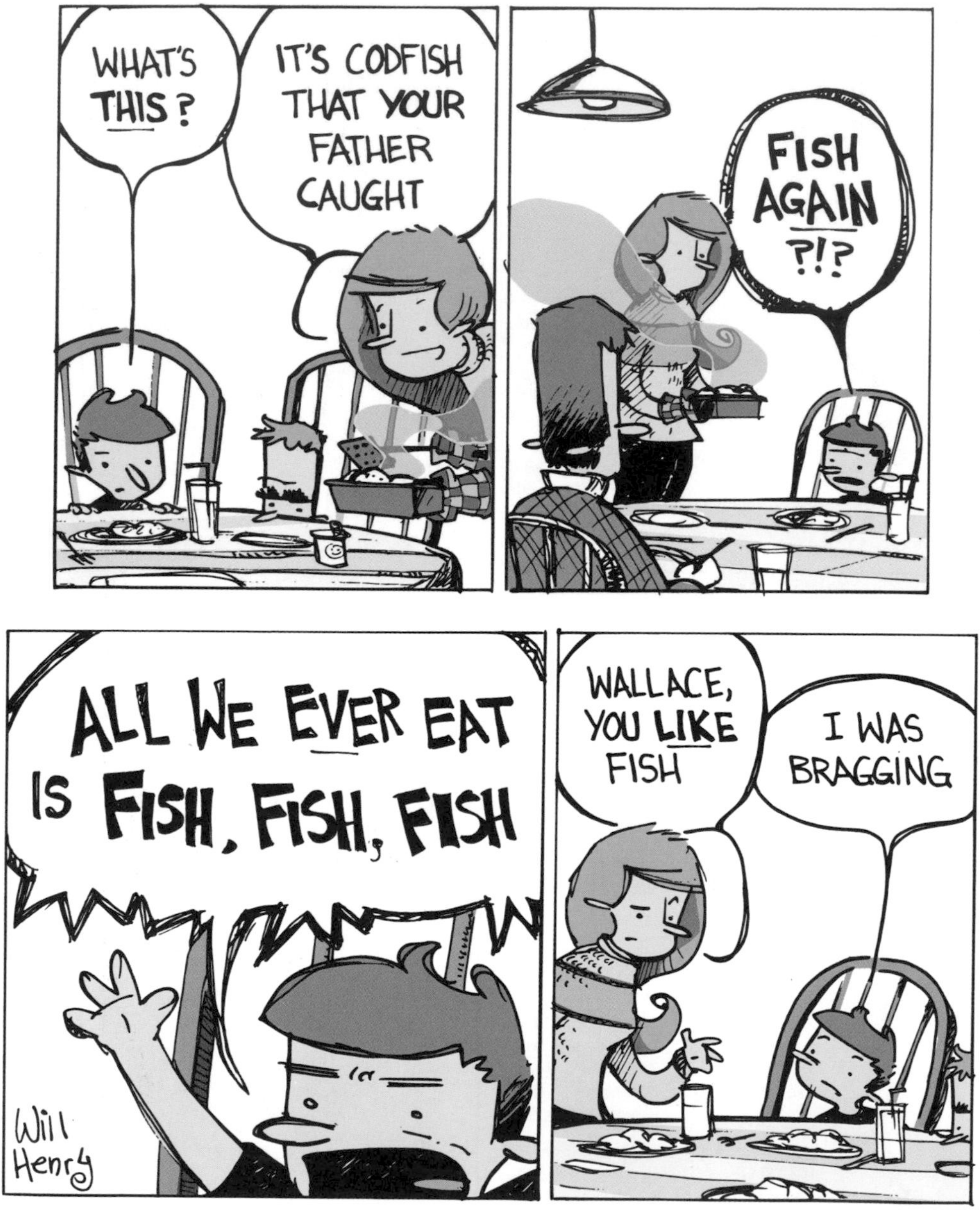
WHAT'S THIS ?
IT'S CODFISH THAT YOUR FATHER CAUGHT
FISH AGAIN ?!?
ALL WE EVER EAT IS FISH, FISH, FISH
WALLACE, YOU LIKE FISH
I WAS BRAGGING
Will Henry

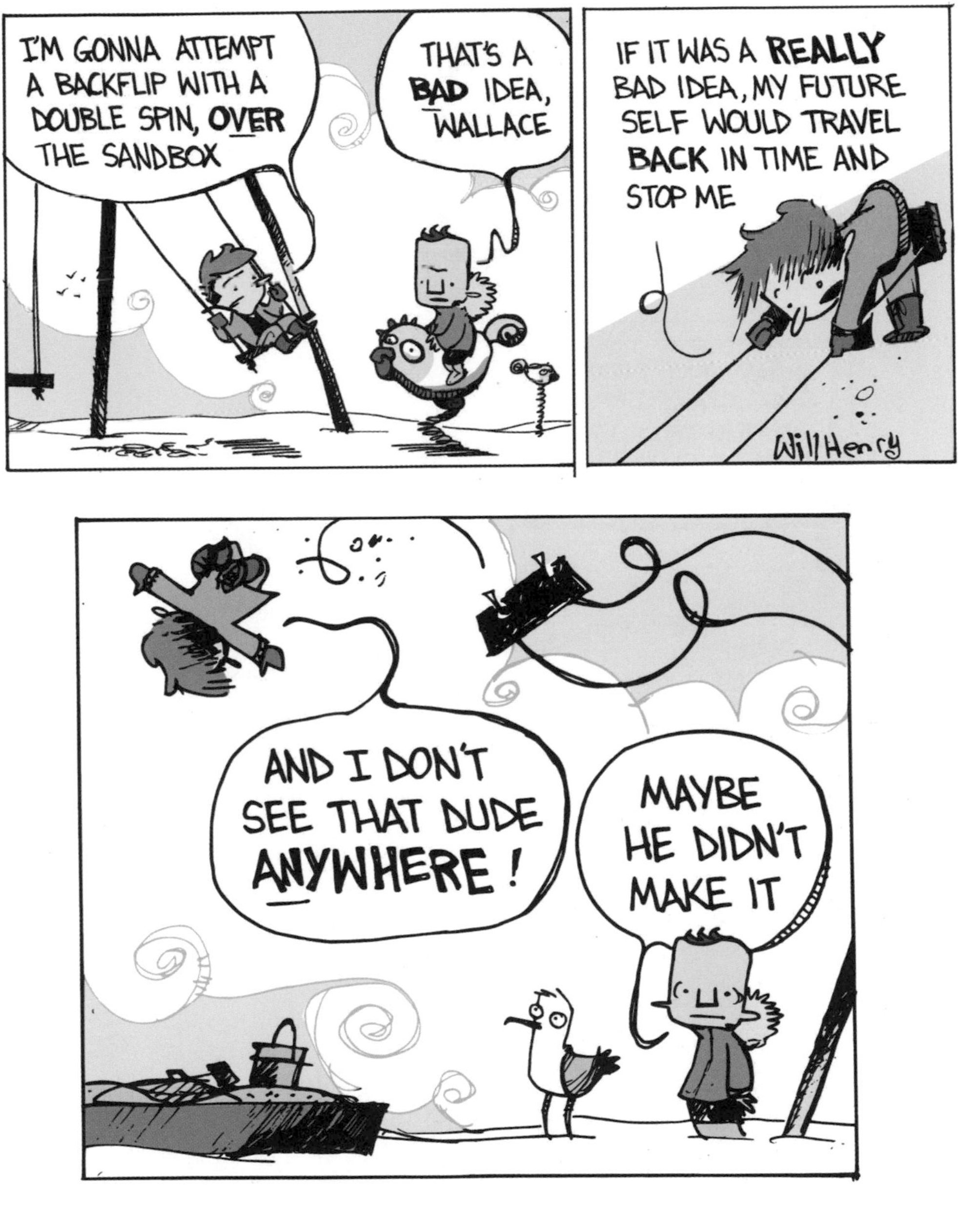
I'M GONNA ATTEMPT A BACKFLIP WITH A DOUBLE SPIN, OVER THE SANDBOX
THAT'S A BAD IDEA, WALLACE
IF IT WAS A REALLY BAD IDEA, MY FUTURE SELF WOULD TRAVEL BACK IN TIME AND STOP ME
Will Henry
AND I DON'T SEE THAT DUDE ANYWHERE!
MAYBE HE DIDN'T MAKE IT

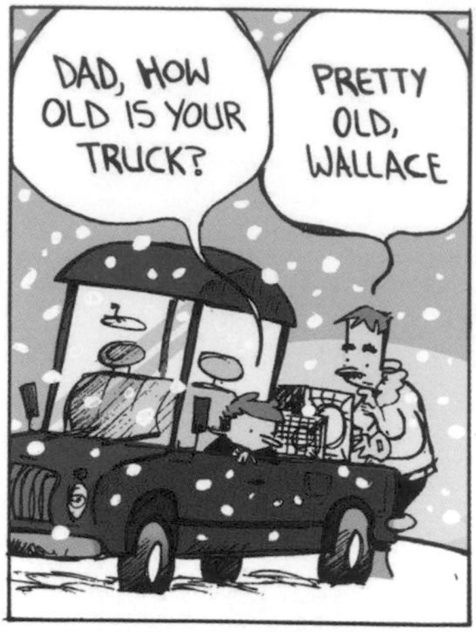
DAD, HOW OLD IS YOUR TRUCK?
PRETTY OLD, WALLACE

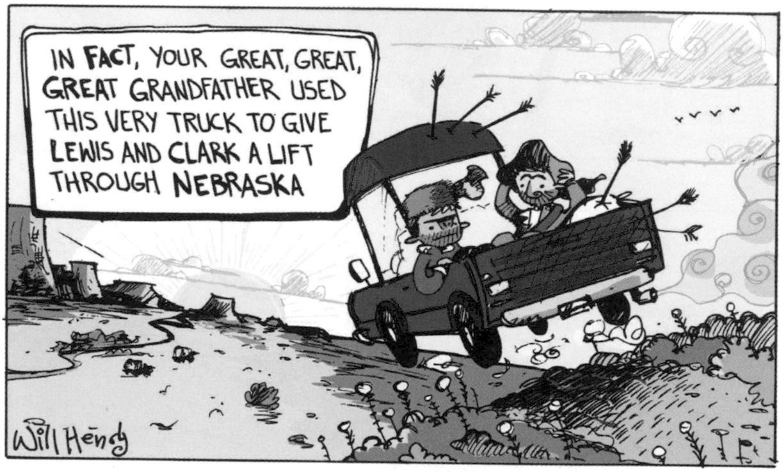
IN FACT, YOUR GREAT, GREAT, GREAT GRANDFATHER USED THIS VERY TRUCK TO GIVE LEWIS AND CLARK A LIFT THROUGH NEBRASKA
Will Hendy

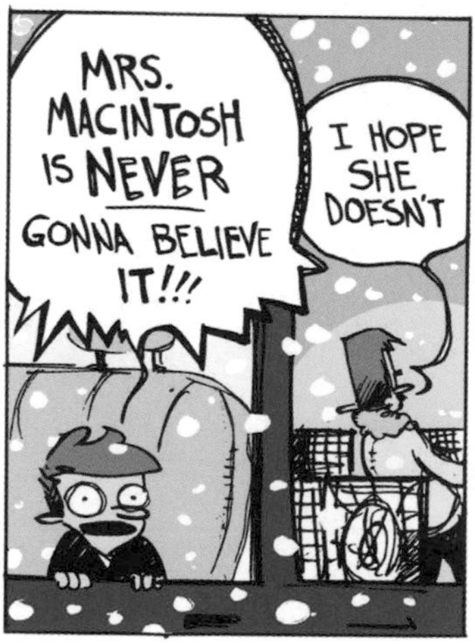
MRS. MACINTOSH IS NEVER GONNA BELIEVE IT!!!
I HOPE SHE DOESN'T

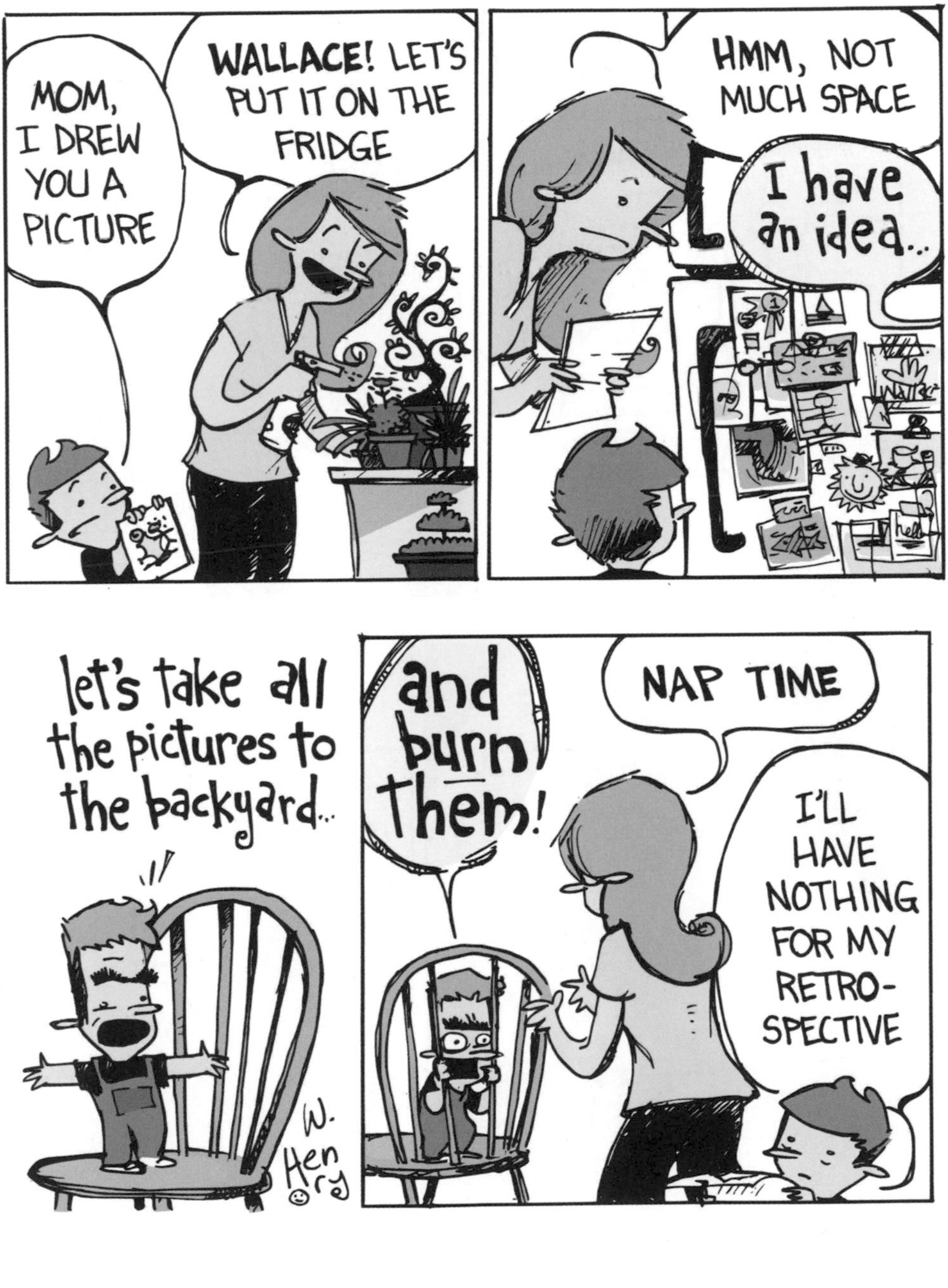
MOM, I DREW YOU A PICTURE
WALLACE! LET'S PUT IT ON THE FRIDGE
HMM, NOT MUCH SPACE
I have an idea...
let's take all the pictures to the backyard...
and burn them!
NAP TIME
I'LL HAVE NOTHING FOR MY RETRO-SPECTIVE
W. Henry

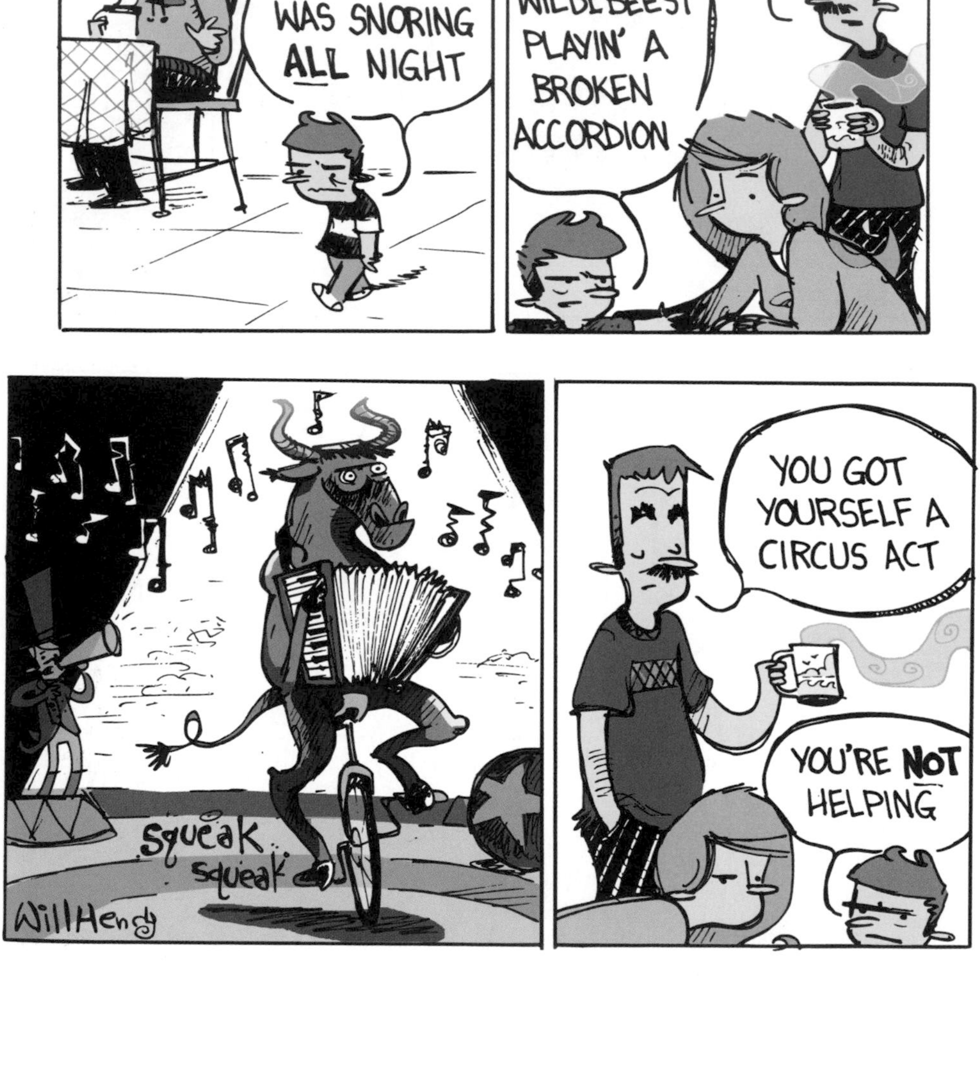
WALLACE, HUN, YOU LOOK TIRED
STERLING WAS SNORING ALL NIGHT
HE SOUNDS LIKE A WILDEBEEST PLAYIN' A BROKEN ACCORDION
YOU THROW A UNICYCLE IN THE MIX...
Squeak... squeak
WillHendy
YOU GOT YOURSELF A CIRCUS ACT
YOU'RE NOT HELPING

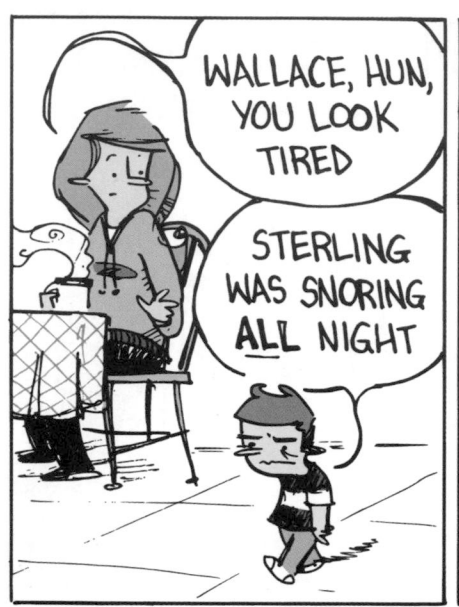

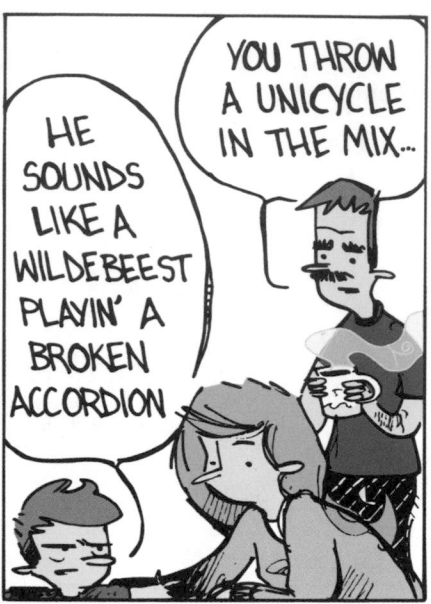

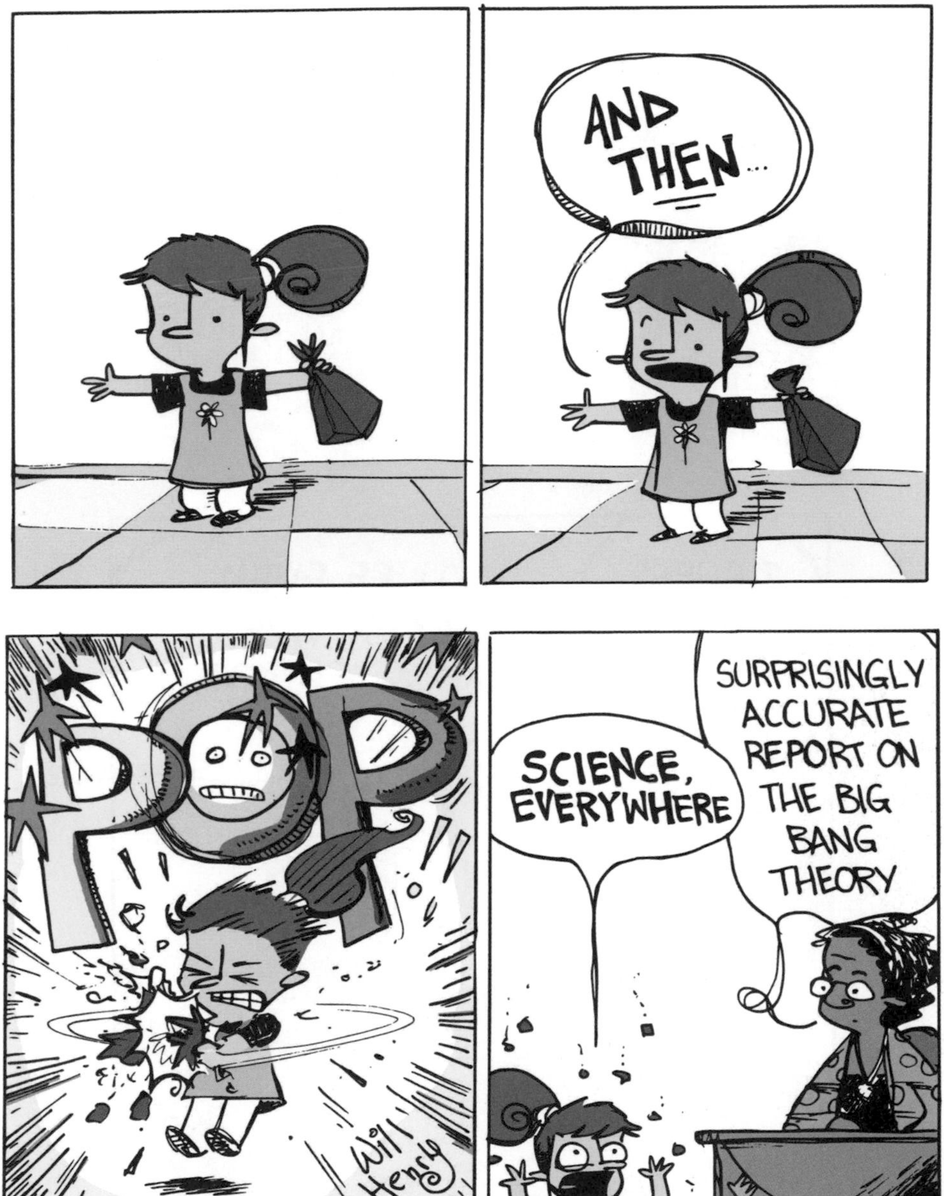
AND THEN...
POP!!
Will Henry
SCIENCE, EVERYWHERE
SURPRISINGLY ACCURATE REPORT ON THE BIG BANG THEORY

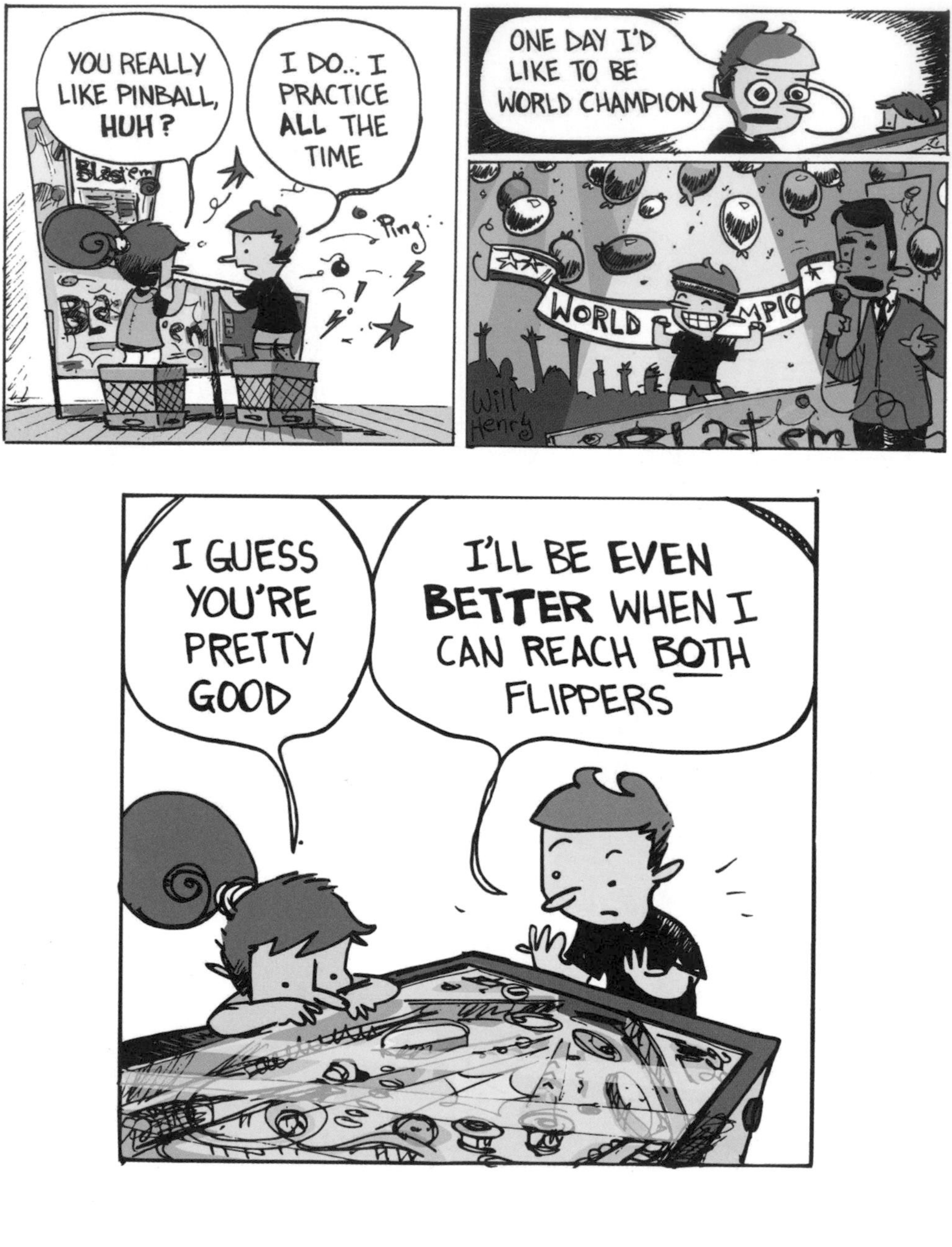
YOU REALLY LIKE PINBALL, HUH?
I DO... I PRACTICE ALL THE TIME
Ping
Blast'em
ONE DAY I'D LIKE TO BE WORLD CHAMPION
WORLD
MPIO
Will Henry
I GUESS YOU'RE PRETTY GOOD
I'LL BE EVEN BETTER WHEN I CAN REACH BOTH FLIPPERS

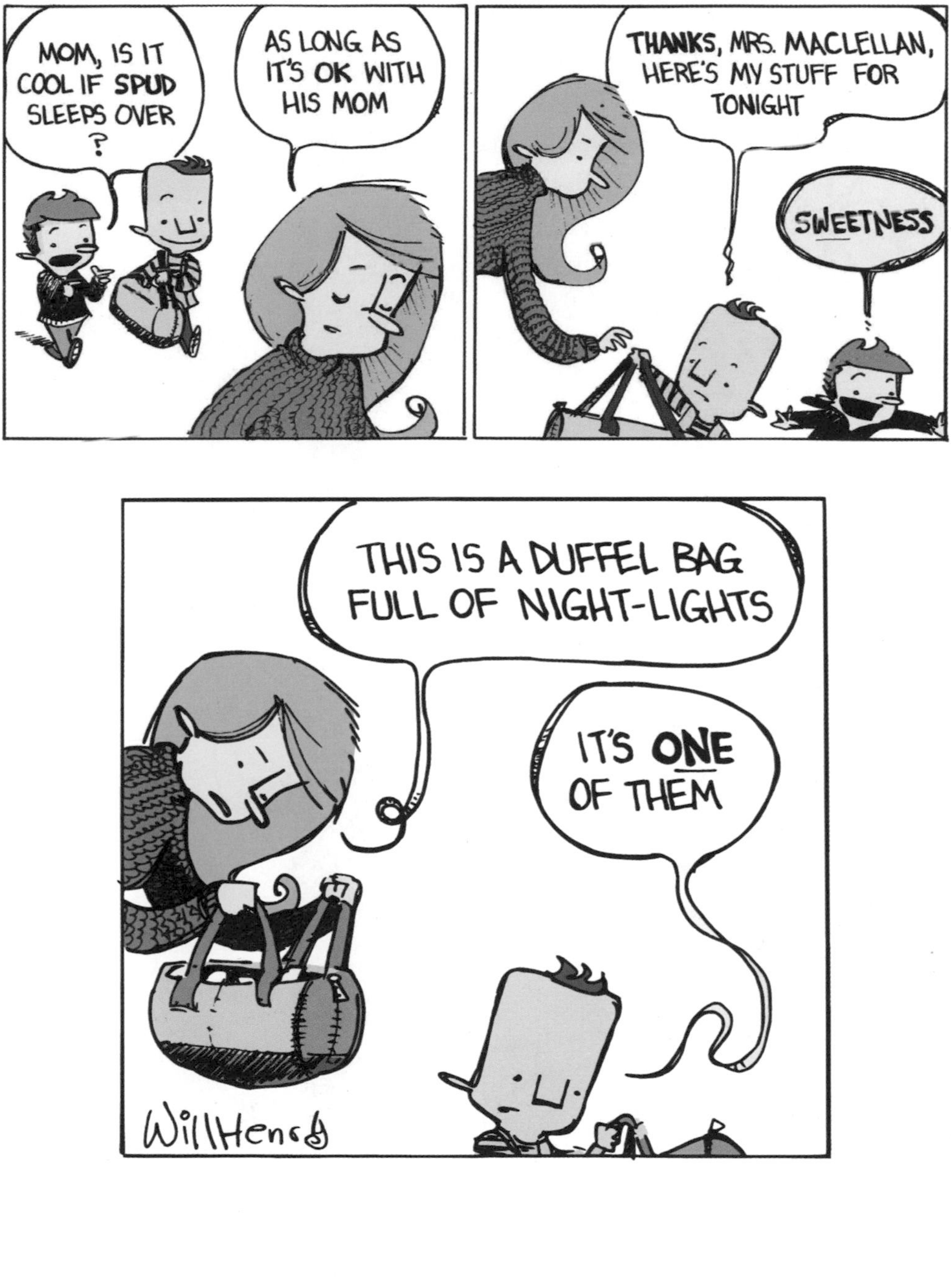
MOM, IS IT COOL IF **SPUD** SLEEPS OVER ?
AS LONG AS IT'S **OK** WITH HIS MOM
THANKS, MRS. MACLELLAN, HERE'S MY STUFF FOR TONIGHT
SWEETNESS
THIS IS A DUFFEL BAG FULL OF NIGHT-LIGHTS
IT'S **ONE** OF THEM
WillHenry

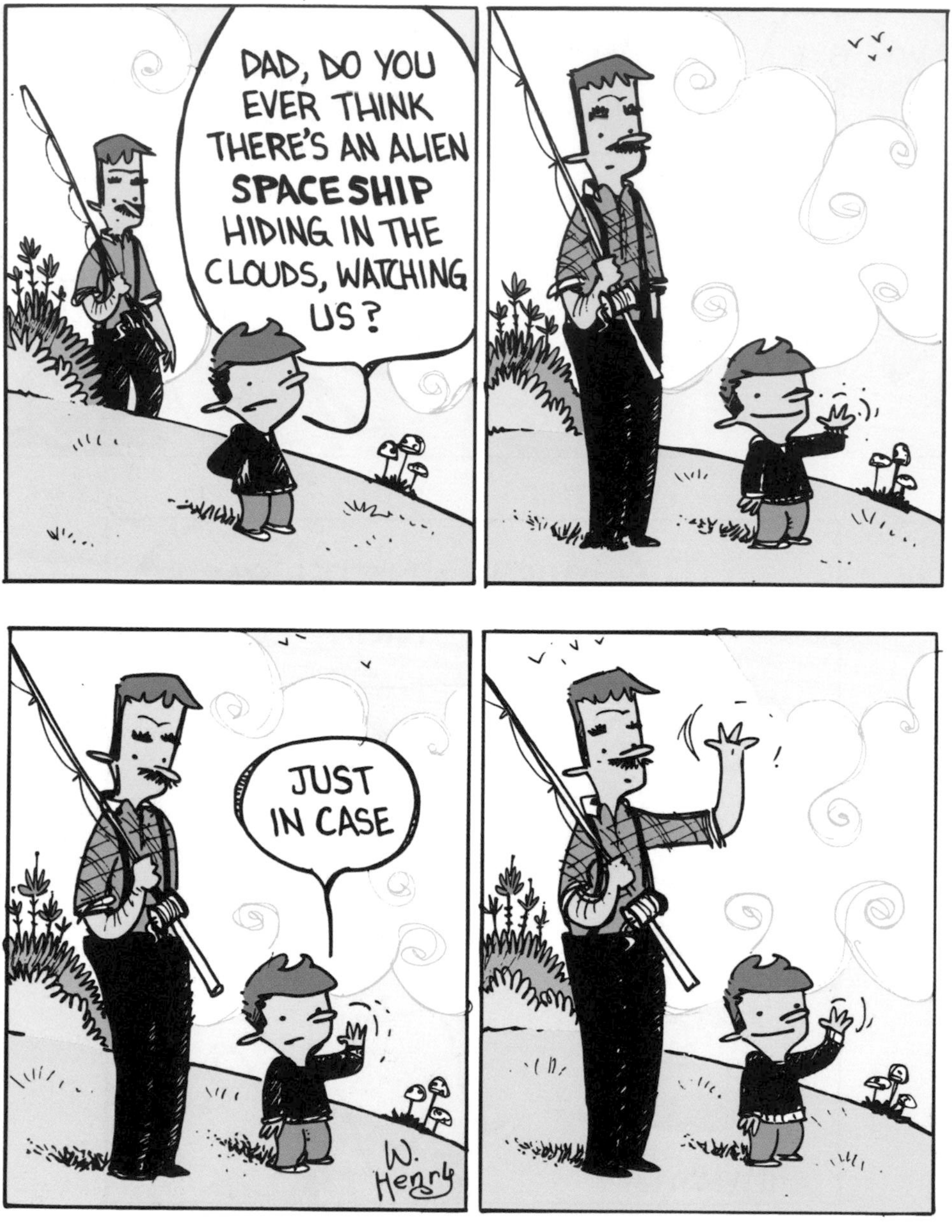
DAD, DO YOU EVER THINK THERE'S AN ALIEN **SPACESHIP** HIDING IN THE CLOUDS, WATCHING US?
JUST IN CASE
W. Henry

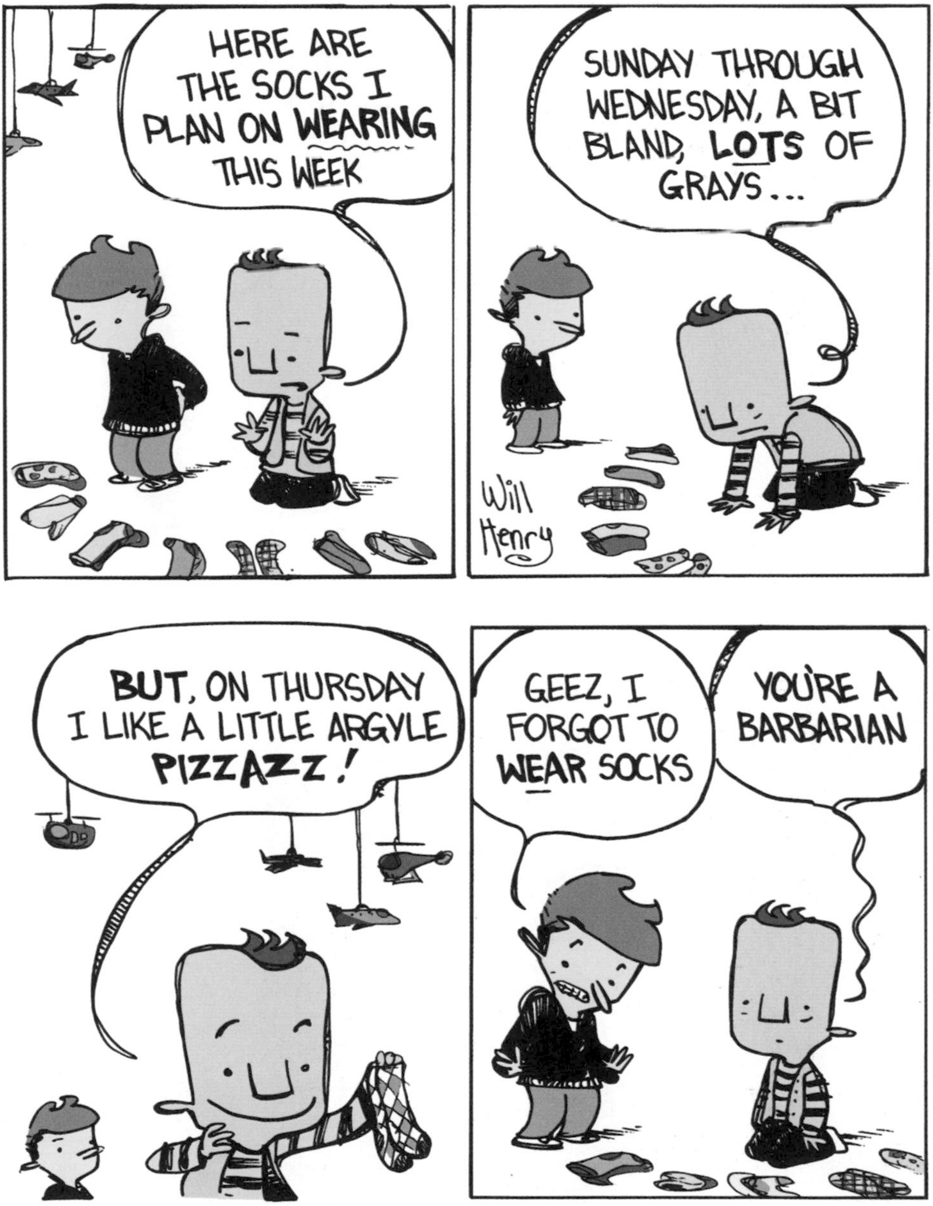
HERE ARE THE SOCKS I PLAN ON WEARING THIS WEEK
SUNDAY THROUGH WEDNESDAY, A BIT BLAND, LOTS OF GRAYS...
Will Henry
BUT, ON THURSDAY I LIKE A LITTLE ARGYLE PIZZAZZ!
GEEZ, I FORGOT TO WEAR SOCKS
YOU'RE A BARBARIAN

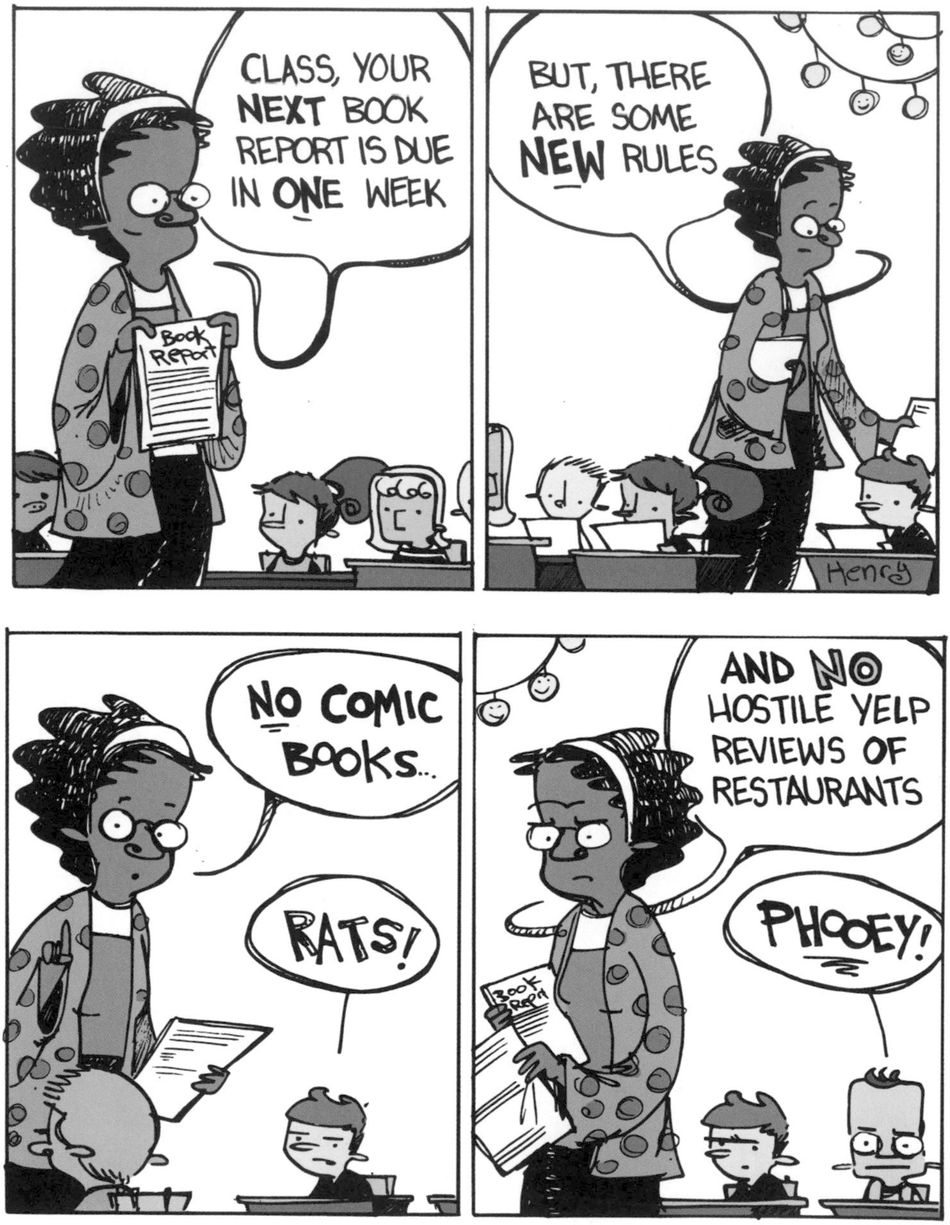
CLASS, YOUR NEXT BOOK REPORT IS DUE IN ONE WEEK
Book Report
BUT, THERE ARE SOME NEW RULES
Henry
NO COMIC BOOKS...
RATS!
AND NO HOSTILE YELP REVIEWS OF RESTAURANTS
PHOOEY!

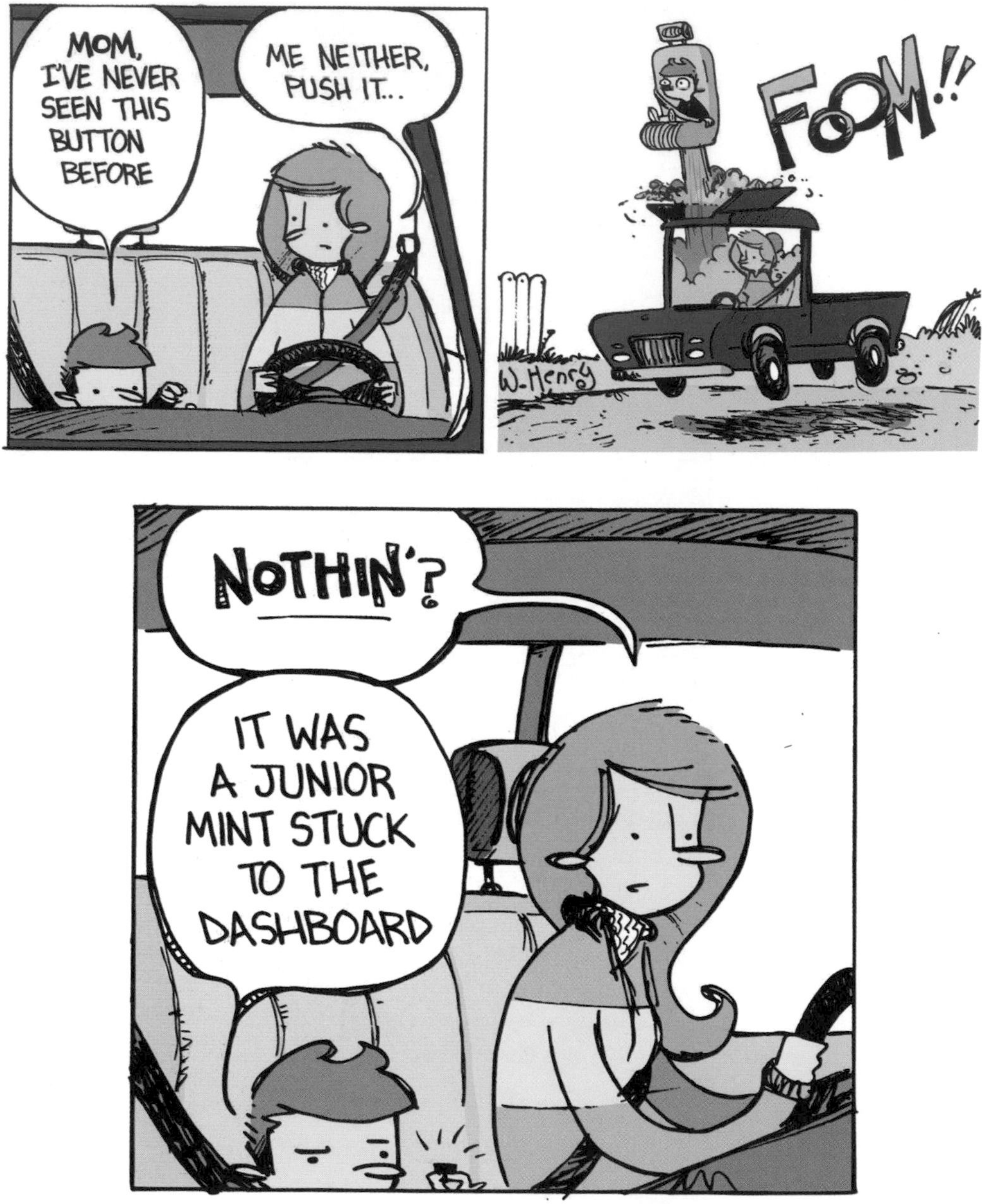
MOM, I'VE NEVER SEEN THIS BUTTON BEFORE
ME NEITHER, PUSH IT...
FOOM!!
W. Henry
NOTHIN'?
IT WAS A JUNIOR MINT STUCK TO THE DASHBOARD

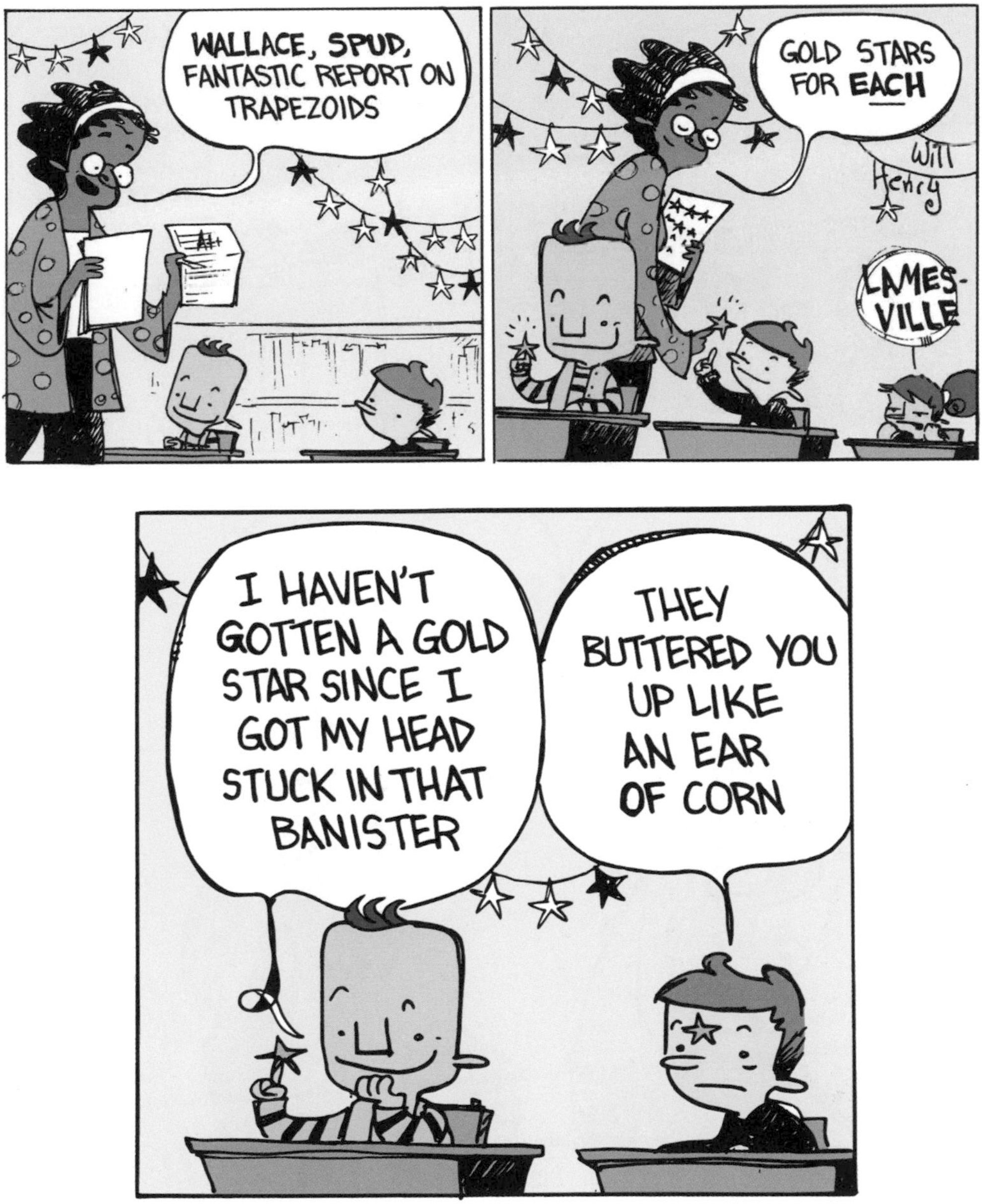
WALLACE, SPUD, FANTASTIC REPORT ON TRAPEZOIDS
A++
GOLD STARS FOR EACH
Will
Henry
LAMES-VILLE
I HAVEN'T GOTTEN A GOLD STAR SINCE I GOT MY HEAD STUCK IN THAT BANISTER
THEY BUTTERED YOU UP LIKE AN EAR OF CORN

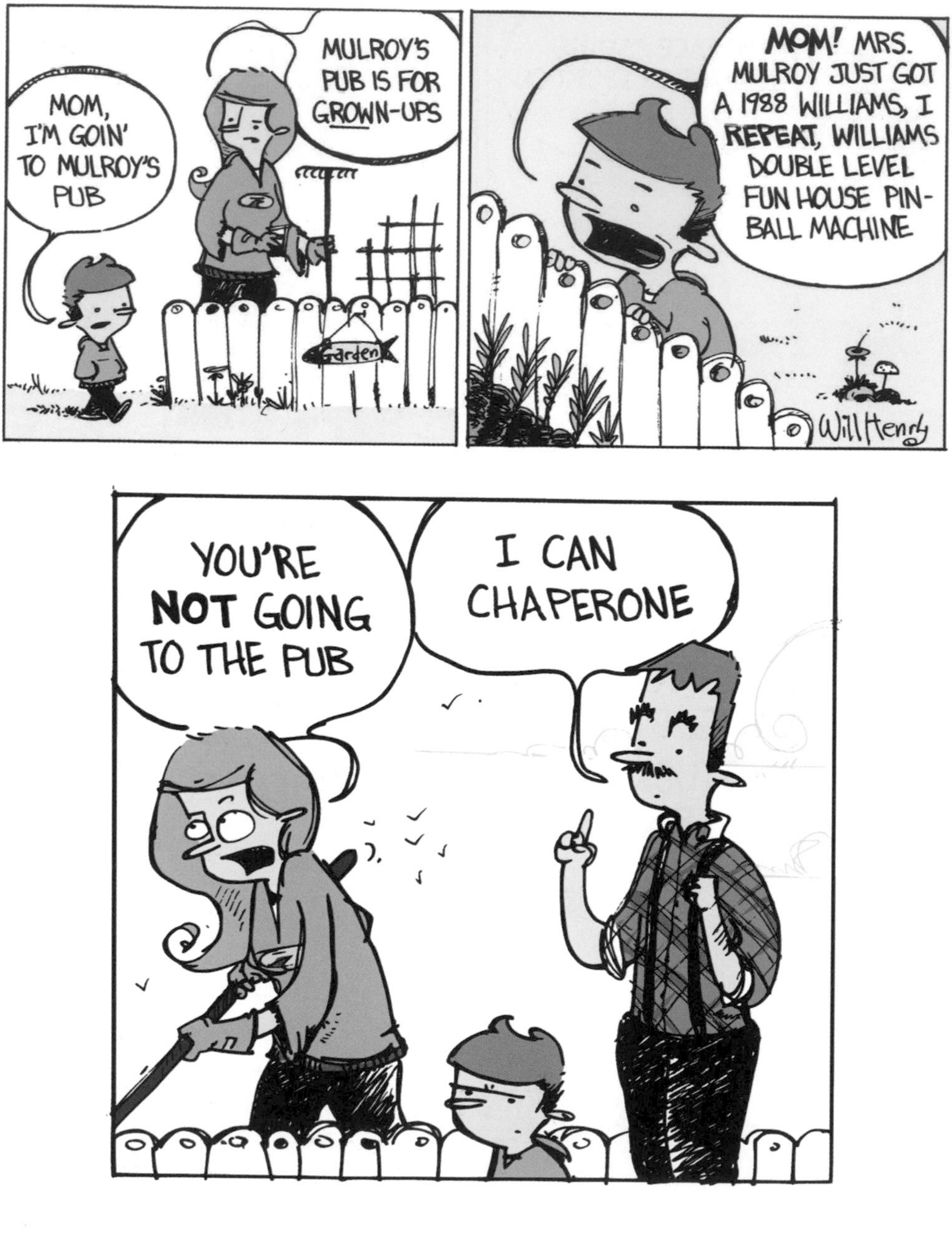
MOM, I'M GOIN' TO MULROY'S PUB
MULROY'S PUB IS FOR GROWN-UPS
Garden
MOM! MRS. MULROY JUST GOT A 1988 WILLIAMS, I REPEAT, WILLIAMS DOUBLE LEVEL FUN HOUSE PIN-BALL MACHINE
©Will Henry
YOU'RE NOT GOING TO THE PUB
I CAN CHAPERONE

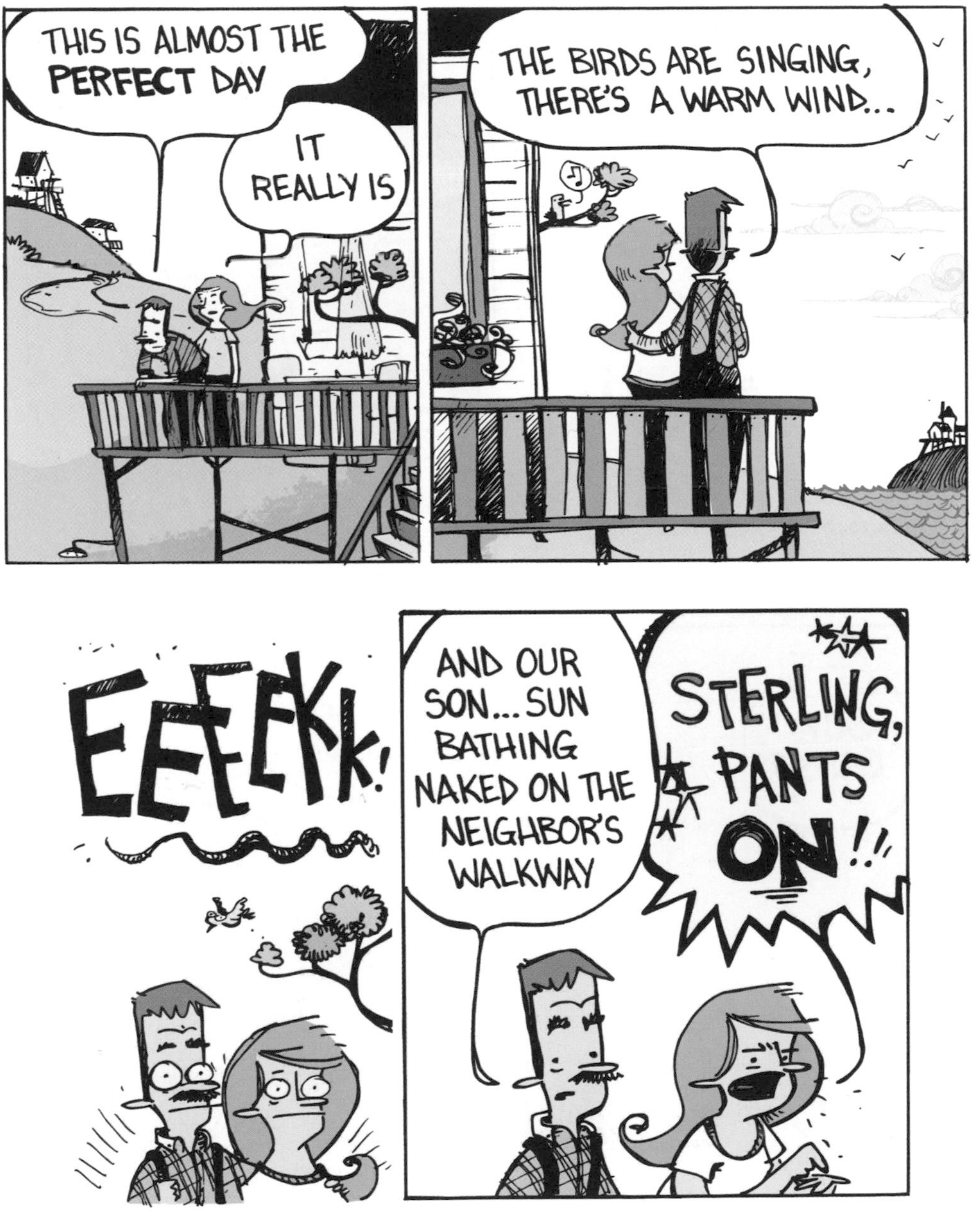
THIS IS ALMOST THE PERFECT DAY
IT REALLY IS
THE BIRDS ARE SINGING, THERE'S A WARM WIND...
EEEEKK!
AND OUR SON... SUN BATHING NAKED ON THE NEIGHBOR'S WALKWAY
STERLING, PANTS ON!!!

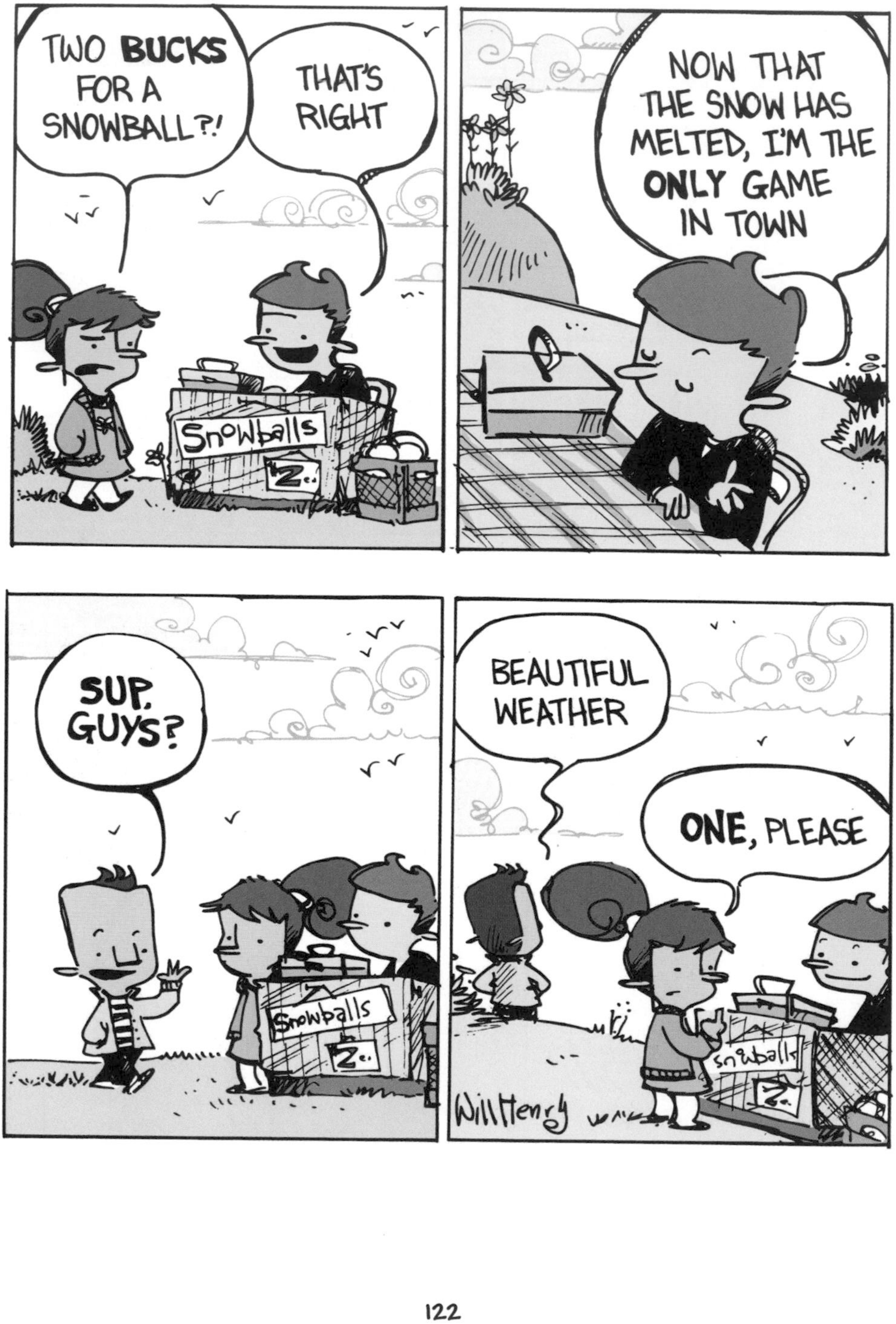
TWO BUCKS FOR A SNOWBALL?!
THAT'S RIGHT
Snowballs
2.
NOW THAT THE SNOW HAS MELTED, I'M THE ONLY GAME IN TOWN
SUP. GUYS?
Snowballs
2.
BEAUTIFUL WEATHER
ONE, PLEASE
Snowballs
2.
Will Henry

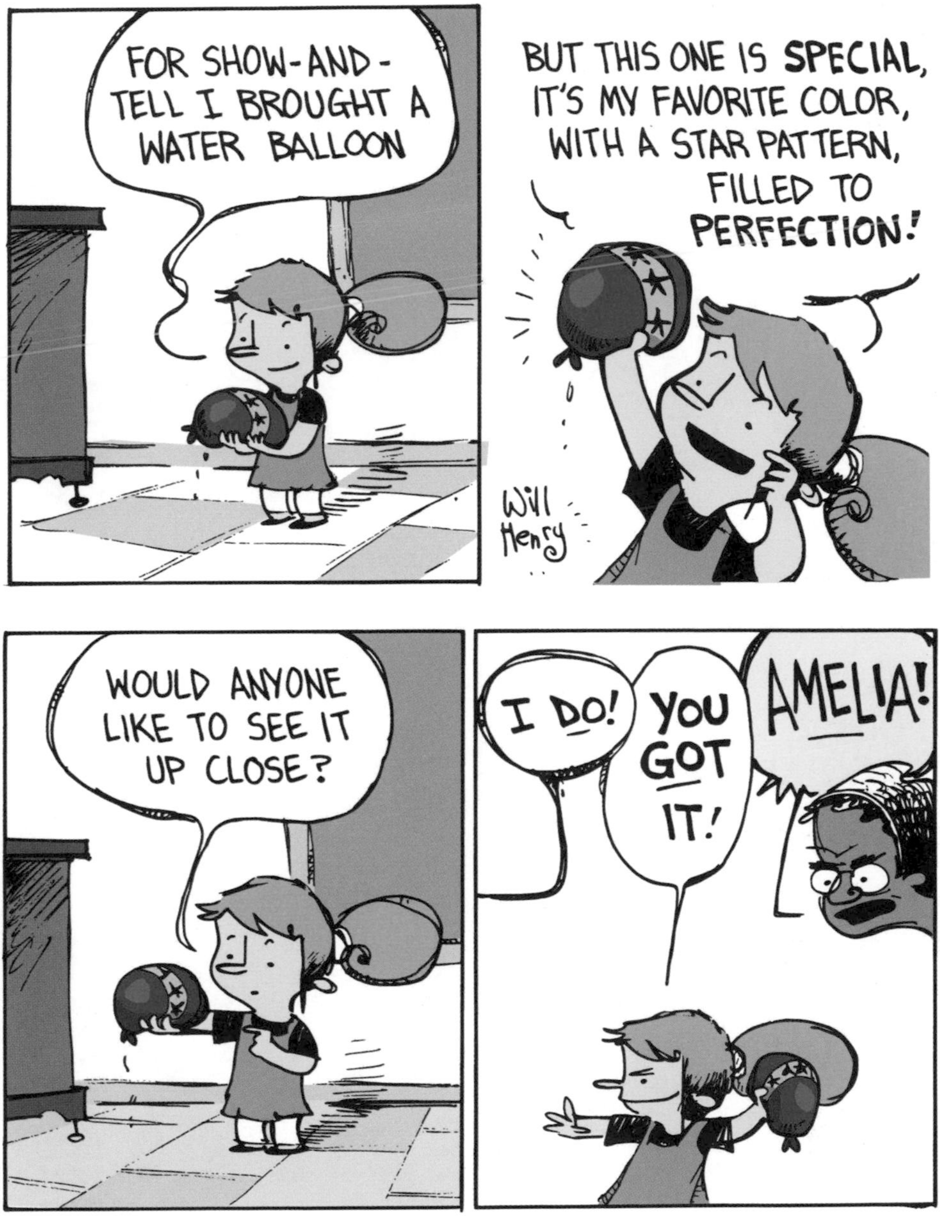
FOR SHOW-AND-TELL I BROUGHT A WATER BALLOON
BUT THIS ONE IS **SPECIAL**, IT'S MY FAVORITE COLOR, WITH A STAR PATTERN, FILLED TO **PERFECTION**!
Will Henry
WOULD ANYONE LIKE TO SEE IT UP CLOSE?
I DO!
YOU GOT IT!
AMELIA!

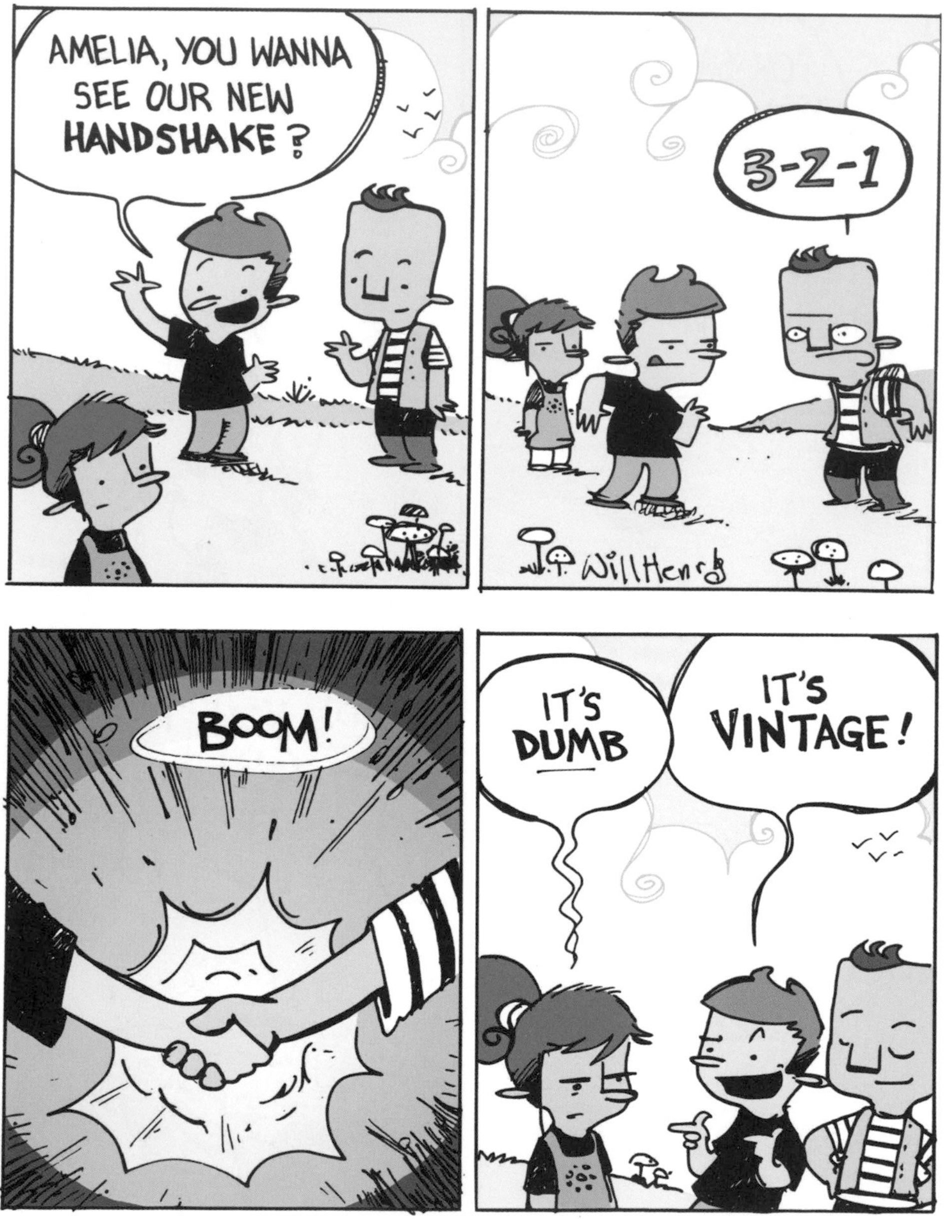
AMELIA, YOU WANNA SEE OUR NEW HANDSHAKE?
3-2-1
WillHenry
BOOM!
IT'S DUMB
IT'S VINTAGE!

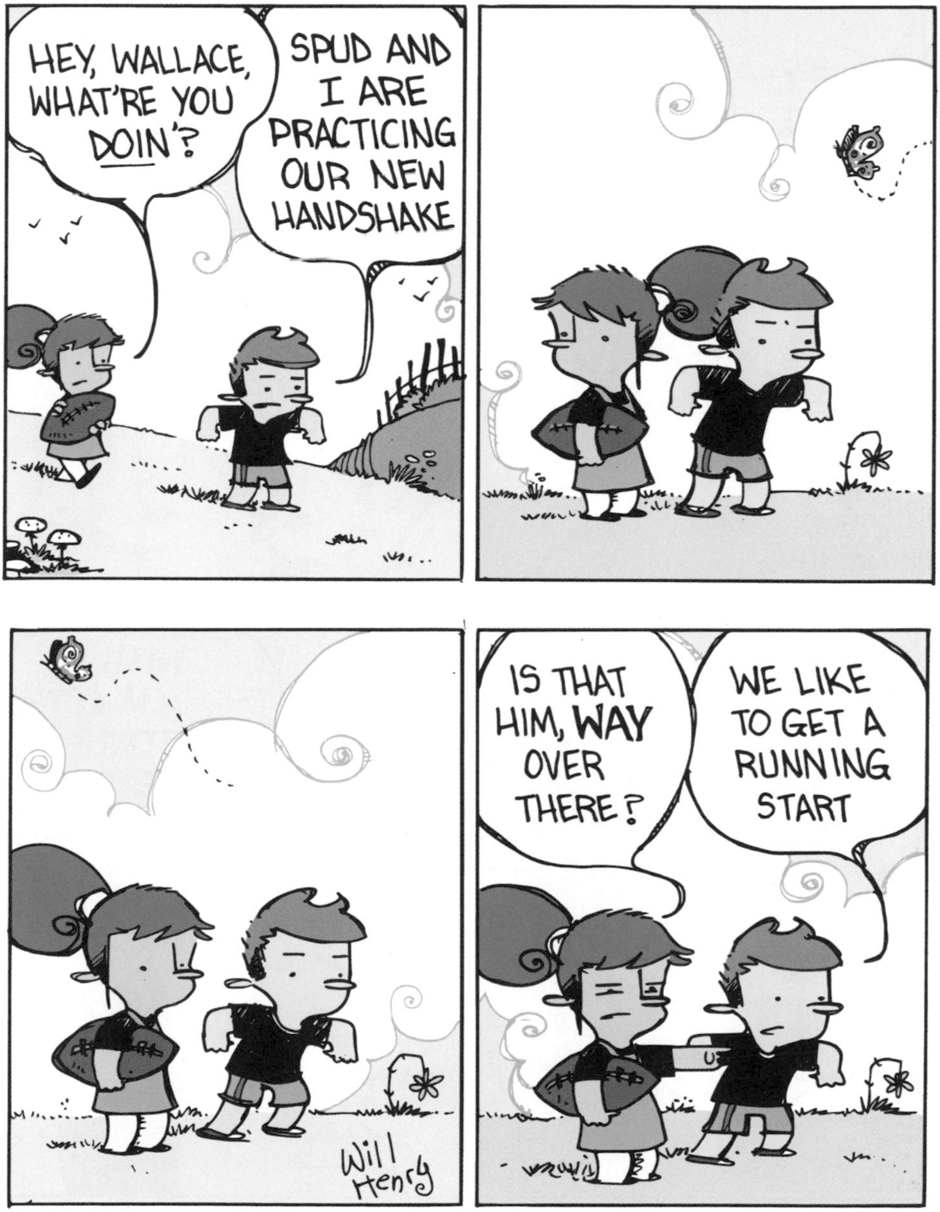
HEY, WALLACE, WHAT'RE YOU DOIN'?
SPUD AND I ARE PRACTICING OUR NEW HANDSHAKE
IS THAT HIM, WAY OVER THERE?
WE LIKE TO GET A RUNNING START
Will Henry

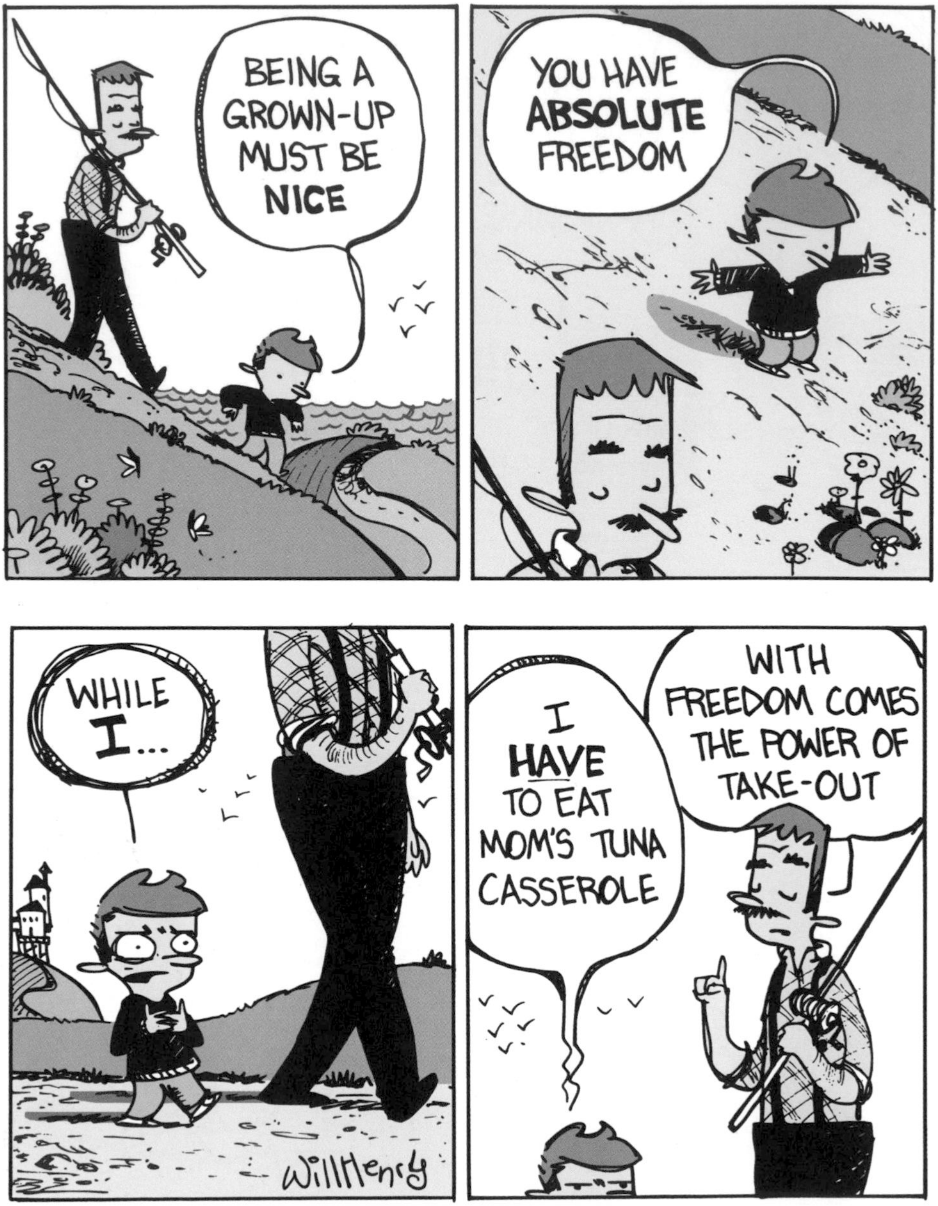
BEING A GROWN-UP MUST BE NICE
YOU HAVE ABSOLUTE FREEDOM
WHILE I...
WillHenry
WITH FREEDOM COMES THE POWER OF TAKE-OUT
I HAVE TO EAT MOM'S TUNA CASSEROLE

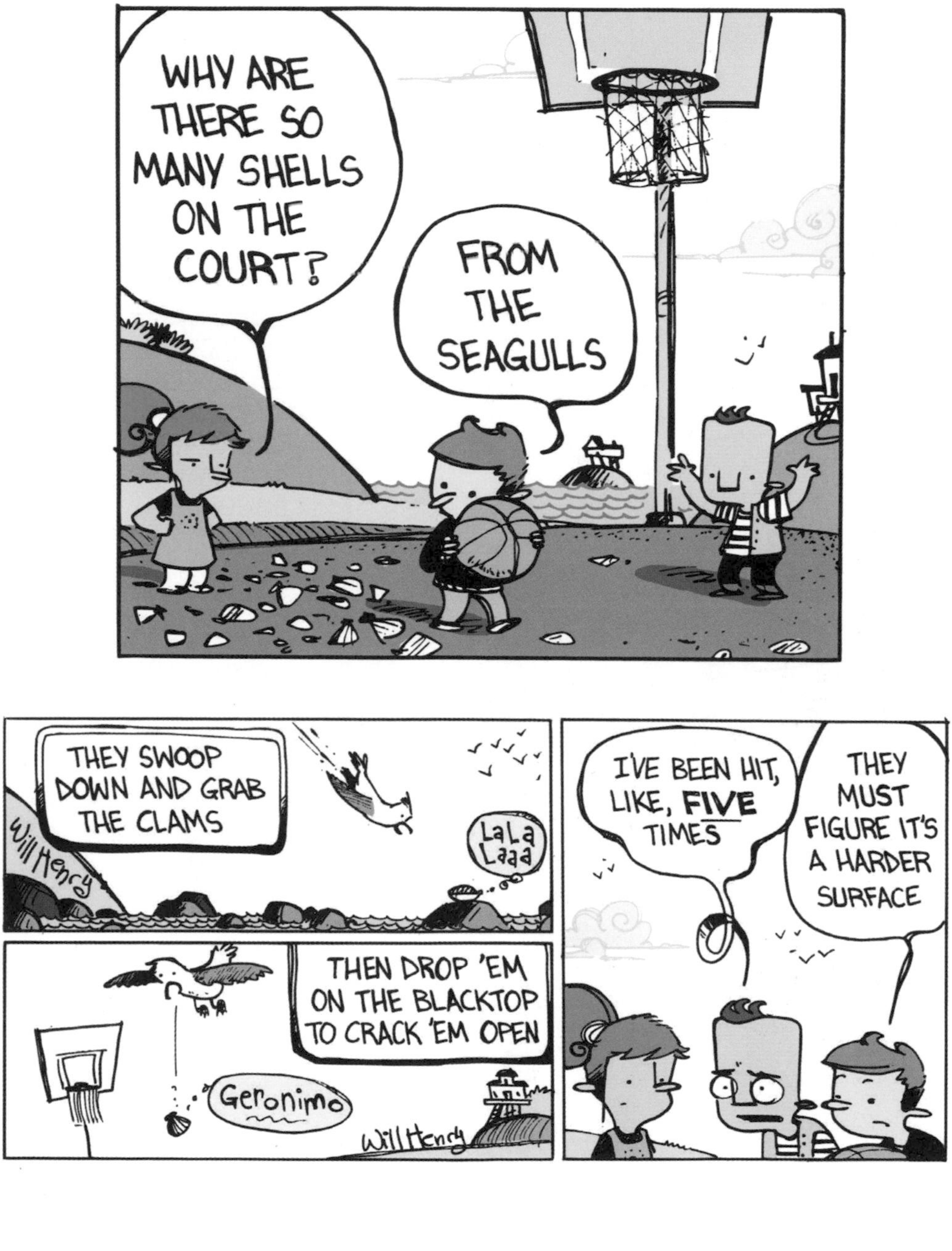
WHY ARE THERE SO MANY SHELLS ON THE COURT?
FROM THE SEAGULLS
THEY SWOOP DOWN AND GRAB THE CLAMS
LaLa Laaa
Will Henry
THEN DROP 'EM ON THE BLACKTOP TO CRACK 'EM OPEN
Geronimo
Will Henry
I'VE BEEN HIT, LIKE, **FIVE** TIMES
THEY MUST FIGURE IT'S A HARDER SURFACE

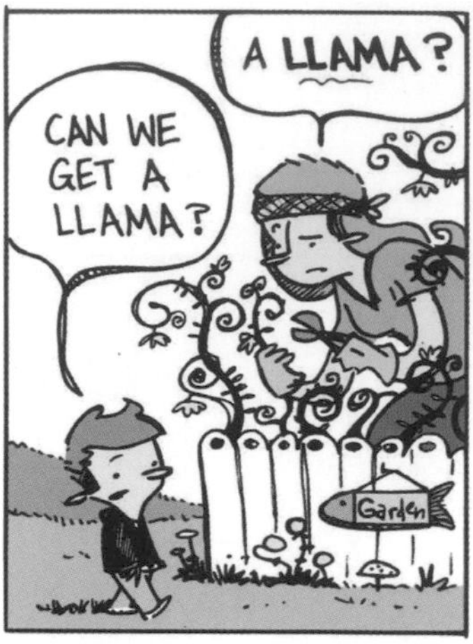
CAN WE GET A LLAMA?
A LLAMA?
Garden

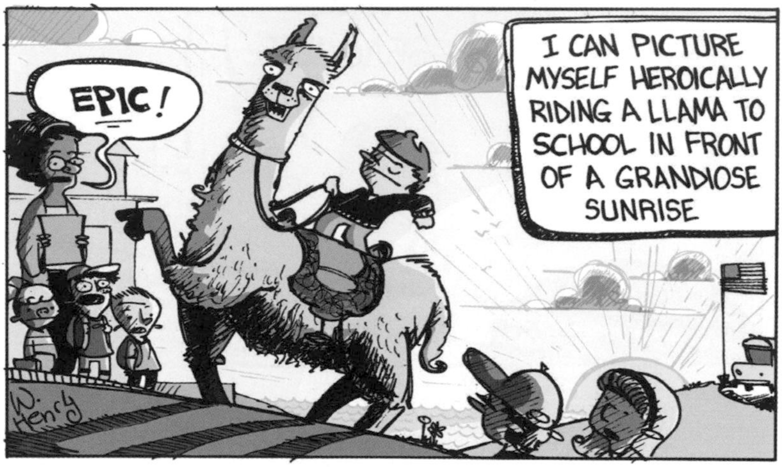
I CAN PICTURE MYSELF HEROICALLY RIDING A LLAMA TO SCHOOL IN FRONT OF A GRANDIOSE SUNRISE
EPIC!
W. Henry

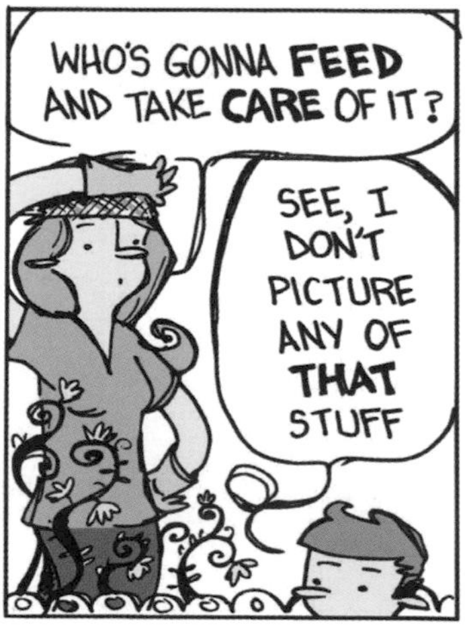
WHO'S GONNA FEED AND TAKE CARE OF IT?
SEE, I DON'T PICTURE ANY OF THAT STUFF

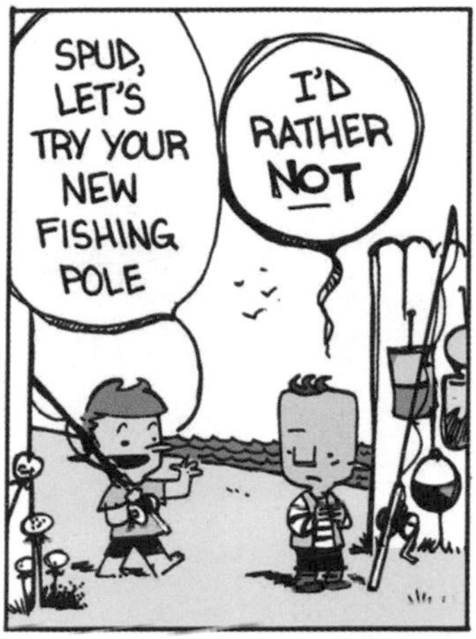
SPUD, LET'S TRY YOUR NEW FISHING POLE
I'D RATHER NOT

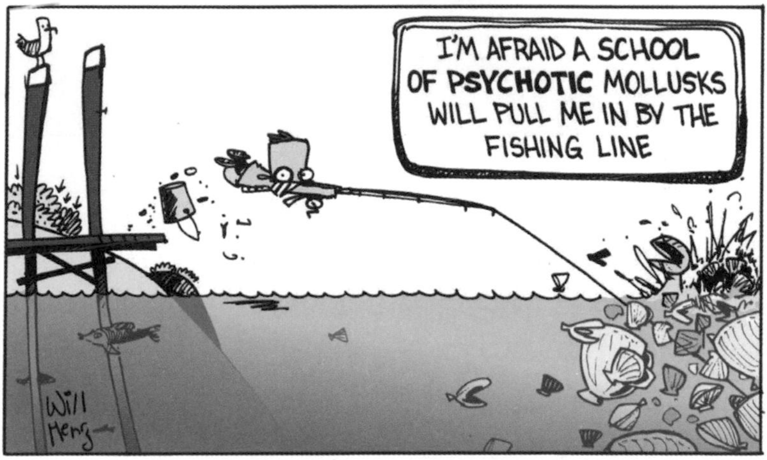
I'M AFRAID A SCHOOL OF PSYCHOTIC MOLLUSKS WILL PULL ME IN BY THE FISHING LINE
Will Henry

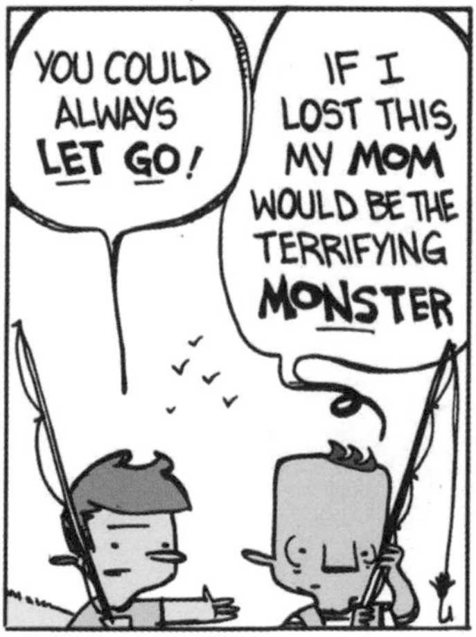
YOU COULD ALWAYS LET GO!
IF I LOST THIS, MY MOM WOULD BE THE TERRIFYING MONSTER

WHY DO YOU CUT SLITS IN THE HOT DOGS ?
IF I DIDN'T...
THE HOT DOG WOULD EXPLODE!
Will Henry
SHOWERING HOT DOG MEAT ONTO THE PEOPLE
I WOULD HATE TO CLEAN THOSE GUTTERS

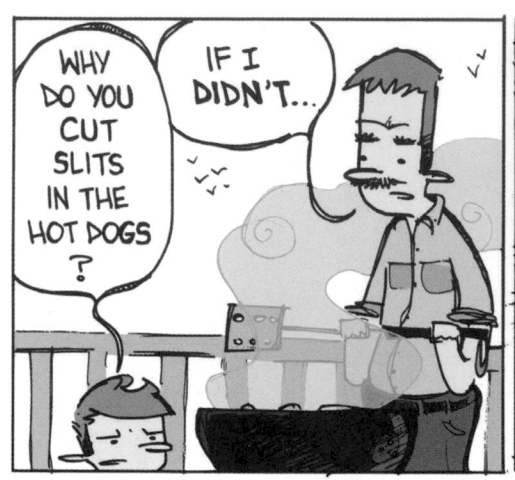

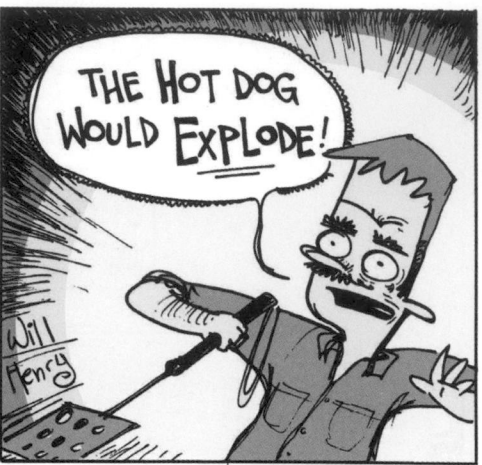

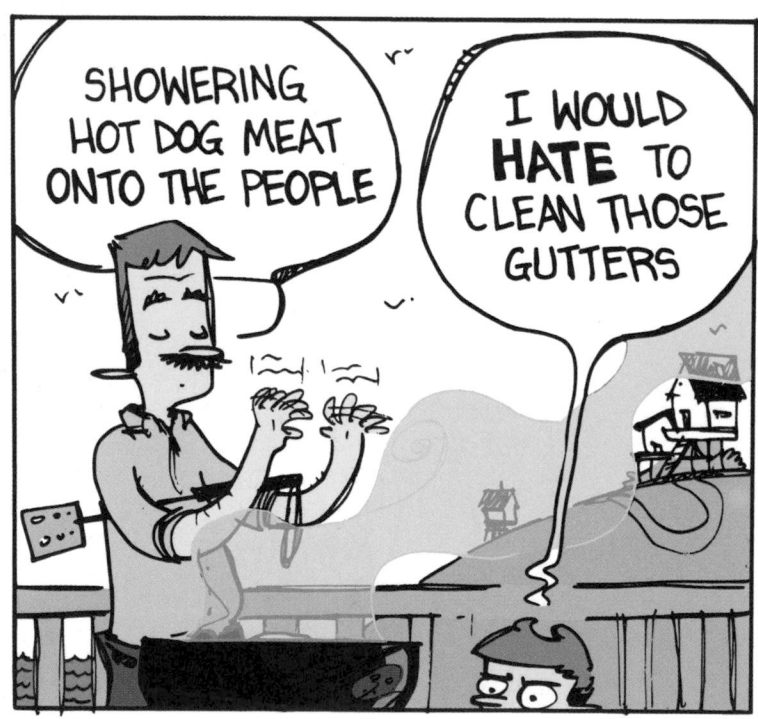

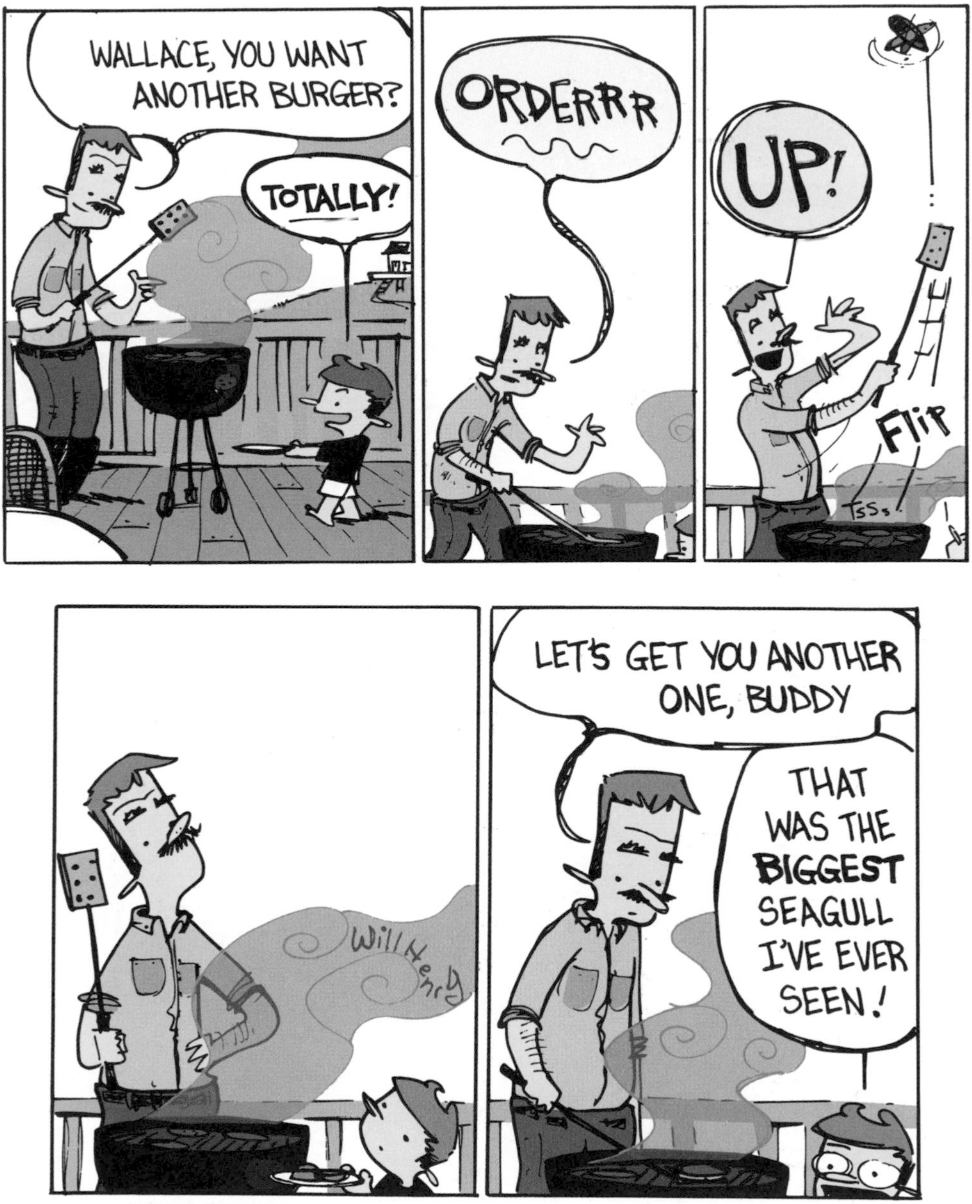
WALLACE, YOU WANT ANOTHER BURGER?
TOTALLY!
ORDERRRR
UP!
FLIP
TSSS
Will Henry
LET'S GET YOU ANOTHER ONE, BUDDY
THAT WAS THE BIGGEST SEAGULL I'VE EVER SEEN!

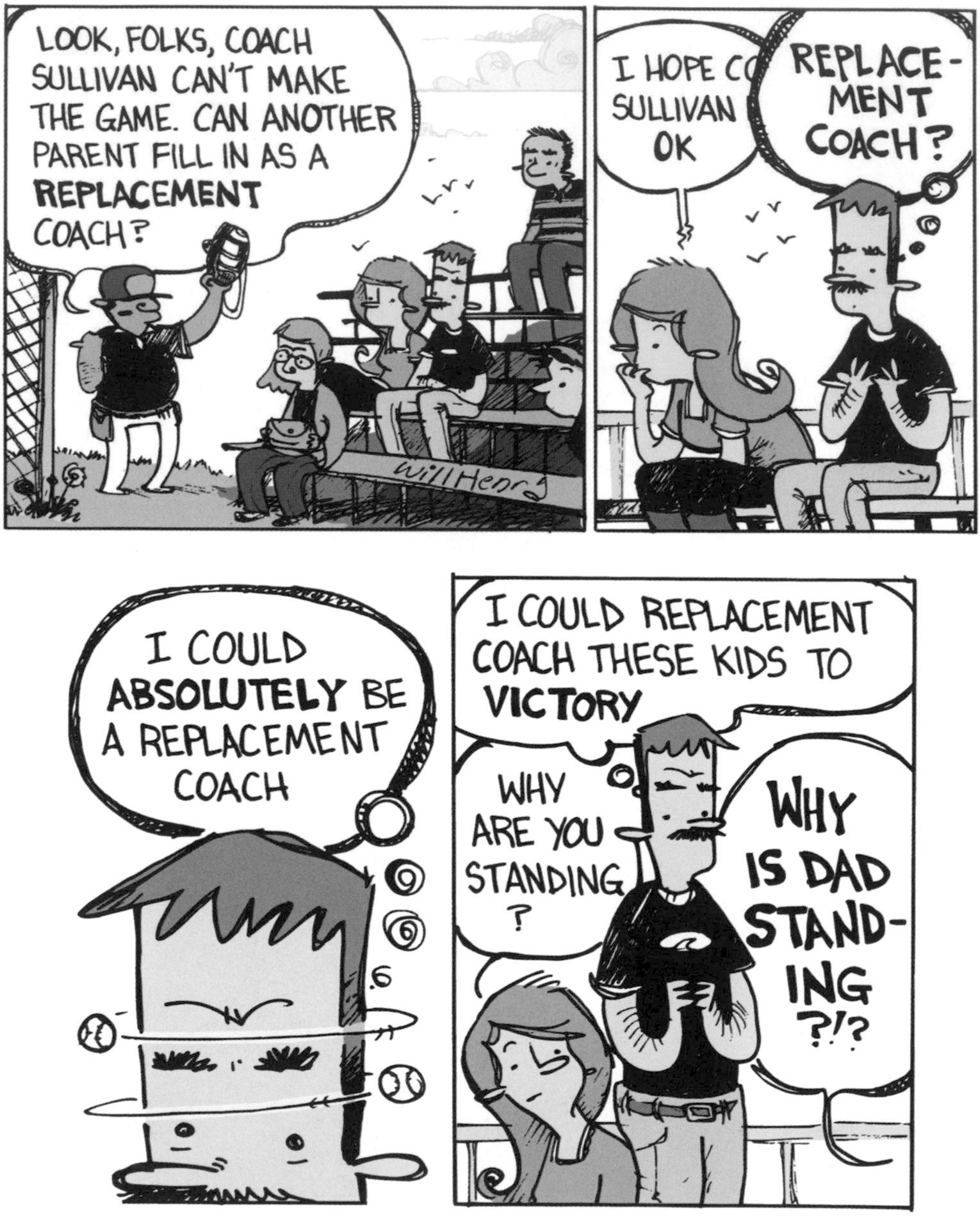
LOOK, FOLKS, COACH SULLIVAN CAN'T MAKE THE GAME. CAN ANOTHER PARENT FILL IN AS A **REPLACEMENT** COACH?
Will Henry
I HOPE C
SULLIVAN
OK
REPLACE-MENT COACH?
I COULD **ABSOLUTELY** BE A REPLACEMENT COACH
I COULD REPLACEMENT COACH THESE KIDS TO **VICTORY**
WHY ARE YOU STANDING ?
WHY IS DAD STAND-ING ?!?

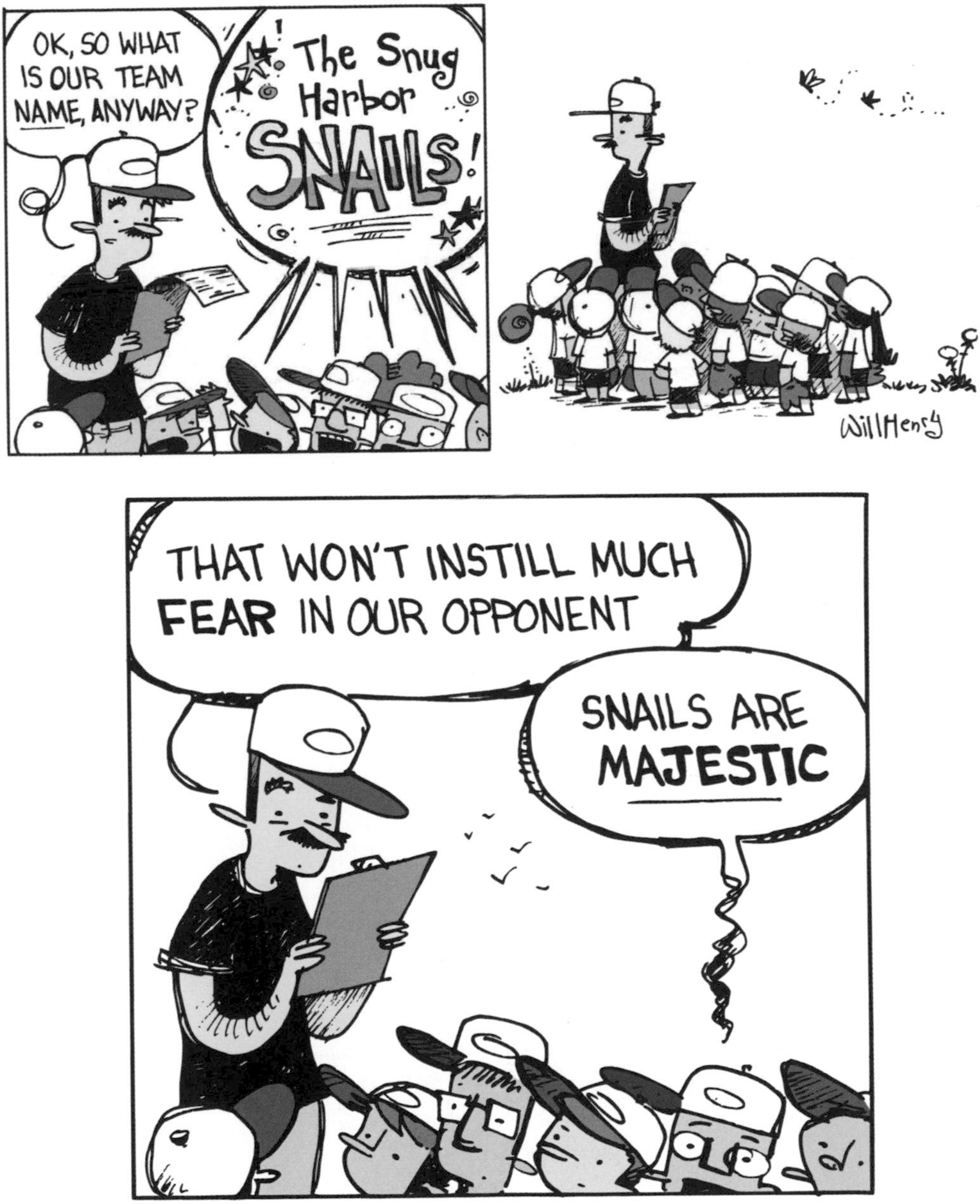
OK, SO WHAT IS OUR TEAM NAME, ANYWAY?
The Snug Harbor SNAILS!
WillHenry
THAT WON'T INSTILL MUCH FEAR IN OUR OPPONENT
SNAILS ARE MAJESTIC

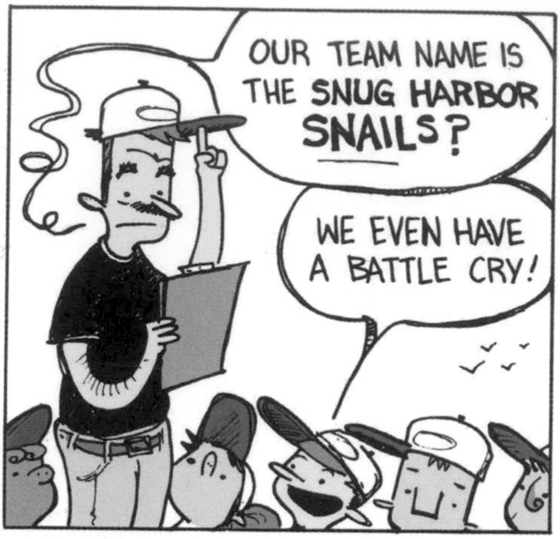
OUR TEAM NAME IS THE SNUG HARBOR SNAILS?
WE EVEN HAVE A BATTLE CRY!

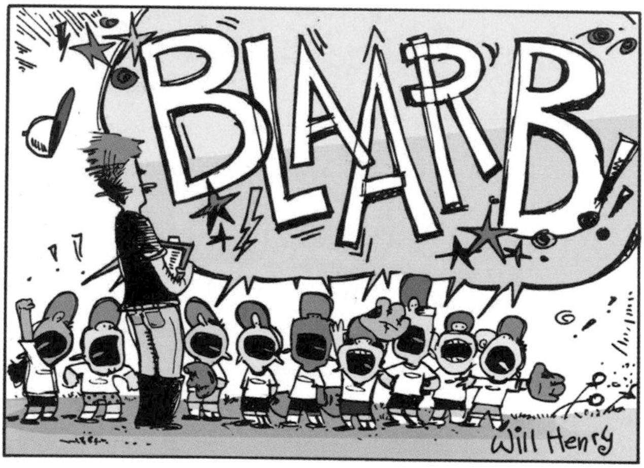
BLAARB!
Will Henry

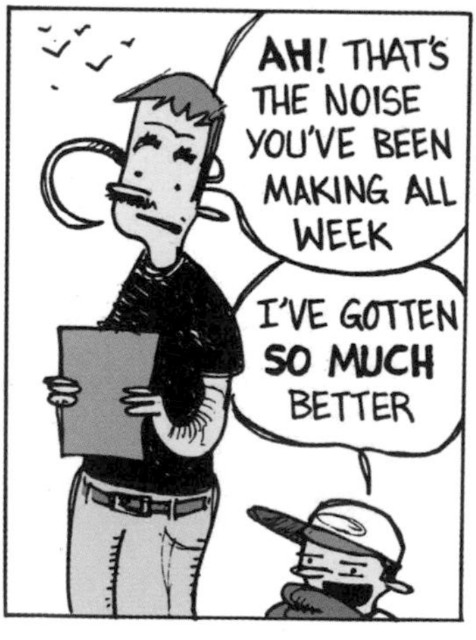
AH! THAT'S THE NOISE YOU'VE BEEN MAKING ALL WEEK
I'VE GOTTEN SO MUCH BETTER

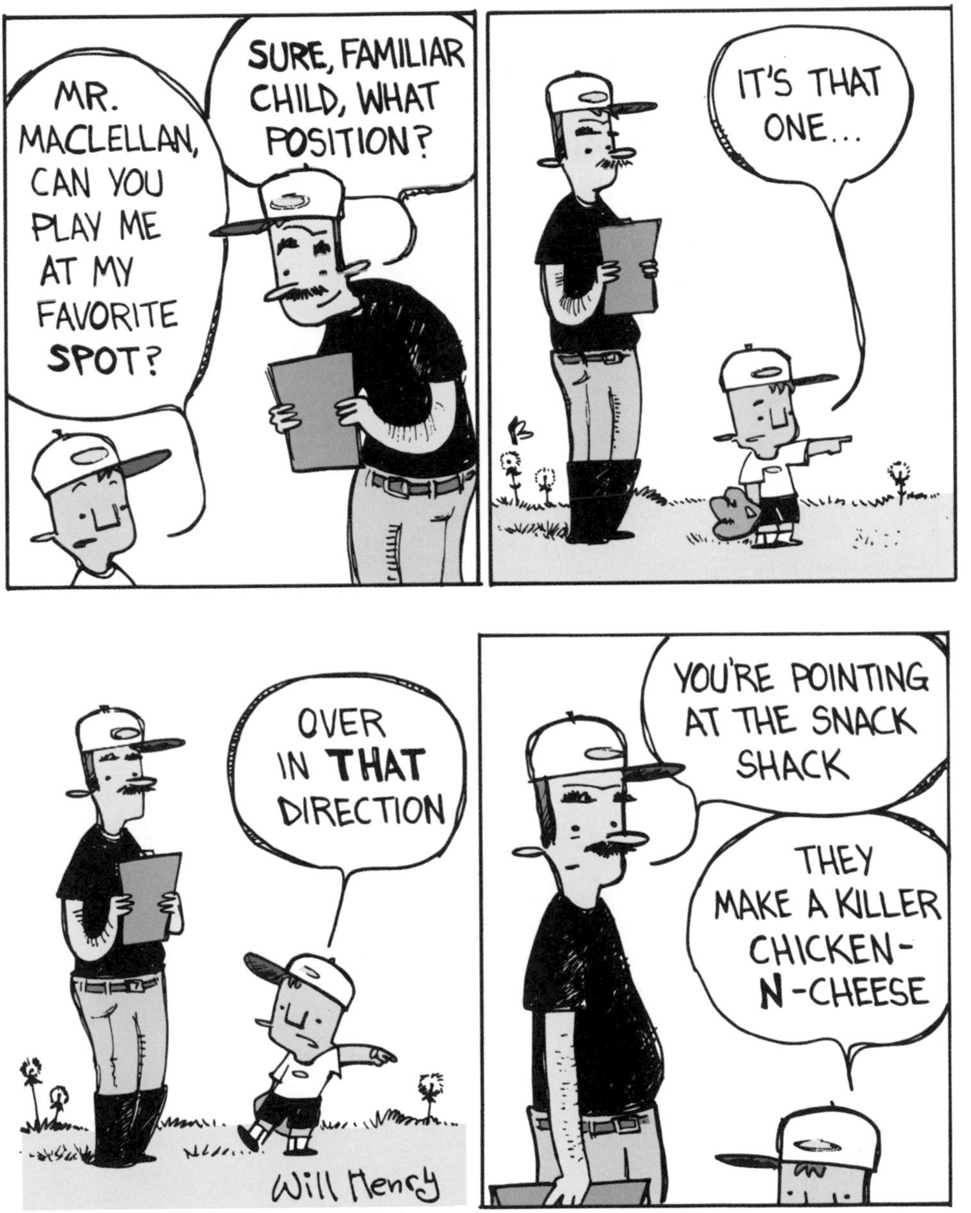
MR. MACLELLAN, CAN YOU PLAY ME AT MY FAVORITE **SPOT**?
SURE, FAMILIAR CHILD, WHAT POSITION?
IT'S THAT ONE...
OVER IN **THAT** DIRECTION
Will Henry
YOU'RE POINTING AT THE SNACK SHACK
THEY MAKE A KILLER CHICKEN-**N**-CHEESE

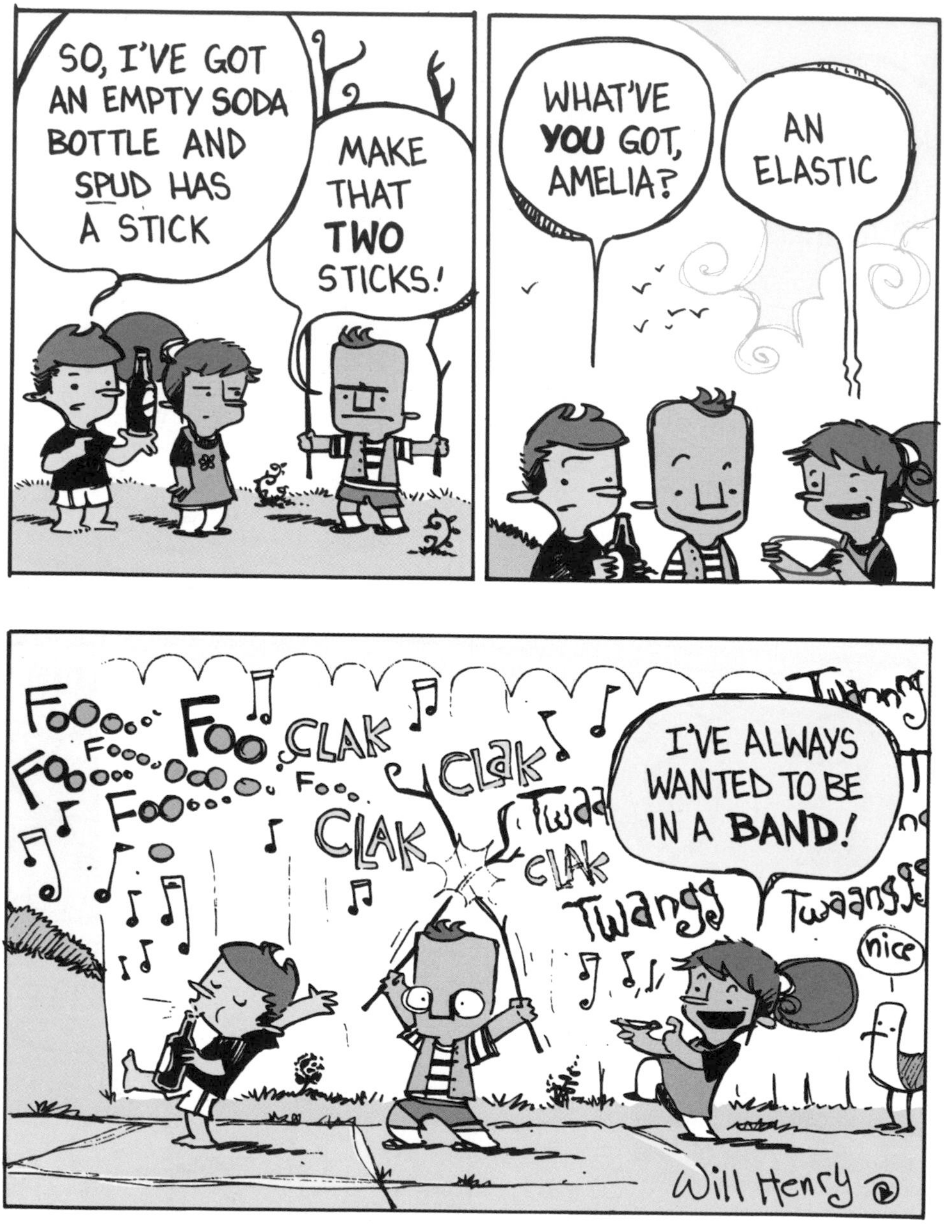
SO, I'VE GOT AN EMPTY SODA BOTTLE AND SPUD HAS A STICK
MAKE THAT **TWO** STICKS!
WHAT'VE **YOU** GOT, AMELIA?
AN ELASTIC
FOOooo FOO
Fooooo
FOOoo FOOooo
Fooo
CLAK
CLAK
CLAK
Twaa
CLAK
Twangg
Twanng
Twaangge
I'VE ALWAYS WANTED TO BE IN A **BAND**!
nice
Will Henry

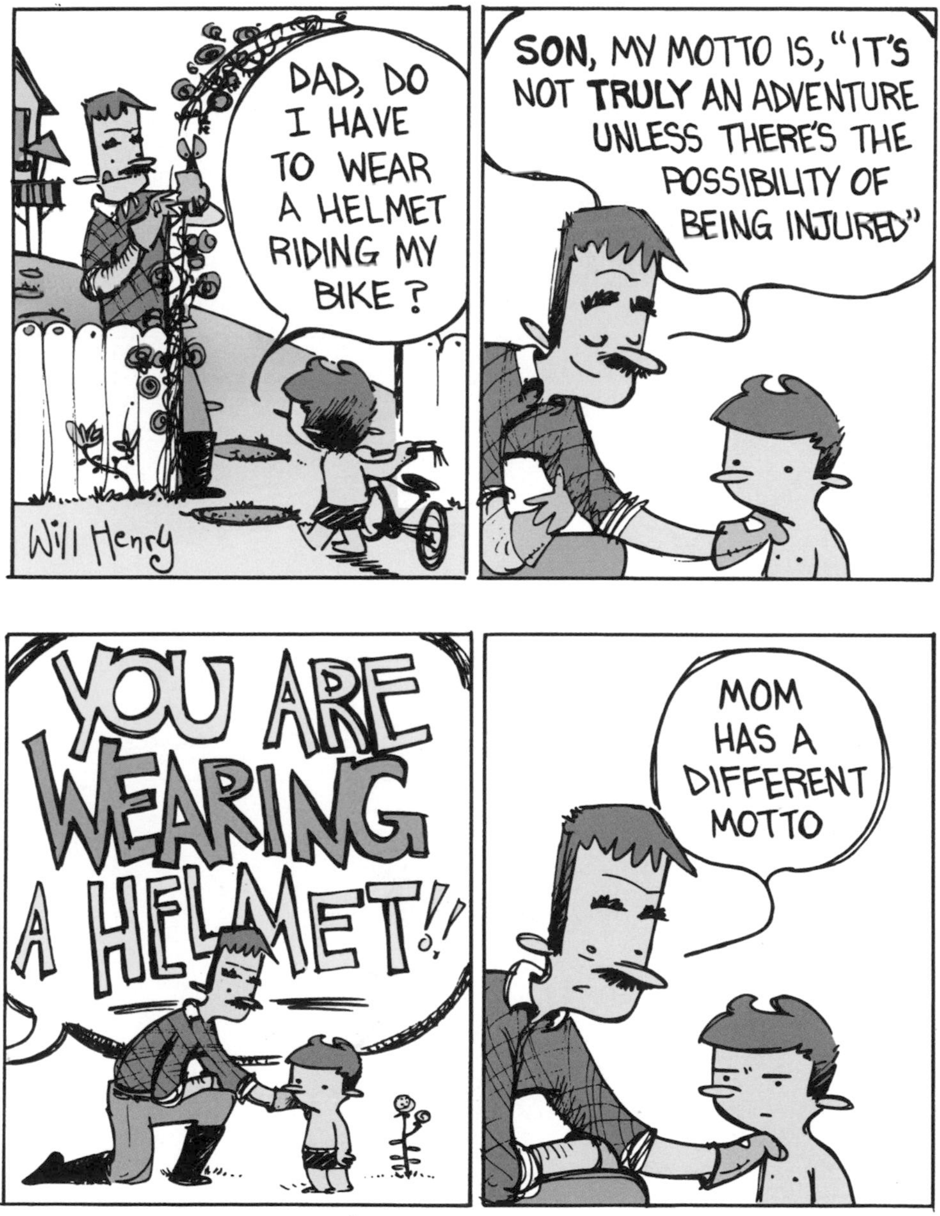
DAD, DO I HAVE TO WEAR A HELMET RIDING MY BIKE?
Will Henry
SON, MY MOTTO IS, "IT'S NOT TRULY AN ADVENTURE UNLESS THERE'S THE POSSIBILITY OF BEING INJURED"
YOU ARE WEARING A HELMET!!
MOM HAS A DIFFERENT MOTTO

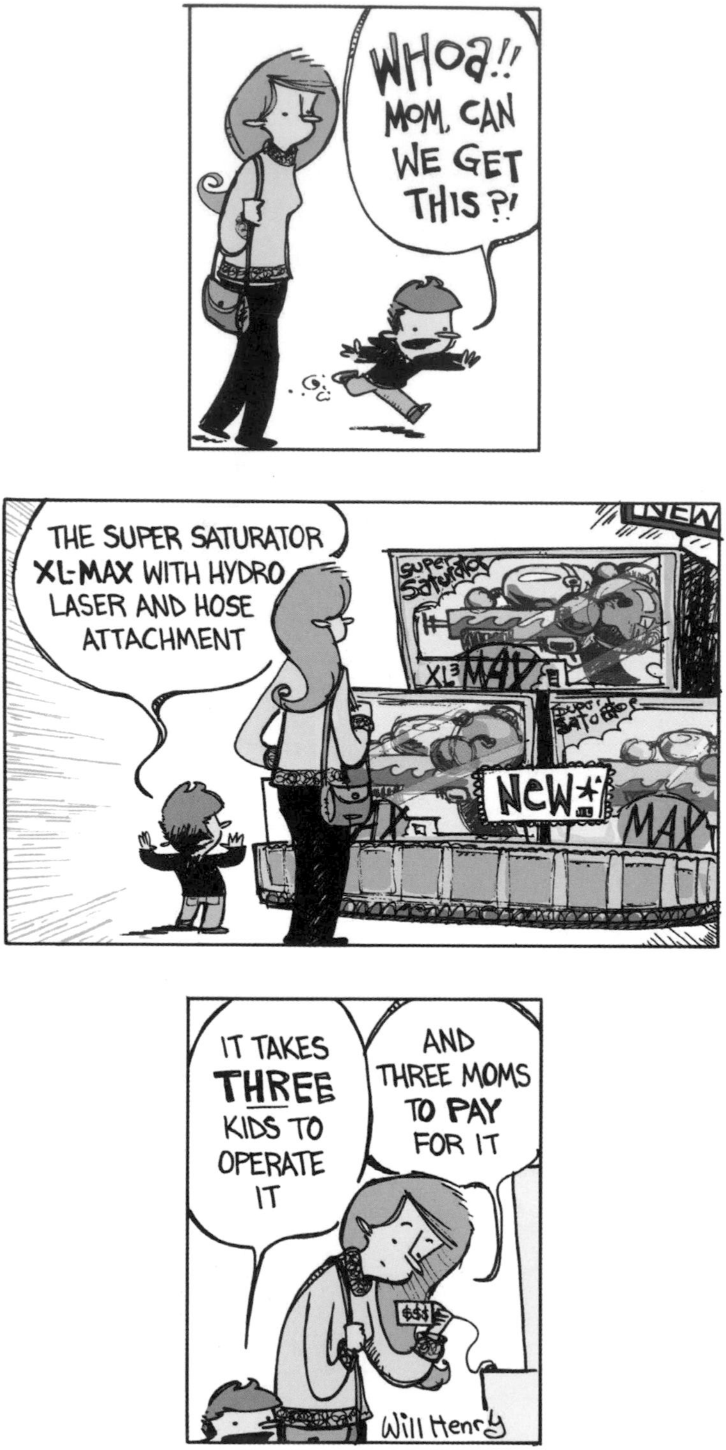
WHoa!! MOM, CAN WE GET THIS?!
THE SUPER SATURATOR XL-MAX WITH HYDRO LASER AND HOSE ATTACHMENT
NEW
MAX
IT TAKES THREE KIDS TO OPERATE IT
AND THREE MOMS TO PAY FOR IT
$$$
Will Henry

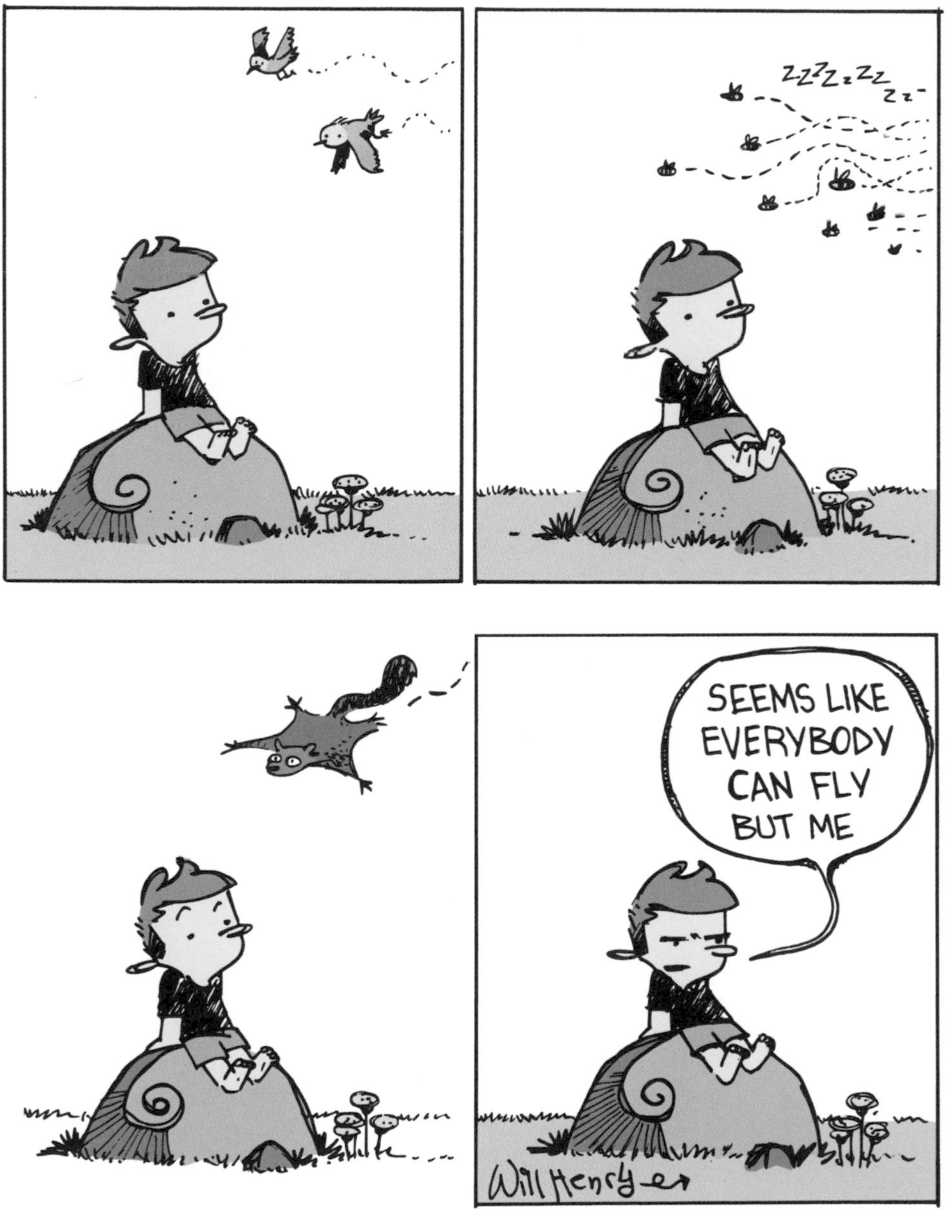
ZZZZzZZ Zz
SEEMS LIKE EVERYBODY CAN FLY BUT ME
Will Henry

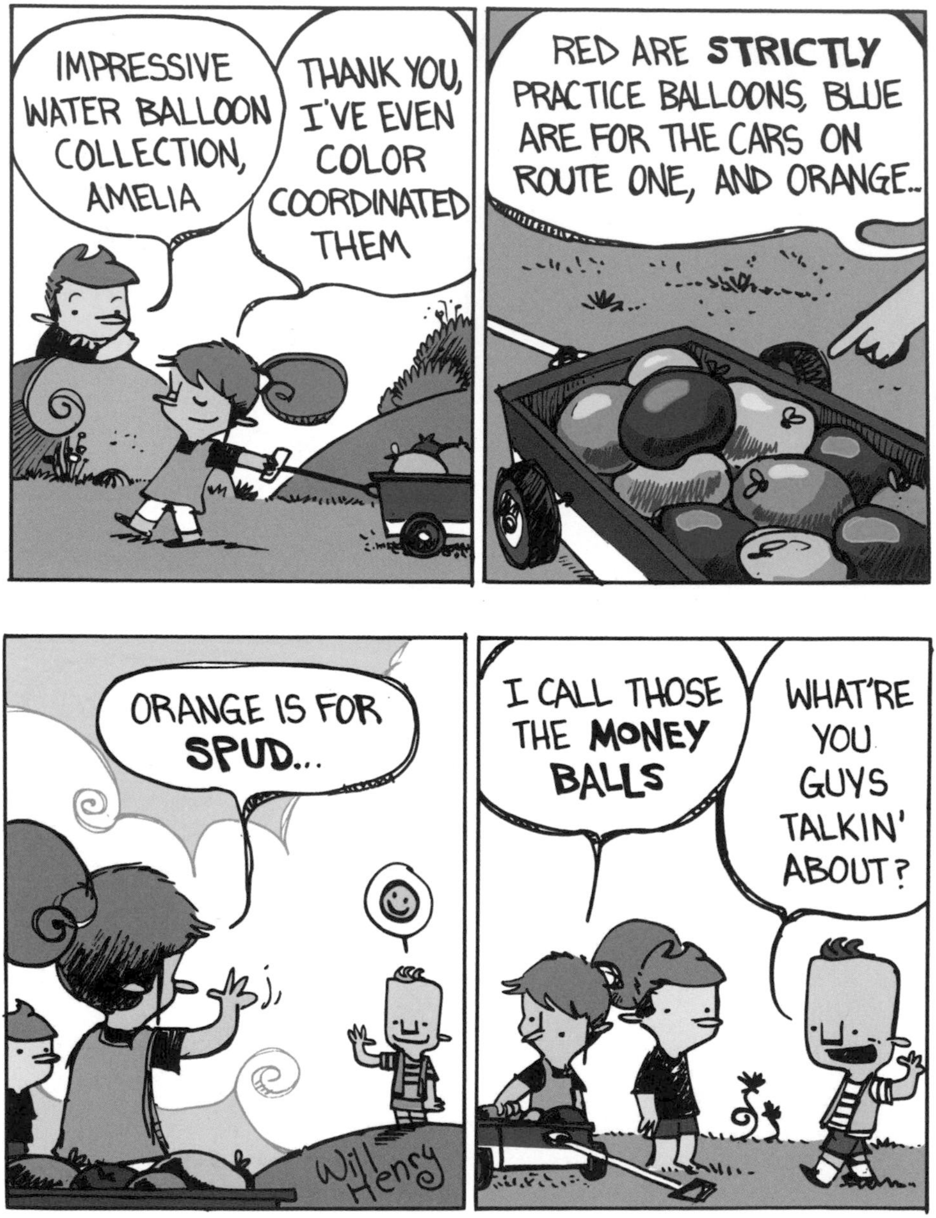
IMPRESSIVE WATER BALLOON COLLECTION, AMELIA
THANK YOU, I'VE EVEN COLOR COORDINATED THEM
RED ARE STRICTLY PRACTICE BALLOONS, BLUE ARE FOR THE CARS ON ROUTE ONE, AND ORANGE...
ORANGE IS FOR SPUD...
Will Henry
I CALL THOSE THE MONEY BALLS
WHAT'RE YOU GUYS TALKIN' ABOUT?

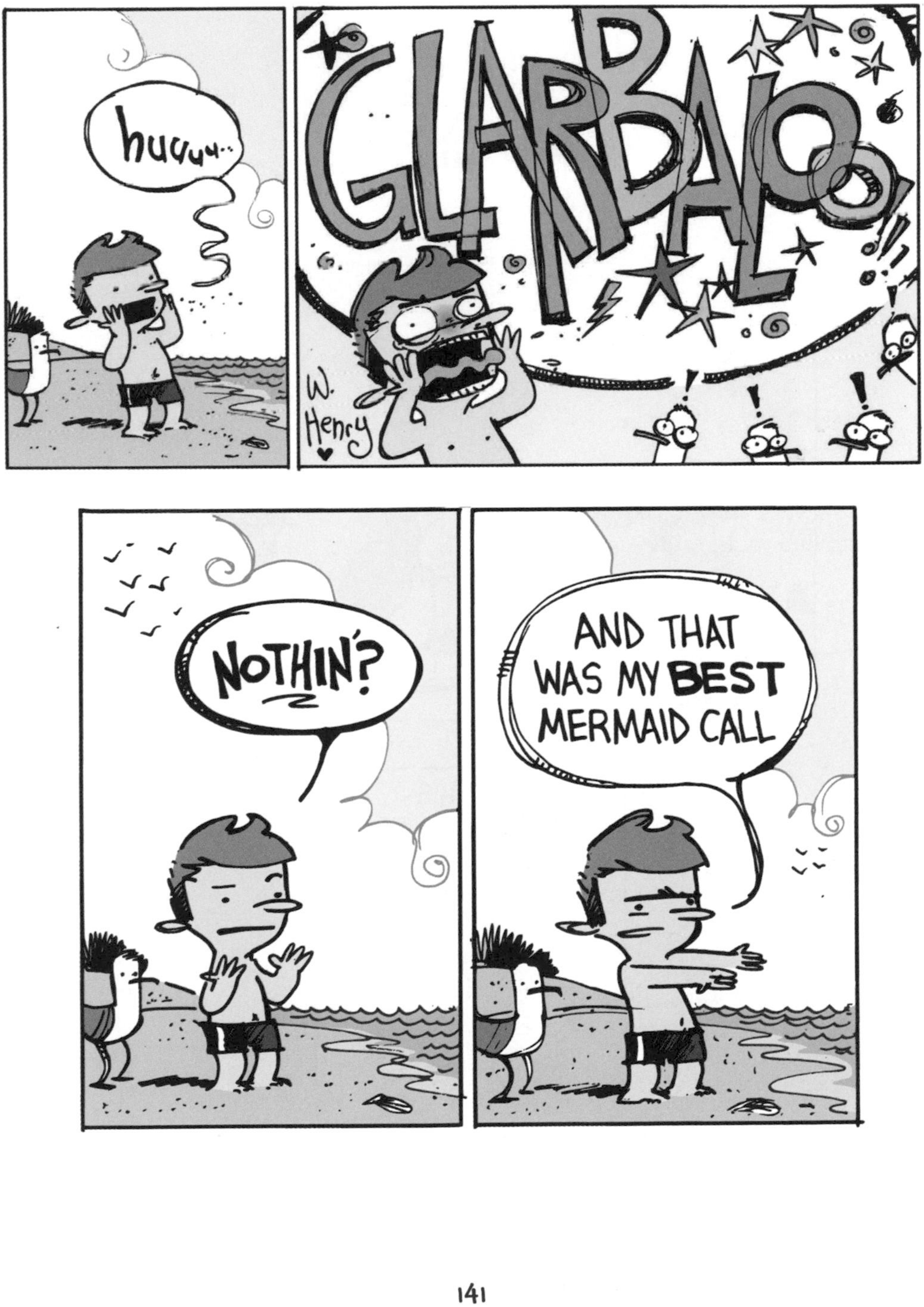
huuuu...
GLARBALOO!!
W. Henry
NOTHIN'?
AND THAT WAS MY **BEST** MERMAID CALL

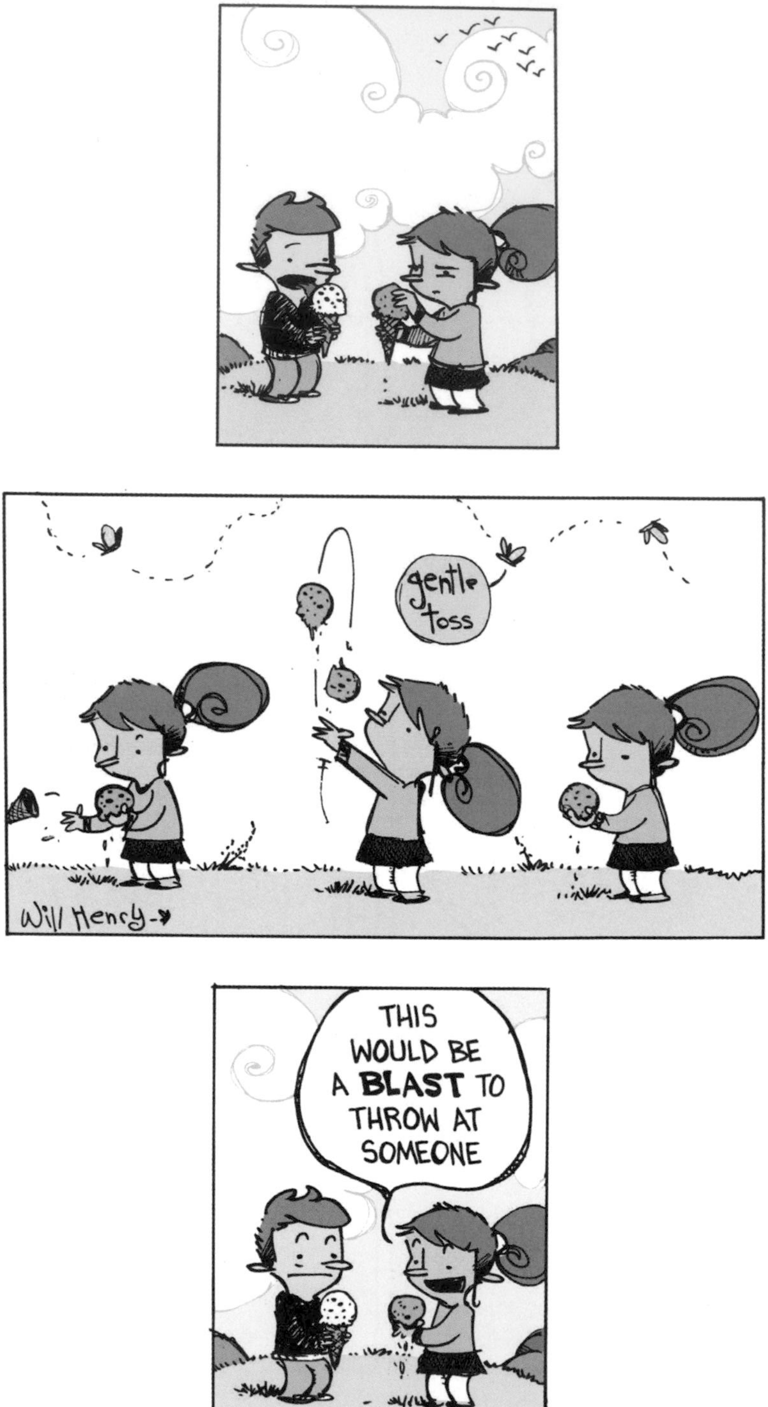
gentle toss
Will Henry
THIS WOULD BE A **BLAST** TO THROW AT SOMEONE

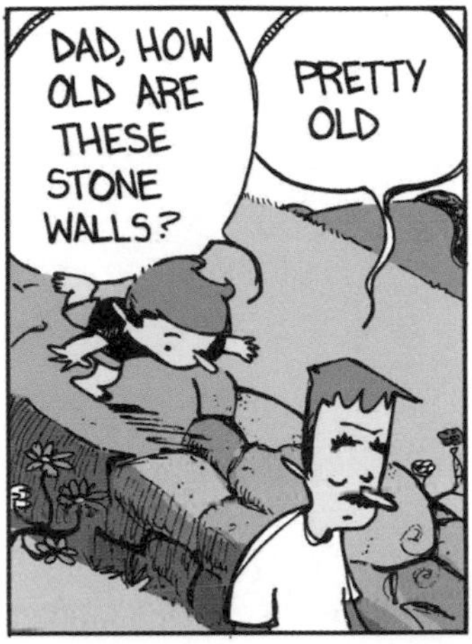
DAD, HOW OLD ARE THESE STONE WALLS?
PRETTY OLD

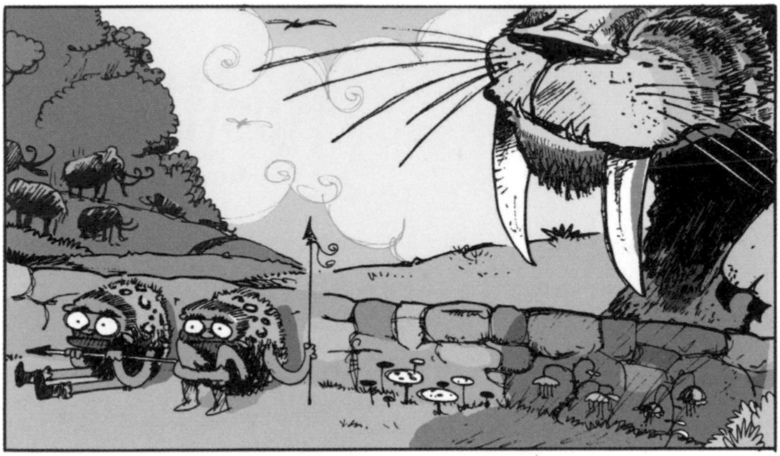

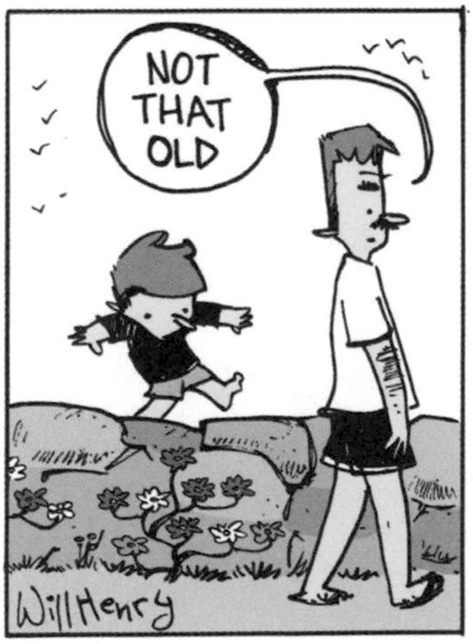
NOT THAT OLD
Will Henry

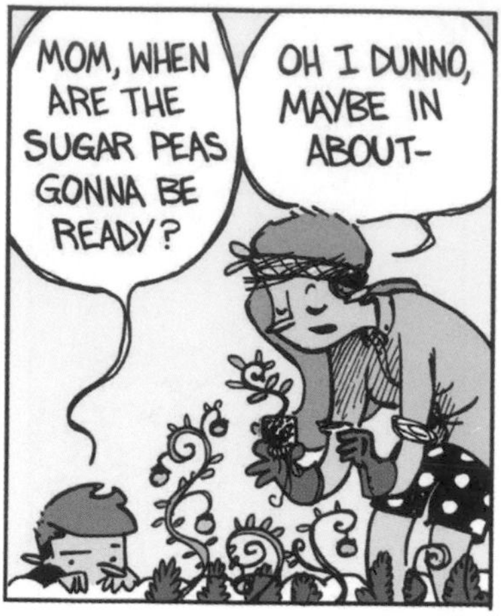
MOM, WHEN ARE THE SUGAR PEAS GONNA BE READY?
OH I DUNNO, MAYBE IN ABOUT-

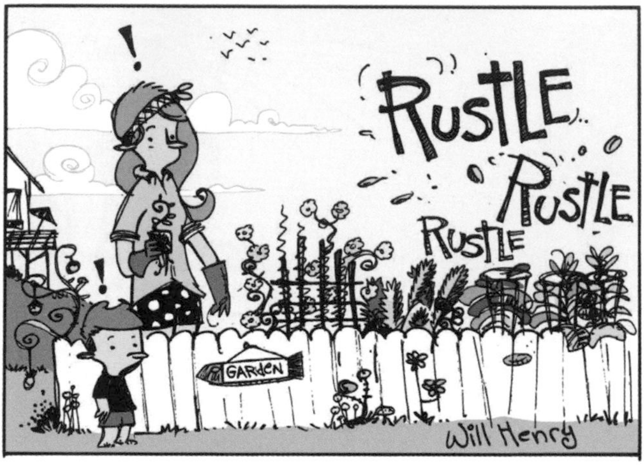
!
RUSTLE
RUSTLE
RUSTLE
!
GARDEN
Will Henry

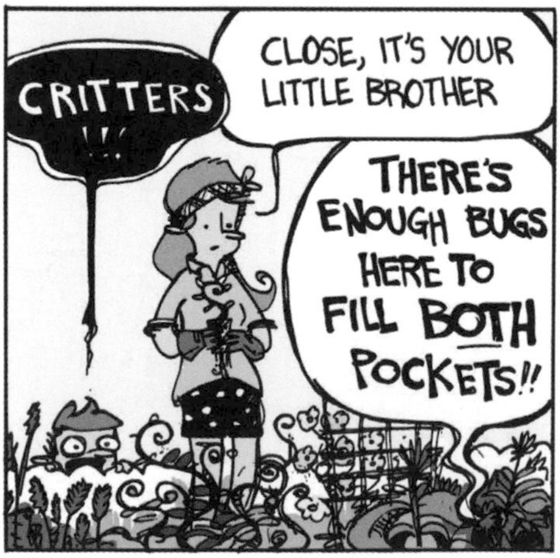
CRITTERS !!!
CLOSE, IT'S YOUR LITTLE BROTHER
THERE'S ENOUGH BUGS HERE TO FILL BOTH POCKETS!!

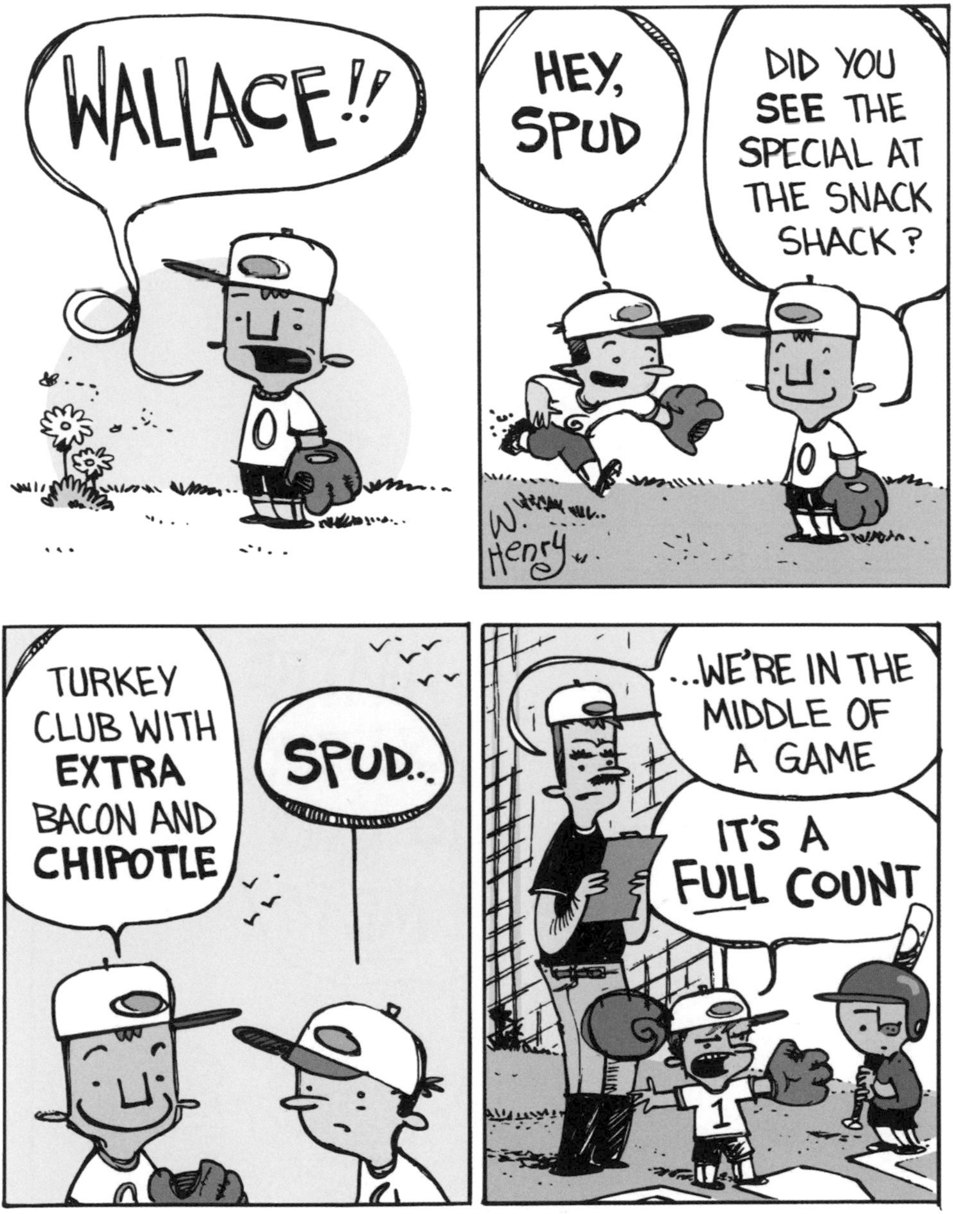
WALLACE!!
HEY, SPUD
DID YOU SEE THE SPECIAL AT THE SNACK SHACK?
W. Henry
TURKEY CLUB WITH EXTRA BACON AND CHIPOTLE
SPUD..
...WE'RE IN THE MIDDLE OF A GAME
IT'S A FULL COUNT

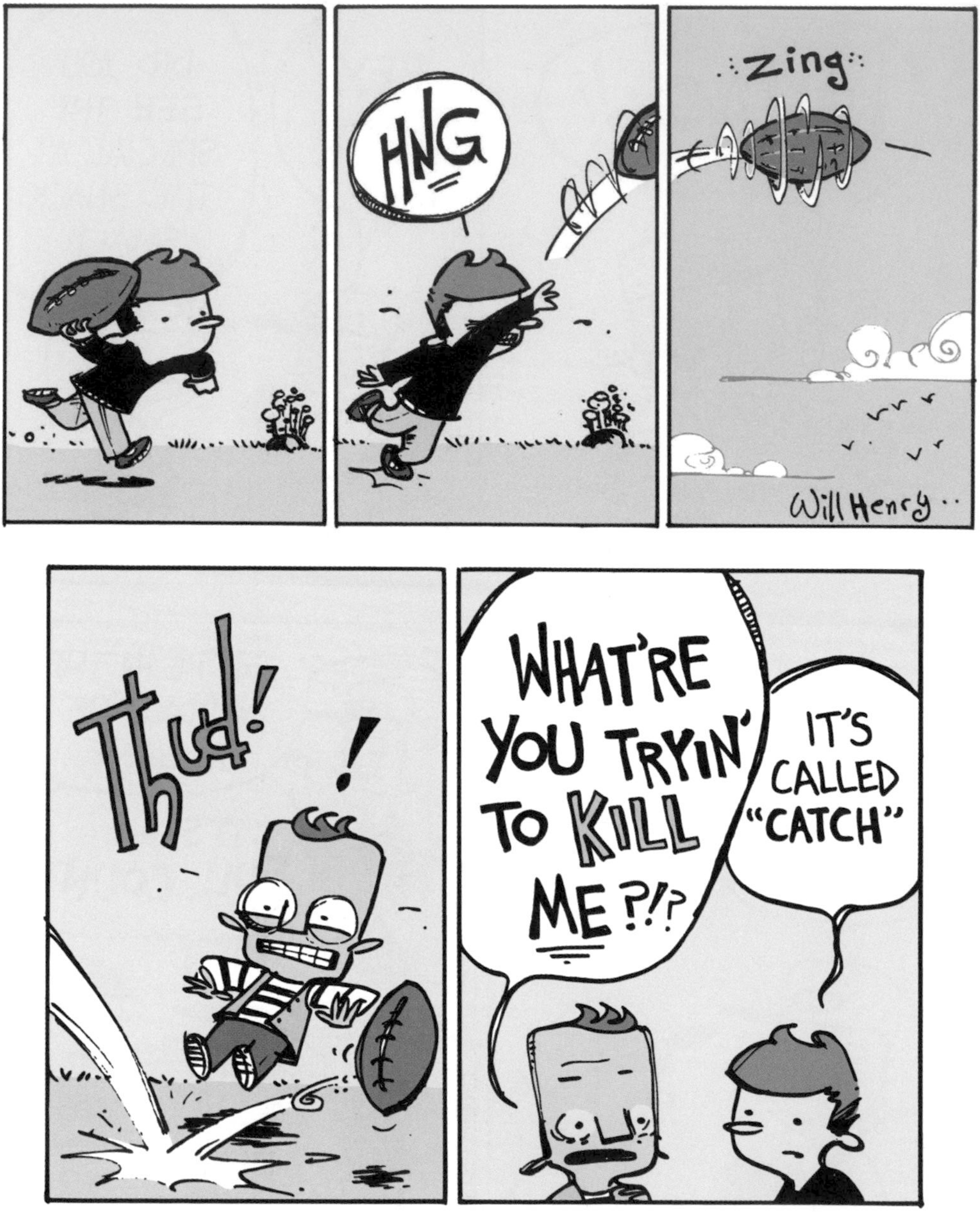
HNG
zing
Will Henry
Thud!
!
WHAT'RE YOU TRYIN' TO KILL ME?!?
IT'S CALLED "CATCH"

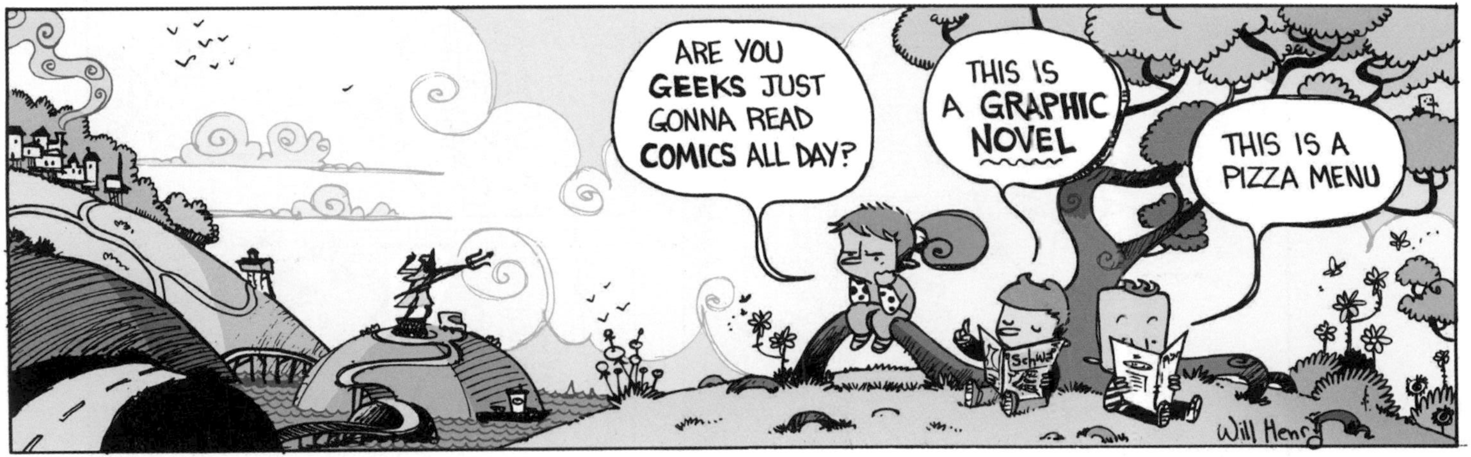
ARE YOU GEEKS JUST GONNA READ COMICS ALL DAY?
THIS IS A GRAPHIC NOVEL
THIS IS A PIZZA MENU
Will Henry

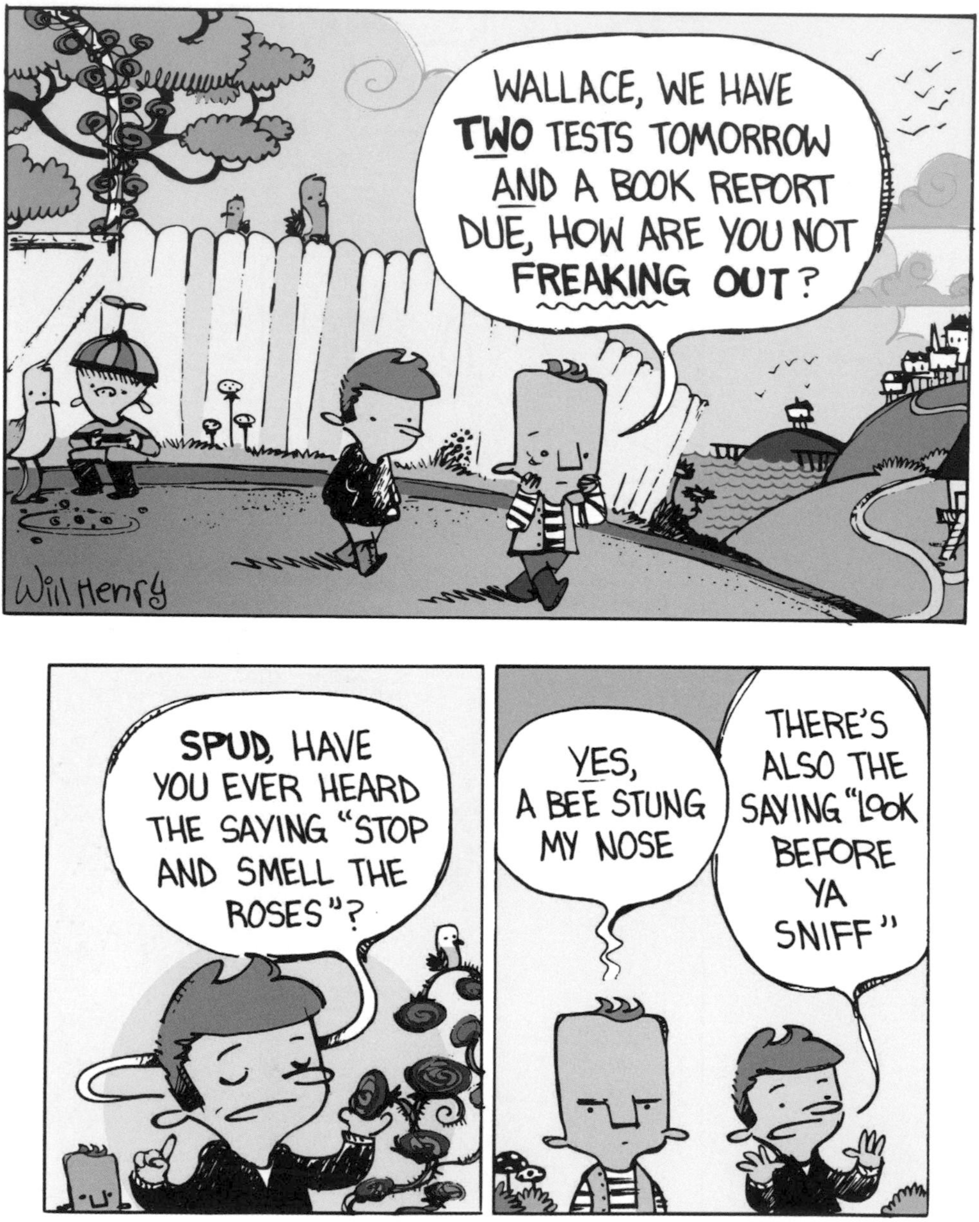
WALLACE, WE HAVE TWO TESTS TOMORROW AND A BOOK REPORT DUE, HOW ARE YOU NOT FREAKING OUT?
Will Henry
SPUD, HAVE YOU EVER HEARD THE SAYING "STOP AND SMELL THE ROSES"?
YES, A BEE STUNG MY NOSE
THERE'S ALSO THE SAYING "LOOK BEFORE YA SNIFF"

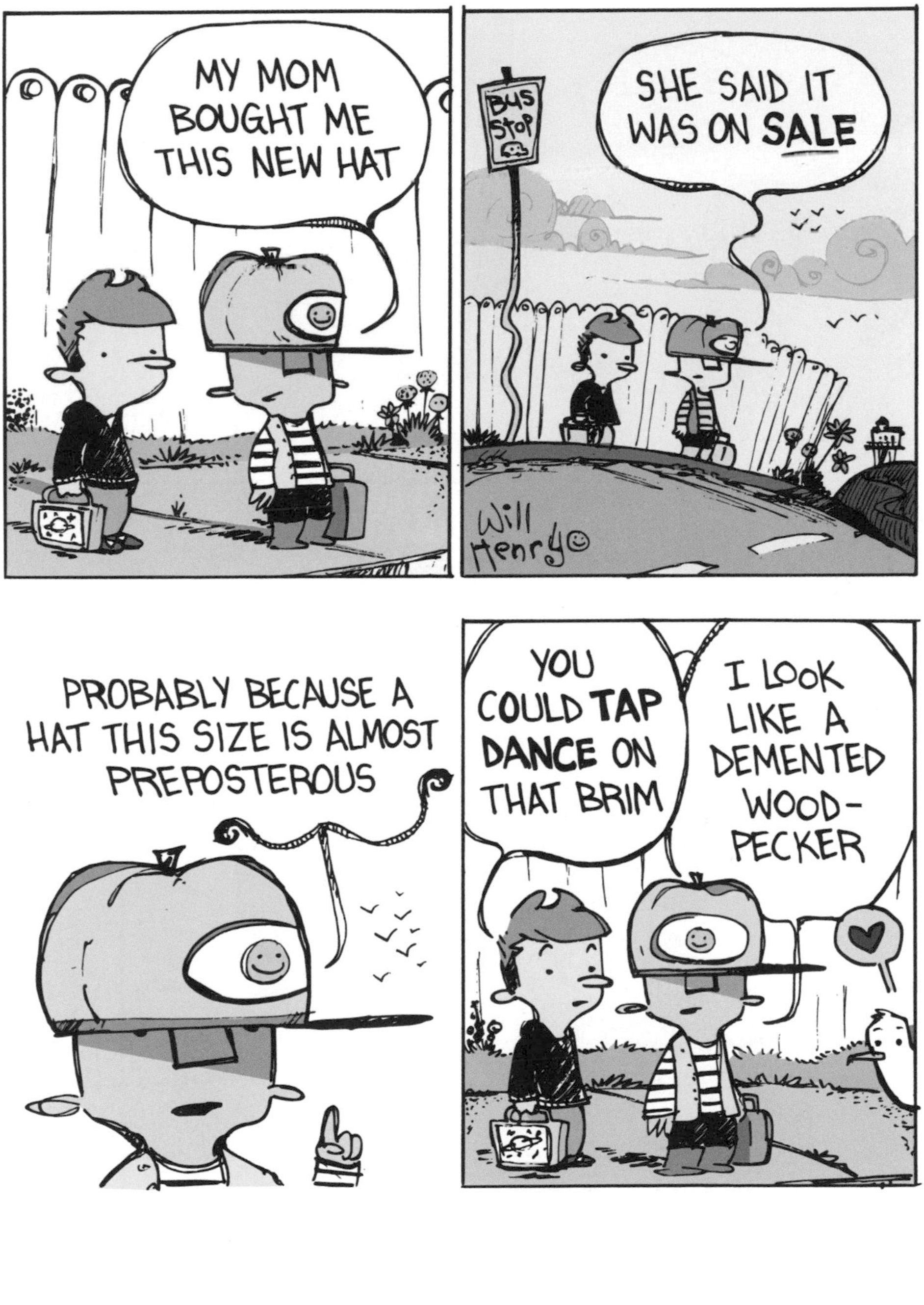
MY MOM BOUGHT ME THIS NEW HAT
BUS STOP
SHE SAID IT WAS ON SALE
Will Henry©
PROBABLY BECAUSE A HAT THIS SIZE IS ALMOST PREPOSTEROUS
YOU COULD TAP DANCE ON THAT BRIM
I LOOK LIKE A DEMENTED WOOD-PECKER

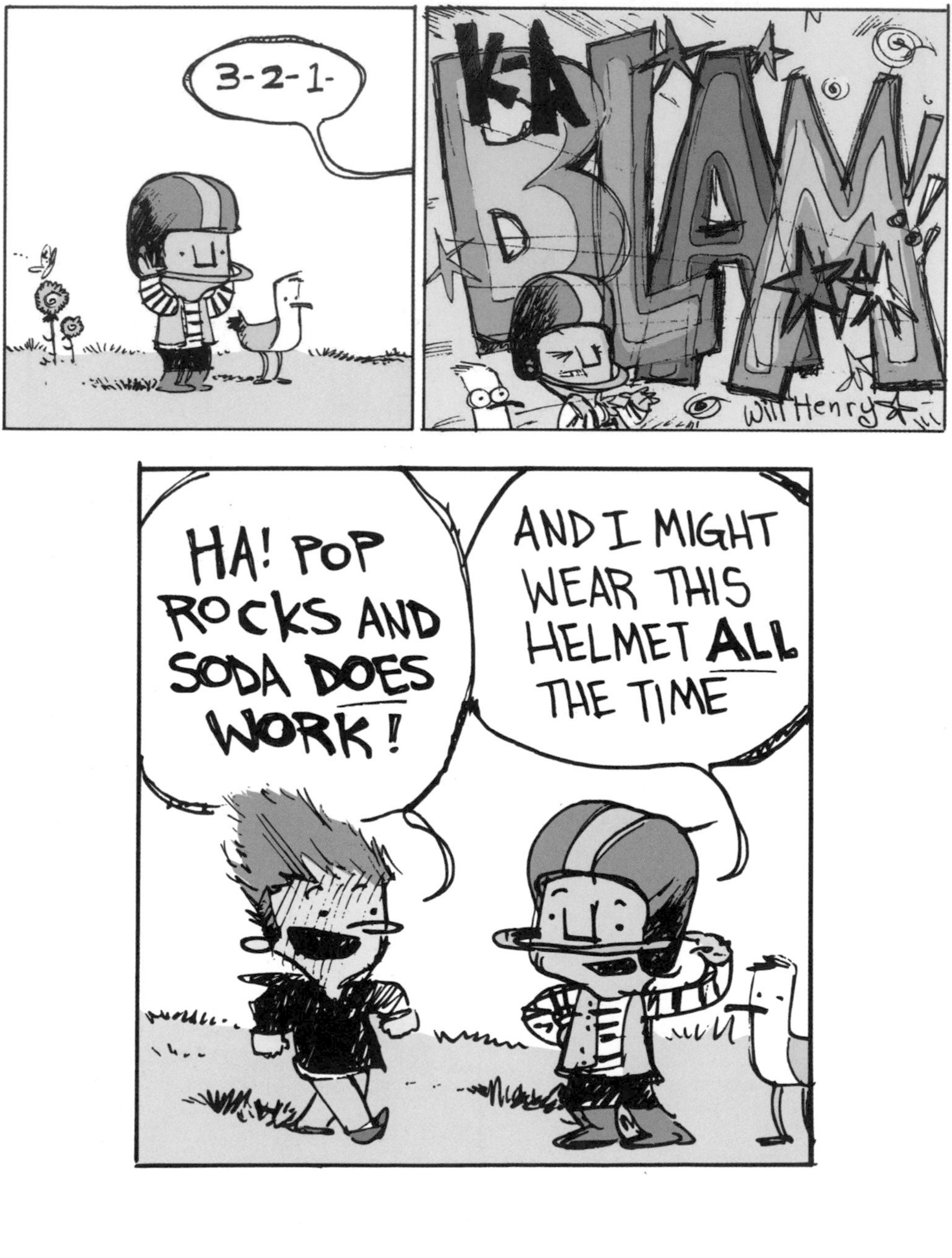
3-2-1-
KA-BLAM!
Will Henry
HA! POP ROCKS AND SODA DOES WORK!
AND I MIGHT WEAR THIS HELMET ALL THE TIME

IF YOU BOYS WATCH ANY MORE OF THAT TELEVISION...
Will Henry
YOU'LL GET SUCKED INTO IT AND BE **TRAPPED**
LET'S CHANGE IT TO THE **FOOD NETWORK**

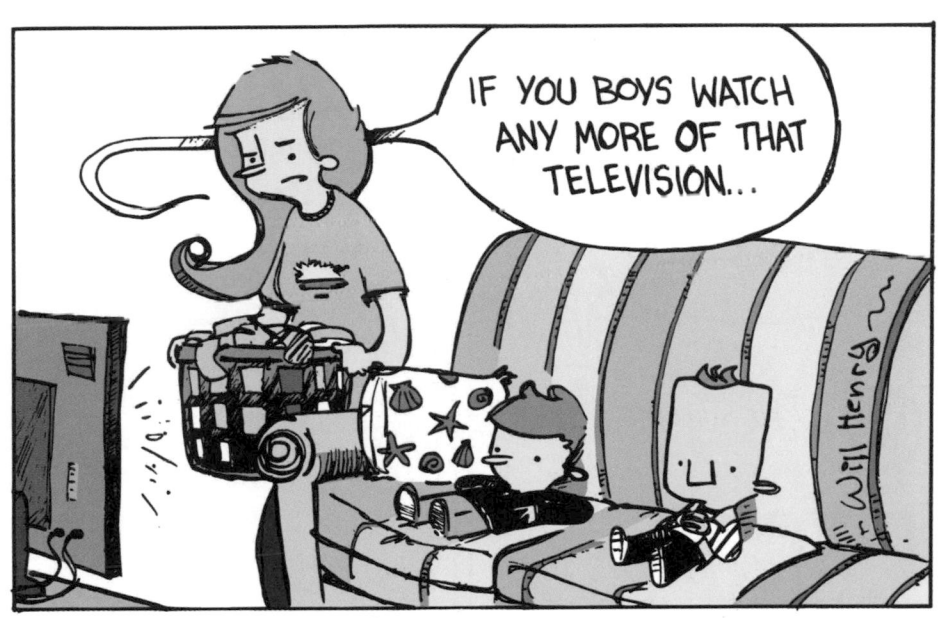

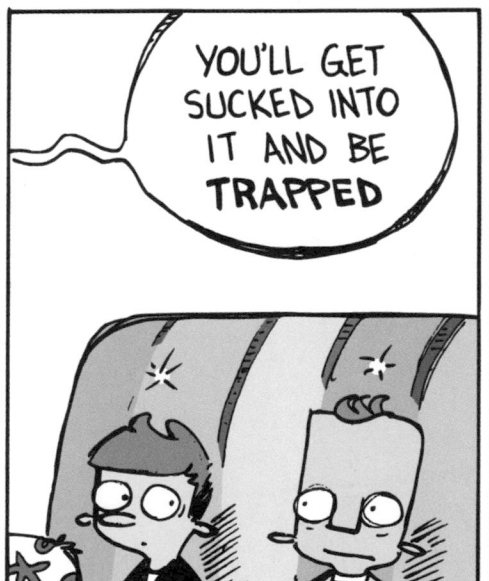

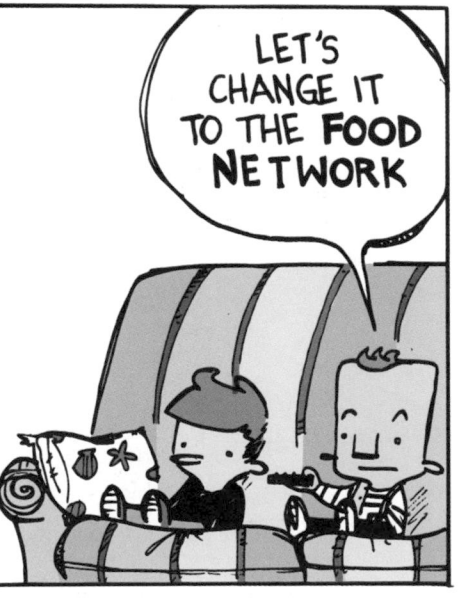

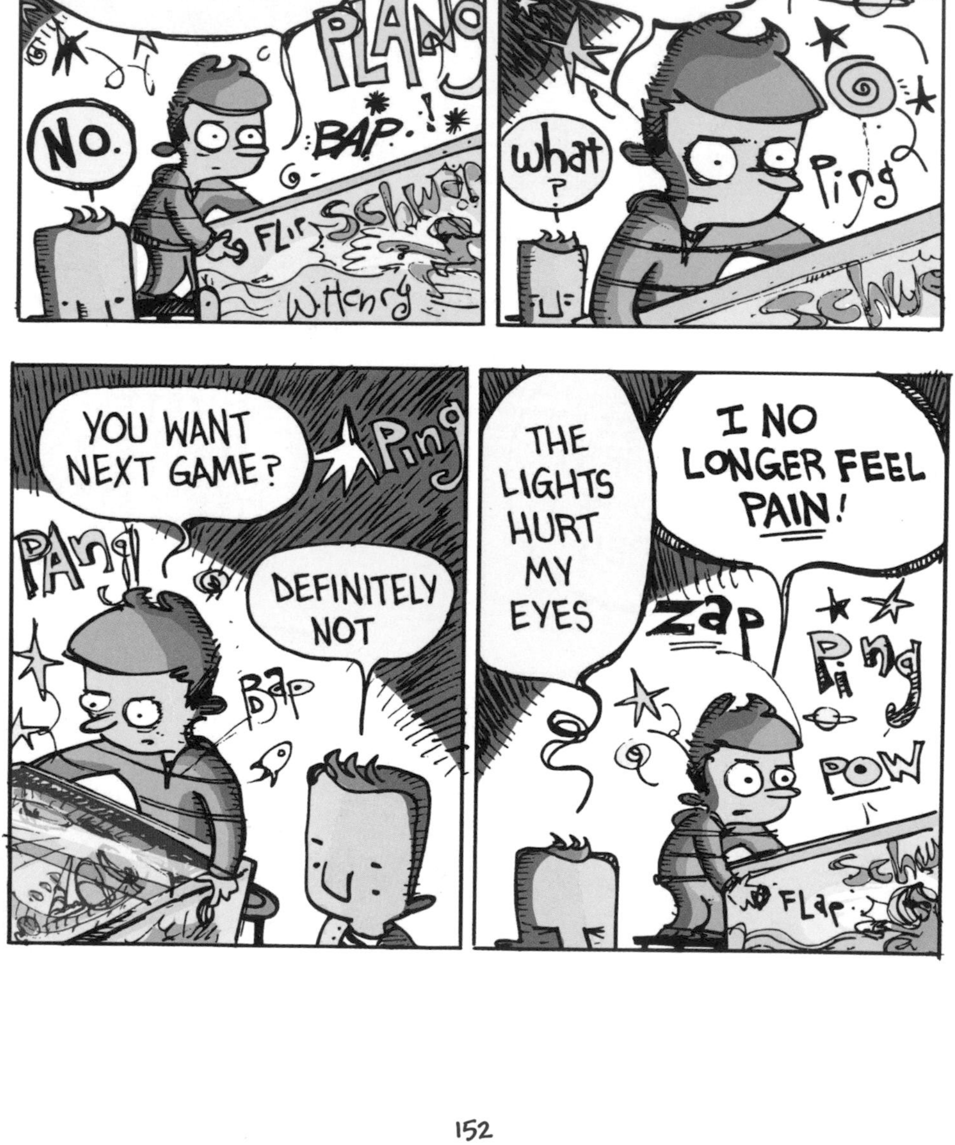
SPUD, WITH THE RIGHT TRAINING YOU COULD BE A PINBALL EXPERT
POW
PLANG
BAP
NO.
FLIP
SCHWAP
W. Henry
ALL WE GOTTA DO IS GET YOU TO TRY IT ONCE!
BLANG
what?
Ping
YOU WANT NEXT GAME?
Ping
PANG
DEFINITELY NOT
BAP
THE LIGHTS HURT MY EYES
I NO LONGER FEEL PAIN!
ZAP
PING
POW
FLAP

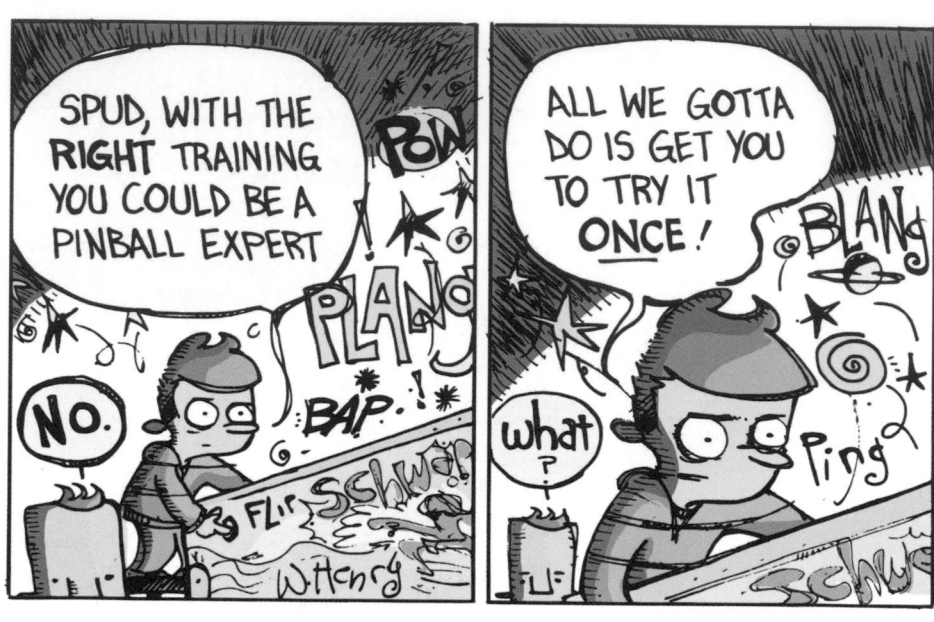

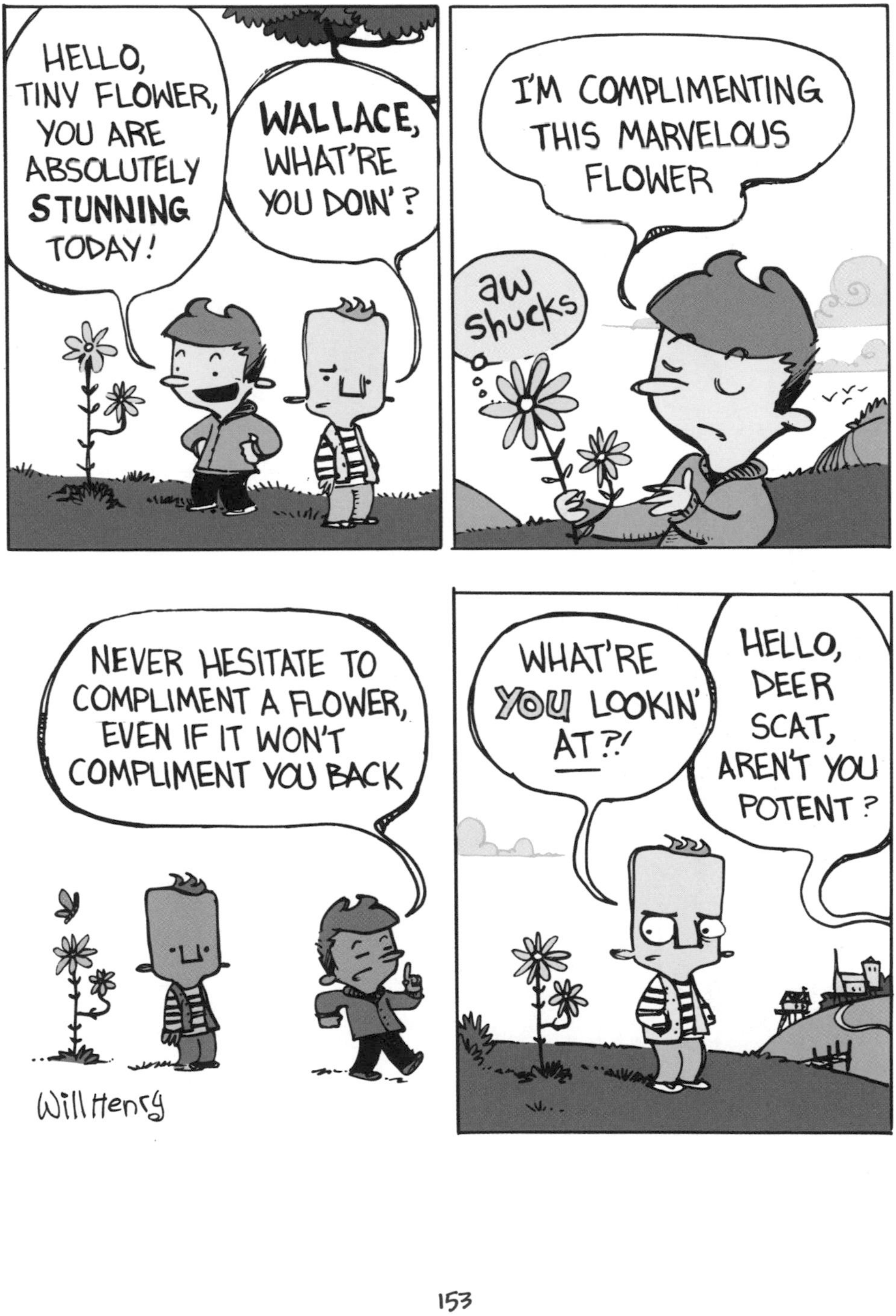
HELLO, TINY FLOWER, YOU ARE ABSOLUTELY STUNNING TODAY!
WALLACE, WHAT'RE YOU DOIN'?
I'M COMPLIMENTING THIS MARVELOUS FLOWER
aw shucks
NEVER HESITATE TO COMPLIMENT A FLOWER, EVEN IF IT WON'T COMPLIMENT YOU BACK
Will Henry
WHAT'RE YOU LOOKIN' AT?!
HELLO, DEER SCAT, AREN'T YOU POTENT?

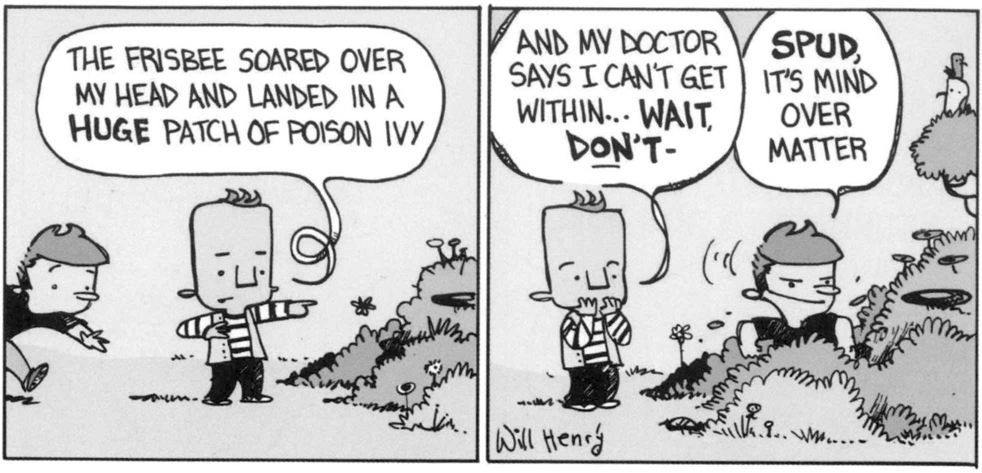
THE FRISBEE SOARED OVER MY HEAD AND LANDED IN A HUGE PATCH OF POISON IVY
AND MY DOCTOR SAYS I CAN'T GET WITHIN... WAIT, DON'T-
SPUD, IT'S MIND OVER MATTER
Will Henry

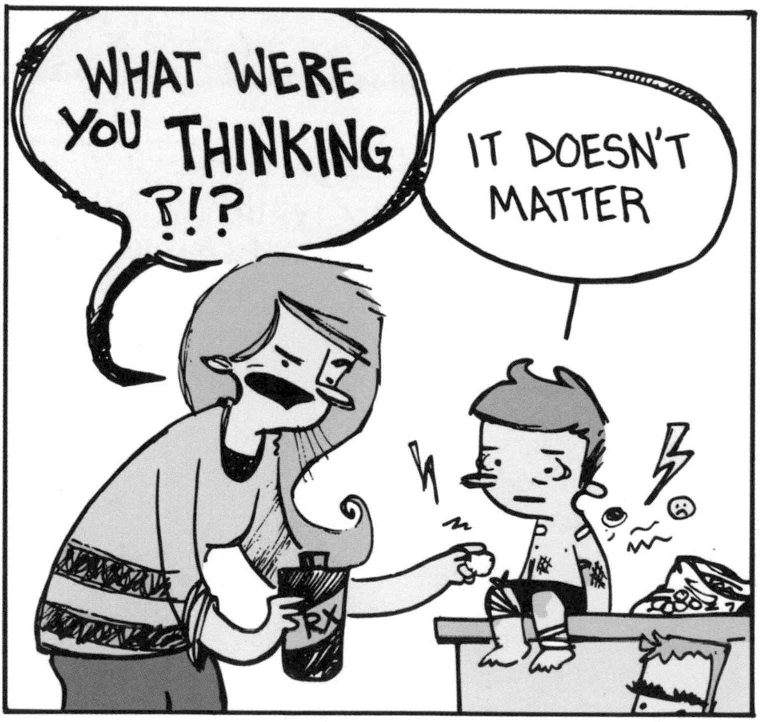
WHAT WERE YOU THINKING ?!?
IT DOESN'T MATTER
RX

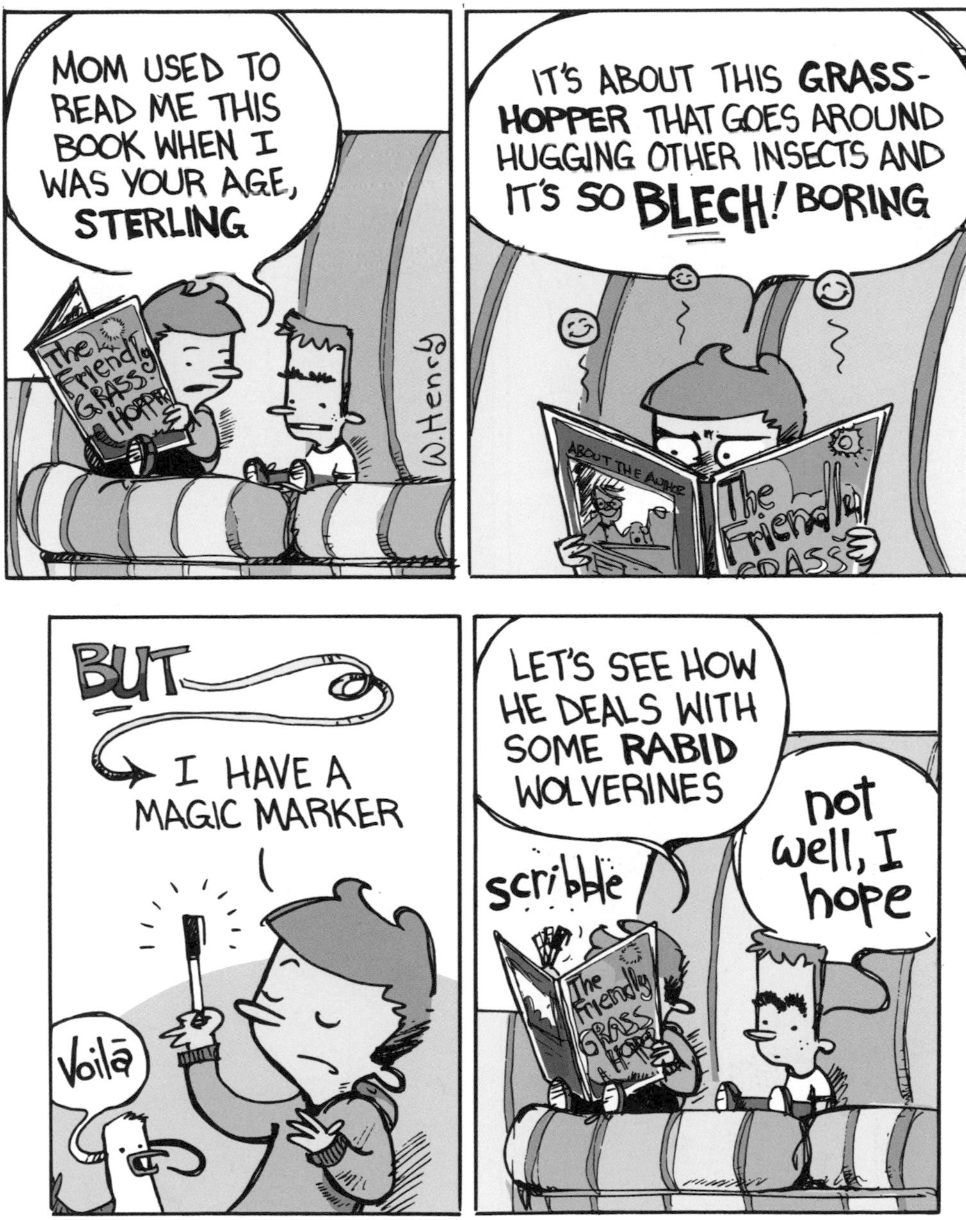
MOM USED TO READ ME THIS BOOK WHEN I WAS YOUR AGE, STERLING
The Friendly GRASS HOPPR
W. Henry
IT'S ABOUT THIS GRASS-HOPPER THAT GOES AROUND HUGGING OTHER INSECTS AND IT'S SO BLECH! BORING
ABOUT THE AUTHOR
The Friendly GRASS
BUT
I HAVE A MAGIC MARKER
Voilà
LET'S SEE HOW HE DEALS WITH SOME RABID WOLVERINES
scribble
not well, I hope
The Friendly GRASS HOPP

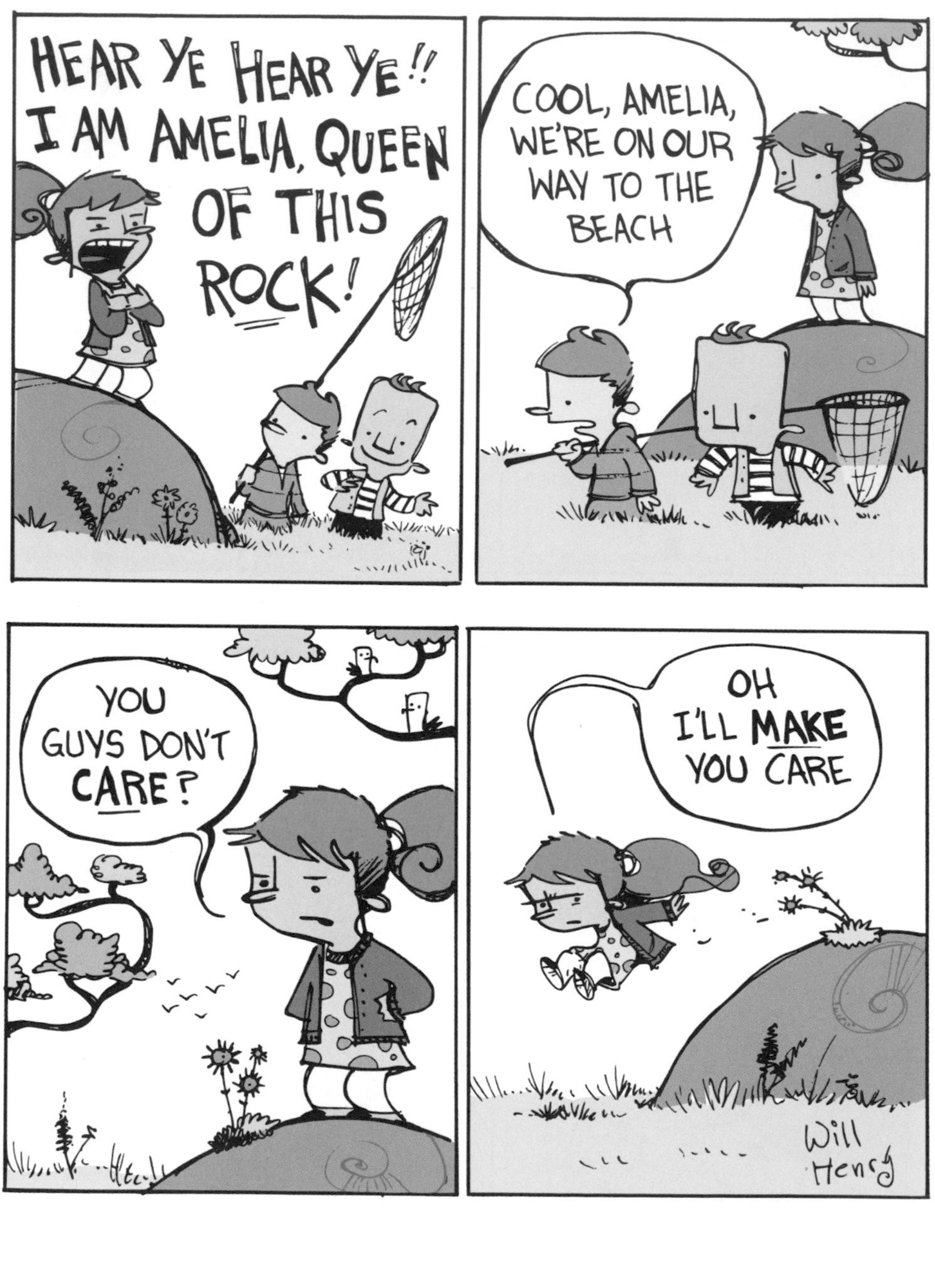
HEAR YE HEAR YE!! I AM AMELIA, QUEEN OF THIS ROCK!
COOL, AMELIA, WE'RE ON OUR WAY TO THE BEACH
YOU GUYS DON'T CARE?
OH I'LL MAKE YOU CARE
Will Henry

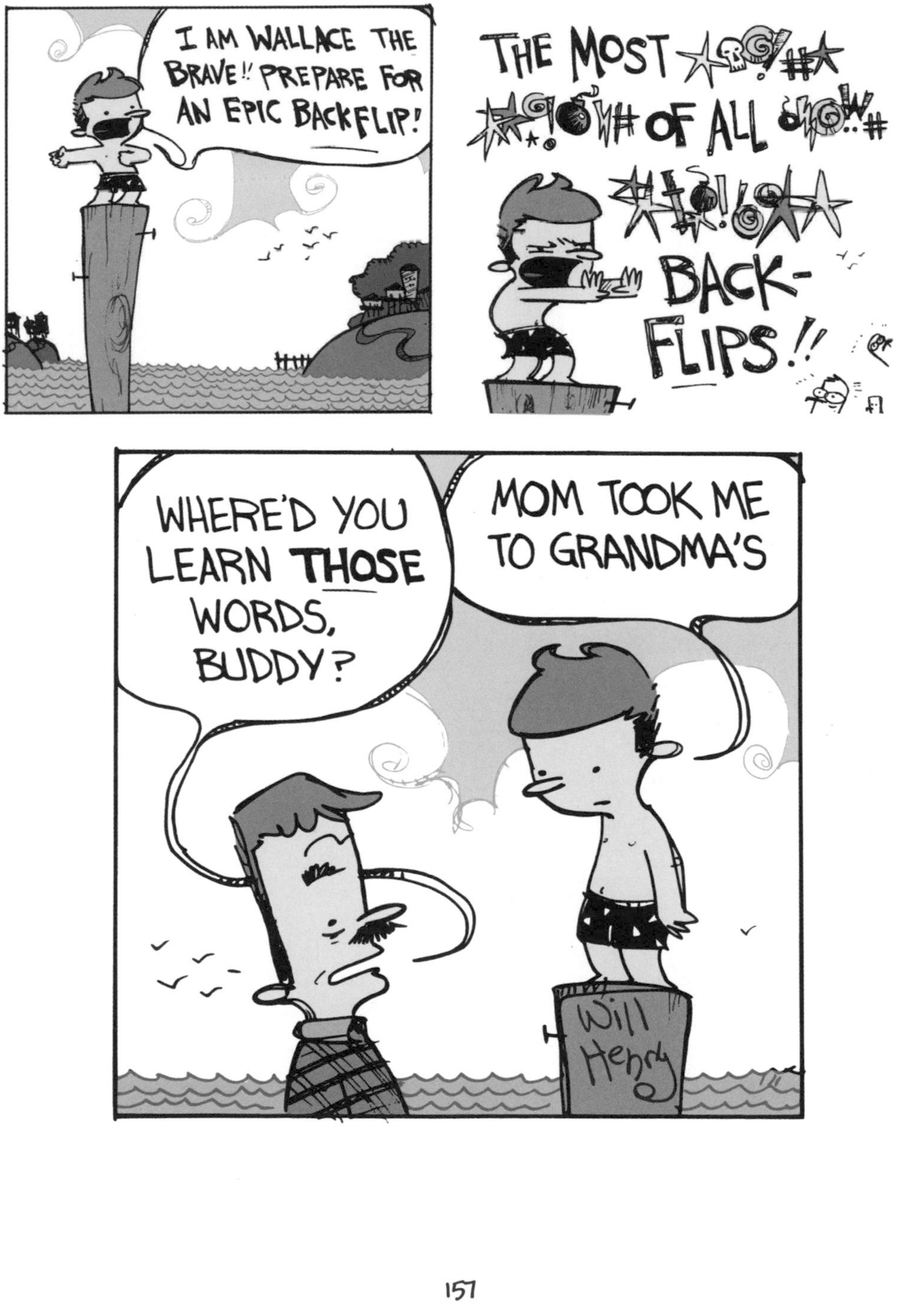
I AM WALLACE THE BRAVE!! PREPARE FOR AN EPIC BACKFLIP!
THE MOST OF ALL BACK-FLIPS!!
WHERE'D YOU LEARN THOSE WORDS, BUDDY?
MOM TOOK ME TO GRANDMA'S
Will Henry

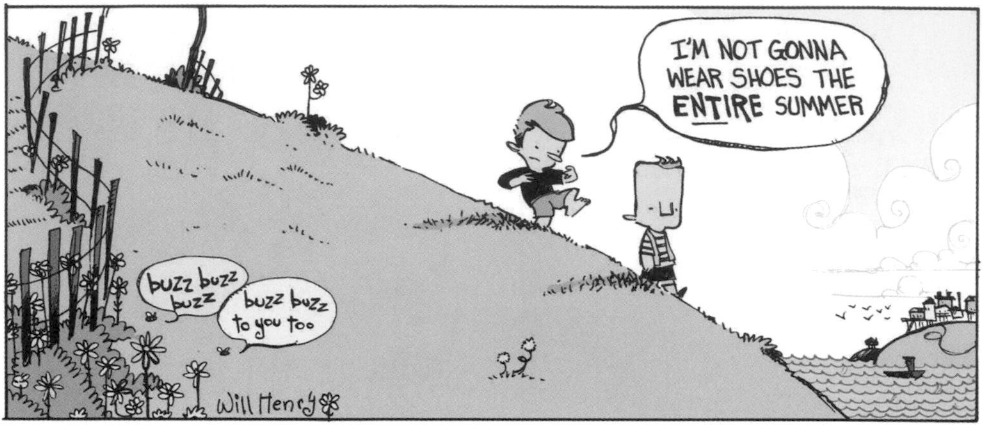
I'M NOT GONNA WEAR SHOES THE ENTIRE SUMMER
buzz buzz buzz
buzz buzz to you too
Will Henry

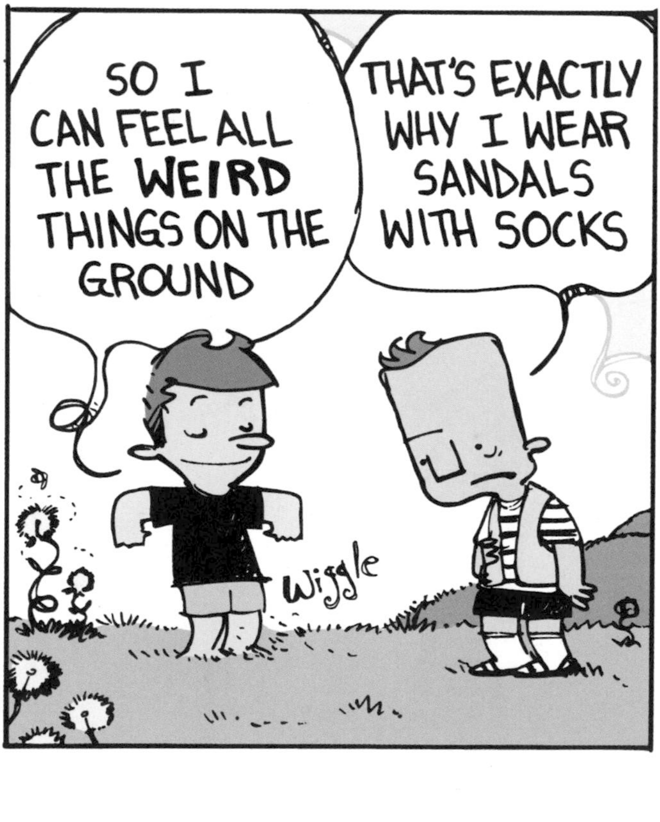
SO I CAN FEEL ALL THE WEIRD THINGS ON THE GROUND
THAT'S EXACTLY WHY I WEAR SANDALS WITH SOCKS
Wiggle

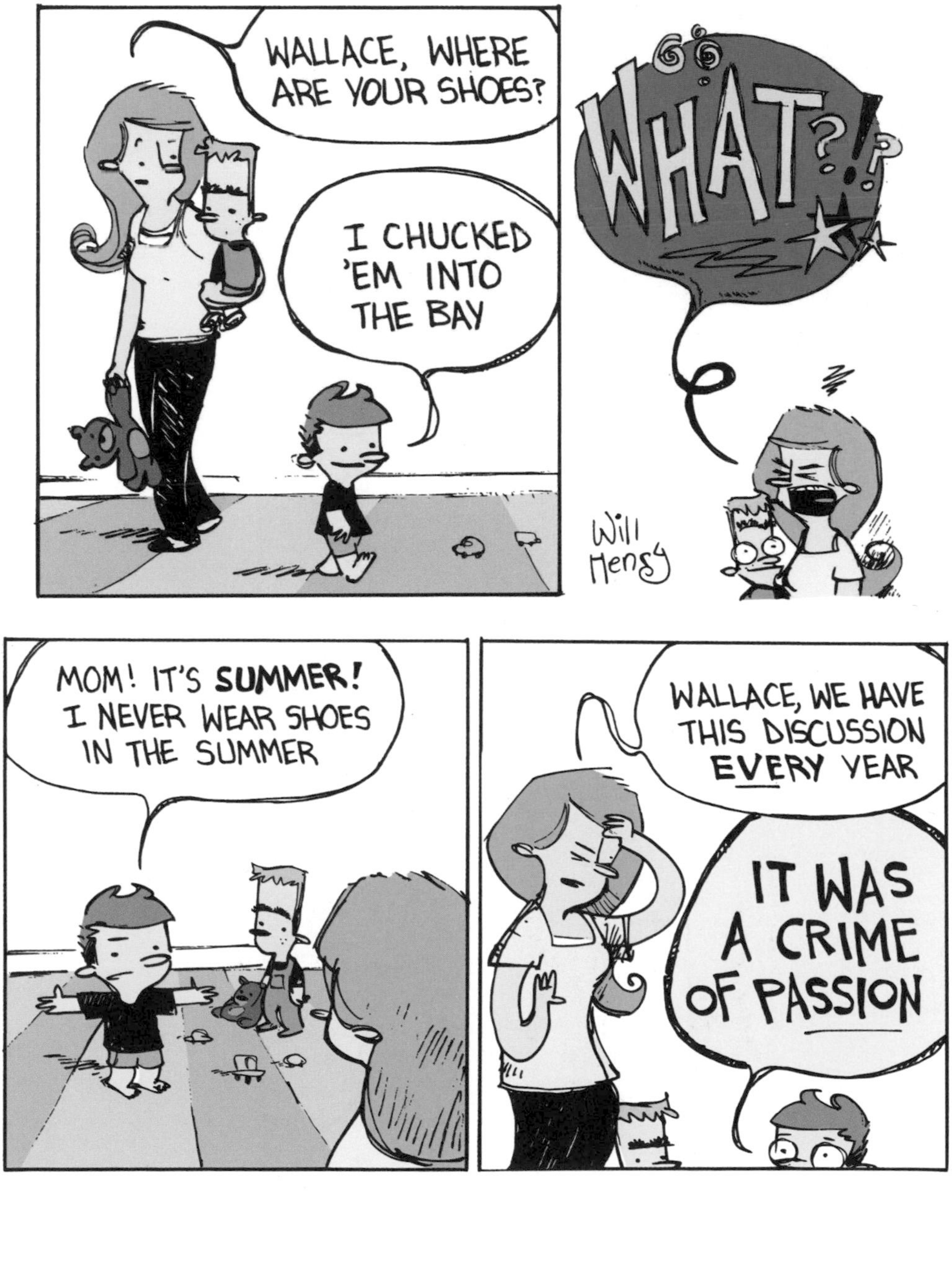
WALLACE, WHERE ARE YOUR SHOES?
I CHUCKED 'EM INTO THE BAY
WHAT?!?
Will Hensy
MOM! IT'S **SUMMER!** I NEVER WEAR SHOES IN THE SUMMER
WALLACE, WE HAVE THIS DISCUSSION EVERY YEAR
IT WAS A CRIME OF PASSION

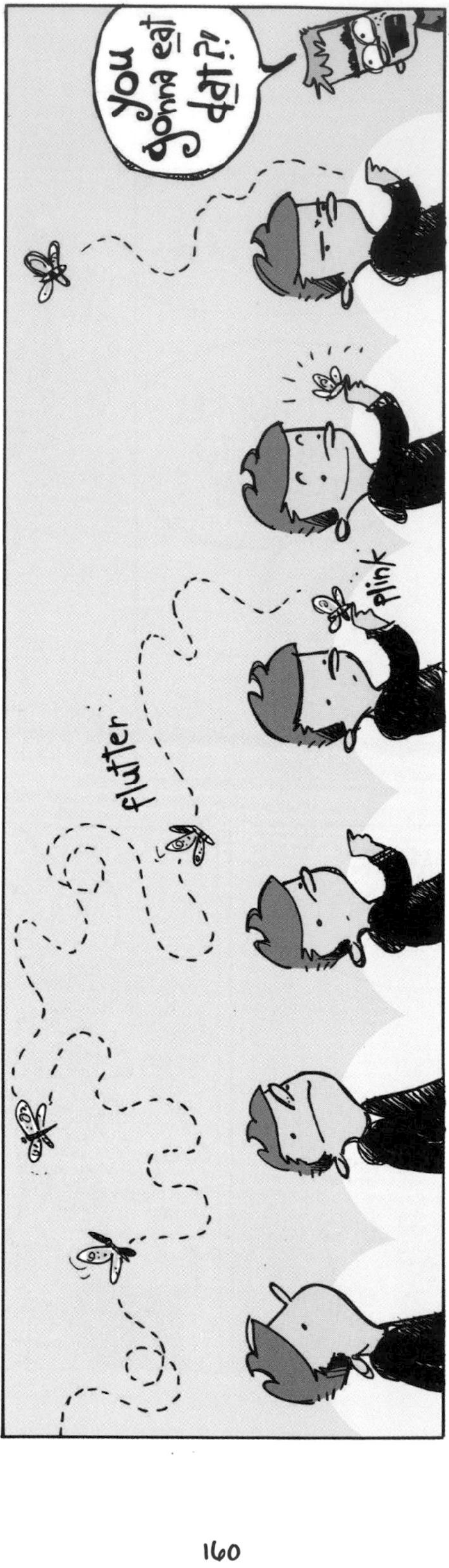
flutter
plink
You gonna eat dat?!

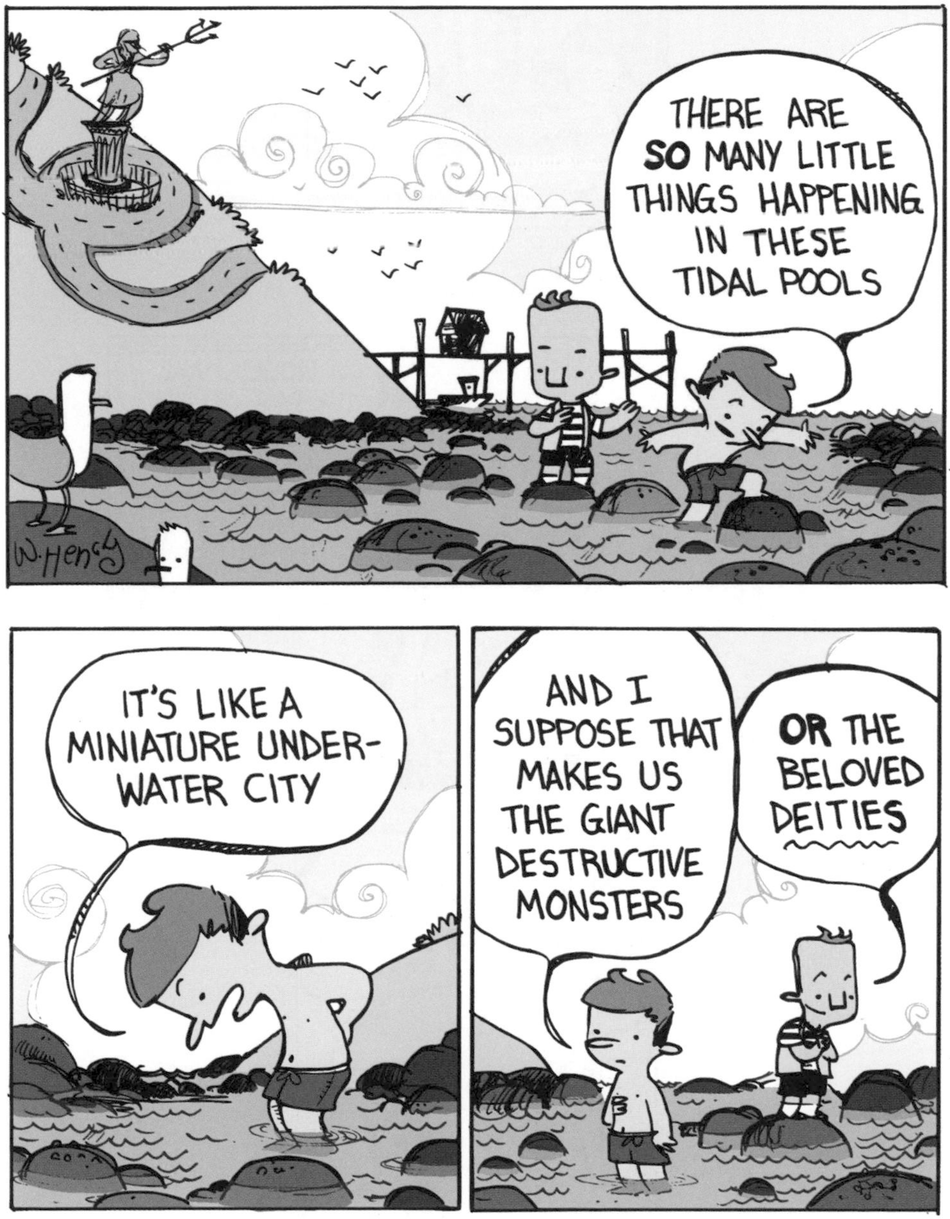
W. Hensly
THERE ARE **SO** MANY LITTLE THINGS HAPPENING IN THESE TIDAL POOLS
IT'S LIKE A MINIATURE UNDER-WATER CITY
AND I SUPPOSE THAT MAKES US THE GIANT DESTRUCTIVE MONSTERS
OR THE BELOVED DEITIES

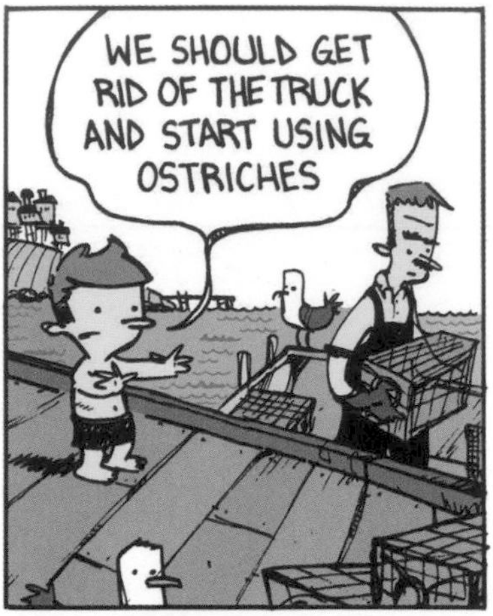
WE SHOULD GET RID OF THE TRUCK AND START USING OSTRICHES

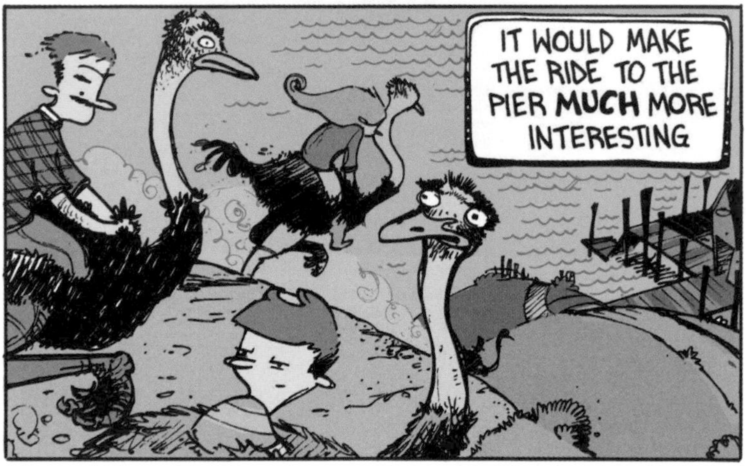
IT WOULD MAKE THE RIDE TO THE PIER **MUCH** MORE INTERESTING

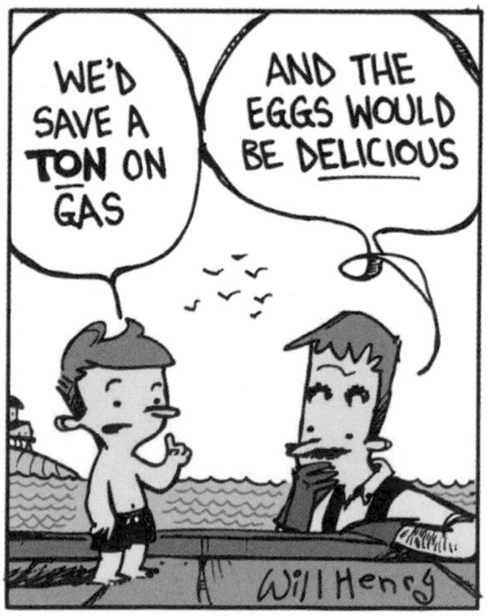
WE'D SAVE A **TON** ON GAS
AND THE EGGS WOULD BE DELICIOUS
Will Henry

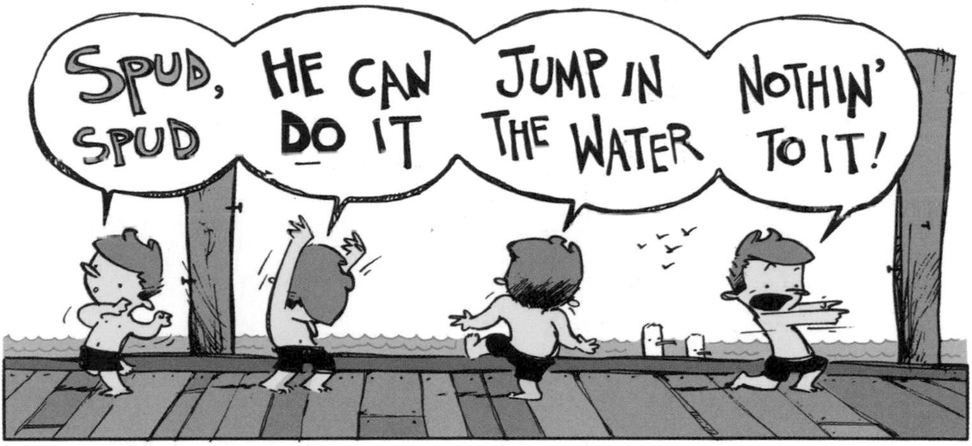
SPUD, SPUD
HE CAN DO IT
JUMP IN THE WATER
NOTHIN' TO IT!

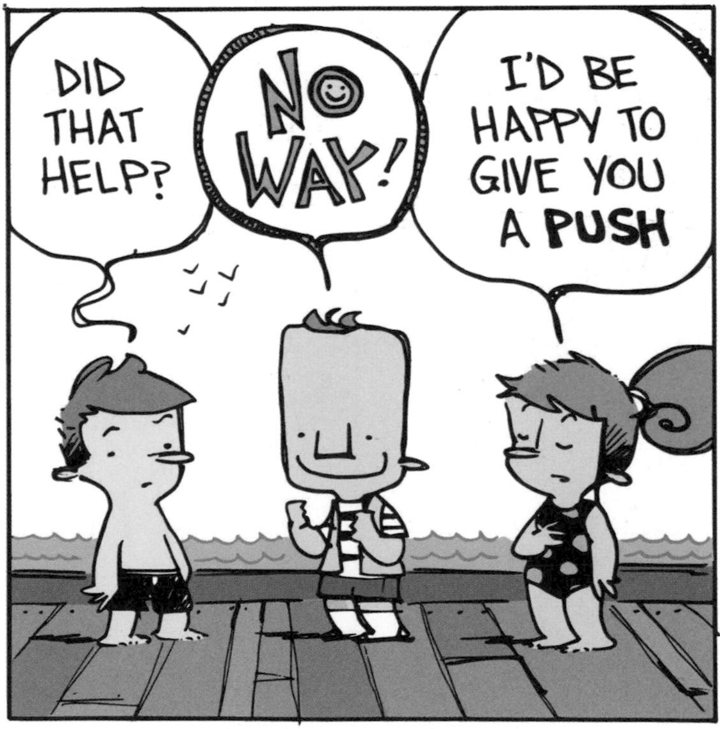
DID THAT HELP?
NO WAY!
I'D BE HAPPY TO GIVE YOU A PUSH

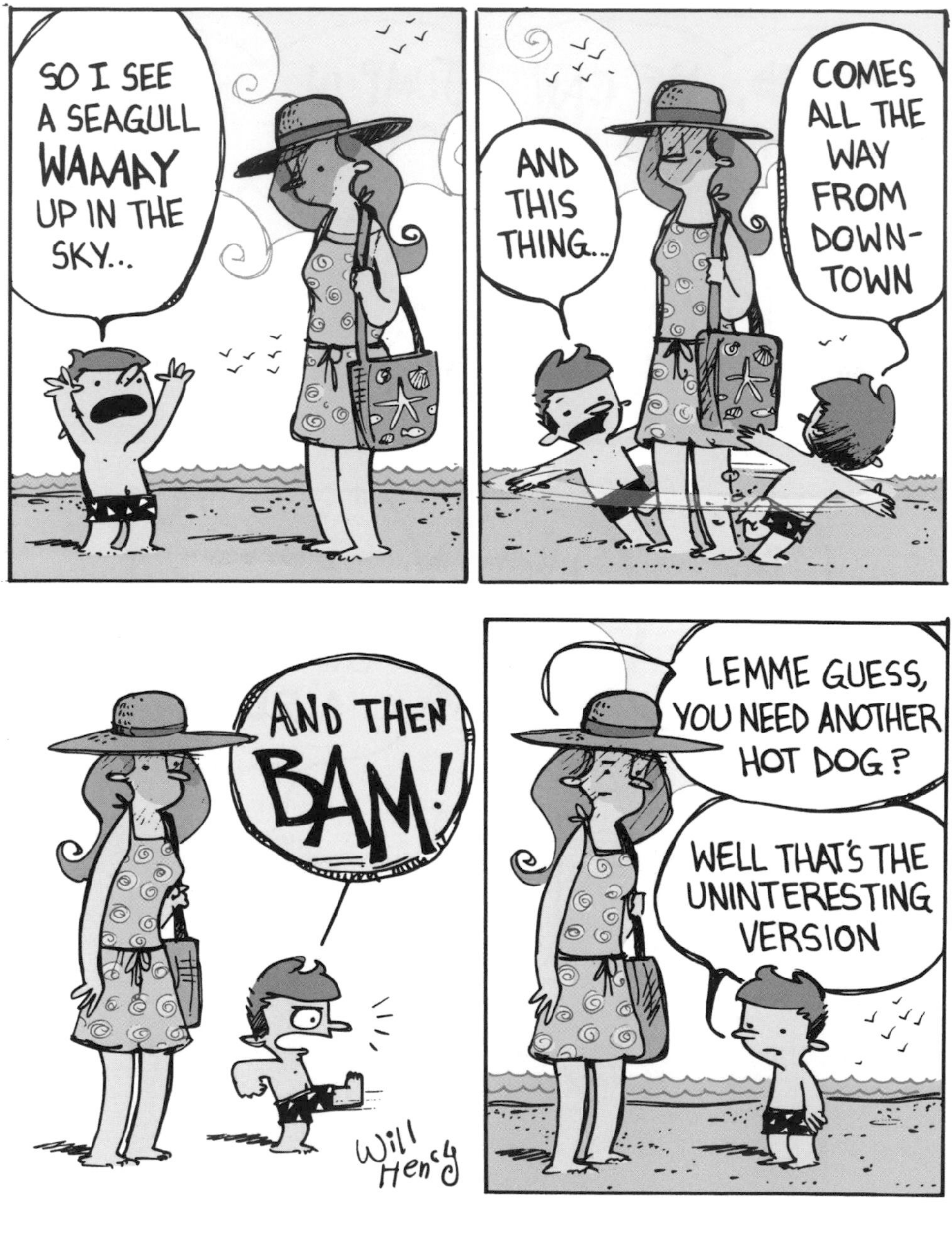
SO I SEE A SEAGULL WAAAAY UP IN THE SKY...
AND THIS THING...
COMES ALL THE WAY FROM DOWN-TOWN
AND THEN BAM!
LEMME GUESS, YOU NEED ANOTHER HOT DOG?
WELL THAT'S THE UNINTERESTING VERSION
Will Henry

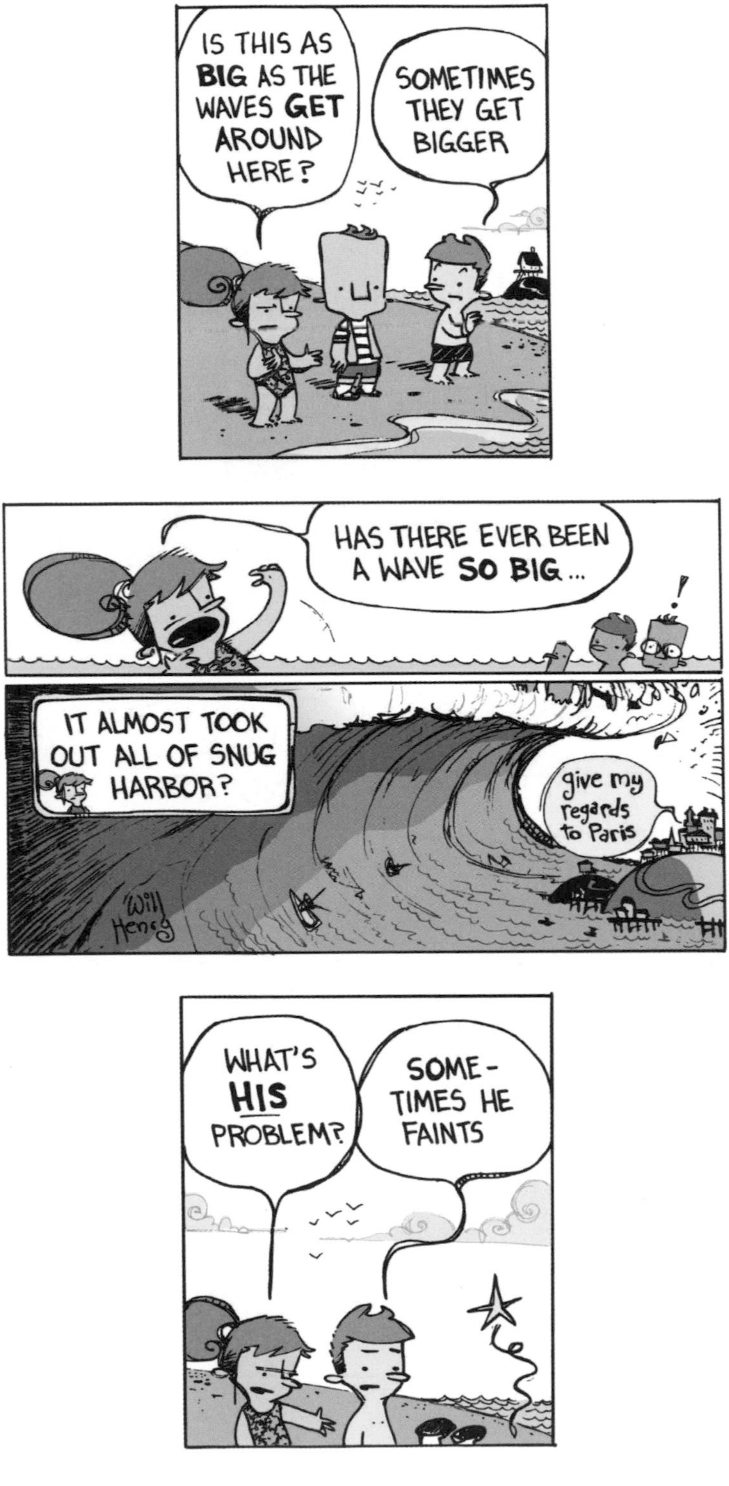
IS THIS AS **BIG** AS THE WAVES **GET** AROUND HERE?
SOMETIMES THEY GET BIGGER
HAS THERE EVER BEEN A WAVE **SO BIG**...
!
IT ALMOST TOOK OUT ALL OF SNUG HARBOR?
give my regards to Paris
Will Henry
WHAT'S **HIS** PROBLEM?
SOME-TIMES HE FAINTS

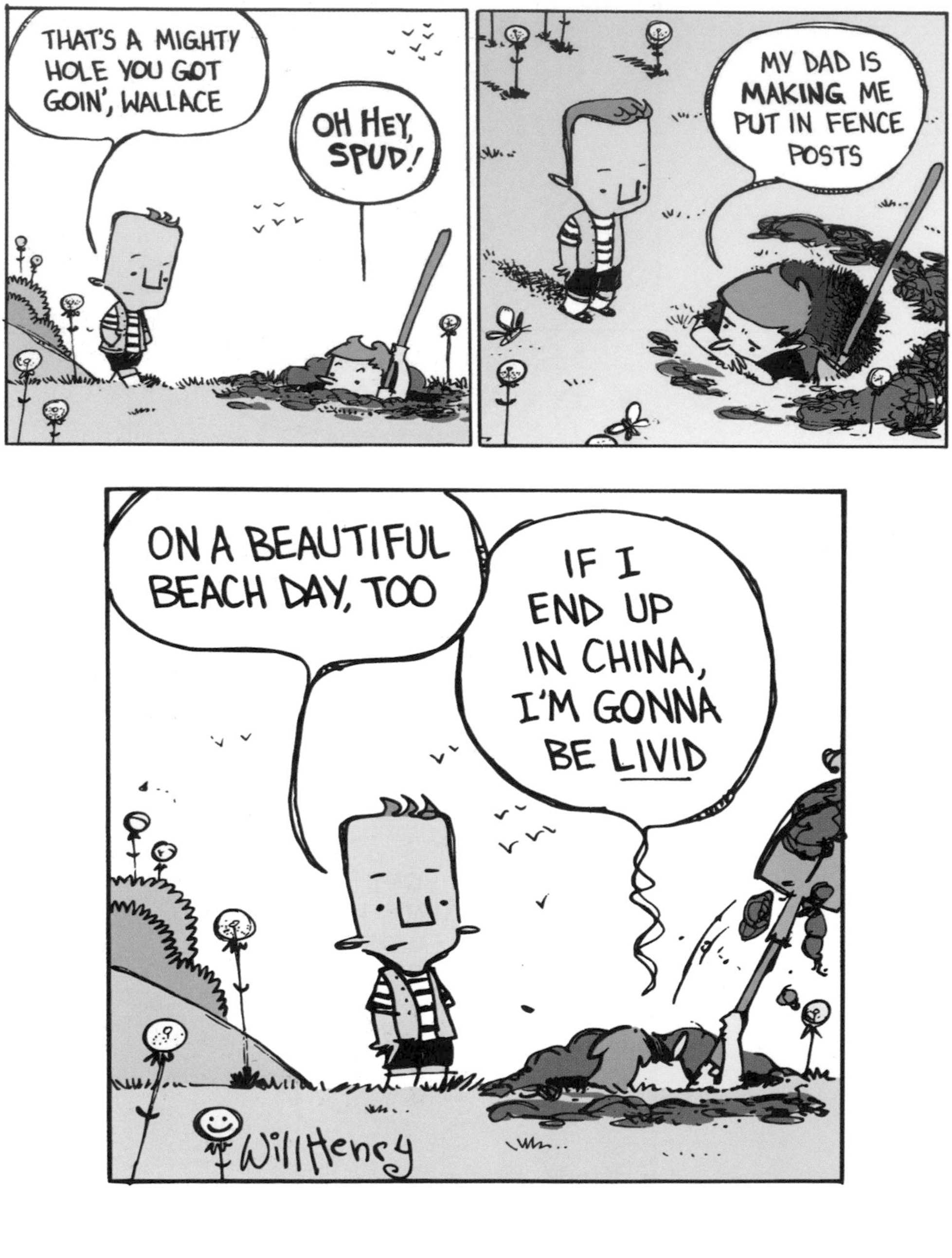
THAT'S A MIGHTY HOLE YOU GOT GOIN', WALLACE
OH HEY, SPUD!
MY DAD IS MAKING ME PUT IN FENCE POSTS
ON A BEAUTIFUL BEACH DAY, TOO
IF I END UP IN CHINA, I'M GONNA BE LIVID
Will Henry

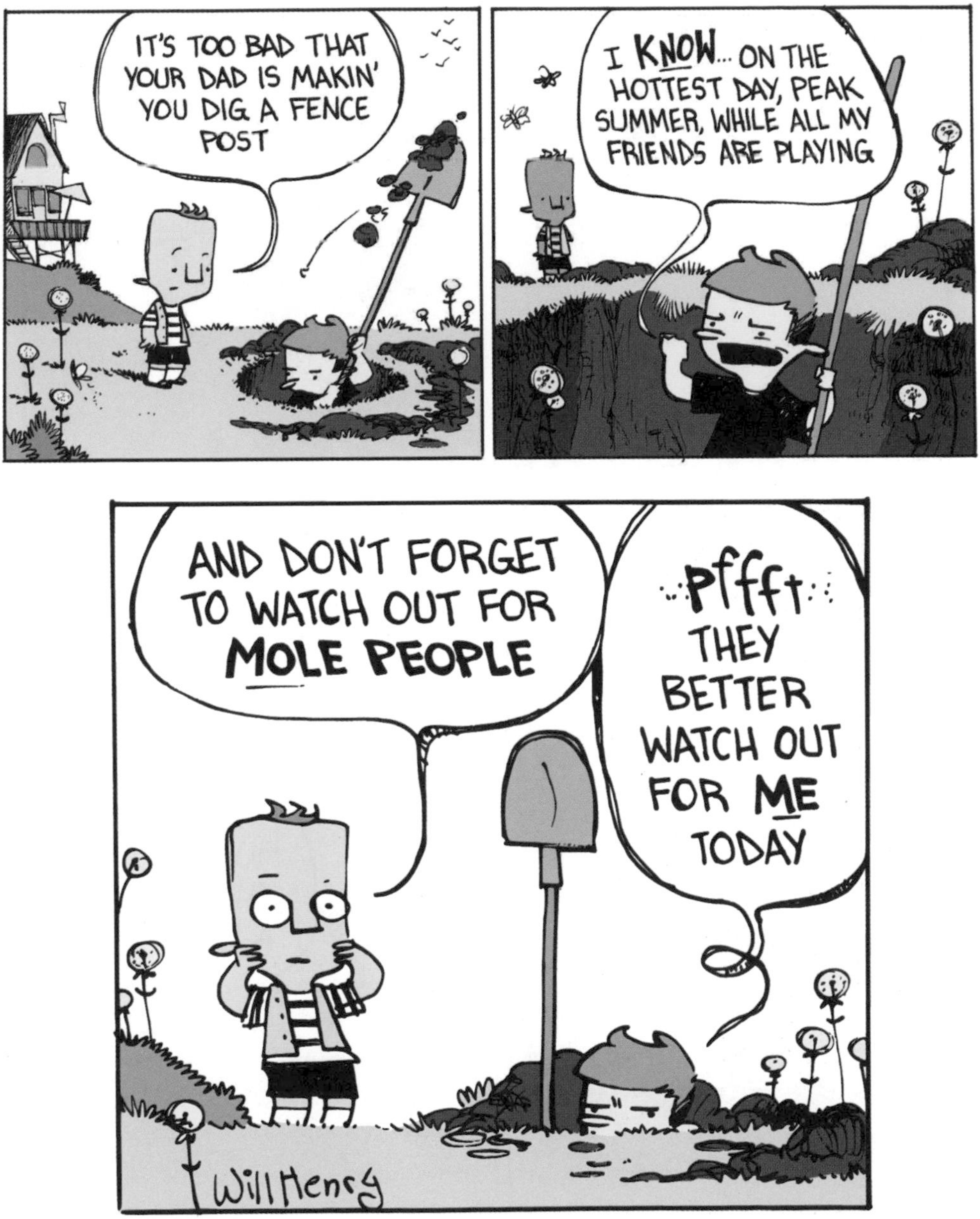
IT'S TOO BAD THAT YOUR DAD IS MAKIN' YOU DIG A FENCE POST
I KNOW... ON THE HOTTEST DAY, PEAK SUMMER, WHILE ALL MY FRIENDS ARE PLAYING
AND DON'T FORGET TO WATCH OUT FOR MOLE PEOPLE
Pffft THEY BETTER WATCH OUT FOR ME TODAY
Will Henry

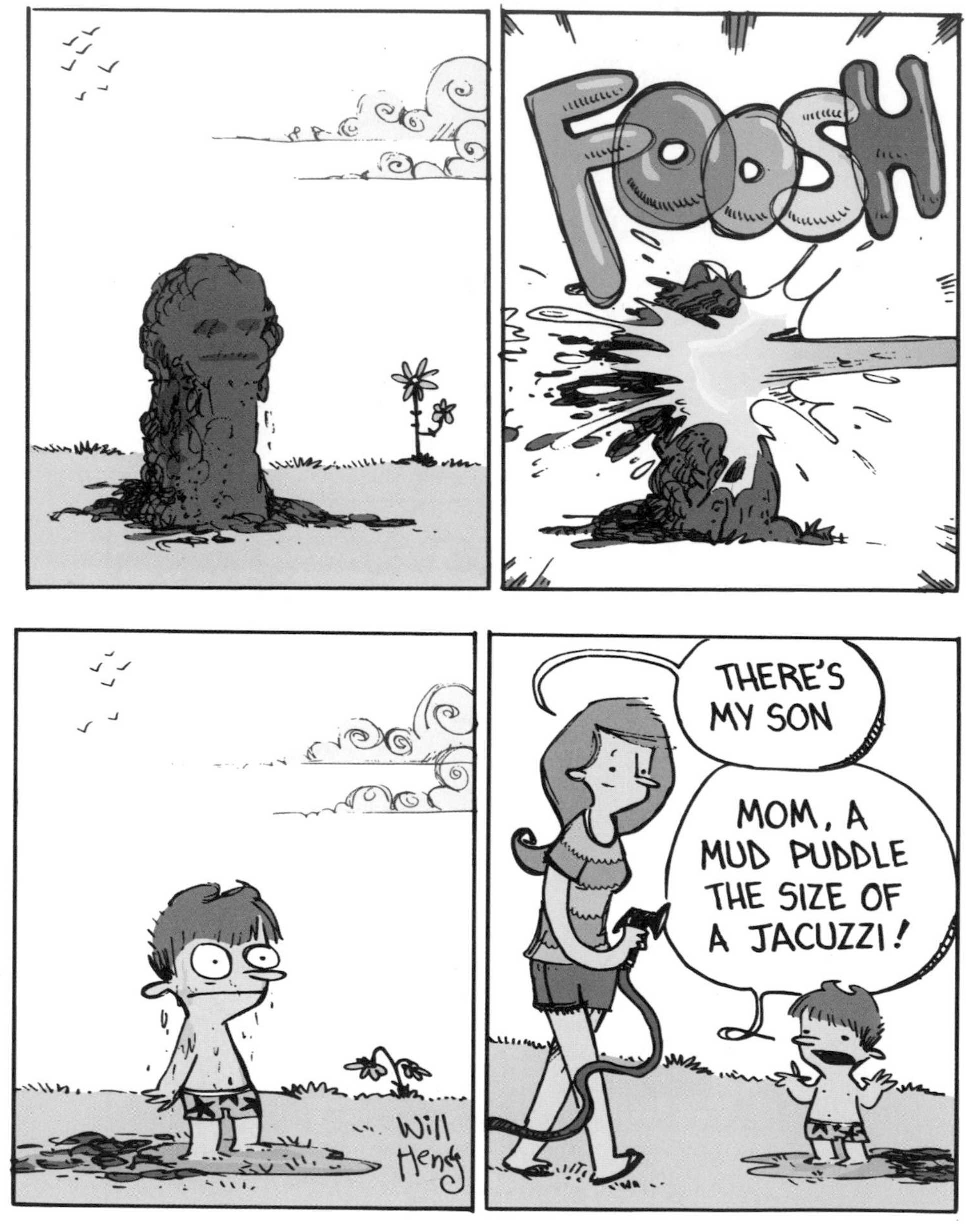
FOOSH
THERE'S MY SON
MOM, A MUD PUDDLE THE SIZE OF A JACUZZI!
Will Henry

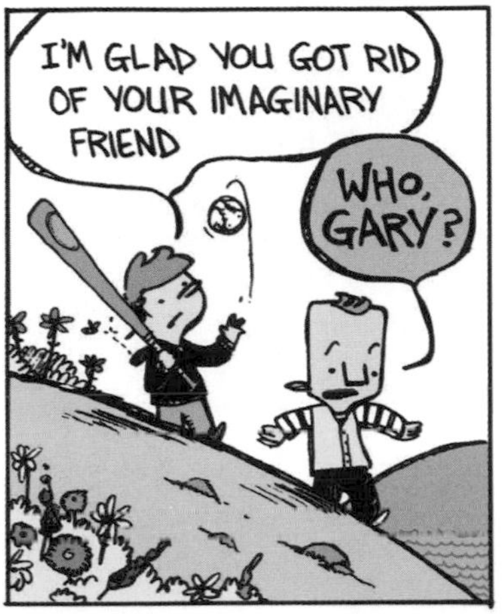
I'M GLAD YOU GOT RID OF YOUR IMAGINARY FRIEND
WHO, GARY?

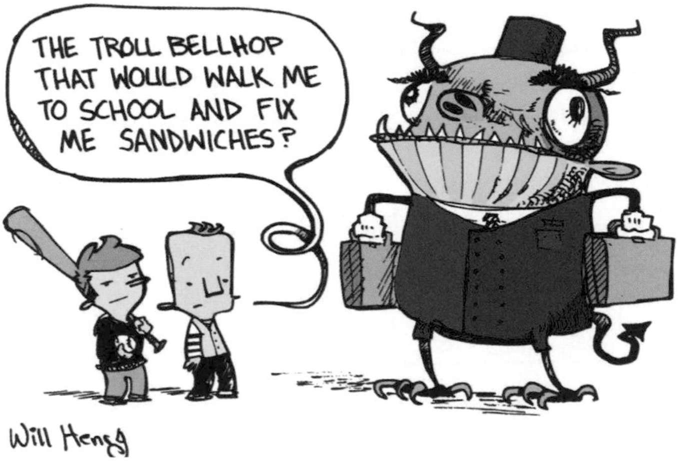
THE TROLL BELLHOP THAT WOULD WALK ME TO SCHOOL AND FIX ME SANDWICHES?
Will Henry

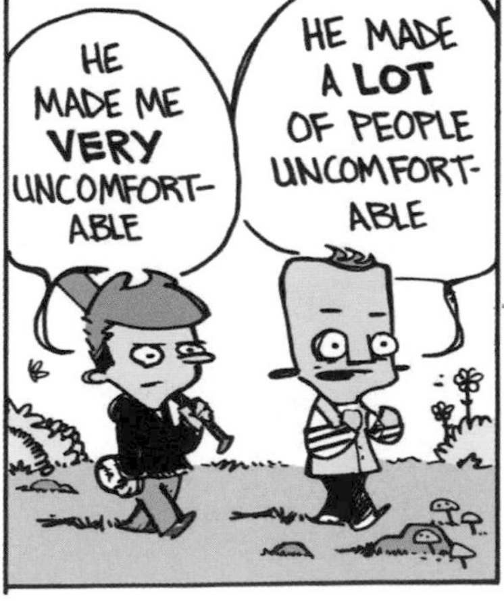
HE MADE ME **VERY** UNCOMFORT-ABLE
HE MADE A **LOT** OF PEOPLE UNCOMFORT-ABLE

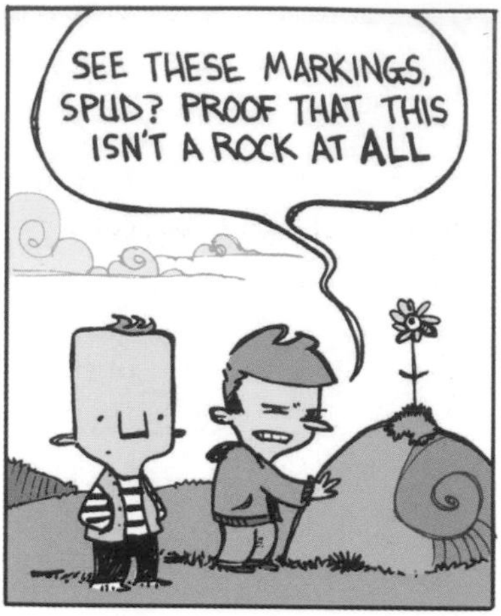
SEE THESE MARKINGS, SPUD? PROOF THAT THIS ISN'T A ROCK AT ALL

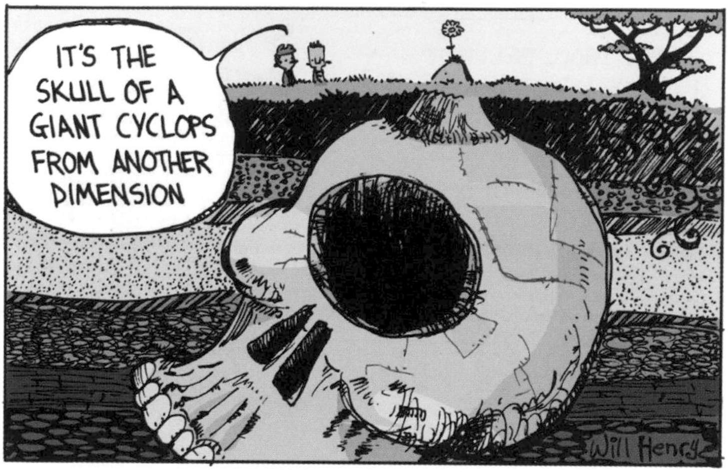
IT'S THE SKULL OF A GIANT CYCLOPS FROM ANOTHER DIMENSION
Will Henry

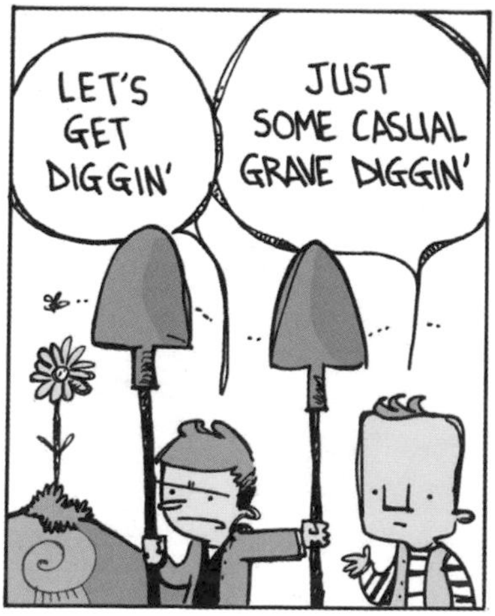
LET'S GET DIGGIN'
JUST SOME CASUAL GRAVE DIGGIN'

MORE TO EXPLORE!
A special section featuring fun activities!

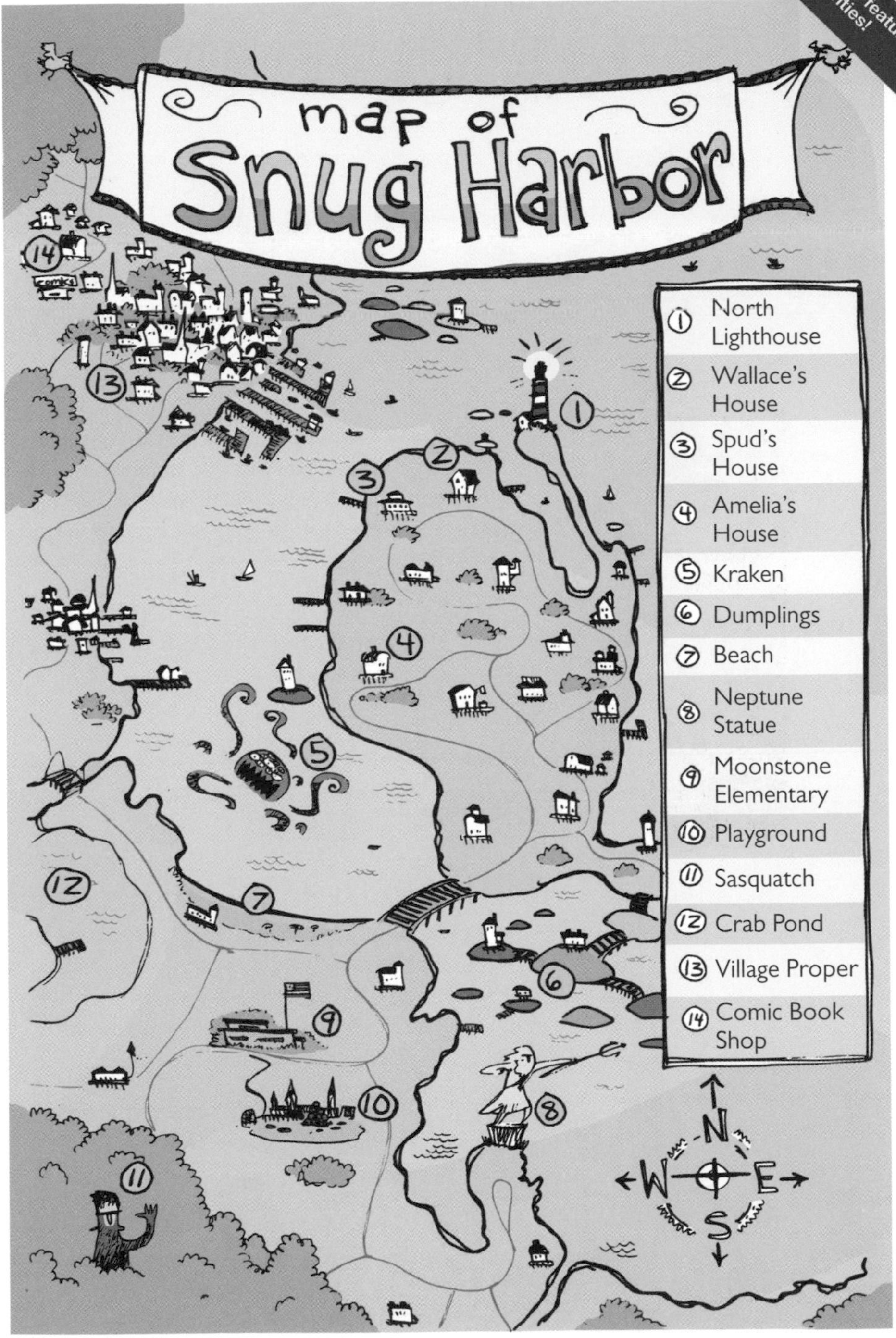

map of
Snug Harbor
comics
1 North Lighthouse
2 Wallace's House
3 Spud's House
4 Amelia's House
5 Kraken
6 Dumplings
7 Beach
8 Neptune Statue
9 Moonstone Elementary
10 Playground
11 Sasquatch
12 Crab Pond
13 Village Proper
14 Comic Book Shop
N
W
E
S

ORGANIZE A
BEACH CLEANUP

much better

...yeck?

Each year, trash in the ocean kills more than one million seabirds and 100,000 marine mammals and turtles. You can do your part by organizing a beach cleanup with you and your friends.

WHAT YOU'LL NEED:

Large buckets or garbage bags

Rubber gloves

Pokey things

An adult

TIPS FOR ORGANIZING A BEACH CLEANUP
- Put up flyers or start a social media campaign
- Bring sunscreen and water, it gets hot out there
- Pick a designated, manageable area to clean
- Go early in the morning or later in the day to avoid crowds
- Dispose collected litter in proper location
- Bring your friends and make it fun!

NATURE CROWN

Make a radical crown from nature's bounty!

WHAT YOU'LL NEED:

Empty cereal box

Scissors

Stapler

Colorful leaves and flowers

Start by unfolding the cardboard cereal box.

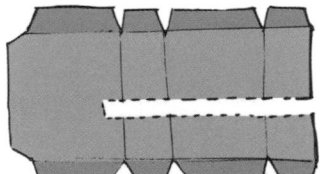

snip snip

Next, cut out a long, cardboard strip.

Perf

Arrange leaves, twigs, and flowers along cardboard strip and staple in place.

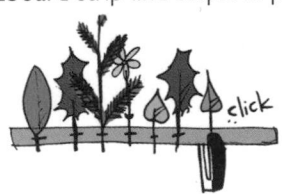

click

Once attached, bend the cardboard in a circle and staple together.

Finally, place crown on head and become kings of the forest.

MONARCH BUTTERFLIES!

Ever wanted to help a monarch butterfly? It's super easy!

oh, hello
hi
munch munch

You can find monarch butterfly larva or caterpillars located on the underside of milkweed plants. They have a soft look with yellow, white, and black stripes.

das me

The caterpillar will feel right at home in a glass jar. Make sure to punch holes in the lid and don't forget to feed the little guy

They are feracious and will devour lots and lots of milkweed. Make sure the caterpillar always has food to eat. Don't forget to clean the jar every so often. A happy home is a clean home.

or girl
like a cheese burger
NO! milkweed leaves

The caterpillar will blissfully eat for 10–14 days before spinning a beautiful cocoon or chrysalis.

Once the caterpillar is in the cocoon, it will take another 10–14 days before it emerges as a brilliant monarch butterfly.

Lastly, give the butterfly a funky name and release it back into the wild!

BYE!
I knew him when

BE FREE, CORNELIUS!
thank you

Andrews McMeel Publishing
a division of Andrews McMeel Universal
1130 Walnut Street, Kansas City, Missouri 64106

www.andrewsmcmeel.com

18 19 20 21 22 SDB 10 9 8 7 6 5 4 3

ISBN: 978-1-4494-8998-4

Library of Congress Control Number: 2017940895

Made by:
Shenzhen Donnelley Printing Company Ltd.
Address and location of manufacturer:
No. 47, Wuhe Nan Road, Bantian Ind. Zone,
Shenzhen China, 518129
3rd Printing—9/17/18

ATTENTION: SCHOOLS AND BUSINESSES

Andrews McMeel books are available at quantity discounts with bulk purchase for educational, business, or sales promotional use. For information, please e-mail the Andrews McMeel Publishing Special Sales Department: specialsales@amuniversal.com.

Look for these books!

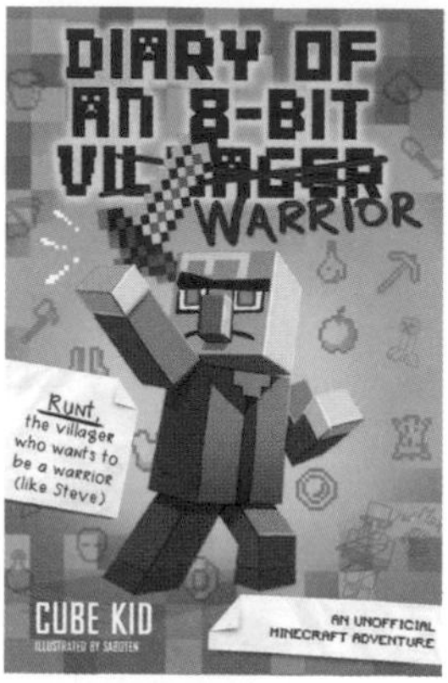
DIARY OF AN 8-BIT WARRIOR
Runt, the villager who wants to be a warrior (like Steve)
CUBE KID
AN UNOFFICIAL MINECRAFT ADVENTURE

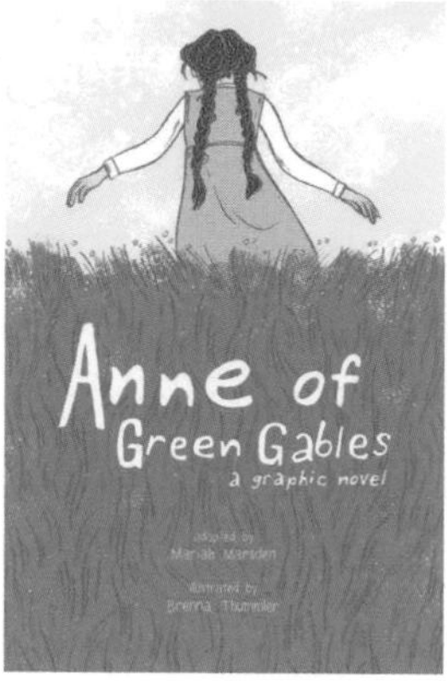
Anne of Green Gables
a graphic novel

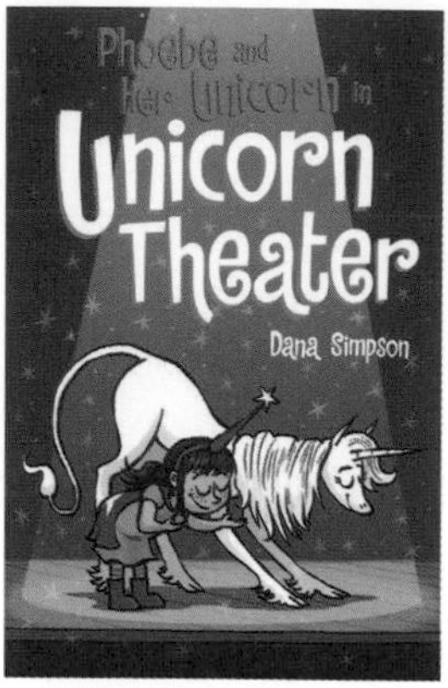
Phoebe and Her Unicorn in
Unicorn Theater
Dana Simpson

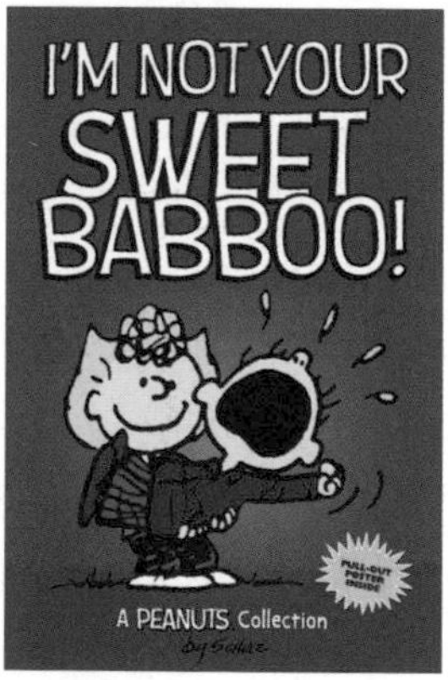
I'M NOT YOUR SWEET BABBOO!
FULL-OUT POSTER INSIDE
A PEANUTS Collection

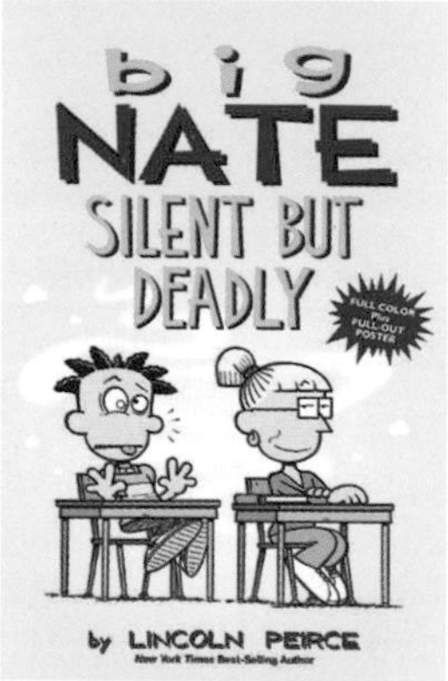
big NATE
SILENT BUT DEADLY
FULL COLOR Plus PULL-OUT POSTER
by LINCOLN PEIRCE
New York Times Best-Selling Author

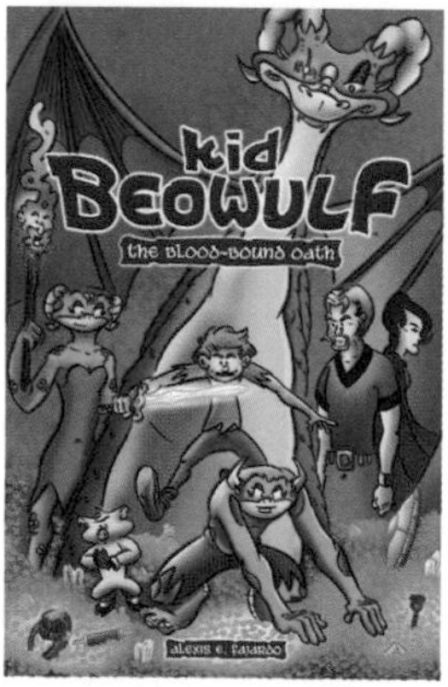
kid BEOWULF
the blood-bound oath
alexis e. fajardo

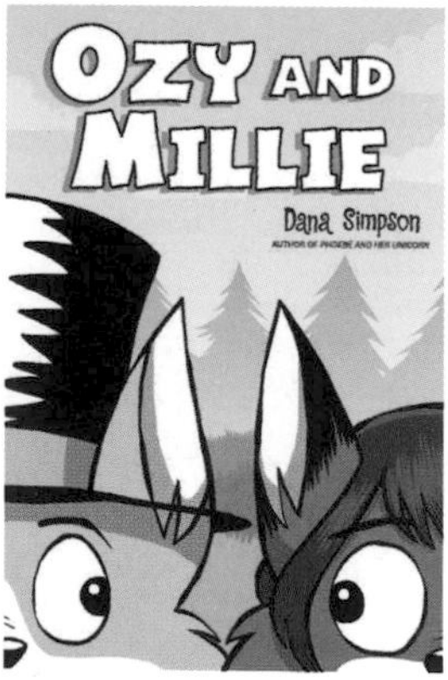
OZY AND MILLIE
Dana Simpson
AUTHOR OF PHOEBE AND HER UNICORN

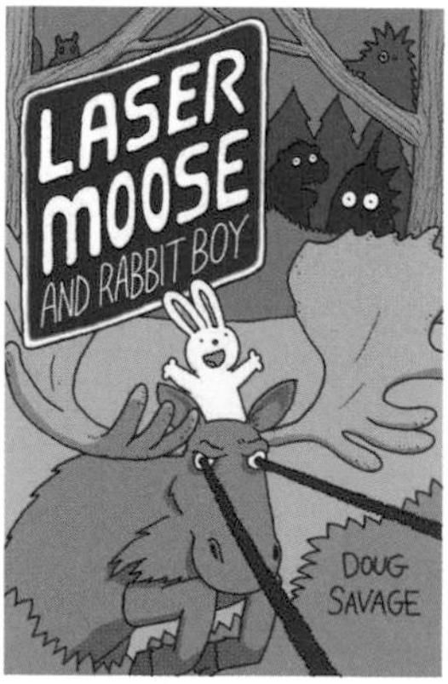
LASER MOOSE AND RABBIT BOY
DOUG SAVAGE

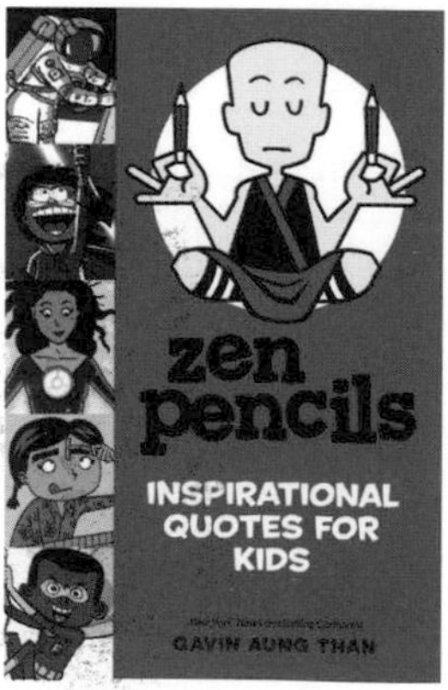
zen pencils
INSPIRATIONAL QUOTES FOR KIDS
GAVIN AUNG THAN